Acclaim for Robert Bryndza's
The Girl in the Ice

"Compelling at every turn! *The Girl in the Ice* grabs us from the first page and simply won't let go, as we follow the brilliantly drawn Detective Erika Foster in her relentless hunt for one of the most horrific villains in modern crime fiction." —Jeffery Deaver, #1 internationally bestselling author

"A riveting page-turner. An astonishingly good plot with perfectly drawn characters and sharp, detailed writing. *The Girl in the Ice* is a winner."
—Robert Dugoni, #1 *Wall Street Journal* bestselling author

"Robert Bryndza's *The Girl in the Ice* has everything I look for in a mystery: an evil antagonist, a clever detective, and a plot that kept me guessing until the very end!" —T. R. Ragan, *New York Times* bestselling author

"I loved, loved, loved this book and Erika Foster is most definitely my kind of heroine. She is smart, tenacious, direct and passionate... I found the writing tight, evocative and enthralling. I CANNOT wait for the next installment." —Angela Marsons, *USA Today* bestselling author

"A compelling read—once you've started, it's hard to put down."
—Rachel Abbott, author of *Sleep Tight*

"An intriguing web of lies, secrets and suspense. I really enjoyed getting to know DCI Foster and am already looking forward to the next book."
—Mel Sherratt, author of *Taunting the Dead*

"Once in a while a book stops you in your tracks... this is THAT book!"
—*Crime Book Junkie*

"A nonstop, edge-of-your-seat, roller coaster of a thriller! The ending, oh the ending! My mind is still blown! This book does not disappoint!"
—*Book Addicted Boy*

"Oh my gosh!... gripping, grimy, hard-core, thrilling... I was hooked!!!... I loved this book... You Have GOT To Read This!"
—*A Page of Fictional Love*

"Hands down, one of the most exciting, dramatic, tense and compelling thrillers that I think I have ever read." —*Bookaholic Confessions*

"Absolute perfection!... Boy are there some sharp turns! There were a few moments when I felt like I had it all figured out and I was so wrong! Fantastic book!"
—*Eternal Optimist*

Also by Robert Bryndza

The Detective Erika Foster crime thriller series

The Girl in the Ice
The Night Stalker (coming soon)

The Coco Pinchard romantic comedy series

The Not So Secret Emails of Coco Pinchard

Coco Pinchard's Big Fat Tipsy Wedding

Coco Pinchard, The Consequences of Love and Sex

A Very Coco Christmas

Coco Pinchard's Must-Have Toy Story

Stand alone romantic comedy novels

Miss Wrong and Mr Right
Lost In Crazytown

THE GIRL IN THE ICE

ROBERT BRYNDZA

GC

GRAND CENTRAL PUBLISHING

NEW YORK BOSTON

This book is a work of fiction. Names, characters, places, and incidents are the product of the author's imagination or are used fictitiously. Any resemblance to actual events, locales, or persons, living or dead, is coincidental.

Cover design and photography by Henry Steadman

Grand Central Publishing
Hachette Book Group
1290 Avenue of the Americas, New York, NY 10104
grandcentralpublishing.com
twitter.com/grandcentralpub

Originally published in 2016 by Bookouture
First Grand Central Publishing Edition: April 2018

Grand Central Publishing is a division of Hachette Book Group, Inc.
The Grand Central Publishing name and logo is a trademark of Hachette Book Group, Inc.

Library of Congress Control Number: 2017961254

ISBN: 978-1-5387-1342-6 (trade paperback)

Printed in the United States of America

LSC-C

10 9 8 7 6

For Ján, who shares my life through the comedy,
and now, the drama.

PROLOGUE

The pavement glittered in the moonlight as Andrea Douglas-Brown hurried up the deserted high street. Her high heels click-clacked in the quiet, frequently breaking rhythm—a result of all the vodka she'd consumed. The January air was sharp, and her bare legs stung from the cold. Christmas and New Year had been and gone, leaving a cold aseptic void. Shop windows slid past, bathed in darkness, broken only by a grimy off-license under a flickering street light. An Indian man sat inside, hunched in the glow of his laptop, but didn't notice as she stalked past.

Andrea was so fueled by anger, so intent on leaving the pub behind, that she only questioned where she was going when the shop windows were replaced by large houses set back from the pavement. A skeleton of elm tree branches stretched above, vanishing into the starless sky. She stopped and leaned against a wall to catch her breath. Blood roared through her body, and the icy air burned as she pulled it into her lungs. Turning back, she saw she'd come quite far, and was halfway up the hill. The road stretched away behind, a slick of treacle bathed in sodium orange with the train station at its base, which was shuttered in darkness. The silence and the cold pressed down on her. The only movement was the stream of vapor as her breath hit the freezing air. She tucked her pink clutch bag under her arm, and, satisfied no one was around, lifted the front of her tiny dress and retrieved an iPhone from her underwear. The Swarovski crystals on the cover glittered lazily under the orange street lights. The screen showed there was no signal. She cursed, tucked it back into her underwear and unzipped the tiny pink clutch. Nestling inside was an older iPhone, it too had Swarovski bling, but several of its crystals were missing. It too showed no signal.

Panic climbed in Andrea's chest as she looked around. The houses were set back from the road, tucked behind tall hedges and iron gates. If she could reach the crest of the hill, she'd probably get reception. And screw it, she thought, she would call her father's driver. She'd think of an explanation why she was south of the river. She buttoned up her tiny leather jacket, wrapped her arms over her chest and set off up the hill, the old iPhone still cradled in her hand like a talisman.

The sound of a car engine rumbled behind and she turned her head, squinting into the headlights, feeling even more exposed as the bright light played over her bare legs. Her hopes that it was a taxi were dashed when she saw the roof of the car was low and there was no "for hire" sign. She turned away and carried on walking. The sound of the car engine grew louder, and then the headlights were on top of her, casting a large circle of light on the pavement in front. A few more seconds passed, but the lights were still on her; she could almost feel their heat. She glanced back into the glare. The car slowed, and crawled along a few feet behind.

She felt furious when she realized whose car it was. With a flick of her long hair, she turned back and carried on walking. The car accelerated a little, drawing level. The windows were tinted black. A sound system boomed and fizzed, tickling her throat, making her ears itch. She stopped abruptly. The car came to a halt seconds later, then reversed the few feet back so the driver's window was now level with her. The sound system fell silent. The engine hummed.

Andrea leaned over and peered at the inky glass of the tinted window, but only her face reflected back. She leaned down and tried the door, but it was locked. She banged on the window with the flat of her pink clutch bag and tried the door again.

"I'm not playing games, I meant what I said back there!" she shouted. "Either open the door or…or…"

The car remained motionless, its engine humming.

Or what? it seemed to say.

Andrea tucked her bag under her arm, gave the tinted glass the finger, and stalked away, climbing the last of the hill to its crest. A huge tree straddled the edge of the pavement and, putting its thick trunk between her and the car's headlights, she checked the phone again, holding it out above her head for a signal. The sky was starless, and the browny-orange cloud seemed so low that her outstretched arm might brush against it. The car slowly inched forward and came to a halt beside the tree.

Fear began to trickle through Andrea's body. Staying in the shadow of the tree, she scanned her surroundings. Thick hedges lined the pavements on both sides of the road, which stretched away up ahead into a blur of suburban gloom. Then she spied something opposite: an alleyway running between two large houses. She could just make out a small sign, which read: DULWICH 1¼.

"Catch me if you can," she murmured. She took a breath, and made to run across the road—but caught her foot on one of the thick tree roots bulging up under the pavement. Pain shot through her ankle as it folded under her. She lost balance, her clutch bag and phone skidding away as her hip hit the corner of the curb and she tumbled into the road, her head hitting the tarmac with a hollow thud. She lay dazed in the glare of the car headlights.

They blinked off, plunging her into darkness.

She heard a door open and tried to get up, but the road under her lurched and spun. Legs came into view, blue jeans…

A pair of expensive trainers blurred and became four. She put out her arm, expecting the familiar figure to help her up, but instead, in a swift move, a leather-gloved hand clamped over her nose and mouth. The other arm encircled her upper arms, pinning them against her body. The glove's leather was soft and warm against her skin, but the power and strength of the fingers inside shocked her. She was yanked up, dragged swiftly to the rear door and slung inside the car, landing lengthways on the backseat. The cold behind her extinguished as the door slammed shut. Andrea lay in shock, not quite comprehending what had just happened.

The car shifted as the figure climbed into the front passenger seat and closed the door. The central locking clicked and whirred. Andrea heard the glove compartment open, a rustle, and then it was snapped shut. The car swayed as the figure clambered through the gap in the front seats and sat down hard on her back, pushing the air from her lungs. Moments later, a thin plastic strip encircled her wrists, pulling them tight behind her back, biting into her skin. The figure shifted down her body, quick and lithe, muscular thighs now pressing on her tied wrists. The pain in her twisted ankle intensified as thick tape was unfurled with a juddering sound and her ankles were bound together. An overpowering smell of a pine tree air freshener mixed with a coppery tang, and she realized her nose was bleeding.

A flash of anger gave Andrea a surge of adrenaline, sharpening her mind.

"What the fuck are you doing?" she started. "I'll scream. You know how loud I can scream!"

But the figure shifted round, knees now on her back, forcing the air out of her. A shadow moved in the corner of her eye, and something hard and heavy came down on the back of her head.

Fresh pain and stars burst in front of her eyes. The arm rose and again came crashing down, and then everything went black.

The road remained silent and empty as the first specks of snow began to fall, twirling lazily to meet the ground. The car, sleek with its tinted windows, pulled away almost soundlessly and slid off into the night.

CHAPTER 1

Lee Kinney emerged from the small end-terrace house where he still lived with his mother, and stared up the high street at the blanket of white. He pulled a packet of cigarettes from his trackies, and lit up. It had snowed all weekend, and was still falling, purifying the churn of footprints and tire tracks already on the ground. Forest Hill train station was silent at the foot of the hill; the Monday morning commuters who usually surged past him, bound for offices in Central London, were probably still tucked up in the warm, enjoying an unexpected morning in bed with their other halves.

Lucky bastards.

Lee had been unemployed since leaving school six years ago, but the good old days of languishing on the dole were over. The new Tory government was cracking down on the long-term unemployed, and Lee now had to work full-time for his dole. He'd been given a fairly cushy work placement as a council gardener at the Horniman Museum, just a ten-minute walk from his house. He'd wanted to stop home this morning like everyone else, but he'd heard nothing from JobCenter Plus to say that work was canceled. In the blazing row that had followed, his mother had said if he didn't show up, his dole would be stopped, and he'd have to find somewhere else to live.

There was a bang on the front window and his mother's pinched face appeared, shooing him away. He gave her the finger and set off up the hill.

Four pretty teenage girls were coming toward him. They wore the red blazers, short skirts and knee-high socks of Dulwich School for Girls. They chatted away excitedly in their plummy accents about how they'd been turned away from school, while simultaneously swiping at their iPhones, the signature white headphone wires swinging against blazer pockets. They crowded the pavement en masse, and didn't part when Lee reached them, so he was forced to step down off the curb into a murky slush left by the road gritter. He felt icy water seep into his new trainers and shot them a dirty look, but they were too absorbed in their tribal gossip, screaming with laughter.

Stuck-up rich bitches, he thought. As he reached the brow of the hill, the clock tower of the Horniman Museum appeared through the bare branches of the elm trees. Snow had spattered against its smooth yellow sandstone bricks, sticking like clumps of wet toilet tissue.

Lee turned right onto a residential street which ran parallel to the iron railings of the museum grounds. The road climbed sharply, the houses becoming grander. As he reached its summit, he stopped for a moment to catch his breath. Snow flew into his eyes, scratchy and cold. On a good day you could see London spread out from here, stretching away for miles down to the London Eye by the Thames, but today thick white cloud had descended, and Lee could only just make out the imposing sprawl of the Overhill housing estate on the hill opposite.

The small gate in the iron railings was locked. The wind was now blowing horizontally and Lee shivered in his trackies. A miserable old git was in charge of the gardening crew. Lee was supposed to wait for him to show up and let him in, but the street was empty. He looked around to make certain, and then scaled the small gate into the museum grounds, taking a thin pathway between tall evergreen hedges.

Sheltered from the shrieking wind, the world around him fell eerily silent. The snow was deepening fast, refilling his crunching footprints as he made his way through the hedgerows. The Horniman Museum and its grounds covered seventeen acres, and the sheds for gardening and maintenance were set right at the back, against a high wall with a curved top. Everywhere was a dazzling blur of white, and Lee lost his bearings, emerging deeper than he had expected in the gardens, beside the Orangery. The ornate wrought-iron-and-glass building took him by surprise. He doubled back, but after a few minutes was again in unfamiliar territory, finding himself at a fork in the path.

How many times have I walked through these bloody gardens? he thought. He took the path to the right, leading into a sunken garden. White marble cherubs posed on snowy brick plinths. The wind gave a low howl as it blew among them, and as Lee passed, it felt as if the blank, milky little eyes of the cherubs were watching him. He stopped and held his hand up to his face against the onslaught of snow, trying to work out the quickest way to the Visitors' Center. The garden maintenance crew weren't usually allowed in the museum, but it was freezing, and the café could be open, and screw it, he would warm up like any other normal human being.

His phone buzzed in his pocket, and he pulled it out. It was a text message from the JobCenter Plus, saying that "due to adverse weather he would not be required to attend his work placement." He stuffed it back in his pocket. The cherubs all seemed to have their heads turned toward him. Were they facing him before? He imagined their pearly little heads slowly moving, tracking his progress through the garden. He shook away the thought and hurried past the blank eyes, concentrating on the snow-covered ground, and emerged into the quiet of a clearing around a disused boating lake.

He stopped and squinted through the whirling flakes. A faded blue rowing boat sat in the center of a pristine oval of snow that had settled on the frozen lake. At the opposite end of the lake was a tiny decaying boat shed, and Lee could just make out the cover of an old rowing boat under its eaves.

Snow was seeping into his already-wet trainers, and despite his jacket, the cold was spreading around his ribs. He was ashamed to realize that he actually felt scared. He needed to find his way out of here. If he doubled back through the sunken garden, he could find the path around the perimeter and emerge onto London Road. The petrol garage would be open and he could buy more fags and some chocolate.

He was about to turn back, when a noise broke the silence. It was tinny and distorted, coming from the direction of the boat shed.

"Hey! Who's there?" he shouted, his voice emerging high-pitched and panicky. It was only when the noise ceased, and seconds later, began to repeat, that Lee realized it was the ringtone from a mobile phone, and could be coming from one of his co-workers.

Because of the snow he couldn't tell where the path ended and the water began, so, sticking close to the band of trees that lined the edge of the boating lake, Lee carefully made his way round toward the sound of the ringtone. It was a desperately light tune, and as he drew nearer he could hear that it was coming from the boat shed.

He reached the low roof, and, ducking down, saw a glow illuminating the gloom from behind the tiny boat. The ringtone stopped, and seconds later the light went out. Lee was relieved it was just a phone. Druggies and dossers regularly scaled the walls at night, and the gardening crew was always finding empty wallets—dumped after the cash and cards were removed—

used condoms, and needles. The phone had probably been dumped... *But why dump a phone... Surely you'd only dump a really crappy phone?* thought Lee.

He circled the little boathouse. The posts of a tiny jetty poked through the snow, and the jetty continued under the low roof of the boat shed. Where the snow couldn't reach, Lee could see that the wood was rotten. He eased along the jetty, ducking down under the eaves of the low roof. The wood above his head was rotten and splintered, and cobwebs hung in wisps. He was now beside the rowing boat, and could see that on the other side of the shed, lying on a little wooden ledge, was an iPhone.

Excitement rose in his chest. He could sell an iPhone down the pub, no probs. He gave the rowing boat a shove with his foot, but it didn't budge; the water was frozen solid around it. He passed its bow, stopping at the opposite end of the jetty. Crouching on his knees, he leaned over, and using the sleeve of his coat he cleared away a powdery layer of snow, exposing thick ice. The water underneath was very clear, and down in the depths he could just make out two fish, mottled with red and black, swimming lazily. A string of tiny bubbles rose up from them, reached the underside of the ice, and rolled away in opposite directions.

The phone started to ring again and he jumped, almost slipping off the end of the jetty. The cheesy ringtone bounced around inside the roof. He could see the illuminated iPhone clearly now against the opposite wall of the boat shed, lying on its side on a lip of wood just above the frozen waterline. It had a sparkly jeweled case. Lee went to the rowing boat and swung a leg over. He placed his foot on the wooden seat and tested his weight, still keeping the other foot on the jetty. The boat didn't budge.

He swung his other leg over, climbing into the boat, but even from here the iPhone was still out of his reach. Spurred on by the thought of folded bank notes, thick in the pocket of his trackies, Lee hooked his leg over the opposite side of the boat and tentatively placed his foot on the ice. Holding on to the edge of the boat, he pressed down, risking a wet foot. The ice held strong. He stepped out of the boat and placed his other foot on the ice, listening for the telltale squeaking sound of tension and weakness. Nothing. He took a small step, and then another. It was like walking on a concrete floor.

The eaves of the wooden roof slanted down. To reach the iPhone, Lee was going to have to get down on his haunches.

As he squatted down, the light from its screen illuminated the inside of the boat shed. Lee noticed a couple of old plastic bottles and bits of rubbish poking up through the ice, then something which made him stop...it looked like the tip of a finger.

His heart racing, he reached out and gently squeezed it. It was cold and rubbery. Frost clung to the fingernail, which was painted a deep purple. He pulled the sleeve of his coat over his hand and rubbed at the ice around it. The light from the iPhone cast the frozen surface in a murky green, and underneath he saw a hand, reaching up to where the finger poked through the ice. What must have been an arm vanished away into the depths.

The phone stopped ringing, and was replaced by a deafening silence. And then he saw it. Directly underneath where he crouched was the face of a girl. Her milky brown swollen eyes stared at him, blankly. A clump of dark hair was fused to the ice in a tangle. A fish swam lazily past, its tail brushing against the girl's lips, which were parted as if she were about to speak.

Lee recoiled with a yell and leaped up, his head crashing against the low roof of the boathouse. He bounced off and landed back on the ice, legs sliding away under him.

He lay for a moment, stunned. Then he heard a faint squeaking, cracking sound. Panicking, he kicked and scrabbled, trying to get up, to get as far away from the dead girl as he could, but his legs slid away under him again. This time, he plunged through the ice into the freezing water. He felt the girl's limp arms tangling with his, her cold slimy skin against his. The more he fought, the more their limbs became intertwined. The cold was sharp, absolute. He swallowed foul water and kicked and flailed. He somehow managed to heave himself away to the edge of the rowing boat. He heaved and retched, wishing that he'd reached that phone, but his thoughts of selling it were gone.

All he wanted now was to call for help.

CHAPTER 2

Erika Foster had been waiting for half an hour in the grubby reception area of Lewisham Row Police Station. She shifted uncomfortably on a green plastic chair, one of a row bolted to the floor. The seats were faded and shiny, polished by years of anxious, guilty arses. Through a large window overlooking the car park, the ring road, a gray office tower, and the sprawling shopping center fought a battle for visibility in the blizzard. A trail of melted slush ran diagonally from the main entrance to the front desk where the desk sergeant sat, regarding his computer with bleary eyes. He had a large jowly face and was absently picking at his teeth, pulling out a finger to inspect the findings before popping it back in his mouth.

"Guvnor shouldn't be long," he said.

His eyes moved down Erika's body, taking in her thin frame, clad in faded blue jeans, woolen jumper, and a purple bomber jacket. His gaze came to rest on the small suitcase on wheels at her feet. She glared back at him, and they both looked away. The wall beside her was a mess of public information posters. DON'T BE A VICTIM OF CRIME! declared one, which Erika thought was a pretty stupid thing to put up in the reception area of an outer London nick.

A door beside the front desk buzzed and Chief Superintendent Marsh came into the reception area. His close-cropped hair had grayed in the years since Erika had last seen him, but despite his exhausted face, he was still handsome. Erika got up and shook his hand.

"DCI Foster, sorry to keep you. Was your flight okay?" he said, taking in what she was wearing.

"Delayed, sir... Hence the civvies," she replied apologetically.

"This bloody snow couldn't come at a worse time," said Marsh, adding: "Desk Sergeant Woolf, this is DCI Foster; she's joining us from Manchester. I'll need you to assign her a car asap..."

"Yes, sir," nodded Woolf.

"And I'll need a phone," added Erika. "If you could find something older, preferably with actual buttons. I hate touch screens."

"Let's get started," said Marsh. He swiped his ID card and the door buzzed and clicked open.

"Snotty cow," murmured Woolf, when the door had closed behind them.

Erika followed Marsh down a long, low corridor. Phones rang, and uniformed officers and support staff streamed by in the opposite direction, their pasty January faces tense and urgent. A fantasy football league pinned up on the wall slid past, and seconds later, an identical pin board held rows of photos with the heading: KILLED IN THE LINE OF DUTY. Erika closed her eyes, only opening them when she was confident she had passed. She nearly crashed into Marsh, who had stopped at a door marked INCIDENT ROOM. She could see through the half-open blinds of the glass partition that the room was full. Fear crawled up her throat. She was sweating under her thick jacket. Marsh grabbed the door handle.

"Sir, you were going to brief me before—" started Erika.

"No time," he said. Before Erika had a chance to respond, he had opened the door and indicated she should go first.

The incident room was large and open plan, and the two-dozen officers fell silent, their expectant faces bathed in the harsh strip lighting. The glass wall partitions on either side faced onto corridors, and along one side there was a bank of printers and photocopiers. Tracks had been worn into the thin carpet tiles in front of these, and between the desks to whiteboards lining the back wall. As Marsh strode to the front, Erika quickly stowed her suitcase by a photocopier which was churning out paper. She perched on a desk.

"Morning everyone," said Marsh. "As we all know, twenty-three-year-old Andrea Douglas-Brown was reported missing four days ago. And what has followed has been a media shit-storm. Just after nine o'clock this morning, the body of a young girl matching Andrea's description was found at the Horniman Museum in Forest Hill. Preliminary ID is from a phone registered to Andrea, but we still need a formal ID. We've got forensics on their way now, but it's all being slowed down by the bloody snow…" A phone started to ring. Marsh paused. It carried on ringing. "Come on people, this is an incident room. Answer the bloody phone!"

An officer at the back snatched it up and started to speak quietly.

"If the ID is correct, then we're dealing with the murder of a young girl linked to a very powerful and influential family, so we need to stay far ahead on this one. The press, you name it. Arses are on the line."

The day's newspapers lay on the desk opposite Erika. The headlines screamed out: **DAUGHTER OF TOP LABOR PEER VANISHES** and **ANDIE KIDNAP TERROR PLOT?** The third was the most striking, with a full-page picture of Andrea under the headline: **TAKEN?**

"This is DCI Foster. She's joining us from the Manchester Metropolitan Police," finished Marsh. Erika felt all eyes in the room turn to her.

"Good morning everyone, I'm pleased to be..." started Erika, but an officer with greasy black hair interrupted.

"Guv, I've been on the Douglas-Brown case, as a missing person and..."

"And? What, DCI Sparks?" asked Marsh.

"And, my team is working like clockwork. I'm following up several leads. I'm in contact with the family..."

"DCI Foster has vast experience working on sensitive murder cases..."

"But..."

"Sparks, this isn't a discussion. DCI Foster will now be taking the lead on this... She'll be hitting the ground running, but I know you will give her your best," said Marsh. There was an awkward silence. Sparks sat back in his chair and regarded Erika with distaste. She held his gaze and refused to look away.

Marsh went on, "And it's mouths shut, everyone. I mean it. No media, no gossip. Okay?" The officers murmured in agreement.

"DCI Foster, my office."

Erika stood in Marsh's top-floor office as he searched through piles of paperwork on his desk. She glanced out of the window, which afforded a more commanding view of Lewisham. Beyond the shopping center and train station, uneven lines of red-brick terraced houses stretched toward Blackheath. Marsh's office deviated from the normal order of a Chief Superintendent. There were no model cars lined along the windowsill, no family photos angled on the shelves. His desk was a mess of paperwork piled high, and a set of shelves by the window seemed to be used as an overflow, crammed with bulging case files, unopened post, old Christmas cards and curling Post-it notes covered in his small spidery handwriting. In one corner, his ceremonial uniform and hat lay draped over a chair, and on top of the crumpled trousers, his Blackberry winked red as it charged. It was a strange mix of teenage boy's bedroom and high authority.

Marsh finally located a small padded envelope, and handed it to Erika. She tore the edge off and pulled out the wallet with her badge and ID.

"So, I suddenly go from zero to hero?" she said, turning the badge over in her hand.

"This isn't about you, DCI Foster. You should be pleased," said Marsh, moving round and sinking into his chair.

"Sir, I was told, in no uncertain terms, that when I returned to service, I'd be put on administrative tasks for six months minimum?"

Marsh indicated she should take the seat opposite.

"Foster, when I called you this was a missing person case. Now we're looking at murder. Do I need to remind you who her father is?"

"Lord Douglas-Brown. Wasn't he one of the main government contractors for the Iraq War? At the same time as serving in the cabinet?"

"This isn't about politics."

"Since when have I cared about politics, sir?"

"Andrea Douglas-Brown went missing on my patch. Lord Douglas-Brown has exerted enormous pressure. He's a man of influence who can make and break careers. I've got a meeting with the Assistant Commissioner and someone from the bloody cabinet office later this morning..."

"So this is about your career?"

Marsh shot her a look. "I need an ID on this body and a suspect. Fast."

"Yes, sir." Erika hesitated. "Can I ask, why me? Is the plan to throw me in first as potential fall guy? Then Sparks gets to clean up the mess and look the hero? Cos I deserve to know if..."

"Andrea's mother is Slovak. And so are you... I thought it might help things, to have an officer her mother can identify with."

"So it's good PR to put me on the case?"

"If you want to look at it like that. I also know what an extraordinary police officer you are. Recently you've had troubles, yes, but your achievements far outshine what has..."

"Don't give me the shit sandwich, sir," said Erika.

"Foster, the one thing you've never mastered is the politics of the force. If you'd done that we might be sitting on opposite sides of this conversation right now."

"Yeah. Well, I have principles," said Erika giving him a hard stare. There was silence.

"Erika... I brought you in because I think you deserve a break. Don't talk yourself out of the job before you've begun."

"Yes, sir," said Erika.

"Now, get over to the crime scene. Report back to me the second you have information. If it *is* Andrea Douglas-Brown we'll need a formal ID from the family."

Erika got up and went to leave. Marsh went on, his voice softer, "I never got the chance, at the funeral, to say how sorry I was about Mark... He was an excellent officer, and a friend."

"Thank you, sir." Erika looked at the carpet. It was still difficult to hear his name. She willed herself not to cry. Marsh cleared his throat and his professional tone returned.

"I know I can rely on you to reach a swift conviction on this. I want to be kept posted every step of the way."

"Yes, sir," said Erika.

"And DCI Foster?"

"Sir?"

"Lose the casual gear."

CHAPTER 3

Erika found the women's locker room and worked fast, changing into a forgotten but familiar ensemble of black trousers, white blouse, dark sweater and long leather jacket.

She was stuffing her civilian clothes into a locker when she noticed a crumpled copy of the *Daily Mail* at the end of one of the long wooden benches. She pulled it toward her and smoothed it out. Under the headline, **DAUGHTER OF TOP LABOR PEER VANISHES**, was a large picture of Andrea Douglas-Brown. She was beautiful and polished, with long brown hair, full lips and sparkling brown eyes. Her skin was tanned and she wore a skimpy bikini top, shoulders back to accentuate her full breasts. She stared into the camera with an intense, confident gaze. The photo had been taken on a yacht, and behind her the sky was a hot blue, and the sun sparkled on the sea. Andrea was being embraced from either side by wide, powerful male shoulders, one taller and one shorter—the rest of whoever they were had been cropped out.

The *Daily Mail* described Andrea as a "minor socialite," which Erika was sure Andrea wouldn't enjoy if she could read it, but it refrained from calling her "Andie" as the other tabloids had done. The paper had spoken to her parents, Lord and Lady Douglas-Brown, and to her fiancé, who had all pleaded for Andrea to get in contact with them.

Erika scrabbled in her leather jacket and found her notebook, still there after all these months. She noted down the name of the fiancé, a Giles Osborne, and wrote: Did Andrea run away? She looked at it for a moment, then scrubbed it out ferociously, tearing the paper. She tucked the notebook in the back of her trousers and went to put her ID in the other free pocket, but paused, feeling it in her hand for a moment: its familiar weight, the leather case cover worn into a curve after years resting against her buttock in the back pocket of her trousers.

Erika went to a mirror above a row of sinks, flipped open the leather case and held it out in front of her. The ID photo showed a confident woman, blonde hair swept back, staring into the camera defiantly. The woman looking back at her, holding the ID, was scrawny and pallid. Her short blonde hair stuck up in tufts, and gray was showing at the roots. Erika watched her shaking arm for a moment, then flipped the ID closed.

She would put in a request for a new photo.

CHAPTER 4

Desk Sergeant Woolf was waiting in the corridor when Erika emerged from the women's locker room. He waddled along beside her, noticing she was a full head taller than him.

"Here's your phone; it's all charged and ready to go," he said, handing her a clear plastic bag containing a phone and charger. "A car will be ready for you after lunch."

"And you've nothing with buttons?" snapped Erika, when she saw a smartphone through the plastic.

"It's got an on/off button," he snapped back.

"When my car arrives, could you put this in the boot?" she said, indicating her suitcase on wheels. She moved past him and through the door of the incident room. Conversation fell quiet when she entered. A short, plump woman approached her.

"I'm Detective Moss. We're just trying to sort you an office." The woman had wiry red hair, and her face was so splattered with freckles that they grouped together in blotches. She went on, "All the info is going up on the boards as it comes in and I'll have hard copies put in your office when—"

"A desk is fine," said Erika. She went over to the whiteboards, where there was a large map of the Horniman Museum grounds, and underneath, a CCTV image of Andrea.

"That's the last known picture of her, taken at London Bridge Station boarding the 8:47 p.m. train to Forest Hill," said Moss, following. In the CCTV photo, Andrea was stepping up into the train carriage with a shapely bare leg. Her face was fixed with an angry expression. She was dressed to the nines in a tight leather jacket over a short black dress, wearing pink high heels and carrying a matching clutch bag.

"She was alone when she boarded the train?" asked Erika.

"Yes, I've got the CCTV video here that we took the image from," said Moss, grabbing a laptop and coming back over. She balanced it on a pile of files and maximized a video window. They watched the time-lapse video, a view of the train platform taken side-on. Andrea walked across into shot and into the train carriage. It only lasted a few seconds, so Moss placed it on a loop.

"She looks really pissed off," said Erika.

"Yeah. Like she's off to give someone a piece of her mind," agreed Moss.

"Where was her fiancé?"

"He's got a watertight alibi, he was at an event in Central London."

Several more times, they watched Andrea move across the platform and into the train. She was the only person in the video; the rest of the platform was empty.

"This is our Skipper, Sergeant Crane," said Moss, indicating a young guy with close-cropped blond hair who was simultaneously on the phone, searching through files and shoving a whole Mars bar in his mouth. He attempted to swallow as much of it as he could. Out of the corner of her eye, Erika saw Sparks put the phone down. He pulled on his coat and made for the door.

"Where are you going?" she asked. Sparks stopped and turned.

"Forensics just gave us the okay to go down to the crime scene. We need a fast ID, in case you'd forgotten, Ma'am?"

"I'd like you to stay here, Sparks. Detective Moss, you're with me today—and you, what's your name?" she asked a tall, handsome black officer who was taking a call at a desk nearby.

"Detective Peterson," he said covering the phone.

"Okay, Detective Peterson. You're with me too."

"What am I supposed to do then, just sit here twiddling my thumbs?" demanded Sparks.

"No. I need access to all CCTV covering the Horniman Museum and surrounding streets—"

"We've got it," he interrupted.

"No, I want you to expand your window to everything in the forty-eight hours leading up to Andrea's disappearance, and everything since, and I want a door-to-door around the museum. I also need anything and everything you can get about Andrea. Family, friends; pull bank details, medical and phone records, e-mail, and social media. Who liked her? Who hated her? I want to know everything. Did she have a computer, a laptop? She must have had, and I want it."

"I was told we couldn't have her laptop; Lord Douglas-Brown was very specific..." started Sparks.

"Well, I'm telling you to get it." The incident room had now fallen silent. Erika went on, "And no one—I repeat, no one—is to talk to the press or share anything in any capacity. Do you hear me? I don't even want people saying 'no comment.' Mouths shut... Is that enough to keep you busy, DCI Sparks?"

"Yes," said Sparks, glaring at her.

"And Crane, you'll get the incident room running smoothly?"

"Already on it," he said, swallowing the last of his Mars bar.

"Good. We'll reconvene here at four."

Erika walked out, followed by Moss and Peterson. Sparks threw down his coat.

"Bitch," he said under his breath, and sat back down at his computer.

CHAPTER 5

Moss peered over the steering wheel at the snowy road ahead. Erika sat beside her in the passenger seat, with Peterson in the back. The awkward silence was broken periodically by the windscreen wipers, hissing and squealing as they passed over the glass, and looking as if they were gummed up with grated coconut.

South London was a palette of grimy grays. Decaying terraced houses slid past, their front gardens paved over for parking. The only dots of color came from the wheelie-bins packed outside in clusters of black, green and blue.

The road turned sharply to the left, and they came to a halt at the back of a line of cars stretching around the first bend of the one-way Catford Gyratory. Moss flicked on the siren, and the cars began to mount the pavement so they could pass. The heating in the squad car was broken and it gave Erika a good excuse to keep her shaking hands deep in the pockets of her long leather jacket, hoping it was hunger making them shake, and not the pressure of the task ahead. She spied a packet of red licorice bootlaces tucked into the slot above the radio.

"Do you mind?" she asked, breaking the uneasy silence.

"Yeah, go ahead," said Moss. She put her foot down and they sped through a gap in the traffic, the back wheels lurching to one side on the icy road. Erika pulled a bootlace from the packet, pushed it into her mouth and chewed. She eyed Peterson in the rearview mirror. He was hunched intently over an iPad. He was tall and slight with an oval, boyish face. He reminded her of a wooden toy soldier. He looked up and held her gaze.

"So. What can you tell me about Andrea Douglas-Brown?" said Erika, swallowing the licorice bootlace and grabbing another.

"Didn't the Super brief you, boss?" asked Peterson.

"He did. But imagine he didn't. I approach every case from the point of knowing nothing; you'd be surprised what new insights come up."

"She's twenty-three years old," started Peterson.

"Did she work?"

"There's no employment history..."

"Why?"

Peterson shrugged. "Doesn't need to work. Lord Douglas-Brown owns SamTech, a private defense company. They develop GPS and software systems for the government. At the last count he was worth thirty million."

"Any brothers and sisters?" asked Erika.

"Yeah, she has a younger brother, David, and an older sister, Linda."

"So you could say Andrea and her siblings are trust fund kids?" asked Erika.

"Yes and no. The sister, Linda, does work, albeit for her mother. Lady Douglas-Brown owns a society florist's. David is doing an MA at university."

They had now reached Catford High Street, which had been gritted, and the traffic was moving normally. They sped past pound shops, payday moneylenders, and independent supermarkets with exotic produce piled high, threatening to spill over onto the slushy pavements.

"What about Andrea's fiancé, Giles Osborne?"

"They are... they *were* due to have a big wedding in the summer," said Moss.

"What does he do?" asked Erika.

"He runs an events company, upmarket stuff: Henley Regatta, product launches, society weddings."

"Did Andrea live with him?"

"No. She lives at home with the parents, in Chiswick."

"That's West London, yeah?" asked Erika. Peterson nodded at her in the rearview mirror.

Moss went on, "You should see the family home. They've knocked four houses together, excavated the basement; must be worth millions."

They passed a Topps Tiles, which looked closed, its car park a large empty square of fresh snow, then a Harvester Restaurant where a tall Christmas tree was being slowly fed into a chipper by a man wearing earmuffs. The drone of its engine vibrated through the car and then receded, as a cluster of run-down pubs rolled into view. In front of one called The Stag, an old woman with a sunken face leaned against a peeling green door, smoking a cigarette. Beside her, a dog had its head in a bin bag, the snowy pavement strewn with old food.

"So what the hell was Andrea Douglas-Brown doing around here, alone? Bit off the beaten track for the daughter of a millionaire who lives in Chiswick, isn't it?" asked Erika.

A flurry of snow briefly enveloped the car, and when it cleared, the Horniman Museum came into view. The sandstone edifice was flanked with tall yucca and palm trees, looking out of place caked in snow.

Moss slowed the car at the iron gates, pulling up beside a young male uniformed officer. Erika wound down the window and he leaned forward, placing a leather-gloved hand on the doorframe. Snow whirled into the car, sticking against the upholstered inside of the door. Erika showed him her ID.

"Take the next left. It's a steep hill. We've sent a gritter up there but take it slow," he said. Erika nodded and wound up the window. Moss took the left and they started up the steep road. As they approached the summit, a roadblock came into view, manned by another uniformed officer. Standing on the pavement to the left of the police tape was a group of journalists, rugged up in winter gear. They took interest in the police car's arrival, and camera flashes bounced off the windscreen.

"Bugger off," growled Moss as she attempted to change up to third. The gears crunched and the squad car lurched forward before stalling. "Shit!" she cried, gripping the wheel. She slammed on the brake, but they continued to slide. Through the rearview mirror Erika saw the road dropping away behind them. The photographers reacted to the drama and fired off more flashes.

"Do a sharp left, now!" shouted Peterson, quickly winding down his window and craning his neck round. Erika gripped the dashboard as Moss leaned into the wheel and managed to halt the slide, guiding the squad car into a recently vacated parking space by the curb, which was free of snow. The wheels caught on the bare tarmac and they skidded to a stop in the parking space.

"That was sheer luck," said Peterson with a dry grin. Snow was pouring in through his window and sticking to his short dreadlocks.

"That was bloody sheer ice," said Moss, taking a deep breath.

Erika undid her belt, embarrassed to feel her legs shaking. They all exited the car as the photographers both jeered with laughter and called out questions about the identity of the dead body. Snow was rushing at them horizontally as they pulled out their ID, and the tape was lifted to let them pass. As Erika crossed underneath she took comfort in being back, the police tape being lifted for her, the feel of the ID in her hand again.

Another uniformed officer directed them toward the iron gate leading into the museum grounds.

A huge white forensics tent now covered the boathouse, its base blurring into the mass of snow. One of the crime scene assistants was waiting with coveralls for Erika, Moss and Peterson, and they suited up before entering.

Floodlights inside the tent gleamed off the snow and illuminated the rotting wood of the low roof. They peered underneath, where three forensics officers were assisting the crime scene manager, combing over every inch of the inside. A rowing boat sat gleaming on the small wooden jetty, and a police diver, slick in his black gear, emerged from the icy water with a spray, bringing with him a warm, bilious smell of stale pond. Rubbish and murk floated around him where chunks of ice were melting under the glare of the lights.

"DCI Foster," said a deep male voice. For once, Erika had to crane her head up to look at the tall figure that appeared from behind the boathouse. He pulled down his mask to reveal a proud, handsome face with large dark eyes. His eyebrows were heavily plucked, resulting in two immaculate lines.

"I'm Isaac Strong, forensic pathologist," he said. "I know Moss and Peterson," he added. They both nodded. He led them round, past the outer wall of the boathouse, and they came to a metal stretcher placed lengthways against the back of the tent. The dead girl lay naked, save for the remnants of a torn and muddy dress bunched around her waist. Below were the torn strips of a black thong. Her full lips were slightly parted, and one of her front teeth was broken off, close to the gum. Her eyes were wide open in a milky death stare, and her long hair was matted with leaves and debris from the water.

"That's her, isn't it?" said Erika quietly. Moss and Peterson nodded.

"Okay," said Isaac, breaking the silence. "Her body was found frozen in the ice. At this early stage I'd hazard—and I repeat, *hazard*—that she'd been in the water for at least seventy-two hours. The temperature dropped below zero three days ago. Also, her phone was still working when she was found; a young guy who works here heard it ringing." He handed Erika an iPhone, bagged up in clear plastic. It had a spray of Swarovski crystals on the cover.

"Do we know who was ringing?" asked Erika, seizing the thought of an early lead.

"No. The battery died shortly after we retrieved it from the water. It's been dusted for prints, but it's a mess."

"Where's the guy who found her?"

"The paramedics are with him in an ambulance by the Visitors' Center. He was in a state when uniform arrived on the scene. He'd fallen through the ice on top of the body; vomited, urinated and defecated in shock, so we're trying to eliminate his DNA fast," said Isaac. He moved to the body on the stretcher.

"Bloating of the face and ligature marks on the neck could indicate strangulation, and her right collarbone is broken," he said, and gently used a latex gloved hand to tilt the head. "Clumps of hair are missing, roughly around the same patch by each temple."

"Whoever did it could have been behind her and pulled at her hair," said Moss.

"Is there evidence of sexual violence?" asked Erika.

"I'll need time to look further. There are weals and scratches on her inner thighs, ribs, and breasts..."

He indicated a bloom of red lines under each breast, and carefully placed his hand over to show the imprint of fingers on her rib cage. "The wrists are lacerated which could indicate her hands were tied, but her arms weren't tied when she went into the water. There is also bruising to the back of the head and we found fragments of tooth enamel embedded in the front corner post of the jetty…We're still looking for the remains of the tooth. She could have swallowed it, so I may find it later."

"When she went missing, she was wearing pink high heels and had a pink bag. Any sign of those?" asked Moss.

"She was only wearing the dress and underwear, but no bra…no shoes." Isaac carefully lifted her legs. "The heels of her feet are badly lacerated."

"Dragged barefoot," said Erika, recoiling at the sight of her feet, angrily scraped and split, the flesh underneath pink.

"One of our divers did pull this out of the water." Isaac handed Erika a small clear plastic bag. It contained a driving license ID card. They regarded the photo, silent for a moment.

"That's an intense photo. It's like she's there, staring at us from beyond the grave," said Peterson.

Erika thought he was right. Often in ID pictures the eyes were glazed over, or the subject looked a little trapped in the headlights, but Andrea had a confident stare.

"Jesus," said Erika, looking from the photo of Andrea to the dead body, wide-eyed and filthy on the stretcher. "How soon can you establish an exact cause of death?"

"I've given you enough to go on. I'll need to do the autopsy," bristled Isaac.

"Which you'll do today," said Erika, fixing him with a stare.

"Yes. Today," said Isaac.

The grounds were quiet outside the forensics tent. The snow had stopped falling, and a group of uniformed officers were silently combing their way around the lake, white bunching up around their dark legs as they waded through the drifts of snow.

Erika took out her phone and called Marsh. "Sir. It's Andrea Douglas-Brown," she said.

There was a pause. "Shit."

"I'm just on my way to talk to the boy who found her, and then I'll go and inform the parents," said Erika.

"Your thoughts? Foster?"

"Without a doubt we're looking at murder, perhaps rape with strangulation or drowning. Everything I have is on its way to the guys back at the nick."

"Do we have any suspects in view?"

"No, sir. I'm hitting the ground running as it is. We need to organize a formal ID with the family. Forensics are going straight from the scene to do an autopsy so I'll keep you posted on the arrangements for that."

"If I can tell the media we have a suspect..." started Marsh.

"Yes, sir. I know. Talking to the family is our first line of inquiry. There is a high chance she knew the killer. When she went missing there were no witnesses, no one saw her being snatched. She could have met the killer here."

"Take it easy, Foster. Don't go in guns blazing, assuming that Andrea was meeting up for some sordid shag."

"I never said she was meeting for a sordid..."

"Remember this is a well-respected family who..."

"I have done this before, sir."

"Yes. But realize who you're dealing with."

"Yes. A grieving family. And I have to ask them the usual questions, sir."

"Yes, but this is an order. Go easy."

When Erika came off the phone she was prickling at Marsh's attitude. The one thing she despised about Britain was its class system. Even in a murder investigation, it seemed that Marsh wanted the family to have some kind of VIP treatment.

Moss and Peterson emerged from the tent with a uniformed police officer, and they made their way past the lake and through the sunken garden. Erika wondered if the blank-eyed statues had watched as Andrea was dragged past, screaming for her life.

A radio on the accompanying officer's lapel hissed static. "We've just recovered a small pink handbag from a hedge on London Road," said a tinny voice.

"Which direction is London Road?" asked Erika.

"The high street," said the officer, pointing past a row of trees.

After months of inactivity, Erika was struggling to get her brain back into gear. Every time she closed her eyes she saw Andrea's body, skin torn and bruised, blank eyes wide open. There were so many variables to a murder investigation. The average-sized house could keep a forensics team busy for days, but this was a crime scene potentially stretching across seventeen acres, with evidence strewn across public areas, trapped under a thick layer of snow.

"Bring it to the Visitors' Center, by the ambulance," said Erika to the officer, who hurried off. Moments later she, Moss and Peterson emerged from the hedgerows. At the bottom of a gentle snow-covered slope was the futuristic glass box of the Visitors' Center. A courtyard out front had been churned up by an ambulance, which was parked with its back doors open. A young man in his early twenties sat in the back under a pile of blankets. He was gray-faced and shaking. A small woman stood by the ambulance doors, watching over a member of the crime scene unit who was carefully processing the boy's clothes, his gloved hand labeling the soiled tracksuit, jumper and trainers in their clear evidence bags. The woman had the same bushy eyebrows as the boy, but with a sharp little face.

"I want a receipt," she was saying, "and I want it in writing what's being taken away. Lee only got those tracksuit bottoms in

November, and those trainers are new too—there's still thirteen weeks of catalog payments to be made on them. How long are you gonna have them for?"

"These are all now evidence in a murder investigation," said Erika, as they reached the ambulance. "I'm DCI Foster, this is Detective Moss and Detective Peterson." They held out their ID and the woman peered beadily at their photos.

"What's your name?" prompted Erika.

"Grace Kinney, and my Lee's done nothing more than turn up for work. And because he's been forced to wait in the cold, he'll be on the sick and they'll stop his money!"

"Lee, can you tell us exactly what happened?"

Lee nodded, his face pale and haunted. He told them how he'd arrived for work, then followed the sound of the phone ringing, which had led to the discovery of Andrea's body under the ice. An officer interrupted him, appearing at the ambulance doors holding a small pink clutch bag in a clear plastic bag. Another plastic bag contained its contents: six fifty-pound notes, two compact tampons, a mascara, a lipstick and a perfume atomizer.

"Did that belong to the dead girl?" said Grace, peering over. The officer quickly placed it behind his back.

"She's seen it now," Erika snapped at the officer. She went on, "Ms. Kinney. You have to understand that this is evidence in a sensitive investigation and…"

"I'll keep my mouth shut, don't you worry," Grace said. "Although what a young girl with a designer bag and a wad of fifties was doing round here, God only knows."

"What do you think she was doing?" asked Erika.

"I'm not doing your job for you. But it don't take Sherlock Holmes to realize she was on the game. She probably brought a punter up here and it all went wrong," said Grace.

"Lee, did you recognize the dead girl?"

"Why would my Lee recognize a prostitute?"

"We don't...we don't think she was a prostitute."

Grace seemed oblivious to Lee's distress. He pulled the blanket around him and furrowed his brow, knitting his bushy eyebrows together. "She was beautiful," he said, quietly. "Even dead, under the ice...It was horrible, how she died, wasn't it?"

Erika nodded.

"I could see it in her face," said Lee. "Sorry, what was the question?"

"Did you recognize her, Lee? Had you seen her around?" repeated Erika.

"No. I've never seen her before," he said.

"We think she could have been out at one of the pubs on the high street when she went missing. Which pubs attract the younger crowd?" asked Peterson.

Lee shrugged. "The Wetherspoon's is busy on a weekend...The Pig and Whistle. That's just up from the station."

"Do you go out much, Lee?" asked Peterson. Lee shrugged. Peterson continued, "The Wetherspoon's, The Pig and Whistle. Any other pubs?"

"He steers clear of those, don't you?" said Grace, throwing Lee a look.

"Yeah, yeah. I do. I mean, I steer clear," said Lee.

Grace went on, "It used to be nice round 'ere. Nothing posh, but nice. That rough old Wetherspoon's used to be a lovely Odeon. The worst are The Glue Pot and The Stag. I tell you, if the world was flooded with piss and those two boozers were above the waterline, you wouldn't catch me in there. And they're swarming with bloody immigrants—no offense, love," she added, to Peterson. Erika noticed Moss suppress a smile.

Grace continued, still oblivious to Lee's distress. "I tell you,

I go out down the high street and feel like a foreigner in me own country: Polish, Romanian, Ukrainian, Russian, Indian, African...And Lee tells me they're all down at the JobCenter, hands out, taking what they can. You should raid those pubs on the high street. Loads of them work behind the bar, and nip out in their tea breaks to sign on. But no, there's a blind eye turned to that. It's my Lee who's got to come out in all weather and work a forty-hour week for sixty quid's worth of benefits. It's disgusting."

"How long have you been working in the museum grounds?" asked Erika. Lee shrugged. "I did four weeks before Christmas."

"And I suppose it'll be Lee's fault he can't work, cos some stupid prostitute went and got herself..."

"That's enough," said Erika.

Grace seemed chastised. "I suppose she's still someone's daughter. Do you know who she is?"

"We can't say at this stage."

This aroused Grace's interest. "It wasn't that girl, the posh one who's gone missing? What was her name, Lee—Angela? Did she look like that girl in the paper?"

Lee was now staring blankly ahead, seemingly reliving the moment he'd come face-to-face with Andrea through a sheet of ice.

"As I said, we still need to identify the body," said Erika. "We'll contact the JobCenter for you, Lee, and let them know what's going on. Do stay in the local area. We might have to talk to you again."

"You think he's going to leave the country, do you?" snapped Grace. "Chance would be a fine thing—although, round here we'd probably be the only ones leaving!"

Erika, Moss and Peterson left as the paramedics began to ready the ambulance for leaving.

"She was a bit of a handful," said Moss.

"But she gave us more information than Lee," said Erika. "Let's check out those pubs. The Glue Pot, The Stag. Could Andrea have been in one of those the night she went missing?"

CHAPTER 6

There was a fresh onslaught of snow when they emerged from the museum, so they ditched the squad car and took the overland train to London Bridge, and then the tube over to Chiswick. The tube was cramped and hot, and they had to stand most of the journey in a tightly packed huddle, with Erika sandwiched between her new colleagues. Peterson's lean frame was contrasted by the dumpy bulk of Moss pressed against her other side. Erika wished she could have five minutes to herself, some space and fresh air to gather her thoughts. In twenty-five years of police investigations, she'd informed what seemed like hundreds of people that they had lost loved ones, but since experiencing the other side of loss, she felt different. The pain was still so raw. And now she was going to have to tell Andrea's parents, and watch the now-familiar grief as it consumed them.

Snow had stopped falling when they emerged from Turnham Green tube station. Chiswick High Road was polished in comparison to South London. The streets were clean, with freshly painted post boxes, and independent butchers and organic stores mingled among the Victorian terraced houses with their spotless sash windows. The banks and supermarkets had a zing and a gleam. Even the snow seemed whiter.

The Douglas-Browns' house was in a large, sweeping cul-de-sac set back from the busy high street. Their super-size Georgian house had been sandblasted, the removal of years of soot and smog exposing brickwork the color of butter. It dominated the other houses, despite being partly hidden by the tall trees growing in a small park at the center of the cul-de-sac. Footprints tracked across the snow where a group of photographers milled about, cameras slung over their warm winter coats, steam rising from their takeaway cups of coffee. Their interest was piqued as Erika, Moss and Peterson approached the house, entering through the front gate. Camera shutters began to click, flashes bouncing off the high-gloss black paint of the Douglas-Browns' stout front door. Erika took a deep breath and pressed the bell. An elegant chime sounded deep inside.

"Are you police?" shouted a voice from behind them.

"The dead body, is it Andie?" shouted another. Erika closed her eyes for a moment, feeling the photographers like a heavy presence behind. *What bloody right did they have to call her Andie? Not even her parents called her that.*

The front door opened, but only partially, and a tiny, dark-haired old lady looked up at them through a gap. She lifted a hand to shield her eyes as the camera flashes intensified.

"Good morning, we need to speak with Simon and Diana Douglas-Brown, please," said Erika, and the three officers flashed their IDs. They expected the lady to usher them in, but she peered up at them from under hooded eyelids, the camera flashes reflecting in her black eyes.

"You're inquiring about the Lord and Lady Douglas-Brown?"

"Yes. It's iegarding the disappearance of their daughter, Andrea," said Erika, quietly.

"I'm the Douglas-Browns' housekeeper. Please give me your identification," said the little woman, "and wait here whilst I confirm who you are." She collected up their IDs and closed the door. Fresh camera flashes bounced off the paintwork.

"Can you confirm she was raped?" shouted a voice.

"Can you confirm it's murder? And if so, do you believe it was politically motivated?" shouted another.

Erika gave Moss and Peterson a sideways glance and they kept facing the door. Seconds ticked by. They could almost feel the heat of the camera flashes on their backs.

"What does she think we're trying to do? Sell them fucking double-glazing?" hissed Moss, quietly.

"Lord Douglas was involved in a hidden camera sting last year," said Peterson, from the corner of his mouth. "The *News Of The World* caught him on film trying to bribe a defense contractor from Tehran."

"The Fake Sheik?" murmured Erika. She was about to say more, when the door opened, a little wider this time. The camera shutters from behind intensified.

"Yes, they all seem in order," said the little woman, returning their IDs and beckoning them through the gap. They followed her inside and she closed the door against the cold and photographers.

The narrow hallway opened out into a gallery, where an elegant, carpeted wooden staircase snaked up around three floors. High above was a round stained-glass skylight, which played a pattern of soft colors over the creamy walls. A glossy grandfather clock sat at the base of the stairs, its pendulum swinging silently. The housekeeper led them down a corridor, past a doorway through which they glimpsed a large steel and granite kitchen, and past an enormous gilt mirror, underneath which sat an equally impressive vase of fresh flowers. They arrived at an oak door, and were led through to a study overlooking the snow-covered back garden.

"Please wait," the housekeeper said, eyeing them as she backed out of the room and closed the door. Underneath a sash window was a sturdy desk of dark wood. Its leather surface was empty apart from a sleek silver laptop. A bookcase filled the wall to the left, and a large leather button-back sofa and two armchairs stood on the right. Above them was a wall covered in framed photographs of Simon Douglas-Brown, who Erika recognized from the press reports of Andrea's disappearance. He was a short virile-looking man, with intense brown eyes.

The photos charted his achievements, beginning with a full head of hair when his technology company was listed on the London Stock Exchange in 1987, progressing, as the hair thinned out, through a series of photos with the Queen, Margaret Thatcher, John Major and then Tony Blair. Erika noted that Her Majesty was a good few inches taller than Lord Douglas-Brown. There were four photos taken with Tony Blair, showing just how involved Douglas-Brown had become in the workings of the Labor government.

Two photos, larger than the rest, had pride of place in the center of the collage. The first was an official portrait, where Douglas-Brown stood among red carpet and wood paneling, wearing a cloak of ermine. A caption underneath showed it was taken on the day of his investiture, when he had been knighted, becoming Baron Simon Douglas-Brown of Hunstanton. In the second photo he struck the same pose, but this time with the addition of his wife, Diana, small and fine-boned beside him in an elegant white dress. She had long dark hair, and looked like an older, more pinched version of Andrea.

"Where is Hunstanton?" asked Erika.

"Norfolk coast. It's got a very nice Sea Life Center," said Moss, leaning into the photo with a deadpan face.

"So his wife became *Lady Diana*," said Peterson.

"Yeah," said Moss. "And it doesn't seem the title has brought her much luck, either!"

"Is this just a laugh for you two?" snapped Erika. "Because I don't remember anything funny about Andrea's body when it was pulled out of the ice."

Moss and Peterson apologized hastily. The three of them looked at the last of the photos in an awkward silence. Lord and Lady Douglas-Brown with President Barack Obama and his wife, Michelle. The Obamas towered over the Douglas-Browns, who had pulled their faces into smiles verging on mania. No doubt, out of shot there was a long line of lords, ladies, diplomats, captains of industry and their skinny wives waiting to step into the frame for an identical picture. A meeting of mere seconds, preserved for eternity on the ego wall.

They were roused from the photo wall by a cough, and turned to see Simon and Diana Douglas-Brown in the study doorway. Erika felt immediate guilt for passing judgment, for the two people standing expectantly in front of them were nothing more than terrified parents.

"Please, just tell us what's going on. Is it Andrea?" asked Diana. Erika detected an accent under Diana's well-spoken English, one much like Erika's own.

"Please sit down," said Erika.

Diana saw their expressions, and put her hands over her face. "No, no, no, no, no! It's not her. Not my baby. Please, not my baby!"

Simon put an arm around his wife.

"I'm very sorry to inform you that your daughter's body was found this morning in the grounds of the Horniman Museum in South London," said Erika.

"And you're sure it's her?" asked Simon.

"Yes. We found Andrea's driving license on her—on her person, and a mobile phone registered to Andrea was at the scene," said Erika. "We're doing everything we can to establish her cause of death, but I need to tell you that we believe it was suspicious. We believe that Andrea was murdered."

"Murdered?" Diana pulled away and sank down into a sofa by the bookcase, her hands still over her face. Simon's olive skin had drained of color, giving him a green pallor. "Andrea, murdered?" Diana repeated. "Who would murder her?"

Erika paused and then said, "I'm afraid we'll need you to come and formally identify Andrea's body."

There was another silence. A clock chimed in the depths of the building. Diana took her hands from her face and looked up at Erika, studying her. *"Odkial ste?"* she said.

"Narodila som sa v Nitre," replied Erika.

"No Slovak, not now. Let's speak English," said Simon.

"What's a woman from Nitra doing telling me that my daughter is dead?" said Diana, fixing Erika with a stare. It was challenging.

"Like you, I've lived in England for longer than I lived in Slovakia," explained Erika.

"You're nothing like me! Where's the other officer, the one who was here before... Sparks? I don't want the fate of our daughter resting on the skills of some Slovakian."

"Mrs. Douglas-Brown," said Erika, feeling anger rise in her.

"It's *Lady* Douglas-Brown."

Erika snapped. "I've been a police officer for twenty-five years. A Detective Chief Inspector for—"

"I can assure you, we're doing everything we can to find the person who did this," said Peterson, stepping in and shooting Erika a look.

Erika composed herself and pulled out her notebook, flicking through to a blank page. "If I may, Lady Diana, I would like to ask you a few questions?"

"No. No, you may not," said Simon, his dark eyes hardening. "Can't you see my wife is... we're... I need to make some phone calls. Where did you say you were from?"

"Nitra is in western Slovakia, but as I said, I've been in England for over twenty years."

"I'm not asking for your bloody life story. I'm asking whether you are Metropolitan police?"

"Yes, we're from Lewisham Row Station," said Erika.

"Right. Well, I want to make some calls. Find out the lay of the land. I've been dealing directly with Assistant Commissioner Oakley—"

"Sir. I'm leading the investigation—"

"And I've worked with Commander Clive Robinson on several police steering committees and—"

"And whilst I respect that, you have to understand that I am now leading this investigation and I need to ask you both some questions!" Too late, Erika realized her voice had risen to a shout. There was a silence.

"Boss. Can I have a word?" asked Peterson. He glanced at Moss and she gave a small, almost imperceptible nod. Erika felt her face flush.

"Boss, a word. Now," said Peterson. Erika rose and followed him out into the corridor. He closed the door. She leaned against the wall and tried to slow her breathing.

"I know," she said.

"Look, I'm not getting up in your face, boss. You've come in to a shit storm and I accept that, but you can't get aggressive with the victim's parents. Because right now, that's all they are. Parents. Let him posture, but we know how it's going to work from here on."

"I know. Shit," said Erika. "Oh, shit..."

"Why did the mother want to know where you were from in Slovenia?"

"Slovakia," corrected Erika. "It's a well-known Slovak attitude. The people who come from Bratislava think they're better than everyone else... I presume that's where she's from."

"And she thinks that makes her better than you," finished Peterson. Erika breathed in and nodded, trying to calm her anger.

Two men in overalls were approaching from the other end of the corridor, pulling a huge Christmas tree. Erika and Peterson parted to let them through. The tree had dried out and was brown in places, and as its branches brushed the walls, pine needles shed and sprayed across the thick blue and green carpet.

Peterson looked as if he was going to say more, then thought better of it, and took a different tack. "It's way past lunchtime. You look like you could use a sugar rush," he said, studying Erika's white face. "I know you're the boss, boss, but how about you go off, and meet us round the corner at a pub or a caff?"

"I'll go in and apologize."

"Boss. Let the dust settle, yeah? We'll get as much info as we can, and come and find you."

"Yeah. Okay. But if you can..."

"I'll arrange for them to do the ID. Yes."

"And we'll need Andrea's laptop... and... Well. Just get as much as you can for now."

Peterson nodded and went back inside the study. Erika paused for a moment. She'd totally blown it, and was coming away with nothing.

She was about to have a look round the house when the housekeeper with the hooded eyes reappeared.

"I'll show you out, shall I?" she insisted.

They followed the trail of dead pine needles to the front door. When Erika was deposited outside on the step, in front of the flashing cameras, she had to bite down hard on her bottom lip to keep herself from crying.

CHAPTER 7

The light was starting to fade when Moss and Peterson caught up with Erika in a coffee shop on Chiswick High Road. She'd spent a frustrating hour sitting by the window, watching the light fade on a day that had seemed so long, but in which she felt she'd achieved nothing. It wasn't like her to go roaring in on an interview and balls it up—especially not with the parents of the victim.

The café had been quiet when Erika had arrived, but had now filled up and was bustling with fashionable singletons, and a pack of yummy mummies who'd marked out a corner of the coffee shop with a barrier of expensive buggies.

Peterson and Moss bought coffee and sandwiches, then came over to the table to join Erika.

"Look, thanks for stepping in there; I don't know what happened. My judgment was off," explained Erika, feeling embarrassed.

"No probs," said Peterson, tearing open a sandwich box and taking a huge bite.

"Diana Douglas-Brown was out of order, but then again, it wasn't the best day of her life, was it?" agreed Moss, taking a bite of her sandwich.

"Yeah, but I shouldn't have…Anyway. What else can you tell me?" asked Erika. She waited for a moment while they both finished chewing.

"Simon and Diana don't know why Andrea was in South London," said Moss. "She'd arranged to go the cinema with David and Linda, the brother and sister. They waited for her at the Odeon in Hammersmith, but she never showed up."

"Were the brother and sister at home?"

"Yeah. David, he was asleep upstairs. Lady Diana didn't want to wake him."

"Wake him? Isn't he in his twenties?" asked Erika.

"David had been awake since the early hours, apparently," said Moss. "They'd been taking it in turns to watch the phones throughout the night, in case Andrea called. It seems she's gone missing before."

"When? Do we have a record?"

"No. They never reported it. A couple of years back she went AWOL over a long weekend. Turned out she went off to France with some guy she'd met in a bar. She came back when she maxed out her credit card."

"Did you get a name of the person she ran off with?"

"Yeah, a Carl Michaels. He was a student at the time. It was nothing dodgy. A dirty weekend, with the added bonus that Andrea had a platinum Visa card," said Moss.

"Did you see the sister, Linda?" asked Erika.

"She came in with a tray of tea. We thought she was the maid. Looks very different to Andrea: frumpy, a bit fat. She works at the mother's florist's," said Peterson.

"And how did she react to the news?" asked Erika.

"She dropped the tray, although..." Moss hesitated.

"What?" asked Erika, wishing again that she didn't have to hear this all second-hand.

Moss looked at Peterson.

"It seemed a bit cod, the way she reacted," he said.

"Cod?" asked Erika.

"You know, like bad acting. I don't know. People react in all sorts of weird ways. The whole family seems a bit screwed up if you ask me," said Peterson.

"Then again, whose family isn't screwed up?" added Moss. "Plus, you throw money into the mix and everything gets heightened."

A phone began to ring, and it took a few moments before Erika realized it was hers. She pulled it out and answered. It was Isaac, telling her that the bad weather had slowed everything right down. The results of the autopsy would be ready in the morning.

"I really wanted them to ID the body tonight," said Erika, when she came off the phone.

"It could work in your favor. It'll give Sir Simon a chance to cool off," said Peterson.

"Did he say anything else?" asked Erika.

"Yeah, he wants Sparks back on the case," said Moss.

They carried on chewing in silence. It was now dark. Car headlights crawled past, illuminating the incessant snow falling outside.

CHAPTER 8

Erika, Moss, and Peterson arrived back at Lewisham Row just after seven p.m. They went straight to the incident room, which was full, the police officers waiting expectantly to share the day's findings. Erika sloughed off her long leather jacket and went to the huge bank of whiteboards lining the back of the room.

"Okay, everyone. I know it's been a long day, but what have we got?"

"How did you get on when you met the family? How did Sir Simon take to you, DCI Foster?" smirked Sparks, leaning back in his chair.

On cue, Chief Superintendent Marsh pulled open the door to the incident room. "Foster. A word."

"Sir, I'm just briefing everyone on the day's events..."

"Okay. But my office, the second you're done," he barked, and slammed the door.

"So it went well, I take it?" needled Sparks, his nasty smile tinted with the white-blue of his computer screen. Erika ignored him and turned back to the whiteboard. Beside Andrea's photo were pictures of Linda and David. She noticed with interest that Andrea and her brother were very attractive, but Linda was overweight and matronly, with a pointed nose and a whiter complexion than her siblings.

"Are the kids all from the same parents?" asked Erika, tapping the board with her marker pen. This took the incident room off guard.

Sergeant Crane looked round in surprise. "We assumed yes..."

"Why did you assume this?" asked Erika.

"Well, they seemed quite..."

"Posh?" asked Erika. "Never forget, we look at family first and foremost as suspects. Don't let yourselves be blinded by the fact that they live in an expensive area of London and have influence and power. Crane, you can look into the children, but of course, be discreet. Now, we know that Andrea was due to meet David and Linda at the cinema last Thursday, the eighth, but she never showed up. Where did she go? Was she meeting a friend, a secret lover? Who was looking specifically into Andrea's life?"

A small Indian woman in her twenties stood up. "PC Singh," she said. She came to the front and Erika handed her the marker pen.

"Andrea's been in a relationship with twenty-seven-year-old Giles Osborne for the past eight months; they'd recently got engaged. He owns Yakka Events, an upmarket events and party planning company, based in Kensington."

"Yakka Events. What does *Yakka* mean?" asked Erika.

"It's the aboriginal word for work. It says on the company website that he spent his gap year in Australia."

"Learning how to serve canapés and champagne from the aborigines?" asked Erika. A flicker of a smile passed through the incident room.

"He's privately educated. Comes from a wealthy family. He has an alibi for the night Andrea went missing."

"I've already interviewed him; we found this out last week," interrupted Sparks.

"What about the records for Andrea's phone, and social media? I take it those have been requested?"

"Yes," said Singh.

"Where are they?"

"I'm on it. I requested them this morning, so we're hoping to get them in the next twenty-four hours," said Crane.

"Why weren't they requested before, when she became a missing person?" asked Erika.

There was silence.

"Worried you were prying into the lives of the influential rich people?"

"I made the call not to go ahead and request those," said Sparks. "The family were still under the impression that Andrea had taken off somewhere; they were monitoring her social media accounts and sharing information with us."

Erika rolled her eyes. "I want those records the second we have them, and anything that gets pulled off the phone hard drive," she said to Crane. "Now, Sparks, you seem full of the joys of late winter. What did you manage to find with the CCTV?"

DCI Sparks leaned back in his chair with a creak. "Not good news, I'm afraid. Until a couple of days ago, three of the CCTV cameras on the London Road were down. So we've got nothing around the train station forecourt, or leading up the high street to the Horniman Museum. Course, the back roads aren't covered either, so we're blind to the events on the night of the eighth."

"Shit," said Erika.

"We have got her coming off the train at Forest Hill Station at"—Sparks flicked through his notes—"9:06 p.m. She comes off the train, goes along the platform and leaves past the ticket office. It was unmanned, and only a couple of other people got off at the same time."

"Can we find out who they are? Maybe they walked up with her."

"I'm already on it," Sparks finished.

"What about the door-to-door?"

Sergeant Crane leaned forward in his chair, saying: "Not a great deal, boss. Most people were either still away after their Christmas break, or asleep."

"What about any pubs?"

"The Wetherspoon's and The Pig and Whistle have CCTV; she didn't go into either of those. There's another four pubs on the high street."

"Grace Kinney mentioned two: The Glue Pot and The Stag."

"We've been to them all. Pretty rough shit-holes they are too, boss, and no one who works there remembers seeing her."

"Look at staff rotas, find out who the locals are. Check again. She was dressed for a night out. There's a high chance she did go into one of those pubs."

"What if she was going to a house party?" asked Singh.

"Okay, then what about off-licenses? Did she go into any to buy fags or booze?"

"Again, the off-licenses do have CCTV, but footage tends to be patchy, and none of them saw her," said Crane.

"What about outside the house where her bag was found?"

"Yes, number forty-nine, and unfortunately, nothing again. Homeowner is a gaga old lady with a live-in carer; neither of them saw or heard anything."

There was an uncomfortable silence.

"Perhaps you should let your team get some rest. It's been a long day," said Sparks.

"Yeah. Okay. Let's meet back here at nine tomorrow. We should have the autopsy results by then, and the phone and social media records."

Erika said goodnight to her officers, and when she was the last in the incident room, she looked over the whiteboards in silence, lingering over Andrea's picture.

"Look at you; just twenty-three. You had your whole life ahead of you." Andrea stared back at her, defiantly, almost mocking her.

Erika jumped as her phone rang,

"Do you want to keep me waiting any longer?" barked Marsh.

"Shit, sir, sorry. I'm on my way up."

CHAPTER 9

"So what you're telling me is, you've got nothing?" said Marsh. He was red in the face as he paced up and down his office. Erika had just underlined the progress made during the first day of investigations.

"This is day one, sir. And as I said, there's a positive ID on the victim; I've kept it out of the press. I think there's one or two pubs where Andrea might possibly be placed the night she vanished."

"*Might possibly be placed*; what does that mean?"

"It means we're hampered by a CCTV black spot all up the London Road and around the train station. We need time and resources to keep on at people, asking questions. Everyone has worked bloody hard, especially when the weather has slowed proceedings…"

"And what the hell did you think you were doing, getting into a row with the Douglas-Browns?"

Erika took a deep breath to steady herself. "I admit, sir, that I should have handled the victim's parents better."

"Too bloody right you should have. I thought Lady Diana would have found some common ground, with you being Slovak?"

"Yes, well, that was the problem. She thought I was common. Not good enough to be leading the murder investigation."

"Yeah, well, you didn't choose to be a police officer so people could be nice to you, DCI Foster. There is a course I can send you on—dealing with the public."

"That's the problem. We're not treating them as members of the public. In fact, is Sir Simon leading the investigation? He seems to think he's in charge…Anyway who told you about what happened? He called you, did he? Knows your direct line number?"

"You're on thin ice, DCI Foster," said Marsh. "He called DCI Sparks, actually, who relayed the message to me."

"How good of him."

Marsh shot her a look. "I've stuck my neck out on this, to get you on this case—"

"I don't want your pity, sir!"

"—and if you're not careful, you'll be gone before you've even started. You need to learn how to keep your mouth shut. I got you on this case because you're a bloody good copper. One of the best I know. Although, right now, I'm questioning my judgment."

"I'm sorry, sir. It's just been a long day—tough conditions, and no sleep. But you know me, I don't make excuses and I will find who did this."

"Okay," said Marsh, calming down. "But you need to apologize sincerely to the Douglas-Browns."

"Yes, sir."

"And get a decent night's sleep. You look like shit."

"Thanks, sir."

"Where are you staying?"

"A hotel."

"Good. Now bugger off, and come to work tomorrow with your head screwed on," said Marsh, waving her away.

Erika was furious when she left Marsh's office; furious that she'd been given a dressing-down, and furious with herself that she'd messed up. She went back down to the incident room and grabbed her coat. Andrea's picture stared boldly back at her from the center of the whiteboard. The handwritten notes on the case blurred in the bright lights, and Erika rubbed her tired eyes. It felt like she was looking at everything through murky glass. She couldn't get a handle on the details. Tiredness and anger washed over her again. She pulled on her coat and left, flicking off the light. When she came out of the incident room she met Desk Sergeant Woolf in the corridor.

"I was just coming to tell you. We've sorted you a car. It's a blue Ford Mondeo," he said, holding out a key fob, his jowly face more sullen than it had been that morning.

"Thanks," said Erika, taking the key. They made for the main entrance, Woolf struggling a little to match her stride.

"I didn't put your suitcase in though; I did my back in a few years ago. Had to have a disc removed. It's behind my desk..."

They emerged into the reception area, where a thin, bedraggled woman was leaning over Woolf's desk, using his phone. She wore filthy ripped jeans, and an old parka jacket that was stained and covered in cigarette burns. Her long gray hair was tied back with an elastic band, and underneath her eyes were deep dark circles. Two unkempt little girls beside her were shrieking encouragement at a little boy with a buzz cut who sat on Erika's suitcase. He wore a pair of stained white tracksuit bottoms and was gyrating his hips with one hand on the suitcase handle and the other in the air, like he was riding a bucking bronco. Woolf hurried behind his desk and put his finger on the phone, cutting off the call.

"I was fuckin' talking!" snarled the woman indignantly, displaying a mouth of crooked brown teeth.

"Ivy. This is a police phone," said Woolf.

"Well, it ain't rung for the past ten minutes. Think yerself lucky the criminals are having a rest!"

"Who do you want to call? I can do it for you," said Woolf.

"I know how to use a fuckin' phone!"

"Who is this woman?" asked Erika.

Ivy held the receiver away from Woolf and gave Erika the once over, saying, "Me and Droopy go way back, don't we Droopy? I call 'im Droopy. Ugly fuckin' bastard, ain't he?"

"You. Get off my suitcase," said Erika to the boy, who couldn't have been more than seven or eight. He ignored her and carried on whooping and riding the suitcase. Woolf grappled with Ivy for the receiver, and finally managed to prize it from her grip.

"I should be allowed to use this bloody phone. It's only a local call and besides, I pay your wages!"

"How do you pay my wages?" asked Woolf.

"I've got money. I pay my taxes, and that's what pays your wages!"

Erika went to lift the little boy off her suitcase, but he leaned over and sank his teeth into the back of her hand. The intensity of the pain surprised her.

"Let go, now," said Erika, trying to keep calm. He looked up at her with a nasty grin, and bit down even harder. Intense pain shot through her hand and she snapped, slapping him hard across the face. He screamed, releasing Erika's hand, and fell off the suitcase, hitting the ground with a thud.

"Who do you think you fuckin' are?" growled Ivy, lunging across at her.

Erika tried to dodge out of the way, but found herself with her back flat against the wall. Woolf caught Ivy just in time, as a long blade glinted inches from Erika's face.

"Ivy, now come on, just cool it..." started Woolf, restraining her under the armpits, but still struggling to hold her back.

"Don't you tell me to cool it, you fat ugly cunt!" said Ivy, dangerously. "You touch my kids and I'll cut your face, no problem, you bitch. I've got nothin' to lose."

Erika tried to control her breathing as she saw the flick-knife inch closer to her face.

"Let go of the knife. Let go," said Woolf, finally gaining a grip on Ivy's wrist, and twisting the flick-knife out of her hand. It clattered to the floor and he put his foot over it.

"You didn't 'ave to be so rough, Droopy," said Ivy, rubbing her wrist. Woolf kept his eye on her as he leaned down and retrieved the knife from the floor. He found the small release button and the blade vanished back into its handle. The little boy and two girls had ceased to be threatening and rowdy. They were just kids, and they seemed more afraid of what Ivy was going to do next. Erika couldn't imagine the life they must lead. She looked at the little boy, who was holding the back of his head.

"I'm sorry, I'm so sorry… What's your name?"

He shrank back from her. What could she say to him? That she'd had a bad day? Erika took in their filthy clothes, their malnourished bodies…

"I want to make a complaint," said Ivy with relish.

"Oh, do you?" said Woolf, moving Ivy toward the main door.

"Yeah, *police brutality*—get yer hands off me—police brutality toward a minor."

"You'll need to fill in a form," said Woolf. "Before you spend a night in the cells for pulling a knife on a police officer."

Ivy narrowed her eyes. "No, I haven't got fuckin' time… Come on, kids. NOW!" She gave Erika a last look, and they followed after her through the main door. There was a flash of coats as they passed the window.

"Shit," said Erika, slumping against the main desk and rubbing at the back of her hand. "I shouldn't have hit that kid."

There was a white and purple ridge of teeth marks deep in her skin, and a blur of blood mingling with the little boy's saliva. Woolf went to a box marked KNIFE AMNESTY where he deposited Ivy's flick-knife. He then moved back round the desk and pulled down a first-aid kit. He placed it on the table beside Erika and opened the lid.

"You know her?" asked Erika.

"Oh, yes. Ivy Norris, or Jean McArdle, Beth Crosby—sometimes she goes by Paulette O'Brien. Bit of a local celebrity." He poured some alcohol solution on a sterile dressing and pressed it against the back of Erika's hand, over the bite marks. The nasty stinging sensation was contrasted by a comforting smell of mint. Woolf went on, "She's a long-term drug addict, prostitute, got a record as long as the Great Wall of China. She used to do a mother-and-daughter specialty, if you know what I mean, until the daughter died of a drug overdose."

"And the kids' fathers?"

"They're actually her grandkids, and who knows? Stick your finger in the phone book."

Woolf removed the dressing and started to clean the bloody bite mark with a fresh one.

"Are they homeless?"

Woolf nodded.

"Could we get them into emergency social services, bed and breakfast?" asked Erika. She could still see Ivy, standing in the car park smoking under the harsh lights and mouthing off to no one in particular. The kids were huddled around her, flinching as she gestured with her arms.

Woolf laughed darkly. "She's banned from most of the B&Bs and hostels for soliciting."

He lifted off the dressing and applied a large square bandage to the back of Erika's hand.

"Thanks," said Erika, flexing her fingers.

Woolf started to pack up the first aid kit. "Now you know what I'm going to tell you. You need to see a doctor about the bite. Get a tetanus jab, and you know... Street kids, not healthy."

"Yeah," said Erika.

"And I have to log this down. Everything what happened. She pulled a knife on you. He bit you..."

"Yes, and I hit him. I hit a bloody kid... It's fine. Do your job, and thank you."

He nodded, took his seat again and pulled out some paperwork. Erika turned back to look outside, but Ivy and the kids were gone.

CHAPTER 10

It was bitingly cold outside. The main entrance of Lewisham Row Police Station was lit up, but the car park was a pool of darkness. Long rows of cars twinkled with frost under the street lamps, and beyond, the traffic crawled steadily by. Erika's hand was still throbbing. She pointed the key fob to her left and clicked, then did the same to her right. A car down the far end of the car park gave two pulses of orange light. She cursed and set off, dragging her case through the deep snow.

She stowed the case in the boot and got inside. The car was freezing, but smelled new. She turned on the engine and activated the central locking. When the heaters had warmed the inside up a little, she pulled out of the parking space and drove slowly toward the exit.

Ivy was standing on the pavement outside. The children were huddled together under her arms, shivering uncontrollably. Erika stopped level with them and opened her window.

"Where are you going, Ivy?" she asked. Ivy turned, the wind catching a wisp of her long gray hair and pressing it against her face.

"What's it got to do with you?" said Ivy.

"I can give you a lift."

"Why would we get in a car with a kiddy-bashing pig?"

"I'm sorry. I was really out of order. I've had a bad day."

"You've had a bad day. Try being me, love," snorted Ivy.

"I can take you wherever you need to go, and the kids can warm up," said Erika, noting the little girls' bare legs underneath their thin dresses.

Ivy narrowed her eyes. "What do I have to do in return?"

"All you have to do is sit in the car," said Erika. She dug out a twenty-pound note. Ivy went to take it, but Erika held it away. "You get it when I drop you off, provided there's no more knives, or biting."

Ivy shot the little boy a look and he nodded obediently. "Fine," she said. She opened the back door and the kids clambered in, crawling across the backseat. When Ivy got in beside Erika, she gave off a nasty, tramp-like whiff. Erika swallowed the fear of Ivy's proximity.

"Seat belts," she said, thinking that it would be safer for her if they were all strapped down.

"Yeah, we wouldn't want to break the law," laughed Ivy, pulling the seat belt round and fastening it with a click.

"Where do you want to go?"

"Catford," said Ivy. Erika pulled out her phone and clicked on her Google maps app. "Bloody hell," said Ivy, "I'll direct you. Go left."

The car was a very smooth drive, and as the street lights played over the windscreen, the unusual combination of Ivy, her grandchildren, and Erika settled into an almost comfortable silence.

"So. You got any kids?" asked Ivy.

"No," said Erika. She put on the windscreen wipers as a dusting of snow hit the windscreen.

"You a lezzer?"

"No."

"Don't bother me. I don't mind lezzers. You can have a good drink with a lezzer, and they're good at DIY…I tried it once, mind. Didn't like the taste."

"Of what? DIY?" joked Erika.

"Very funny. Sayin' that, I'm thinking of going lezzer again. I'll have to split the money but I'm getting sick of the taste of cock."

Erika looked across at her.

"Come on love, you didn't think I worked in Marks and Spencer's, did yer?"

"Where do you live?" asked Erika.

"Why should I tell you where I fuckin' live?" Ivy lurched toward her, but her seat belt locked, holding her in place.

"Easy... You just told me that you're 'sick of the taste of cock.' I thought asking for your address wouldn't be too impolite?"

"Don't you try and be clever with me. I know you. Like your job, do you? Got any friends?" There was a silence. "No I thought not, never off duty, are you? You lot would shop your own mother... Left here."

Erika put on the indicator and turned. "I don't live anywhere, right now," she said, figuring she could offer up some info of her own. "My husband died recently, and I've been away, and..."

"And you lost your marbles, yeah?"

"No, but I came close," said Erika.

"My 'usband was stabbed. Years ago. Bled to death in my arms... Go right here. You're all right though, ain't yer? Good job. I could've been a police officer, or something better," sneered Ivy.

"You know this area well, then?" asked Erika

"Yeah. Bin 'ere me whole life."

"What bars do you recommend?"

"What bars do I recommend?" she said, mimicking Erika.

"Okay, what bars do you know?"

"I know 'em all. As I just said, I've been round 'ere for years. Seen places come and go. The rough ones last the longest."

They passed the Catford Broadway Theatre, the front lit up, still advertising the Christmas pantomime.

"Drop us here," said Ivy.

Catford High Street was deserted. Erika pulled up by a pedestrian crossing, next to a Ladbrokes betting shop and a branch of Halifax.

"There aren't any houses," said Erika.

"I told you, I ain't got a house!"

"Where are you staying then?"

"I've got business to attend to. Come on, wake them up," snapped Ivy to the boy. Erika looked through her rearview mirror. The two girls were asleep, their heads leaned together. The boy stared back at her with a white face.

"I'm sorry I hit you," said Erika. His face remained impassive.

"Leave it out, just give me the money," said Ivy, unclipping her seat belt and opening the car door. Erika fumbled in her coat and brought out the twenty. Ivy took the note, stuffing it in the folds of her parka.

"Before you go, Ivy, what do you know about pubs in Forest Hill? The Stag?"

"There's a stripper there who'll do anything once her pint glass is full of pound coins," said Ivy.

"And what about The Glue Pot?" asked Erika.

Ivy's whole body language changed. Her eyes went wide. "I don't know nothin' about that place," she said hoarsely.

"You just said you knew all the bars around here. Come on, tell me about The Glue Pot?"

"I don't ever go in there," Ivy whispered. "And I don't know nothin,' you hear me?"

"Why not?"

Ivy paused and looked at Erika. "I'd get that hand looked at. Little Mike, he's HIV positive…"

She got out, slamming the door, and vanished in between the shops, the kids trailing after her. Erika was so focused on Ivy's reaction to hearing the name of the pub that she didn't take in what Ivy had just said. She quickly opened her door and followed them to the entrance of a dank alley. She peered down, but it was too dark to make them out in the shadows. "Ivy," she shouted. "Ivy! What do you mean, you don't ever go in there? Why don't you?"

Erika started down the alley, the street lights quickly fading. She felt something soft and squelchy under her feet.

"Ivy. I can give you more money, you just have to tell me what you know…"

She pulled out her phone and flicked on the light. The alley was filled with empty needles, condoms, and discarded packaging and price tags. "I'm investigating a murder," she continued. "The Glue Pot was the last place this girl was seen…"

Her voice echoed. There was no response. She reached a ten-foot high chain-link fence with metal spikes on top. Beyond, she could just make out a scrubby yard with some discarded gas canisters. She looked around.

"Where the hell did they go?" she said under her breath. She doubled back down the alleyway, but she could see no way out—just the high brick walls of the buildings either side.

When Erika came back to the car, her door was still open, the warning alarm gently chiming. She looked around and got back in. Had she imagined them? She spent a few seconds worrying that she had hallucinated the whole episode—Ivy, the kids—and then she felt a throb of pain in the back of her hand, and saw the square bandage.

She quickly activated the central locking, then pulled away with a squeal of tires. Fresh adrenaline surged through her body. Something wasn't right about Ivy's reaction to The Glue Pot. She had been terrified. Why?

Erika didn't care how late it was, or how deprived she was of sleep. She was going to check out that pub.

CHAPTER 11

Erika drove back over to Forest Hill, and parked a couple of roads back from the high street in a quiet residential area. The pub was halfway up the high street, a two-storey brick building with a wine-colored frontage. The Glue Pot was written in white, the "t" trailing away to a cartoon of a paintbrush hovering above a pot of white glue. It was an irritating sign, both naff and clueless. There were four windows, two on each storey, with thick stone sills. The windows on the first floor were dark. Of the two below, one was boarded up, leaving the other to glow murkily behind a net curtain.

Despite the cold, the outer door was wedged open. A sign promised that if you bought two glasses of house wine, you could get the rest of the bottle free. Erika went inside and found the bar was accessed via an inner door with badly cracked safety glass.

The bar was almost empty, with just two young men sitting smoking at one of the many Formica tables. They glanced up at her as she passed, taking in her long legs, and then returned to their beer. A small dance floor to one side was filled with old stacking chairs, and a Magic FM jingle played over the sound system, introducing the opening bars of *Careless Whisper*. Erika went to a long, low bar at the back that was framed by hanging glasses. A dumpy young girl was sitting watching *Celebrity Big Brother* on a tiny portable television.

"Double vodka with tonic, please," Erika said.

The girl heaved herself up, reached for a wineglass, then pushed it against an optic, keeping her eye on the screen. She was wearing a faded Kylie *Showgirl* tour T-shirt stretched to capacity over her large bosom and dumpy frame. She adjusted the back of the T-shirt, pulling it down over her large backside.

"You looking for an au pair? Childcare?" the girl asked, presumably having picked up on Erika's slight accent. Erika detected the hint of an accent in the girl, too, Polish? Russian? She couldn't place it. The girl pushed the glass against the optic again.

"Yes," said Erika, deciding to play along. The girl pulled out a plastic bottle of tonic water, and filled the wineglass up to the brim. She placed the drink down on the bar, then slid across a square of card and a biro.

"You can put a card on the board for twenty pounds. New cards go up every Tuesday. Twenty-three fifty for that and the drink," she said.

Erika paid and sat down, taking a gulp of the drink. It was warm and flat.

"Why didn't you send your husband?" asked the girl, watching to see what Erika wrote on the card.

"Like I need my husband to drink more!"

The girl nodded with familiarity. Erika moved over to the small corkboard the girl had indicated, which was on the wall beside the bar. It was plastered with hundreds of cards, one over the other, handwritten in Slovak, Polish, Russian, Romanian—all advertising construction jobs, childcare, or au pair positions.

"Is it always this quiet?" asked Erika, looking around at the empty bar.

"It's January," shrugged the woman, wiping ashtrays with an old cloth. "And no football."

"My friend got her au pair from an advert here," said Erika, coming back to her bar stool. "Do you get many women in here? Young girls? Looking to be au pairs?"

"Sometimes."

"My friend said that there was a girl looking for work, that I might meet her here?"

The girl stopped wiping an ashtray and regarded her with a cold eye. Erika took another sip of her drink then pulled out her phone. She scrolled through to the picture of Andrea and turned it round.

"This is her."

"Never seen her," said the girl, a bit too quickly.

"Really? My friend did say she was in here just a few days ago..."

"I didn't see her." The girl lifted up a wire tray half-filled with empty glasses and went to leave.

"I'm not done yet," said Erika, placing her police ID on the bar.

The girl hesitated and put the wire tray back. When she turned, she saw the ID and looked panicked.

"No it's okay, I just need you to answer my questions. What's your name?"

"Kristina."

"Kristina...?"

"Just Kristina," she insisted.

"Okay. Just Kristina. I'll ask you again. Have you seen this girl in here?"

The girl looked down at the picture of Andrea on the phone and shook her head so furiously that her cheeks wobbled.

"Were you working here the night of the eighth? It was a Thursday, just over a week ago."

The girl thought about it, and shook her head again.

"Are you sure? She was found dead earlier today."

The girl chewed her lip.

"Are you the landlady?"

"No."

"You just work here?"

"Yes."

"Who's the landlady, or landlord?"

Kristina shrugged.

"Come on, Kristina. I can find out this information easily, with the brewery. And those men were smoking in here, despite the smoking ban. Do you know how much that would cost in fines? Thousands of pounds. And then there's the illegal employment agency. You just charged me twenty pounds to advertise. I could make a call and have a team of officers here in five minutes, and you'd be responsible..."

Kristina started to cry. Her huge chest heaved, her face went red and she scrubbed at her beady little eyes with a corner of a tea towel.

"If you can just answer a couple of questions," said Erika, "I can make sure that you are seen as an innocent employee."

Kristina stopped crying and caught her breath.

"Okay... It's okay, Kristina. Nothing bad is going to happen. Now, please, look at this photo again. Did you see this girl here on the night of the eighth? That was last Thursday. She was abducted and murdered. If you can tell me anything, you might help me find whoever did this."

The girl looked down through swollen eyes at the picture of Andrea. "She sat there, in the corner," she said, finally. Erika turned and saw the small table by the dance floor. She also noticed that the two men drinking had gone, leaving half-full pints.

"You're sure it was this girl?" said Erika, holding up the picture on the phone again.

"Yeah. I remember how beautiful she was."

"Was she alone? Did she meet anyone?"

Kristina nodded. "There was a young woman with her, short blonde hair."

"As short as mine?" asked Erika.

The girl nodded.

"Anything else?"

"They had a drink, or two, I don't know, it was a really busy night...and...and..."

Erika could see she was becoming more worked up and scared. "Go on, Kristina. It's okay, I promise."

"Then I don't know when she went, her friend—but when I looked again, there was a man sitting with her."

"What did he look like?"

The woman shrugged. "Tall, dark...They argued."

"What do you mean, tall and dark? Can you be a bit more detailed?" said Erika, trying to hide her frustration. This was a real breakthrough, but Kristina was being too vague. She made a decision and pulled out her phone.

"Kristina, I want you to come with me to the station, and do what we call a photofit of the woman and man you saw Andrea sitting with."

"No, no, no, no," Kristina started, backing away.

Erika dialed the number for the duty desk at Lewisham Row. It started to ring. "Your information could lead to us finding out who killed this woman, Andrea."

"But I'm at work...and..."

"I can get the officers to come here. We can do this now." The duty officer picked up the phone. "It's DCI Erika Foster. I need uniform and a squad car to The Glue Pot pub on London Road in Forest Hill, and who do we have on duty who can do a photofit?"

There was a movement, and Erika realized Kristina had vanished through a door at the back of the bar.

"Shit! Hang on, I'll call you back." Erika swung herself over the bar and through the doorway to a filthy little back kitchen. A door stood open. Erika stepped into the alleyway. It stretched away long and empty in both directions. A light dusting of snow began to fall. It was eerily silent.

Erika walked the length of the alley in both directions. The houses backing onto it were dark, and the roads at either end were empty. The snow started to fall more heavily, and the wind whistled through the buildings. Erika pulled her coat around her against the freezing cold.

She couldn't shake off the feeling she was being watched.

CHAPTER 12

Two uniformed police officers were called to The Glue Pot, but an extensive search came up with nothing. Kristina had vanished. The flat above the pub was unoccupied, filled with a mess of junk and old broken furniture. It was gone midnight by the time that the officers told Erika to knock off, and get some sleep. They would remain stationed at the pub, and at first light they would track down the landlord. If Kristina came back, they would bring her in.

Erika still felt spooked when she returned to her car, parked a few streets away. The streets were silent, and every noise seemed amplified, the wind keening as it blew around the buildings, a wind chime on the porch of a house... It was as if she could feel a gaze from one of the black windows of the houses all around.

From the corner of her eye, she saw a shadow move in one window. She turned, but there was nothing. Just a dark bay window. Was someone watching her from the shadows? She realized she was in desperate need of rest. She would find the first hotel and book in. She unlocked her car and climbed in, activating the central locking. She sank into the comfort of the seat, leaned back her head, and closed her eyes.

It's a baking hot day on a run-down street in Rochdale, and Erika's protective police gear sticks to her skin. She shifts uncomfortably, crouched against the low wall of a terraced house looming tall in the heat. Two officers are beside her, mirrored by three officers on the other side of the front gate. Mark is with them. Second along.

From weeks of surveillance, the terraced house is burned into her brain. Bare concrete out front, overflowing wheelie bins. A gas and electric meter on the wall with its cover ripped off.

Through the front door, up the stairs, a door to the left of the landing leads through to the back bedroom. That's where they cook the meth. A woman has been seen going in with a little kid. It's a risk, but they are prepared. Erika has drilled the routine over and over to her team of eight officers. Only now, they are stationed outside. It is real. Fear threatens to roll over Erika, but she pulls back from it.

She gives the nod, and her black-clad team moves stealthily, surging down the path to the front door. The sun glints off the disc in the meter as it spins. Once, twice, almost matching the thunk of the battering ram. On the third attempt, the wood splinters, and the front door bursts inward with a clatter.

Then all hell breaks loose.

Shots are fired. The window above the electricity meter explodes inward. Shots are coming from the house behind them. Erika's head spins round. The nice house across the street. Sash windows. Brass numbers on the door. Farrow & Ball paint on the walls inside. The couple had been so welcoming, so unassuming when the police had carried out their surveillance.

It falls into place as Erika's eyes are drawn to their upstairs window. She sees a dark shadow, then pain explodes in her neck and she tastes blood. Mark is suddenly beside her, crouching down to help. She tries to speak, to tell him, "It's behind you"*—but blood fills her throat. In the hysteria it's almost funny. Then there is a cracking sound, and the side of Mark's head is blown open…*

Erika woke with a gasp, trying to catch her breath. She was surrounded by an eerie brightness, pressing down. She exhaled, and her breath came out in a long stream. It was only when she saw the steering wheel in front of her that she got her bearings. She was back in the present. Sitting in the car. A fresh layer of snow had fallen, completely covering the windows.

It was a familiar dream. She always woke up at the same point. Sometimes the dream was in black and white, and Mark's blood looked like melted chocolate.

She breathed in and out, her heart rate slowing, the reality sinking in. She heard muffled voices and footsteps; people walking past the car. The voices grew louder and receded.

She looked at the digital clock on the dashboard. It was now almost five in the morning. She'd slept for hours, although she felt no better for it. She shifted in the seat, her body stiff and freezing, and started the engine. The air from the heaters came out in an icy jet.

When the car had warmed up, Erika flicked on the windscreen wipers and waited as the road appeared, washed white by the fresh layer of snow. Noticing the bandage on the back of her hand, she remembered that she had to see a doctor, but the events of last night compelled her to keep going, for now.

Andrea was in that pub... Who were the woman and man she had she spoken to? And why had the barmaid vanished?

It was easier to force the dream to the back of her mind, now that she had a problem to solve. Erika put the car in gear and set off for the police station.

CHAPTER 13

Lewisham Row Police Station was quiet at five-thirty in the morning. The only sound was the far-off hammering along the corridor from the cells. The women's locker room was empty, and Erika stripped off her grubby clothes and went through to the huge communal showers, turning on the water as hot as she could bear. She stood under it, savoring the warmth, and as the steam rose, the tiled Victorian showers vanished, and Erika with them.

By six, she was dressed in clean clothes, and alone in the incident room, nursing a cup of coffee and some chocolate from the vending machine. Andrea Douglas-Brown stared back at her from the wall, over-confident.

Erika went to the desk she'd been allocated, located her password and logged on to the intranet. It had been eight months since she'd looked at her work e-mail—not through any kind of abstinence; she'd not had access. Scrolling through, she saw messages from former colleagues, newsletters, junk mail, and a notice to attend a formal hearing. That almost made her laugh: she'd been notified of a formal disciplinary hearing through an internal mail system that she'd been barred from accessing.

With a long sweep of the mouse, she highlighted all the old e-mails and pressed delete.

There was now just one e-mail from Sergeant Crane, sent late the previous night:

Find attached Andrea DB's full Facebook
profile history 2007–2014. Plus records from her
phone recovered at the crime scene.
CRANE

Erika opened the attached file and clicked "print." Moments later, the printer by the door whirred into life, rapidly spitting out paper. Erika grabbed the pile of pages and took them down to the staff canteen, hoping to find it open for a decent coffee—but it was in darkness. She found a chair at the back, clicked on the lights, and started to sift through Andrea Douglas-Brown's Facebook profile.

It spanned 217 pages, almost nine years, taking Andrea from a fresh-faced fourteen-year-old to a sultry siren of twenty-three. In her early posts she was quite a conservative young woman, but once boys had come on the scene, she had started to dress more provocatively.

Andrea's seven years of Facebook posts were an endless blur of party photos and selfies. Hundreds of photos with handsome men and beautiful girls, rarely the same people more than a few times. It seemed that she was a party animal, and one who partied at the expensive end of the spectrum. The clubs she frequented were the type where you needed to book a table, and there never seemed to be a shortage of champagne bottles littering those tables in the photos.

Throughout the years, there was little interaction on Facebook with her siblings. Her older sister, Linda, seemed to "like" a few of the family-related posts, as did her younger brother, David, but these tended to be only the posts associated with the annual holidays the Douglas-Brown family took to Greece, and in later years, to a villa in Dubrovnik, Croatia.

The holidays interested Erika the most. Taken every August for three weeks, they followed a similar pattern. At the start of each, Andrea would post some family-friendly pictures—a group photo during a meal in a nice restaurant, or the family gathered round a cabana having a casual lunch in their swimming costumes. At these lunches, Andrea always wore a bikini, and was striking a pose, her dark hair tumbling over one shoulder as she artfully picked at her food. In contrast, Linda would be hunched down, plate piled high, looking a little annoyed that she was being distracted from tucking in. Linda seemed to grow in girth as each holiday passed, and she always covered up in long T-shirts and leggings. David, in contrast, started out as an extremely skinny thirteen-year-old wearing glasses, huddled under his mother's thin arm, and slowly morphed into a handsome young man.

Andrea seemed closer to David; in many of the photos she had drawn him into a reluctant bear hug, his glasses askew. There were barely any photos of Linda and David together. Sir Simon and Lady Diana seemed to give nothing away in photographs, pulling the same faces year in, year out: broad, yet vacant smiles. Here was Lady Diana in a swimming suit and sarong combo. There was Sir Simon in baggy board shorts, pulled a little too high over his hairy belly.

As each holiday progressed, Andrea would quickly lose interest in family time and start to post pictures she'd taken of local boys. At first they'd be a bit stalker-ish, the groups of boys unaware they were being photographed as they stood around smoking, or played football on the beach with their shirts off. Then Andrea would zone in on one boy in particular, spending the last week of the holidays seemingly obsessed, taking endless photos. She apparently liked the bad boys: older and darker with muscly torsos, tattoos and piercings. In one picture, taken in the summer of 2009, Andrea was pictured posing on the back of a giant Harley Davidson, wearing the tiniest bikini and miming driving, while a dark haired lad, who presumably owned the bike, was relegated to riding pillion. He had one hand on her bikini bottoms, and was holding a cigarette, its tip glowing close to Andrea's tanned skin. She fixed the camera with a look that said, *I'm in control.*

Erika wrote in the margin: Who took this picture?

She barely noticed when the shutters went up on the canteen serving-hatch, and bleary-eyed officers began to file in for breakfast. She read on, fascinated by Andrea's life.

In 2012, a new friend appeared on the scene, a girl called Barbora Kardosova.

Slovak name?? wrote Erika, in the margin.

Barbora was dark and beautiful like Andrea, and rapidly seemed to become a close friend, even joining the family holiday in 2012 and 2013. In Barbora, Andrea seemed to have found a boy-hunting partner in crime. Although they now sought boys in a more sophisticated way, pictured together with a string of dark-haired hunks in expensive nightclubs, or around equally expensive sun loungers.

Andrea seemed to have made Barbora a genuine friend, posting pictures where they shared downtime, in which Andrea wore no makeup and was much less conscious of the camera. In many ways, Andrea was prettier without her war paint, larking about with a genuine smile on her face. In one picture, the girls posed side-by-side in front of a mirror, wearing oversized pullovers that hung down to their knees. The huge pullovers were old lady-ish. Barbora's was embroidered with cats chasing balls of wool, while Andrea's was embroidered with a giant ginger cat reclining in its basket. The phone camera flash was reflected in the top corner of the mirror. Andrea's sister, Linda, had commented, "*Get out of my bedroom you fucking cow!*"

Andrea had liked the comment and posted ☺

Then, in late 2013, Barbora abruptly vanished without explanation, defriending Andrea. Erika flicked back through the pages to check nothing was missing. Barbora didn't appear once in a photo after this point. She didn't so much as "like" a post. Around six months later, in June 2014, Andrea's Facebook profile was deactivated. There was no explanation, or message to her friends saying she intended to leave Facebook.

Erika shifted her attention to the phone records. In comparison, they were bland and sparse. Crane had annotated the numbers, which consisted of regular calls to Andrea's fiancé, Giles Osborne; to a local Chinese takeaway on a Saturday; and on the same seven Saturdays leading up to Christmas, phone votes for *The X Factor*. The rest of the phone calls were to her family, to the florist her mother ran in Kensington, and to her father's secretary. There were no calls the night she vanished, even though the phone was found with her at the murder scene. The phone records covered eight months, only going back to June 2014.

There was a clattering as a cup was dropped and shattered on the stone floor. Erika looked up, realizing that it was now light and the canteen was filling up. She checked her watch and saw that it was ten to nine. Not wanting to be late for the briefing, she gathered up her papers and left. She ran into Chief Superintendent Marsh in the corridor.

"I read last night's log," he said, raising an eyebrow.

"Yes, sir. All will be explained. I have a strong lead."

"Which is?"

"I'll tell you in the briefing," she said, as they reached the incident room. When they entered, Erika could see that the whole team had assembled at their desks. They fell silent.

"Okay. Morning everyone. I'll start by saying that Sergeant Crane managed to pull a full Facebook history for Andrea, and phone records, which is great, fast work. Andrea was very active on the site, and then last June she deactivated the profile. Also, her phone records only go back to June 2014. Why? Did she change her number?"

"She met Giles Osborne last June," said DCI Sparks.

"Yes. Now, why would she change her number and deactivate her profile around the same time?"

"Maybe she was turning over a new leaf. Some guys get jealous if a woman has exes and a history," said Singh.

"She obviously used Facebook to meet blokes, and then she got engaged and didn't need it any more," said Sparks.

"But her phone records are—well they're almost too robotic. Are you telling me she met the man of her dreams and her life was complete; she needed no other interactions?"

"I didn't say that," said Sparks.

"No, but there's something fishy about it. She made no calls the night she vanished. Let's dig around. Find her old phone and pull the records, and see if she had a second phone we don't know about? Also, find out everything you can about a girl called Barbora Kardosova, pronounced 'kardosh-ova.' She was a very close friend of Andrea between 2012 and 2013 and then she vanished. Did they fall out? Where is she now? Can we talk to her? Check her out. Find her. And also, any old boyfriends. Andrea wasn't short of male attention; see what you can dig up."

"But be discreet about that," added Marsh, from the back of the room.

Erika went on, "I paid a visit to The Glue Pot pub last night. I got a positive ID from a barmaid called Kristina that Andrea was there the night she vanished. She says that Andrea was with a short-haired blonde woman, and then later, a dark-haired man."

"Are you going to bring this Kristina in, get her to do a photofit?" asked Sparks.

"She got scared off when I suggested this."

"Okay, what's her surname?" asked Sparks.

"Well, I didn't get that far before…"

Sparks smirked and nodded his head.

Erika went on, "Another woman I spoke to, Ivy Norris—"

Sparks interrupted, "Jeez. I wouldn't believe anything Ivy Norris tells you. That old slapper is a known bullshitter and trouble maker."

"Yes, but Ivy Norris had a very weird reaction when I mentioned The Glue Pot. She was scared. Now, I want everything you can get on that pub. Find that barmaid, and interview the landlord. I believe there's a link here to Andrea and we need to find it, fast, before things evaporate."

"DCI Foster. Can I have a word please?" said Marsh.

"Yes, sir…Moss and Peterson, I want you with me today; we're going to get the results of the autopsy and the Douglas-Browns are doing the formal ID of the body."

The incident room burst into busy chatter. Erika followed Marsh up to his office. She closed the door and took a seat opposite him.

"The Douglas-Browns are coming in for the formal ID this morning?"

"Yes. At half-ten."

"I'll be issuing the official police statement at this time. Our press officer, Colleen, is very good, and of course we want to emphasize that this is the murder of an innocent girl. However, we need to be prepared that the press will find a political angle," said Marsh, ruefully.

"Well, they need to sell papers," said Erika. There was a pause, and Marsh drummed his fingers on the desk.

"I need to know what angle your investigation is taking," he said, finally.

"I'm looking for the murderer, sir."

"Don't be flippant."

"Well you were just there, in the incident room. This witness, Kristina, saw Andrea in The Glue Pot on the night she went missing. She says Andrea was with a blonde-haired woman and a dark-haired man. I'm looking for those people."

"And where is she now. This Kristina?"

"Well, she ran away, and I didn't get the chance to pursue any more information."

"Was she aware you were a police officer?"

"Yes."

"Do you think she could have felt it was in her best interest to give you a positive ID of Andrea?"

"Sir?"

"Look, Erika. She is more than likely an illegal immigrant, terrified of being deported. She probably would have told you she saw Elvis at the juke box if she thought it might save her arse."

"Sir, no, I think I have a lead here. And another woman, a local, Ivy Norris. Her reaction to The Glue Pot was..."

"I read last night's duty log, Erika. It says you hit Ivy Norris's grandson and then she pulled a knife on you."

"Yes, the boy bit me, and I reacted badly. But that's not relevant. Sir, Ivy Norris knows this area, and something about that pub scares her."

"Did you know that last month four people were beheaded at the Rambler's Rest in Sydenham? She's probably not keen on going there for a drink either."

"Sir!"

Marsh went on, "I've had the Assistant Commissioner up my arse; I have to report to someone at the bloody cabinet office with updates on this investigation. They want assurances that unsavory or unsubstantiated details of the

Douglas-Brown family won't be dredged up and played throughout the media."

"I don't control the media. Nor do I leak details of investigations. You know that, sir."

"Yes but I need you to—"

"Sir, I need to do my job. Be straight with me. Are you telling me there are things I can't investigate?"

Marsh screwed up his face. "No!"

"Then what are you telling me?"

"I'm telling you to stick to the facts. We've long suspected The Glue Pot is involved in placing illegal immigrants in work, and it's a regular hang-out for prostitutes. You need concrete facts before you start saying Andrea Douglas-Brown was in there on the night she vanished."

"What if I find that barmaid and get her on record with a photofit ID?"

"Well, good luck with that, because she's probably already packed in the back of some lorry and bound for Calais!"

"Sir! We've got Andrea on CCTV. She did board a train to Forest Hill the night she vanished, and her body was found close to the high street. Christ, is it any more obvious that I could be right?"

Marsh looked exasperated. "Okay. Just tread easy; be subtle in your investigation. The press is watching us."

"I will, sir."

"And I want to be kept informed. Everything, you understand?"

"Yes, sir."

Marsh gave her a look and she left his office.

CHAPTER 14

The morgue seemed to leach what little warmth Erika had left in her body as they walked down the long, fluorescent-lit corridor. They reached a metal door, where Moss buzzed through on an intercom. Forensic pathologist Isaac Strong buzzed them in.

"Good morning," said Isaac softly, projecting an aura of calm and order. The white lab coat covering his tall frame was neatly pressed and spotless, a dark leather mobile phone case poking from its top pocket. He wore black skinny jeans and Crocs, and his dark hair was swept away from his high forehead. Again, Erika was drawn to his soft brown eyes below his thinly arched eyebrows. His autopsy room was a heady mix of steel and Victorian porcelain tile. Along one wall was a row of stainless steel doors, and in the center of the room, three autopsy tables also of stainless steel, surrounded by gutters. Andrea Douglas-Brown lay under a white sheet, on the table closest to where they had entered. Andrea's eyes were now closed. Her hair had been washed and neatly brushed back from her forehead. The bruising had darkened, but her face was still swollen. Erika had hoped, for her family's sake, that Andrea would look as if she were sleeping, but despite the efforts to clean her up, her body still looked battered.

Isaac moved around the trolley and gently removed the sheet. In addition to the bruising and lacerations over her naked body, there was now the coarse, neat stitching from where the

Y-shaped incision had been made, running from each shoulder, converging at the chest and moving down between her full breasts to the sternum.

"There was no fluid in the lungs, so she was dead when she went into the water," said Isaac. "The ice preserved decay, but you'll note the blanching of the skin from prolonged exposure to water. Ligature marks on the neck and a fractured collarbone indicate death by strangulation. As I hypothesized, the bruising around the neck indicates a medium-sized hand, no unusual features such as missing fingers."

He paused.

"Toxicology results show there was a high level of alcohol in her blood, plus a small amount of cocaine. She hadn't eaten for several hours; her stomach was empty apart from the broken front tooth, which she probably swallowed, unintentionally, during the attack."

He picked up a small plastic phial containing the broken tooth and held it up to the light.

"I found a residue of an adhesive chemical, found in most brands of masking tape, on her mouth and teeth."

"So she was gagged?" asked Erika.

"It would indicate so. There was no sign that she'd been raped. It does appear, however, that she had anal sex close to the time she died, and it appears to have been consensual. Again, I swabbed the anus for semen and blood, but there was none. But there was latex residue, and small amounts of lubricant."

"She used a condom?" asked Erika.

"Whoever had anal sex with her used a condom," corrected Isaac.

"But how can you be sure that the anal intercourse was consensual?"

There was an uncomfortable pause.

Isaac explained: "There is a marked difference between consensual penetrative sex and non-consensual. With consensual sex, the body is usually relaxed. Non-consensual sex is often coupled with extreme stress, panic and resistance, causing muscles to tense and clench, which in turn can lead to internal bruising and abrasion of the flesh. There was no damage whatsoever to the lining of her rectum. Of course, another theory is that intercourse could have occurred post-mortem."

"Please God, no," said Erika. "I hope not."

"It's possible, yes, but I doubt it. This appears to be a crazed and frenzied attack. The killer set upon her like an animal. Her hair has been pulled out at each temple—would he have had the will and control to stop to put on a condom?"

"Were any condoms found at the scene?" asked Erika.

"The area around the boathouse and boating lake was littered with condoms. We're working on analyzing them all, but it's taking time."

They paused for a moment.

"Do you think Andrea was the kind of girl who did that kind of thing, anal sex?" asked Peterson.

"That's a little judgmental," said Isaac.

"Yeah, well you know, we can be politically correct here, or we can say it like it is. Doesn't just a certain type of girl go in for anal sex?" asked Peterson.

"I don't like that train of thought," said Erika.

"But we have to think like this," said Peterson.

"You're saying, only slutty girls love it up the arse. Ones who put themselves in dangerous situations?" asked Moss.

"Do you think this was al fresco sex gone wrong?" Erika asked Isaac.

"As I say, it's not my job to hypothesize who a person was. When they come to me, I have to make my conclusions as to how they died. You can see here that her hands were tied with a cable tie. It cut into the skin quite deep. Also her legs were tied, and the ankle of the left leg has a small hairline fracture."

"This wasn't naughty outdoor sex that went too far. This was an abduction," said Erika. "She could have had sex earlier in the day with the fiancé, and then . . . Jeez. We're going to have to ask the fiancé. Is there any other DNA evidence at all?"

"If there was, it was most likely destroyed by the water, when she was under the ice," said Isaac.

When they had finished, there were a few minutes of down time before the Douglas-Browns were due to arrive and identify Andrea's body. Moss and Peterson took the opportunity to have a cigarette, and Erika found herself accepting an offer to join them, even though she had given up years ago. They stood in the doorway of a fire exit, looking out over the back at an auto-repair shop. They could see inside the long row of garages where the cars were jacked up, men working in glowing pits underneath.

Erika had dealt with more cases of rape and murder than she could remember. As they smoked in silence, she regarded the young men working opposite. They were young and strong. How close did the average man come in his life to raping women, killing them? How many held back? How many got away with it?

"The key is Andrea. Was it someone she knew?" asked Erika, exhaling cigarette smoke into the cold air, the long-forgotten rush of nicotine roaring through her blood.

"Do you think she was lured into the museum grounds, or did she go of her own free will?" asked Peterson.

"There's so little evidence to go on. No DNA. The CCTV cameras were down."

"Could that have been arranged?" asked Moss. "The CCTV. Could it have been someone on the inside? Someone who'd a grudge against Sir Simon or the family?"

"That's government cutbacks, the crappy CCTV. And if it were a professional kidnapping and execution, would they really leave her phone and her ID at the scene? That seems messy," said Peterson.

"They could have wanted her to be identified fast. Sending a message," said Moss.

"She got plenty of male attention. What about a scorned lover?" asked Erika.

"It's possible. But who? She was engaged. She seemed to have turned into a nun since she met this Giles Osborne. We need to talk to him," said Moss.

Isaac appeared at the doorway.

"The Douglas-Brown family have just pulled into the car park," he said.

"I hate this part of the job," said Moss, stubbing out the half-smoked cigarette on the bottom of her shoe, and replacing it in the packet.

Simon and Diana Douglas-Brown arrived with their daughter, Linda, and son, David. It seemed strange to Erika that she was seeing Andrea's brother and sister for the first time. She felt she knew so much about them from Andrea's Facebook profile.

Diana and Simon were immaculately dressed in black, and Diana looked as if she was being held up by Simon and David. David was very tall and thin and wore a fashionably tight black suit and glasses. Linda was next to her father, and appeared very matronly in a black A-line skirt and a thick winter coat. They all had red eyes from crying.

"Good morning. We're ready for you through here," said Erika, taking them to the door of the identification room.

Simon put a hand over his wife's. "You stay here, David, and Linda, you too. I'll do this."

"Dad, we're here. Together," said David. His voice had a rich forceful command, like his father's, which contrasted with his geeky appearance. Linda chewed her lip for a moment and then nodded in agreement. Erika showed them through. The identification room was small and institutional, with two chairs and a wooden table decorated with a hopelessly cheery bunch of plastic daffodils.

"Please take your time," said Erika, leading them to a large glass window. On the other side of the glass, a curtain was closed. Erika noticed that the curtain had been hung the wrong way round, with the yellowing lining on show, some of the stitching coming away at the top. It was ironic that the dead were the ones who were shown the good side, while relatives and friends waited on the other, as if they were back stage.

Diana visibly tensed as a mortuary assistant drew the curtain back, revealing Andrea, who lay under a sheet, shrouded in white. A soft yellow light played over the wood paneling of the viewing room. Erika had never lost the feeling that viewing a body was almost abstract; theatrical. Some relatives remained impassive, others cried uncontrollably. One man, she remembered, had pounded on the glass so hard that it had cracked.

"Yes. It's her, that's Andrea," said Diana. She gulped and her eyes watered. She pressed a neat square of white handkerchief to her beautifully made-up face. Linda didn't blink, didn't flinch. She just tilted her head, eyes wide with a morbid curiosity. David stared grimly, fighting back tears.

It was Simon who lost control and, with a wail, broke down. David went to embrace his father, but he shook the boy off violently. It was only then that David cried too, leaning over, sobs heaving out of him.

"Let me give you some privacy. Take as long as you need," said Erika. Diana nodded as she retreated.

Five minutes passed, and the family finally emerged with bloodshot eyes. Erika was waiting in the corridor with Moss and Peterson.

"Thank you for doing that," said Erika, softly. "Would it be possible for us to talk to all of you, later this afternoon?"

"What do you want to talk to us about?" asked Simon. His bloodshot eyes were now cautious and embarrassed.

"We'd like to find out some more about Andrea. So we can discover if she knew the killer."

"Why would she have known the killer? You think someone like Andrea would mix with killers?" said Simon.

"No, sir. I don't. But we have to ask these questions."

"Where is Andrea's fiancé?" asked Moss.

"Giles understood that we wanted to be left as a family. I'm sure he will pay his respects when…" Lady Diana's voice trailed off, perhaps realizing she now had to organize a funeral.

They watched as the family walked slowly across the snowy car park to a waiting car. As they got in, Simon Douglas-Brown stared across at Erika. His bloodshot eyes bored into hers. Then he got into the car, and it drove away into the snow.

CHAPTER 15

Yakka Events was based in a futuristic office block on a residential street in Kensington. It rose up between rows of ordinary terraced houses, like a pretentious sculpture that had been delivered to the wrong address. Erika, Peterson and Moss had to buzz in at two separate smoked glass doors before they were allowed access to the front desk. A young receptionist sat typing at her computer, wearing earphones. She saw them, but didn't say a word and carried on typing. Erika leaned across and removed one of her earphones.

"I'm DCI Foster, this is Detective Moss and Detective Peterson. We'd like to talk to Giles Osborne, please."

"Mr. Osborne is busy. One moment, I'll just finish this and get you booked in for an appointment," said the receptionist, making a show of replacing the earphone.

Erika leaned over again and pulled down on the cable, yanking both of the earphones out of the girl's ears. "I'm not asking you, I'm telling you. We'd like to see Giles Osborne."

They all showed her their police ID. The girl's attitude remained, but she picked up the phone on her desk. "What's it regarding?"

"The death of his fiancée," said Erika. The girl dialed a number.

"What did she think we were here about? A cat stuck up a fucking tree?" murmured Peterson. Erika shot him a look.

The receptionist replaced the receiver. "Mr. Osborne will be out in a moment. You can wait through there."

They moved through to a chill-out area with sofas and a low wooden coffee table, where design magazines were neatly fanned out. In the corner was a small bar with a giant fridge, lit up and stocked with rows of beers, and beside that was a giant, silver espresso machine. Along the wall hung a montage of photos, taken at various Yakka Events, which mostly seemed to involve gorgeous young girls and guys handing out free champagne.

"He'd never employ me with my fat arse," muttered Moss as they sat. Erika gave her a sideways glance and saw, for the first time, that Moss was grinning. Erika returned the grin.

Moments later, Giles Osborne emerged through a smoked glass door next to the bar. He was short and plump with dark greasy hair, parted to one side. His beady eyes were close set, and he had a large nose but no chin. He had poured himself into skinny jeans and wore a V-necked T-shirt far too tight for his bulging belly. A strange pair of little pointed ankle boots, which gave him a Humpty-Dumpty-ish quality, completed the outfit. Erika was surprised that this was the man Andrea had chosen to marry.

"Hello, I'm Giles Osborne. What can I do for you?" he said, his accent confident and plummy.

Erika introduced everyone, adding, "We'd firstly like to offer our condolences."

"Yes. Thank you. It was a great shock. Something I'm still trying to process. I don't know if I ever will..." He looked pained, but didn't invite them further.

"Could we go somewhere a bit more private? We'd like to ask you a few questions," said Erika.

"I've already spoken at length, yesterday, with a DCI Sparks," he said, narrowing his eyes suspiciously.

"Yes, and we appreciate your time, but do understand this is a murder investigation and we really need to make sure we have all the information..."

Giles regarded them for a moment and then appeared to snap out of his suspicion. "Of course. Can we get you a drink? Cappuccino? Espresso? Macchiato?"

"I'll have a cappuccino," said Moss. Peterson nodded in agreement.

"Yes, thank you," said Erika.

"Michelle, we'll be in the conference room," Giles said to the receptionist on the front desk. He held the glass door open, and they passed through a communal office where six or seven young men and women were working at computers. None of them looked over twenty-five. Giles opened another glass door, which led into a conference room with a long glass table and chairs. A large plasma television on the wall was mirroring a website, which showed rows of thumbnail images. On closer inspection, Erika realized the images were of coffins. Giles hurried to a laptop on the glass table and minimized the browser, the Yakka Events logo appearing on the television instead.

"I can't imagine how terrible this time must be for Lord and Lady Douglas-Brown. I thought I would make some inroads into planning Andrea's funeral," he explained.

"Andrea was only formally identified an hour ago," said Moss.

"Yes, but you had identified Andrea, correct?" he replied.

"Yes," said Erika.

"One is never certain how to react to sudden bereavement. It must seem strange to you..." He broke down and put a hand over his face. "I'm sorry. I just need a focus... I need to do something, and arranging events is in my blood, I suppose. I just can't believe this has happened..."

Erika pulled a tissue from a box on the conference table and handed it to Giles.

"Thank you," he said, taking it and blowing his nose.

"I take it your company is successful?" said Erika, changing the subject as they took their seats at the conference table.

"Yes, I can't complain. There are always people who want to tell the world about their new product. Recessions come and go, but there is always a need and a want to communicate a concept, a brand, an event. I'm here to help convey that message."

"What message do you hope to convey when you arrange Andrea's funeral service?" asked Moss. Before he could answer, the receptionist came in with the coffees and set them down.

"Thanks, Michelle, you're an angel," said Giles to her back as she left. "Um, that's a really good question. I want people to remember Andrea for what she was: a beautiful young girl, pure and wholesome, innocent, with her whole life ahead of her…"

Erika turned that over in her brain for a moment. She saw Moss and Peterson do the same.

"That's really good coffee," said Moss.

"Thank you. We did the product launch. It's all completely Fairtrade. The farmers are compensated far above the market value for what they grow; their children are given places in schools. They have access to sanitation, clean water. Full healthcare."

"I didn't know I was doing so much good, just drinking a cappuccino," said Peterson, his voice heavy with sarcasm. Erika could tell Peterson and Moss shared her dislike for Giles Osborne. This wasn't going to work if he knew it too.

"We've come here today," said Erika, "to try and build a bit of a picture about Andrea. We believe the best way to catch whoever did this is to piece together her life, and her final movements."

"Sure," said Giles. "It was a shock—a terrible shock." His eyes began to fill with tears again, and he scrubbed at them angrily with the balled-up tissue. He sniffed a couple of times. "We were due to be married this summer. She was so excited. She had already started fittings for the dress. She wanted a Vera Wang, and I always gave my Andrea what she wanted…"

"Didn't her parents want to pay?" asked Erika.

"No. The Slovak tradition is that each family pays half…Are you Slovak? I think I hear an accent?" asked Giles.

"Yes, I am."

"Married?"

"No. Can I ask where you and Andrea first met?"

"She came to work for me, last June."

"As what?"

"One of our sampling girls, although I don't think she really knew the meaning of the word 'work.' I'd known Lady Diana for a few years. We often partner with her floristry business for our events. She said she had a daughter who was looking for a job; then she showed me her picture and that was it."

"How do you mean, 'that was it'?" asked Peterson.

"Well, she was beautiful. The kind of girl we love to employ—and of course, very soon I was in love, ha."

"And did she work for you for long, before a relationship developed?" asked Peterson.

"No—well, the love took a bit longer than her period of employment. She only did one shift, giving out samples of Moët. She was terrible: she behaved like she was at the party, not working—and she got so drunk! So that didn't work out, but, er, *we* did…" Giles trailed off. "Look, is any of this relevant? I would have thought you'd want to be out looking for the killer."

"So it was quite a rapid courtship. You only met eight months ago, last June?" said Erika.

"Yes."

"And you proposed very quickly into the relationship."

"As I said. It was love at first sight."

"And you think it was love at first sight for Andrea too?" asked Moss.

"Look, am I under suspicion?" asked Giles, shifting uncomfortably in his seat.

"Why would you think you were under suspicion? We said we were asking questions," said Erika.

"But I've answered all this before. If you want to cut to the chase, I am able to demonstrate where I was the night that Andrea disappeared. From three p.m. on Thursday, January eighth, until three a.m. the morning of the ninth, I was running a product launch at Raw Spice in Soho, 106 Beak Street. I then came back here to the office with my team; we had some drinks to wind down. I have all this on CCTV. We then went out for breakfast at six a.m.—the McDonald's on Kensington High Street. I have more than a dozen staff that can verify this, and no doubt there is CCTV footage of most of the places. The doorman on my building saw me arrive home at seven a.m., and I didn't leave again until midday."

"What is Raw Spice?" asked Peterson.

"It's a sushi fusion experience."

"Sushi fusion?"

"I really don't expect someone like you to know what that is," said Giles, impatiently.

"Someone like me?" asked Peterson, reaching up to twist one of his short dreadlocks.

"No, no, no; what I meant was, someone who . . . who might not move in central London society . . ."

Erika then stepped in. "Yes, that's all fine. Look, Mr. Osborne—"

"Please call me Giles. This is a first-name office."

"Giles. Are you on Facebook?"

"Of course I'm on Facebook," he bristled. "I run an events company. We're very active on all social media."

"And Andrea?"

"No, she was one of the few people I've ever met who didn't have a Facebook profile. I've tried... I tried to get her on Instagram a couple of times, but she's... she was clueless with technology."

Erika stood and pulled out a couple of screenshots from Andrea's Facebook profile. She laid them out on the glass table in front of him.

"Andrea did have a Facebook profile. She deactivated it in June 2014. I'm guessing this was around the time you two met?"

Giles pulled the paper toward him. "Maybe she wanted to have a fresh start?" he said, confused, clearly trying not to react to a picture of Andrea draped over a handsome young man, his hand cupping one of her breasts through her white halter-neck top.

"So she lied to you about not having a Facebook profile."

"Well, lie is a strong word, is it not?"

"But why keep this from you?"

"I—I don't know."

"Giles. Do you know of The Glue Pot, in Forest Hill?" asked Peterson.

"No, I don't think I do. What is it?"

"It's a pub."

"Then I definitely don't. I don't stray south of the river, in fact, ever."

"Andrea was last seen at this pub on the night she disappeared. She was in the company of a girl with short blonde hair, then later a dark-haired man. Do you have any idea who they could have been? Did she have any friends in South London, around Forest Hill?"

"No. Well, none that I knew of."

"Can you think of anyone who would want to hurt her? Did she owe somebody money?"

"No! No; between Sir Simon and myself, Andrea never wanted for anything. The night she vanished, she told me she was going to the cinema with Linda and David. I was encouraging her to spend more time with her brother and sister; they're not close as siblings."

"Why not?"

"Oh, you know—rich families. The parents delegate the childcare to nannies and teachers. There is always competition for affection among siblings... Well, David and Andrea seemed to get much more attention than Linda. I was lucky. I'm an only child."

The Humpty-Dumpty image came back to Erika again. Giles, small and podgy, sitting alone on a wall, his legs not quite reaching the ground.

"Did you ever meet a girl called Barbora Kardosova? She was a friend of Andrea's." Erika slid a picture of Barbora across the table.

Giles leaned in to examine the picture. "No. Although Andrea did mention Barbora. It seemed she dropped Andrea as a friend, most cruelly. It happened a little while before I met her."

"How well did you know Andrea's friends?"

"She didn't have many female friends. She'd try and get close to other girls and they became jealous of her. She's—she was—so beautiful."

"Did you and Andrea have an active sex life?" asked Peterson.

"What? Yes. We'd just got engaged..."

"Did you have sexual intercourse with Andrea the day she went missing?"

"What has this got to do with—?" Giles started.

"Please can you answer the question," said Erika.

"Um, I think we might have, in the afternoon? Look, I don't know what this has got to do with her going missing. Asking me about our sex life! It's none of your bloody business!" Giles was now red in the face.

"Did you partake in anal as well as vaginal sex?" asked Peterson.

Giles stood up so quickly that his coffee spilled over and his chair fell back. "That's it! Get out now! Do you hear me? This is an informal chat, yes? I don't have to talk to you. It's voluntary."

"Of course it is," said Erika. "But would you please answer the question? Andrea suffered a prolonged and brutal attack before her death. We are asking these questions for a reason."

"What? If we had—if we took part in an unnatural act? No. NO! I wouldn't marry a girl who..." Giles tugged at the neck of his T-shirt, unable to voice the words. "I'm sorry, but I need you to leave. If you want to ask me any more questions I want a lawyer present. This is most distressing and unsavory."

The spilled coffee had reached the edge of the glass table. There was a spattering sound as it began to drip over onto the carpet.

"Was she raped? Was she hurt badly?" he asked, quietly now, dissolving into tears. He leaned against the table and sobbed into the sleeve of his T-shirt.

"We don't believe Andrea was sexually assaulted, but this was a sustained and brutal attack," said Erika, softly.

"Oh, my God," Giles said, taking a deep breath and scrubbing again at his eyes. "I just can't think—I can't imagine what she went through."

Erika gave him a moment before she continued. "Could you tell me, Giles, did Andrea have more than one phone?"

Giles looked up, confused. "No. No, she had a Swarovski iPhone. Sir Simon's secretary sorts out the bill. The same with Linda and David."

Erika looked at Moss and Peterson, and they got up.

"I think we'll end it there, Mr. Osborne, thank you. I'm sorry about the line of questioning, but your answers to these difficult questions will really help our investigation." Erika touched his sleeve. "We'll see ourselves out," she added.

They passed Michelle coming into the glass conference room, carrying a large handful of tissues. She gave them a disapproving look.

"What do you think?" asked Erika, when they emerged out onto the street.

"I'm gonna say it. Cos I know we were all thinking it. What the hell was she doing with him? Talk about out of his league!" said Peterson.

"And I don't think he knew her at all," said Moss.

"Or, she only let him know what she wanted him to know," added Peterson.

CHAPTER 16

By lunchtime, the official news of Andrea's death was playing across the media. As Erika, Moss and Peterson approached the Douglas-Brown residence, the bank of photographers had grown on the green outside, churning up the melting snow. This time they didn't have to wait on the doorstep and were shown straight through to a large drawing room with a double-aspect view of the tree out front and a large garden behind. Two large pale sofas and several armchairs surrounded a long, low coffee table. An open fireplace was decorated in white marble, and in the corner sat a baby grand piano covered in an assortment of framed photographs.

"Hello, officers," said Simon Douglas-Brown, rising from one of the sofas to shake their hands. Diana Douglas-Brown was sitting beside him, and didn't get up. Her eyes were red and swollen, and her face bare of makeup. David and Linda sat at opposite sides of their parents. Simon, Diana and David were still dressed in black, but Linda had changed into a tartan skirt and a baggy white woolen jumper, on the front of which embroidered kittens chased balls of wool. Erika recognized the jumper from the picture on Facebook. Andrea had worn it with Barbora.

"Thank you for seeing us," said Erika. "Before we begin, I would just like to apologize to you if my manner yesterday was rude. It wasn't intentional, and I apologize unreservedly if I caused you any offense."

Simon looked surprised. "Yes, of course, it's forgotten. And thank you."

"Yes, thank you," echoed Diana, croakily.

"We'd just like to find out a little more about Andrea's life," said Erika, taking a seat on the sofa opposite the family. Peterson and Moss sat either side of her. "May we ask you a few questions?"

The family nodded.

Erika looked at David and Linda. "I understand Andrea was supposed to meet you on the night she disappeared?"

"Yes, we were due to meet at The Odeon in Hammersmith, to watch a film," said Linda.

"Which film?"

David shrugged and looked to Linda.

"Gravity," Linda said. "Andrea kept saying how much she wanted to see it."

"Did she say why she canceled?"

"She didn't cancel; she just didn't turn up," said Linda.

"Okay. We have a witness who saw Andrea in a pub in South London, The Glue Pot. Does that mean anything?"

The family all shook their heads.

"That doesn't sound like somewhere Andrea would go," said Diana. She sounded a little woozy and vacant.

"Could she have been meeting someone? Did Andrea have any friends around there?"

"Goodness, no," said Diana.

"Andrea did get through a lot of friends," said Linda, flicking her short fringe out of her eyes with a twitch of her head.

"Linda, that's not fair," said her mother, weakly.

"But she did. There was always someone new she'd met in a bar or a club—she had so many memberships. She'd be crazy about them one minute, and the next they'd be cut off. Excommunicated for some minor misdemeanor."

"Like what?" asked Erika.

"Like, looking nicer than she did, or talking to the guy she wanted to talk to. Or talking about themselves too much..."

"Linda," said her father, warningly.

"I'm telling them the truth!"

"No, you are slating your sister, who is dead. She isn't here to fight with you, anymore..." Simon tailed off.

"Did you go out with Andrea to bars and clubs?" asked Moss.

"No," said Linda, pointedly.

"When you say 'memberships,' what do you mean?"

"Memberships to clubs. I'm not sure they'd be the kind of clubs *you'd* go to," added Linda, looking Moss up and down.

"*Linda*," said Simon.

Linda shifted uncomfortably on the sofa, her broad backside spilling over the edge. "I'm sorry, that was rude," she said, flicking her fringe again. Erika wondered if it was a nervous tic.

"No probs," said Moss, amiably. "This isn't a formal interview; we merely want information to help catch Andrea's killer."

"I can give you the list of clubs where Andrea had memberships. I'll talk to my secretary, get her to e-mail them over," said Simon.

"Linda, you work at a florists, yes?" asked Peterson.

Linda looked him up and down approvingly, as if noticing him for the first time. "Yes. It's my mother's business. I'm assistant manager. Have you got a girlfriend?"

"Um, no," said Peterson.

"Pity," said Linda, unconvincingly. "We've got some lovely stuff coming in for Valentine's Day."

"What about you, David?" asked Peterson.

David had sunk down into the sofa, and he stared ahead vacantly with the neck of his jumper pulled up over his bottom lip. "I'm doing my MA," he said.

"Where?"

"Here in London, at UCL."

"And what are you studying?"

"Architectural History."

"He's always wanted to be an architect," said his mother proudly, putting her hand on his arm. He pulled it out from under her touch. For a moment, Diana looked like she might break down again.

"When did you last see Andrea?" asked Erika.

"The afternoon before we were due to go out," said David.

"Did you go out with Andrea much in London?"

"No. She was more Kardashian bling. I'm more into Shoreditch, y'know?"

"You mean the bars and clubs in Shoreditch?" asked Peterson. David nodded. Peterson added, "I live in Shoreditch. I got a mortgage just before the property prices went mad."

Linda regarded Peterson, as if he were a cream cake waiting to be devoured.

David went on, "Yeah. When I finally get access to my trust fund, I'm buying my own place in Shoreditch."

"David," warned his father.

"Well, I am. He asked me a question and I answered."

There was an almost imperceptible shift in the room. A look passed between Simon and Diana, and then there was silence.

"So, Linda, you are a florist, and David is studying. What did Andrea do?" asked Moss.

"Andrea was engaged to be married," said Linda, her voice heavy with irony.

"Enough!" roared Simon. "I will not have you two talking like this, filling the room with this horrible atmosphere. Andrea is dead. Brutally murdered! And here you are taking pot shots at her!"

"It wasn't me, it was Linda," said David.

"Oh yes, it's always me. Always Linda..."

Their father ignored them. "Andrea was a beautiful girl. But not only that, she lit up a room when she walked in. She was beautiful, and vulnerable and...and...a light has gone out in our lives."

The atmosphere in the room changed. The family seemed to shift on their chairs to move into each other and become a unit.

"What can you tell us about Andrea's friend, Barbora Kardosova?" asked Erika.

"I think she was the closest Andrea ever had to a best friend," said Diana. "She even came on holiday with us. They were so close for a time, and then she just vanished. Andrea said Barbora just moved away."

"Do you know where she went?"

"No. She didn't leave a forwarding address; didn't answer any of Andrea's e-mails," said Diana.

"Do you think that's odd?"

"Of course it was odd. I think she came from a broken home, though. Her mother was unwell. Then of course, people inevitably have a habit of letting you down..."

"Did they have a falling out?"

"It's possible, but Andrea was—well, she wouldn't lie about things like that. She'd have told us. Andrea thinks—thought—that Barbora had become jealous of her."

"Andrea's phone records only go back to June 2014," said Erika.

"Yes, she lost her other phone. She'd had it since she was thirteen or fourteen," said Simon.

"And you replaced it for her?"

"Yes."

"Have you got the number for the old phone?"

"Why would you need that?"

"It's just routine."

"Is it? I would have thought having eight months of phone records would suffice..." They could see that Simon was starting to grow uncomfortable.

"Did Andrea have a second phone?"

"No."

"Could she have had a second phone and you were unaware?"

"Well, no. The family manages her trust fund. She mainly used credit cards. We would have known if she'd bought a phone, but why would she?"

"It would be very helpful if we could have her old phone number."

Simon looked at Erika. "Yes, okay, I'll speak to my secretary. She can pull the details."

Erika went to ask another question, but Diana began to speak.

"I don't know why Andrea would go all the way over across the river! And then she's taken by someone and killed. My baby... *My baby*. She's *dead*!" Diana became hysterical, gulping and retching. Simon and David began to comfort her, but Linda did another nervous flick of her fringe and picked at a piece of lint on her cat jumper.

"Officers, please, that's enough questions," said Simon.

Erika found it hard to hide her exasperation. "Would it be possible to look at Andrea's bedroom?"

"What? Now? Your people have already been and had a look."

"Please. It would help us," said Erika.

"I can take them, Daddy," said Linda. "Come with me, officers."

They followed Linda out, past Diana, who was still hysterical. David gave Linda a nod and a weak smile and then turned back to comfort his mother. On the way out of the door, they passed the piano littered with family photographs of the Douglas-Browns and their three children—all smiling, all happy.

CHAPTER 17

Andrea's bedroom was large and, like the rest of the house, beautifully furnished. Three sash windows along one wall looked out over the green where the press were milling about. Linda marched in ahead of them and moved close to the blinds. The photographers below leaped into action, clicking away. Linda yanked the blinds down with a clatter.

"Those beasts. We can't do anything. We're trapped in here. David's been moaning that he can't even have a cigarette on the terrace. Daddy says it would look bad."

The blinds were thick and cast the bedroom in gloom. Linda flicked on the light. The middle window was the largest. Underneath, there was a huge desk of polished wood. The desk was neatly organized with an astonishing amount of makeup: a big pot of brushes and eyeliner, nail polish lined up in many colors, powder compacts stacked, boxes of lipstick standing to attention in rows. Over the corner of the mirror hung scores of lanyards and tickets from concerts: Madonna, Katy Perry, Lady Gaga, Rihanna, Robbie Williams.

A wardrobe lined the length of the wall on the right. Erika slid the mirrored door across, and the scent of Chanel Chance perfume floated out. Inside was an expensive wardrobe of designer clothes, mostly short skirts and dresses. The bottom was covered in shoeboxes.

"So Andrea got an allowance?" asked Erika, thumbing her way through the clothes.

"When she turned twenty-one she gained access to her trust fund, like I did. Although David still has to wait, which has caused... issues," said Linda.

"What do you mean, issues?"

"Males born into the family have to wait until their twenty-fifth birthday."

"Why is that?"

"David is like any twenty-one-year-old boy. He wants to spend his money on girls and cars and booze. Although, he's much more considerate than Andrea, even though he has less money. He still gets me nicer birthday presents." Linda flicked her fringe again, crossing her arms over her large be-kittened bosom.

"What do you spend your money on?" asked Moss.

"That is a rude question that I don't have to answer," said Linda, tartly.

To one side of the wardrobe was a neatly made four-poster bed with a blue and white blanket, and some soft toys lined up on the pillow. Above the bed was a poster of One Direction.

"She didn't really like them anymore," said Linda, following their gaze. "She said they were just boys and she liked men."

"She was engaged, though?" prompted Erika. Linda gave a bitter laugh. "What's so funny, Linda?"

"Have you seen Giles? When they feed up the ducks for foie gras, he's always at the front of the queue..."

"Why do you think Andrea was with Giles?"

"Come on officers, isn't it obvious? Money. He's due to inherit a fabulous estate in Wiltshire and a house in Barbados. His parents are worth squillions, and they're on their last legs. They had him very late. His mother thought he was the menopause."

"Was Andrea unfaithful to Giles?" asked Moss.

"Boys were always drawn to Andrea. They turned into drooling, pitiful creatures in her presence. She got a kick out of the attention."

"But was Andrea having an affair?" pressed Moss.

"I don't know what she did half the time. We weren't close. But I loved her, and I'm devastated that she's dead..." For the first time, Linda looked as if she might cry.

"What about you, Linda?" asked Moss.

"What about me? Are you asking if I make the boys drool? What do you think?" snapped Linda, cutting her off.

"I wanted to ask if you have a boyfriend," explained Moss.

"That's none of your business. Have *you* got a boyfriend?"

"No. I'm married," said Moss.

"What does he do?" asked Linda.

"She. She's a teacher," said Moss, breezily. Erika tried not to look surprised.

"No, I haven't got a boyfriend," said Linda.

"Can these windows be opened fully?" asked Peterson, moving to the middle sash window, bending over to peer around the closed blinds. "Have they got suicide locks?"

"No, they open all the way," said Linda, admiring Peterson's backside as he bent over. Erika joined him at the window and saw that there was a fire escape leading down to ground level.

"Did Andrea ever climb out of her window to meet friends, if she was grounded?" asked Erika.

"My mother and father never had the time or inclination to ground us. We use the front door if we want to go out," said Linda.

"And you can come and go as you please?"

"Of course."

Erika kneeled down and looked under the bed. There were wispy clumps of dust on the polished wood floor, but one area stood out as a little cleaner than the oth tention to the chest of drawers and we pausing with her hand on the handle. "Wo waiting outside, please Linda?" she asked.

"Why? I thought you were here just to chat?"

"Linda, have you got any photos of Andrea you can show me? It could help us," said Peterson. He came over and touched Linda lightly on the arm. Her round white face blushed scarlet.

"Um, yes, I think I have some," she said, staring up at Peterson with a smile. They left, and Erika closed the door.

"Good old Peterson, taking one for the team," joked Moss, adding, "What is it?"

Erika crossed back to the bed. "Did forensics come in when it was a missing persons?"

"No, Sparks came and had a poke round. I think Simon or Diana was with him though, so it wasn't thorough."

"There's something underneath the bed that looks fishy," said Erika.

They knelt down, pulling latex gloves out of their coats and slipping them on. Erika got down on her front and slid under the bed. Moss flicked on a torch and shone it under the bed as Erika examined a floorboard which was cleaner than the rest, tracing its seams. Erika pulled out her car keys, fitting a key between the floorboards, and levered it up. However, the board was long and the bed was low, so it wouldn't properly lift out. Erika replaced the board and shuffled back out. They took an end of the bed each and pulled it out a few feet with great difficulty.

"Jesus, that's no IKEA shit," grimaced Moss. Erika moved round and got the floorboard up.

Inside a cavity underneath was a mobile phone box. Erika gently lifted it out, and opened the lid. The molded cardboard

,using was still inside, but there was no phone. There was, however, a bag of small white pills, a small dark block of what looked like cannabis resin wrapped in cling film, a pack of large Rizlas and a box of Swan Vestas filters. There was also a small instruction booklet for an iPhone 5S, and a hands-free kit that was still in its little plastic bag. Erika lifted out the molded cardboard. A small white receipt was nestled in the bottom. It was printed on thin shiny paper, and along one edge was a sticky yellow substance that had blurred the ink. On the reverse it was blank, apart from the words "*your my baby x"* written in blue ink, in a childish hand.

"It's a mobile phone top-up voucher," said Erika, turning it back over.

"But there's only half a transaction number," said Moss. "What is that gunk?"

Erika put it to her nose. "Dried egg yolk."

"What about the stash?" asked Moss, looking back in the mobile phone box.

"I don't know. Sadly, it's fairly run-of-the-mill. Six tablets could be ecstasy. An ounce or two of cannabis resin? That's personal use," said Erika. "Let's bag this up and call in a CSI to check out the rest of her bedroom."

When they came back downstairs, Simon and David were showing a doctor to the front door.

"Is everything okay?" asked Erika. Simon thanked the doctor and opened the door. The doctor hurried down the path through the rain of camera flashes, clutching at his leather bag, eager to get out of the firing line. Peterson and Linda joined them as Simon closed the front door.

"No, everything is not *okay*. My wife is suffering severe trauma. I think I'd like to ask you to leave, please."

"We found this under Andrea's bed," said Erika, holding up a plastic evidence bag with the mobile phone box, and the drugs.

"What? No, no, no, no, no," he snapped. "My children do not do drugs! How do I know you didn't plant this?"

"Sir, we're not interested in the drugs. What we are interested in is the fact we think Andrea had a second phone. In this box was a mobile phone top-up voucher dated four months previously. Were you aware of its existence?"

"No. Let me see that..." Sir Simon took the thin plastic bag housing the receipt, and studied it. David and Linda watched with curiosity.

"Whose writing is this?"

"We don't know. Could Giles have written it?"

"He went to Gordonstoun. He'd know the different between 'your' and 'you're.' How do you know this is even hers? It could be an old box."

"Could your secretary have organized a second phone for Andrea?"

"No! Not without telling me about it," said Simon. "What do you two know about this? Was Andrea taking drugs?" he added, turning on David and Linda.

"We don't know anything, Daddy," said Linda, flicking her hair. David shook his head along with her.

"Okay, thank you, sir. Please let us know if you find out anything more. In the meantime, I've asked a forensics team to take a look at Andrea's bedroom."

"What? You're asking my permission?"

"I'm informing you that in the interest of furthering this investigation and finding who killed Andrea, I need a team of forensic officers to look at Andrea's bedroom, sir," said Erika.

"You people do what you want, don't you?" snapped Simon. He walked off to his study and slammed the door.

When they reached Erika's car on Chiswick High Road, her phone rang.

"It's DCI Sparks. I'm at The Glue Pot. It's about the e-fit you tried to arrange with that witness, Kristina."

"Yes? Did you find her?" asked Erika, hope rising in her chest.

"No, and according to the landlord, there's no one called Kristina who works here."

"Where did you find the landlord?"

"He lives in a flat two doors down."

"Then who was the girl I talked to?"

"I asked the bar staff. A girl matching her description, called Kristina, works casually, cash-in-hand, covering when the other bar staff need nights off. One of them had an address for her, so we checked it out. It's a bedsit near the train station, but it's empty."

"Who owns the bedsit?" asked Erika.

"Landlord lives in Spain, and as far as he and the letting agent were aware it's been unoccupied for three months. So this Kristina was either squatting, or gave it as a fake address."

"Shit. Get forensics into that bedsit, dust for prints. So far she's the only one who saw Andrea with this mystery man and woman."

CHAPTER 18

They arrived back at Lewisham Row Station just after five. The team in the incident room looked to be flagging when they returned, but heads rose expectantly from their desks when they caught the smell of coffee.

"Grab a cup, and there's doughnuts," said Erika. They had stopped at Starbucks on their way back to the station. People stretched and pushed themselves away from their desks. Crane came over from where he'd been reviewing the CCTV images.

"You're a star, boss. Decent coffee!" he said, rubbing his eyes.

"I'm hoping you've got some good news about the CCTV coverage of London Road?" asked Erika hopefully, offering him the bag of doughnuts.

"We've been cross-checking bus timetables and routes, and we've requested CCTV from TFL for all the buses that traveled along London Road, past the museum and train station, on the night Andrea went missing. Also, loads of black cabs now have CCTV, so we're working on tracking those down—but we won't get the bus CCTV until tomorrow at the earliest." Crane's hand hesitated above the bag of doughnuts.

"Go on," said Erika, and he plunged his hand in. "Put pressure on them, time is ticking. I take it you've heard about the vanishing barmaid, Kristina?"

The team nodded, chewing on their doughnuts and sipping coffee.

"What about Andrea's phone and laptop? Did you pull off anything interesting?" asked Erika.

"No. Well, we found most of the photos we've already seen on her old Facebook profile, and there are endless games of Candy Crush Saga. She seemed to be obsessed with that game. She appeared to just use her laptop for games and the usual iTunes. The iPhone recovered from the crime scene is virtually empty. No photos or video, and barely any texts."

Chief Superintendent Marsh poked his head around the door to the incident room. "DCI Foster, can I have a word please?"

"Yes, sir. Moss, Peterson—can you brief everyone on what we found under Andrea's bed?" asked Erika. She put the last of her doughnut in her mouth and left the incident room, following Marsh to his office, where she brought him up to speed about the mobile phone box under the bed with the receipt, and the vanishing barmaid from The Glue Pot.

When she had finished, Marsh looked outside the window into the dark night. "Just don't burn your team out. Okay, Foster?"

Marsh seemed a little more relaxed. Erika wondered if it was the newspaper headlines, which had moved focus from the progress the police were making to the tragedy of Andrea's death. For today, at least, the focus was on a beautiful young girl who had had her life snatched away from her.

"The press office has done a great job of shaping the news cycle," said Marsh, as if following Erika's thoughts.

"Is that what you call it these days? *Shaping the news cycle*?" asked Erika with a wry grin.

"Look, there's even a bit about you," he said, reading: "'*The case is being led by DCI Erika Foster, an experienced officer who successfully brought multiple-murderer Barry Paton to justice. She was also commended for her success in conviction rates for honor killings within Manchester's Muslim community…*' And they've used a good photo; the one of us at Paton's trial."

"Why didn't you go the whole hog and give them my address, too?" snapped Erika. "I haven't had a letter from Barry Paton for a few months. He did send me a letter to congratulate me on having my own husband killed, though."

There was a silence.

"I'm sorry," said Marsh. "I thought you'd be pleased, but I didn't think. I'm sorry, Erika."

"It's okay, sir. It's been a long day."

"I've had HR on to me. They say you still haven't provided them with an address," said Marsh, changing the subject.

"So you're now running errands for Human Resources?"

"You are also required to see a doctor; you had exposure to body fluids last night," added Marsh, indicating the now grubby bandage on the back of Erika's hand. For the first time, she thought back to what Ivy had said, about the little boy being HIV positive. She was shocked by how little she cared.

"I haven't had time, sir."

"To what? Go to a doctor? Or find a place to live?"

"I will see a doctor," said Erika.

"So where are you staying?" asked Marsh. "We need to know where to contact you."

"You've got my mobile..."

"Erika. Where are you staying?"

There was an awkward pause.

"I'm not staying anywhere, yet."

"So what did you do last night?"

"I worked through."

"You are leading a major murder investigation. Pace yourself. This is day two. If you carry on like this, what are you going to be like on day seven?"

"There won't be a day seven, not if I have anything to do with it," said Erika, defiantly.

Marsh handed her a card. "It's for a drop-in clinic. Also, we've got the flat Marcie inherited from her parents. The tenants have just left. It's close to the station and it would save you going through all the bureaucracy of renting. Come by my house later, if you're interested. You can get the keys."

"Okay, thank you, sir. I've got some more work to do here first."

"Before nine, if possible. I try to get an early night during the week."

When Erika came back into the incident room, she was met by PC Singh, who was triumphantly holding a piece of paper.

"Simon Douglas-Brown's secretary just faxed through the contract for Andrea's old phone. The one she lost in June. We've put in a request with the network for the records. They should be here first thing tomorrow."

"I think that deserves another doughnut," said Erika, shaking the bag and offering it round.

"And that top-up receipt you found in the box under Andrea's bed? It was from a Costcutter's supermarket near London Bridge," said Crane. "There's a date and time stamp. I've just got off the phone with the manager. He's going to go back through the CCTV. He only keeps it for four months so it could be tight, but fingers crossed."

"Fantastic," said Erika. Crane grinned and grabbed a doughnut from the bag.

"Shouldn't we save one for DCI Sparks?" asked Moss.

"I don't know. I think he's sweet enough already," grinned Erika, which got a big laugh from her colleagues. She felt comfortable now in the incident room—the atmosphere, the camaraderie—but she was conscious that her team had been on the go for a long time, so she told them to call it a day.

"Night, boss," chimed voices as they grabbed coats and bags. The incident room slowly emptied out until Erika was left alone. She picked up the phone on her desk and dialed the number Marsh had given her. A recorded voice told her that the drop-in clinic was now closed and that it would reopen at seven the next morning.

Erika put the phone down and pulled at the grubby bandage on the back of her hand, wincing as the adhesive came away from the skin. Underneath, it was healing fast with very little bruising, a curve of pale little scabs marking out the teeth marks where the boy had bitten her.

Erika binned the bandage and went back over to the whiteboards at the back of the incident room. The whoosh of excitement she had felt earlier had drained away. She felt exhausted. A low hum of a headache was forming at the back of her head. She stared at the evidence: maps and pictures; Andrea alive in her driving license photo; Andrea dead, her eyes wide and hair knotted with leaves against the side of her face. Usually Erika could get a handle on a case early on, but this one seemed to be opening wider and wider, the contradicting facts blooming and multiplying like the cells of a tumor.

She needed sleep, and for that, she realized, she would need to find a bed.

CHAPTER 19

Erika had been starving when she left the station, so she stopped off at an Italian restaurant in New Cross and surprised herself by clearing a giant plate of spaghetti carbonara, followed by a large wedge of tiramisu. It was just after nine when she turned into the road where Marsh lived, in a leafy, affluent corner of South London.

Erika parked the car and found Marsh's front door, number eleven. She was pleased when she saw that the house was in darkness. She'd much rather get a hotel for a few days while she looked for a flat than let Marsh take pity on her. The curtains were open in a large bay window on the ground floor, and she could see right through the double-aspect room to Hilly Fields Park and, beyond, the lights of the London skyline.

She was about to turn round and go back to her car when water began to whoosh down an ornate iron drainpipe at the front of the house. A light clicked on in a small upstairs window and Erika found herself squinting as she was bathed in a perfect square of light. Marsh looked down from the window and, noticing her, gave an awkward wave. She returned the wave, and waited by the front door.

When Marsh opened the door he was wearing tartan print pajama bottoms, a faded Homer Simpson T-shirt, and was drying his hands on a pink Barbie towel.

"Sorry, sir, I've left it a bit late to come over," said Erika.

"No, it's fine. It's bath time."

"I like your towel," said Erika.

"Not *my* bath time, it's..."

"It was a joke, sir."

"Ah, right," he grinned. On cue there was a scream and two tiny, giggling girls with long dark hair ran into the hallway. One was wearing just a pink jumper, knickers and socks. The other was wearing an identical outfit, but her tiny jeans were bunched around her ankles. She tottered forward, lost her balance and fell, hitting the wooden floor with a thunk. There was a moment where she looked up at Marsh, her big brown eyes trying to work out if she should cry. A dark-haired woman in her mid-thirties came rushing in after them. She was dressed casually in tight powder-blue trousers and a white blouse, which showed off her full breasts and hourglass figure. Where her sleeves were rolled up, bath foam clung to her bare arms. She was beautiful, much like her twin daughters.

"Oh dear," she said, matter-of-factly putting her hands on her narrow waist. "Did you go bump?"

The little girl decided it was far more serious than it was, screwed up her face and began to wail.

"Hello, Erika. Welcome to the mad house," said the woman.

"Hi, Marcie... You look wonderful," said Erika.

Marsh scooped up the crying girl in his arms and kissed her face, which was now puce and shiny with tears. Marcie picked up the other little girl, who was staring at Erika, and parked her on a curvy hip.

"Really? You're too kind. My only beauty regime is running after the twins." Marcie blew a wisp of hair away from her flawless creamy skin. "If you're staying, could we close the door? All the heat is rushing out."

"Sorry. Yes," said Erika, coming into the hall and closing the door behind her.

"This is Sophie," said Marsh, cradling the crying girl.

"And this is Mia," said Marcie.

"Hello," said Erika. Both little girls stared. "Gosh, how pretty you both are."

Erika had never quite mastered how to talk to children. Rapists and murderers she could deal with, but children she found a little intimidating.

Sophie stopped crying and joined Mia in staring at Erika.

"Sorry, this is obviously a bad time," said Erika.

"No, it's fine," said Marsh.

Marcie took Sophie and balanced her on her other hip. "Right, say night-night to Erika, girls."

"Night, night," they both squeaked.

"Night!" said Erika.

"It was nice to see you, Erika," added Marcie and sashayed off. Erika and Marsh both regarded her pert behind for a moment.

"Can I get you a glass of wine?" he asked, turning back.

"No. I've just come to take you up on your offer, the flat..."

"Yes, come through. But shoes off."

Marsh moved to a door at the end of the hall as Erika fumbled with her bootlaces. She then followed. The wooden floor was cold and she felt strangely vulnerable in just socks. Through the door at the end was a country-style kitchen with a long wooden table and chairs. In the corner, a red Aga pumped out heat. A large fridge next to the door was covered in splodgy paintings with splashes of random color, all fastened with magnets. An equally splodgy painting dominated the wall above a wooden dresser.

"It's one of Marcie's," said Marsh, following Erika's gaze. "She's very talented; just doesn't get the time anymore."

"Did she do the ones on the fridge, too?" asked Erika, and regretted it the moment it came out of her mouth.

"No. The twins did those," Marsh said.

There was an awkward silence.

"Well, here's all the stuff," Marsh said, handing her a large envelope from the kitchen counter. "The flat isn't too far—Foxberry Road in Brockley, close to the train station. There's a contract, drawn up on a rolling monthly basis, so we can decide how long we want this to last. Just give me a check in the next few days."

Erika opened the envelope and pulled out a bunch of keys, pleased that this wasn't a favor on Marsh's part.

"Thank you, sir."

"It's getting late," said Marsh.

"Of course. I should be off, and get settled in," said Erika.

"Oh, one more thing. Sir Simon got in contact with Colleen, our police media liaison. He wants to make a press appeal, whilst the images of Andrea on the front pages are fresh in people's minds."

"Of course, it's a good idea."

"Yes. We're going to put something together for tomorrow afternoon, so we can hit the evening news and the papers."

"Very good, sir. I'm hoping to have more information tomorrow that we can put to use."

When the front door was closed behind her, Erika walked back to her car, away from the homely warmth of Marsh's life. She bent her head and bit her lip, determined not to cry. That life, with the cozy husband and kids, had been within her grasp. She'd even delayed it a few times, much to Mark's distress.

Now it was gone forever.

CHAPTER 20

When Erika drove into Foxberry Road it was still and quiet. She passed Brockley Train Station, the platform dazzlingly lit-up and empty. A train streaked out from under a footbridge and clattered on toward central London. Erika drove on, past a long row of terraced houses, and found the flat down the far end, perched on a corner where the road led off sharply to the right. There was a vacant parking space outside, but her triumph was short-lived when she saw it was residents' parking only. She would need a permit. Screw it, she thought, parking anyway.

The communal front door opened against a swish of junk mail that was piled up behind. The hall light was on a timer, and it whirred softly as she climbed the narrow staircase, her suitcase bumping along.

The flat was on the top floor, and when she reached the landing she saw that she had a neighbor—there was another front door opposite.

Inside the flat, it felt like the heating had been off for a long time. There seemed to be no electricity. A long, freezing search ensued, using the light on her phone as a torch. She finally found the electricity box, tucked away at the back of a cupboard in the hall, and the lights sprang on.

The first door leading off the hall was a bathroom. It was small, white and clean, with just a shower cubicle. Next to it was a small bedroom with a pine double bed and a wobbly IKEA wardrobe. Above the bed was another blotchy painting. Erika lit a cigarette and peered at the bottom of the canvas, where a small signature read MARCIE ST. CLAIR. Holding the cigarette between her lips, she grabbed the painting off the wall and stashed it behind some plastic buckets in the hall cupboard.

At the end of the hall was a combined living room and kitchen. It too was tiny, but modern, and furnished in an impersonal IKEA style. Impersonal was perfect for right now. Erika pulled open the cupboards, searching for an ashtray. There wasn't one, so she grabbed a teacup.

There was a coffee table and a small blue sofa by a bay window. Erika slumped down in the sofa and looked across at a tiny television, the screen covered in dust. It was unplugged, the lead and aerial lying on the floor beside the TV stand.

Erika turned to the window, and stared out into the darkness, the sparse room and her reflection staring back at her. Once she had finished her cigarette, she stubbed it out in the teacup and lit another.

CHAPTER 21

Several houses down from Erika's flat, tucked in a crease where the road curved sharply, a figure crouched at the end of an alleyway, clad head-to-toe in black, blending in with the darkness. The figure watched Erika in the window as she lit up another cigarette and exhaled, the smoke curling around the bare lightbulb above her head.

I thought she would be harder to find, mused the figure *but here she is, DCI Foster with her lights blazing, displaying herself in the window like a whore in the red light district.*

In the photo the newspapers used, Erika had a fuller, more youthful complexion; here in the window she looked scrawny, exhausted... almost boyish.

Erika stared in the figure's direction, tilting her head to one side and resting it on her chin, the cigarette glowing inches from her face.

Can she see me? The figure shrank back a little into the shadows. *Is she watching me like I'm watching her? No. Impossible. The bitch isn't that good. She's looking at her own reflection from the light inside, no doubt feeling fucking depressed about what she sees staring back.*

DCI Foster's assignment to Andrea's murder had caused major concern. A scroll through Google had shown that Foster had been hailed as a rising star during her time in the Manchester Metropolitan Police. She'd been promoted to the DCI rank aged just thirty-nine, when she'd caught Barry Paton, a youth club caretaker who'd killed six young girls.

But Barry Paton wanted to get caught. She won't catch me. She's officially washed-up. A fuck-up. She led five police officers to their deaths, including her dumb husband. They've assigned her to this case because they know she'll fail. They want a fall guy.

The temperature was dropping fast. It was going to be another freezing night. But being so close, watching DCI Foster, was thrilling.

A car appeared at the top of the road and the figure shrank back further into the alleyway, waiting for its headlights to pass. There was a soft purr as a black cat slunk along the top of the wall. It stopped and froze when it noticed the figure.

"We're almost twins," the figure whispered, lifting a gloved hand and gently moving closer. The cat let itself be stroked. "Good kitty... good."

The cat locked eyes with the figure, then leaped soundlessly off the wall, disappearing over the other side. The figure regarded its leather gloved hands; turning them over, flexing the fingers.

I'd taken Andrea's shit for so long, but I never expected I'd do it. Live out the fantasy of strangling her, choking the life from her body...

As the days had passed, the figure had grown confident, cocky almost, that Andrea's body wouldn't be found. That she would remain frozen under the ice. Winter would pass, and with the warmth of spring she would rot down—rot down until her mask of beauty was gone and she looked more like who she really was.

But four days later, she'd been found. Intact...

There was the sound of a door slamming. Looking back up, the figure saw that the light had gone out in DCI Foster's window. She had left her flat and was stepping out onto the pavement to her car.

The figure smiled. It ducked down and retreated rapidly, melting into the shadows of the dark alley.

CHAPTER 22

Erika liked driving. It wasn't so much the type of car—it didn't have to be anything exotic. It just had to be secure and warm. As she drove through the empty streets of South London, the car felt like a cocoon around her, and more like home than the flat.

She turned her head away slightly as she drove past Brockley Cemetery, the headstones glimmering under the street lights. The car lurched to the right, and she realized she had to slow down. The snow had melted a little during the day, but at night a freeze had descended, making the roads dangerous.

She put her phone on hands-free and put a call in to the nick. Sergeant Woolf answered, and she asked him to give her a list of the dodgiest pubs in the area.

"Can I ask why?" he said, his voice tinny on the end of the line.

"I fancy a drink."

There was a pause. "Okay. There's The Mermaid, The Bird In The Hand, The Stag, The Crown—not The Crown that's a Wetherspoon's, there's another Crown on the brink of the brewery pulling the plug. It's at the top of Gant Road. And of course, there's The Glue Pot."

"Thanks."

"DCI Foster, keep me posted where you are. If you need backup..."

Erika hung up, cutting him off.

She spent the next three hours making her way round some of the roughest pubs she'd seen in her long career. It wasn't the squalor, the dirt, or the drunken people that bothered her. It was the despair in people's faces as they propped up the bar. The hopelessness as they sat slumped in a corner, or poured what little money they had into fruit machines.

What was even more disturbing was that the pubs weren't miles from affluent suburbs. A horrible dive called The Mermaid was next to an Indian fusion restaurant, which was advertising it had recently been awarded a Michelin Star. The bright interior, on show for everyone to see, was filled with happy, well-dressed people dining in groups. The Bird In The Hand, where Erika gave a haunted-looking young girl begging with a baby twenty pounds, was next to a posh wine bar filled with glossy women and their rich husbands.

Was she the only one who noticed this?

At midnight, Erika arrived at The Crown in Gant Road. It was an old-fashioned looking public house with brass lamps over a red frontage. A lock-in was underway, but Erika managed to get in, giving a lad on the door a crisp twenty-pound note.

The inside was packed and the atmosphere rowdy. The windows were steamed up and there was a smell of beer, sweat and cheap perfume. Everyone seemed rather rough round the edges, but had made the effort and was dressed in their best. Erika was questioning exactly what the party was in aid of, when she spied who she'd been looking for.

Ivy sat on a small bar stool at the back, next to a flashing fruit machine. Beside her sat a large young woman who had long black roots in her blonde hair and her lip pierced. Erika slowly made her way over, squeezing through groups of people who looked pretty far-gone. When she reached Ivy, she could see her pupils were dilated. Her eyes were now hideous pools of black.

"What the fuck are you doin' here?" asked Ivy, struggling to focus.

"I just wanted a word," shouted Erika, over the noise.

"I paid for all this," shouted Ivy, waving a finger around. Erika noticed that there were several bags of shopping pooled around the stools.

"It's not about that," said Erika.

The girl beside Ivy glowered. "Everything all right, Ive?" she said, leaning in, not taking her eyes off Erika.

"Yeah," said Ivy. "She's buying the next round."

Erika passed the girl a twenty, realizing she'd parted with a lot of cash that evening. The girl heaved herself off the little stool and vanished into the crowd.

"Where are the kids?" asked Erika.

"'Oo?"

"Your grandkids?"

"Upstairs. Asleep. Why, do you want to hit 'em?"

"Ivy..."

"Well you can get in the queue, love. They've bin fuckin' me off today something proper."

"Ivy. I need to talk to you about The Glue Pot," said Erika, perching on the warm, vacated stool.

"What?" said Ivy, trying to focus.

"You remember? The pub we talked about. The Glue Pot, on London Road."

"I don't go there," slurred Ivy.

"I know you don't go there. *Why* don't you go there?"

"Cos..."

"Please. I need more. Why not, Ivy?"

"Fuck you!"

Erika held up yet another twenty. Ivy attempted to focus, and then grabbed it, tucking it under the waistband of her grotty jeans.

"So, what you wanna talk about?"

"The Glue Pot."

"Bad stuff there. Bad man…bad…" said Ivy, shaking her head.

"There's a bad man?"

"Yeah…" Ivy's eyes were now rolling in her head and she seemed to be seeing things—things that weren't in the bar. Her head snapped to one side.

"Ivy. The bad man. What's his name?"

"He's bad, I tell you, love…"

"Did you hear about the girl who died, Andrea?" Erika pulled out her phone and found the picture of Andrea. "This is her, Ivy. Her name was Andrea. She was beautiful, with dark hair. Do you think Andrea knew this bad man?"

Ivy managed to focus on the phone picture for a moment. "Yeah, she was beautiful."

"You saw her?"

"Few times."

"You saw this girl, a few times, in The Glue Pot?" said Erika, holding the phone up to Ivy.

"I was beautiful once…" Ivy's eyes rolled in her head and she started to slide off the bar stool.

"Come on, Ivy. Stay with me," said Erika, grabbing her and righting her on the stool. "Please look at this picture once more."

Ivy stared at it. "The bad ones are always the worst, but the best, too. You let them do anything to you, even if it hurts, even if you don't want to…"

Erika looked over at the bar and could see that the large girl with the pierced lip wasn't buying any drinks. She was talking to a group of men, and they kept looking at Erika and Ivy.

"Ivy, this is important. Are you talking about Andrea? Did she meet with this bad man at The Glue Pot? He had dark hair. Please. I need anything, a name..."

Ivy drooled, and blew out a bubble of saliva, which popped. She rolled her tongue over her chin and Erika caught sight of her rotten teeth.

"I saw her, with him and some blonde bitch. Stupid girls, they both got in too deep with him," said Ivy.

"What? Ivy? A dark man and a blonde woman?"

"Is this an official visit?" asked a voice. Erika looked up to see a large bear of a man with wispy strawberry-blond hair.

"I didn't invite her," said Ivy, adding, "she's a fucking pig."

"No, it's not an official visit," said Erika.

"Then I'd like you to go," the man said, his voice menacingly calm and quiet.

"Ivy, if you think of anything, see anything, here's my number." Erika pulled out a pen and scrap of paper from her leather jacket, scribbled down her mobile number, and tucked the scrap of paper into the pocket of Ivy's jeans. The man hooked his hand under Erika's arm. "Excuse me," she said, "what do you think you're doing? Who do you think you are?"

"The landlord. Everyone here is invited, and I'm giving away complimentary drinks. You are *not* invited, and therefore I have to tell you to leave or I'm breaking the law."

"I said I wasn't here on an official visit, but my visit could become official at any moment," said Erika.

"This is a wake," said the man, matter-of-factly. "And we have a no-pigs door policy."

"What did you just call me?" asked Erika, trying to remain calm. A short guy with strange gnomic features joined them.

"Did you know my muvver?" he asked accusingly.

"Your mother?" asked Erika.

"Yeah, that's what I said. My muvver, Pearl."

"Who are you?"

"Don't fucking ask me who I am at my own fucking muvver's wake! Who the fuck are you?"

"So this is your mother Pearl's wake, is it?" asked Erika.

"Yeah, and what you gonna fucking do about it?"

Erika looked around the room; people were starting to take notice.

"Cool it, Michael," said the landlord.

"I don't like her attitude, stuck-up lanky bitch," said Michael, looking her up and down.

"You need to calm down, sir," said Erika.

"*Sir?* Are you taking the piss?"

"No, I'm a police officer," said Erika, pulling out her ID.

"What's a pig doing here? You told me you'd had a word..."

"I did have a word, Michael. This *police officer* is just leaving."

"There's a fucking pig 'ere!" cried a weedy, red-haired woman who had tottered over, wearing only one pink slip-on shoe. There was a crack of glass, and then two blokes started to fight. The red-haired woman threw her pint over Erika and wiggled her fingers in a "come and get it" gesture. Erika felt herself being grabbed around the waist. At first she thought she was being attacked, but the landlord was carrying her, holding her up in the air as people swore and spat at her. Through the force of his sheer weight and height he pulled her through the throng and got her behind the bar.

"Get the fuck out. Go through there, to the kitchens. The back door leads out to an alley behind," he said, putting out a hand to stop people from the crowd who were trying to squeeze through the small hatch to get behind the bar. A glass exploded above Erika's head, shattering a vodka optic. At the far end of the bar, the woman who'd thrown the drink pulled up another hatch, and people poured behind the bar and began to rush at Erika.

"Get out!" said the landlord. He pushed her through a stinking pair of curtains. She stumbled down a dimly lit hallway, crashing into boxes of crisps, tripping over a crate of empty bottles. The music blared but barely drowned out the sound of the chaos and breaking glass from the bar behind. She could see that the landlord was being pushed and shoved as he tried to block the doorway. Erika found a door into a kitchen of filth and hellish grease, and at the back she pushed open a fire exit. The cold air hit her wet skin, which was already feeling sticky from the beer, and she saw she was in an alleyway.

Erika dashed back toward the road, past the steam and chaos emanating from the bar windows, and out to her car, which was thankfully still waiting on the road out front.

She got in and drove away with a squeal of rubber. She felt relieved, elated, adrenaline surging through her. And then she remembered that Ivy was still inside the pub. Ivy had seen Andrea, with the dark-haired man and the blonde-haired woman.

Had Ivy been in The Glue Pot the night Andrea vanished? Did this mean the barmaid at The Glue Pot was telling the truth?

CHAPTER 23

Erika was called to Chief Superintendent Marsh's office when she arrived the next morning. She carried with her a check for the rent and the signed contract for the flat. She was surprised, when she entered the office, to see DCI Sparks sat opposite Marsh. Sparks had a smug look on his face.

"Sir?"

"What the hell were you playing at, going into The Crown last night?" demanded Marsh.

Erika looked between Sparks and Marsh. "I stuck to orange juice…"

"This isn't funny! You crashed the wake for Pearl Gadd, and caused no end of chaos. Do you know the Gadd family?"

"No. Should I?"

"They're a bunch of low-life scum who own a massive lorry transportation network in the south of England. However, they've been working with us."

"Working *with us*, sir? Do you want me to allocate one of them a desk in the incident room?"

"Don't get smart."

Sparks was trying not to enjoy this, watching their exchange with his chin resting on the heel of his hand. Erika noticed how he'd let the nail grow long on each index finger.

"Sir. If you've called me in here for a bollocking, I'd rather be bollocked in private."

"You don't outrank DCI Sparks, and he's here as part of the investigation. You're supposed to be working together. I take it your visit to The Crown was part of your inquiries?"

Erika paused, and took the seat next to Sparks.

"Okay. If this is a meeting, fine. Tell me all about our colleagues in the South London underworld."

Sparks removed the hand from under his chin. "The Gadd family has been feeding us information for the past eight months. Information that will hopefully lead to the seizure of millions of pounds' worth of counterfeit cigarettes and alcohol."

"In return for what?" asked Erika.

Marsh interrupted, "I don't have to spell it out, DCI Foster. We're stretched to the fucking limit with what we can and can't do. Do you know what a delicate ecosystem it is here in South London? In return for this information we've been turning a blind eye to . . . well, lock-ins and things. Then you barrel in there last night with your ID and your attitude."

"They said it was a wake, sir."

"It was a fucking wake!"

"Okay, I'm sorry. It seems you do things a little bit differently here than when we were in Manchester."

"We don't do things differently," said Sparks, with an annoying calm. "Although we do thoroughly check our intelligence before we move in."

"What did you just say?" said Erika.

"I'm talking about last night."

"You're sure about that?"

"That's enough!" shouted Marsh, slamming his fist on the table.

Erika swallowed down her anger, and her hatred for Sparks. "Sir. My visit to The Crown had a purpose. It helped me secure new information about Andrea's killer."

Marsh sat down. "Go on," he said.

"I now have a second witness who saw Andrea on the night she died in The Glue Pot, talking to a tall dark man and a blonde woman. This new witness went so far as to hint that Andrea could have been in a relationship with the man."

"Who is this new witness?"

"Ivy Norris."

Sparks rolled his eyes and looked at Marsh, "Do me a favor—Ivy Norris? Also goes by the names Jean McArdle, Beth Crosby, Paulette O'Brien?"

"Sir, she—"

"She's a known time-waster," said Marsh.

"But sir, I got the feeling she was scared when I pressed her about this man. It was genuine fear. I also believe, especially now we've found the phone packaging under Andrea's bed, that Andrea had a second mobile phone, a phone she didn't tell anyone about. I think she had friends that she didn't want her fiancé, Giles Osborne, to know about..."

"The records from Andrea's old phone, the one she lost last year, came in last night," said Sparks.

"No, I think Andrea had another phone. One she was still using. She bought a top-up voucher four months ago, we found it under her bed with the box," explained Erika.

"It means nothing. It could've been for a friend," said Sparks. "Anyway, back to the records for the old phone that actually exist. I took the opportunity to go through them last night, and some interesting information has come to light."

"What's that?" asked Erika.

"Several names come up in her call log, which I've cross-checked with Andrea's Facebook messenger account. One of them is a bloke called Marco Frost... Ring any bells?"

Marsh looked at Erika.

"Yes. He's a barista who Andrea was, I dunno, dating a while back. An Italian guy, works at a coffee place in Soho?"

Sparks nodded and went on, "He made hundreds of calls to Andrea's old phone. The calls were over a period of ten months, between May 2013 and March 2014."

"Why wasn't I told that the phone records had come through?" demanded Erika.

"It was late last night. I thought you might have wanted to get your beauty sleep," said Sparks.

"Sparks, get on with it," said Marsh.

"Okay. So I went back through the interview I did with the Douglas-Browns, when Andrea had first gone missing. And they mentioned this Marco Frost. Andrea did date him briefly for a month at the beginning of 2013. Then she ditched him, and the phone calls started. He turned up at the house several times. Wouldn't take no for an answer. Sir Simon actually had a police officer visit Marco Frost and speak to him about his unhealthy interest in Andrea."

"Why wasn't this mentioned to me before?" asked Erika.

"My notes were available in the file."

"I never got them."

"Well, they were available."

"All right, all right, all right. Let's act like adults," said Marsh, impatiently. "Go on, DCI Sparks."

"Okay. So I went back to Andrea's new phone, where, as we know, there's not much to go on. She checked her e-mails on that phone too, and there was a load of e-invites to parties and events—"

"Yes, the team has been through them, there are hundreds. She had memberships with lots of private clubs," said Erika.

Sparks continued, "There was an e-invite for an event at the Rivoli Ballroom on Thursday, January eighth, the night she vanished. It was a fancy burlesque show organized by one of the clubs where she was a member."

"Yes, and on that same night Andrea had invites to several other parties in London. As I say, she was on loads of mailing lists...And she had already arranged to meet her brother and sister at the cinema."

"But the whole family have said she was a flake; she changed her mind with the wind. It wouldn't be out of character for her to just decide to do something else," said Sparks.

Erika reluctantly had to agree with this.

Sparks went on, "The Rivoli Ballroom is actually bang opposite Crofton Park train station, which on the map looks fairly close to Forest Hill station—to be precise, it's just under two miles away. To get to Forest Hill or Crofton Park you need to take a train from London Bridge, but the two train stations are on completely different lines. What if Andrea got on the wrong train? She rarely used public transport. That could be why she was all dolled-up in Forest Hill."

There was a silence from Erika and Marsh.

"And I saved the best bit until last," said Sparks. "Last night, I got onto the organizer of this burlesque party at the Rivoli Ballroom, and he sent me though their mailing list. Marco Frost was also on that list and was sent the same e-invitation. This gives us an opportunity..."

Erika could see Marsh turning it over in his head.

"This is very promising," he said, getting up and starting to pace. "My next question is, where is this Marco Frost?"

"I don't know. I've been up all night putting this together," said Sparks.

"Look, Sparks, we've had our differences, and I'd like nothing more than this to be a strong lead. But it's hardly a motive. How many people were on that mailing list of invites?" said Erika.

"Three thousand."

"Three thousand. And what makes you think Andrea went anywhere near this Rivoli Ballroom? Her body was found within half a mile of Forest Hill train station, where she got off the train."

Marsh continued to pace up and down, thinking.

Erika continued. "I now have two witnesses who saw Andrea in The Glue Pot the night she vanished."

"One of whom has vanished into thin air, and the other a known drug-addicted, alcoholic prostitute," said Marsh.

"But sir, I think Ivy Norris is—"

"Ivy Norris is scum," said Sparks. "One of her specialities is to shit on the bonnets of the squad cars in the car park."

"Sir, at least acknowledge that we have two lines of inquiry," said Erika. "If you think mine is unreliable, then you must admit that Sparks's is purely circumstantial! I think that we could use this press appeal this afternoon for information about Andrea being seen with the man and the woman in The Glue Pot."

Marsh shook his head. "DCI Foster, we're dealing with people here who the media are itching to hang out to dry. Lord Douglas-Brown, his wife and family, and of course Andrea, who isn't lucky enough to still be here to defend her character from these accusations."

"Sir, it's not an accusation!"

"Sir, The Glue Pot is a known hangout for prostitutes," said Sparks. "It's been raided repeatedly. A bloke got sent down for making kiddie porn in the flat upstairs."

"I agree with Sparks," said Marsh. "Anything we put out there about Andrea Douglas-Brown will instantly be twisted and shredded by the press. We have to be sure it's fact."

"What if I can get Ivy Norris in here to make a statement?"

"She's unreliable. She's made false statements before," said Marsh.

"But, sir!"

"That's enough, DCI Foster. You will work with DCI Sparks to pursue the line of inquiry relating to Marco Frost and Andrea both receiving an invitation to this party at the Rivoli Ballroom. Is that clear?"

"Yes, sir," grinned Sparks.

Erika nodded.

"Right, you can go Sparks. And don't be too happy. There's still a dead girl; that hasn't changed." Sparks looked chastised and left the office.

Marsh eyed Erika for a moment. "Erika, try and cultivate some semblance of a private life. I'm all for my officers taking initiative, but you need to do things by the book and keep me informed of what you are doing. Take a night off, and perhaps do your laundry."

Erika realized she still had a sticky layer of beer on her leather jacket from the previous night.

"Did you visit the doctor yet?" Marsh added.

"No."

"When you finish tonight, I want you to see our duty doctor. That's an order."

"Yes, sir," said Erika. "Here's the contract for the flat."

"Okay, good. How did you find it, all okay?"

"Yes."

When Erika emerged from Marsh's office, Woolf was waiting for her in the corridor.

"I didn't grass you; he got a call from the landlord at The Crown. Then he demanded the logbook from the front desk."

"It's okay. Thank you."

As Woolf went off to get changed and go home after a long night shift, Erika wondered who else from London's criminal underworld was able to pick up the phone and call Chief Superintendent Marsh.

CHAPTER 24

By mid-morning, the incident room at Lewisham Row was hectic. Phones rang, faxes and printers churned, and police officers rushed in and out. Erika and Sparks were sitting in a corner with Marsh and Colleen Scanlan, the stern and rather matronly police media liaison officer. They were working through what was going to be covered at the press appeal.

"So I finish with my introduction and then we'll hear from Sir Simon," said Marsh. "I think he wanted to use autocue for this, if we can arrange that?"

"That shouldn't be a problem. We'll need his final text within the next couple of hours to get it e-mailed over and loaded up," said Colleen.

"Okay," said Marsh. "So, Sir Simon will say: 'Andrea was an innocent, fun-loving twenty-three-year-old with her whole life ahead of her…' Then we've got her picture flashing up on the screens behind us. 'She never hurt anyone, never caused anyone pain, and yet here I am, a heartbroken father, making an appeal for witnesses to a horrific crime, the murder of my daughter…' Shouldn't that be 'an' horrific crime?"

"'An' would actually be incorrect," said Colleen. "Although it's a common misconception. You only use 'an' when the following word begins with a vowel sound…"

"We want this press conference to be an open, down-to-earth line of communication to the public," snapped Erika. "Let's not waste time debating the correct bloody grammar!"

"Okay, so, 'a horrific crime,'" said Marsh.

It pained Erika that the press conference was being built around evidence she felt was circumstantial, and that the team who she thought she'd bonded with had seized upon Sparks's weak theory with such zeal. She had to admit that to an outsider, the Rivoli Ballroom theory had more credence. She cursed herself for being so stupid and going off on her own to pursue The Glue Pot barmaid and Ivy Norris. She should have taken Moss or Peterson. She looked over at them both working the phones, trying to track down Marco Frost.

She turned the Frost theory over in her brain, and a sliver of doubt flashed through her—but then her gut instinct kicked in. Her gut was telling her she was on to something with Andrea meeting the dark-haired man and blonde girl in The Glue Pot. Even if her two witnesses had been unreliable, was it likely that they would be unreliable in exactly the same way? Both Ivy and Kristina were people who existed uncomfortably on the wrong side of the law. It would be easier for them to say they knew nothing, that they hadn't seen Andrea . . . Erika suddenly realized that Marsh was talking to her.

"DCI Foster, what do you think? Should we mention the Tina Turner video? Colleen thinks yes."

"What?"

"The Rivoli Ballroom. It's a very famous old venue, and Colleen thinks a fact like that will stick in the public's memory, make them remember the appeal, and it could lead to increased word-of-mouth."

Erika still looked nonplussed.

"Tina Turner filmed her *Private Dancer* video at the Rivoli Ballroom back in 1984," said Colleen.

"She did?" asked Erika.

"Yes. So shall we put that in with the appeal, with the photo of the venue?"

Erika nodded and looked down at the itinerary they were compiling. "Where are we going to say that Andrea was in Forest Hill? Her clutch bag was recovered on London Road."

"With media appeals we need to narrow things down, present a clear concise message. If we say she was in one place and then another, people will get confused; they need continuity," explained Colleen, a little condescendingly.

"I understand how these things work, thank you. But this appeal is a great opportunity to gather information. This skates over vital clues as to how Andrea went missing," said Erika.

"We're aware that she may have been in the location in question, but we have no hard evidence. There is no CCTV footage, or witnesses. The killer must have used a car; he could have thrown that bag out of the car window on London Road," stated Marsh.

"I know the details of my own case, sir!"

They finished an hour later, with Erika having reluctantly agreed to the content of the press conference, which made no mention of Andrea being anywhere near The Glue Pot, and played down the fact she could have been on the London Road.

Erika came out to the vending machine and saw Sergeant Crane feeding in coins and selecting a cappuccino.

"All right, boss? We got the bus footage through from TFL, and some stuff from a couple of black cabs who went along London Road," he said. The machine beeped and he bent down and pulled out the plastic cup, blowing on the froth.

"Let me guess, nothing?"

Crane took a gulp of coffee and shook his head. "But this Marco Frost seems tough to track down. The last place of work we have is the Caffè Nero on Old Compton Street, and he doesn't work there anymore. His mobile number's been disconnected too."

"Keep trying. Perhaps he went off with Barbora Kardosova."

"Ha! That's another theory, boss."

"Well, add it to the list," said Erika darkly, as she fed coins into the machine and selected a large espresso.

CHAPTER 25

The incident room at Lewisham Row had been set up as the response center for the appeal, which would be going out live on the BBC, Sky and other rolling news channels. Six uniformed officers had been drafted in to man the phones.

Erika, Sparks, Marsh and Colleen had left Lewisham Row an hour before, to go over to the Thistle Hotel near Marble Arch, where the appeal would be taking place.

Moss and Peterson were using the time before the appeal to work on the whereabouts of their prime suspect, Marco Frost. They had been working off address and payroll information from the Caffè Nero where he had worked in Old Compton Street. This had proved to be a dead end; Marco had quit working for them a year ago. They had tried his parents' address, but Marco's parents had died within six months of each other the previous year. Marco had been living with them in a rented flat, but had now moved. Moss had just been given a phone number from the landlord. Marco was now living with his aunt and uncle. Moss dialed the phone number, and the uncle answered after only a couple of rings.

The conference room at the Thistle Hotel in Marble Arch was huge and windowless. An endless patterned carpet covered the floor, and the rows of chairs in front of a small platform were almost full. Members of the press waited with their cameras.

Lights were being set up, and already a couple of TV journalists were standing practicing their pieces to camera. Two large flat-screen televisions were on stands at the side of the room, and they showed live feeds from the BBC News Channel and Sky News. The sound was muted, but across both screens was a banner, trailing that there would shortly be a live press conference and police appeal about the murder of Andrea Douglas-Brown.

On the platform was a long table, dotted at intervals with small microphones. A woman from the hotel staff moved along with a tray, placing a glass and a small carafe of water at each chair. Behind were three video screens showing the blue Met Police logo against a white background.

It never failed to make Erika feel uncomfortable, the relationship the police had with the media; one day pushing them away, accusing them of intruding and twisting the facts, and the next inviting them to a press conference which had all the hallmarks of a theatrical performance.

On cue, Colleen appeared at Erika's side and asked her to come to the staging area for makeup.

"Just a little powder to take the shine off your face," she added. But the way she looked at her watch indicated it might take a lot longer to get Erika to look half-decent on live television.

The hotel had set aside a smaller conference room next door for police and family. A group of sofas had been pushed together and there was a table with water and orange juice.

Marsh sat wearing his Chief Superintendent uniform. A young girl was working on his face with a tube of foundation and a triangular-shaped sponge. Beside him, another young girl was making up DCI Sparks. They were deep in conversation with Simon and Diana, who sat opposite. Again, Andrea's parents were both clad in black, and while Simon did most of the talking, Diana held on to his hand, nodding and dabbing at her eyes. They looked across and Erika nodded respectfully. Diana nodded back, but Simon ignored her and turned back to Marsh and Sparks.

"They shouldn't be a moment, then it's your turn," said Colleen. Erika went over to get a glass of water from the table, which was under a window looking out over the traffic grinding its way around Marble Arch. Linda and David appeared through the door at the back of the room, and approached the table.

"Hello," said Erika, pouring herself some water.

"Hi," said David. He held out his glass and let Erika fill it. He was dressed in jeans and a royal blue jumper and looked very white. Linda wore a long black skirt and a bright red sweater with a plastic molded panel on the front, depicting a row of thin white cats standing on their hind legs, wearing can-can dresses. Above them was written, "WE'RE DOING THE CAT-CAT!" It seemed garish and inappropriate.

Colleen came back and told Erika they were almost ready.

"I hate wearing makeup, too," said Linda, pouring herself a glass of orange juice.

"You're not going to be on telly," said David, sipping his water.

"Did you know Jimmy Savile always refused to wear makeup on television? He said he wanted people to see the real him...A horrible irony, don't you think?" said Linda, flicking her fringe away from her eyes with a twitch. Erika didn't know what to say, and just nodded.

"I wrote to his show when I was seven," Linda continued. "I wanted him to fix it for me to visit the Disney studios and draw a cat for an animation film. You know, they make animations with loads of pictures drawn with tiny differences..."

"I'm sure DCI Foster knows how animation works," said David, rolling his eyes at Erika conspiratorially.

"Of course, I never got a reply... Even Jimmy Savile rejected me." Linda laughed dryly.

"Jesus. Can you just try and be normal for once? You come wearing that stupid jumper, making sick jokes!" snapped David. Linda jumped as he slammed his empty glass on the table and walked away.

"It wasn't a joke. I really did want to visit the Disney studios," said Linda, blushing and twitching her hair off her forehead. Erika was glad when Colleen appeared and took her to the makeup girl.

Marsh and Sparks were now standing near the door to the larger conference room with Simon and Diana. The makeup girl worked fast on Erika, and just as she finished, a young guy wearing earphones approached and said there were two minutes to go. Erika's phone rang.

"Sorry, I need your phone off, it interferes with the sound," he said.

"I'll just take this quickly," said Erika, seeing Moss's name flash. She moved over to the window and answered the call.

"Boss, it's me," Moss said. "Are you there with the Super and Sparks? I've been trying their phones..."

"They've switched them off; something to do with the microphones and sound," said Erika, realizing she'd been third on Moss's list.

"We've tracked down Marco Frost. He lives with his uncle in North London."

Erika could see the press conference was about to start. Moss went on, "Marco Frost was in Puglia in Italy until two days ago. He went with his uncle and aunt for an extended Christmas break to visit relatives. They drove in the uncle's car. The uncle owns a convenience store near Angel, and they brought back a shedload of olive oil and meats, etcetera, etcetera."

"So Marco Frost has an alibi," said Erika, the excitement rising in her.

"Yup. He even used his credit card when he was abroad. He can't have killed Andrea."

Colleen appeared at Erika's elbow. "We have to go, DCI Foster, and that has to be turned off," she said.

"Good work, Moss."

"Is it? This means we're none the wiser about who killed Andrea… Well, there's your theory."

"I've got to go Moss, I'll talk to you later," said Erika, and hung up. She switched off her phone as she saw the others move toward the conference room. Simon went first, followed by Marsh, then Sparks.

So Marco Frost didn't kill Andrea, thought Erika. *Sparks's theory has just fallen apart.* The conversations she'd had with The Glue Pot barmaid and Ivy needled at her brain. *Andrea had been seen with a dark-haired man and a blonde woman… They were still out there. Whoever did this was still out there.*

Marsh, Sparks and Simon had now disappeared into the press conference. Diana remained on the sofa. She was crying again and was being comforted by Linda and David.

"We need you in there, *now*," hissed Colleen to Erika.

Giles Osborne burst through the door at the back. He was rugged up in a huge winter coat. He rushed over to Diana, unwinding his scarf and apologizing for being late.

"Have I missed the appeal?" he said. Diana shook her head through her tears.

"Now, DCI Foster!" said Colleen.

Erika made a decision—a decision which would have far reaching consequences… She took a deep breath, smoothed down her hair, and went into the press conference.

CHAPTER 26

Moss, Peterson, Crane, and the rest of the team were back at Lewisham Row, gathered around a large flat-screen television. The BBC News channel counted down to the hourly bulletin, and then a wide shot of the press conference came onto the screen. Seated at the long table were DCI Sparks, DCI Foster and Chief Superintendent Marsh. Next to Marsh sat Simon Douglas-Brown, who looked haunted and drawn.

Simon read his statement from the prepared script, and footage of him was interspersed with the driving license photo of Andrea that had been doing the rounds in the press, plus a newer photo: Andrea on her last family holiday with Linda, David and their parents. They were all smiling at the camera, with a backdrop of the sea behind. David smiled bashfully. Linda's face remained set in the same pudgy-faced scowl.

"DCI Foster was right, this is all very touching," said Crane. "But it's like a well-packaged display of grief. Will it prompt anyone to call in?"

On the screen, Simon Douglas-Brown finished his statement, and the camera pulled out to a wide shot. Chief Superintendent Marsh was about to speak, when Erika leaned over and shifted his microphone toward her. She addressed the camera and started to speak.

"The events leading up to the disappearance of Andrea are confusing, and we need your help. We would appreciate anyone coming forward who saw Andrea on the night of the eighth of January. It was a Thursday night. We believe Andrea spent some time between eight p.m. and midnight in a pub called The Glue Pot on London Road—that's South London, in Forest Hill. Andrea was seen by a member of the bar staff talking to a dark-haired man and a blonde-haired girl. Members of the public may have also seen Andrea walking up London Road between eight p.m. and midnight, toward the Horniman Museum, where her body was found. If you have any information, however small, please come forward. Phone the incident room number which will be coming up shortly."

"Was that planned?" asked Peterson, back in the incident room.

"Nope," said Moss.

On screen there was a moment where Chief Superintendent Marsh couldn't find his place, or what to say next. He shot Erika a look and pulled back the microphone. "We'd like to, erm, add that this is, um, er... it's a lead that Andrea was seen... We also believe that Andrea could have been on her way to a party at the Rivoli Ballroom, which is close to Forest Hill Station, where she alighted on the night of the eighth of January," countered Marsh, more forcefully. There was a moment of silence. The camera cut again to a wide shot of the press conference.

"Jeez, he's making a mess of it. It's like he's making it up, not Foster," said Moss.

The cameras flicked between wide shots of the conference room and the gathered press, which added to the confusion, before settling back onto Superintendent Marsh, who finally got back on track and finished the scripted appeal. He ended with: "We have officers standing by now to answer your calls and e-mails. Thank you."

The camera then cut away from the press conference to the anchor in the BBC News studio. The screen behind her was filled with the contact number and e-mail address for the incident room. She read out the details, asking again for anyone who had information, and repeating the name of both The Glue Pot and the Rivoli Ballroom, apologizing that they only had a photo of the Rivoli Ballroom.

The officers back in the incident room at Lewisham Row looked at each other uneasily, and then the phones started to ring.

CHAPTER 27

The moment the press conference disbanded and the live camera feed was off, Erika stood up. Her heart was pounding. The journalists and photographers were crowding toward the exits. Simon turned to Marsh, a furious look in his brown eyes.

"What were you lot fucking playing at?" he hissed. "I thought we were clear about this and how it would work?" He looked out, almost despairingly, at the press leaving.

Marsh and Sparks stood up. "DCI Foster, a word, now," said Marsh. Erika took a deep breath and left the platform, ignoring their voices behind her as she crossed the carpet, speeding up toward the doors at the back of the conference room. Once through, she found a fire exit and clattered down three flights of stairs before bursting outside onto a side street.

She stood and caught her breath, the rain pricking at her clammy skin. She knew there would be consequences for what she had just done, but didn't she always stand by her convictions? Her convictions had told her this was the right thing to do. She had done something good, something for Andrea, who didn't have the right to reply.

She started to walk, not noticing the rain, and joined the bumping and jostling of the crowds on Oxford Street, lost in a cocoon of thoughts. Her gut feeling, the certainty she'd felt, began to fade. She should have stayed and faced the music. In her absence, they would be discussing what she had done, reaching conclusions. They were making decisions without her, planning what they would do next.

She hesitated, then stopped. The rain pounded down on the pavements, and people streamed around her, their heads down, hoods and umbrellas up. They tutted and cursed as their smooth passage to the bus or tube was blocked. It was now the peak of rush hour. Erika needed to think, to plan what she would do next. If she went back, it would look weak. She set off again, moving with the crowd.

Behind her, a few people back, followed a figure. The same figure that had watched Erika smoking at her window. This time, the figure wasn't completely clad in black, but easily blended in among the crowd with their hoods and umbrellas. The crowd seemed to swell and slow as they approached Marble Arch tube station, the figure shadowing Erika with a gap of just two people between them.

Erika was one of the few people on the street without a hood, and was walking with her head down, the collar of her leather jacket up.

She is, indeed, a worry to me. She's been to that fucking pub and talked to people. She knows a great deal more than I thought. Has it been an act, all that angst and despair? Until that press conference I thought she was damaged goods. The burned-out wreck of a once brilliant cop.

The figure was close to Erika now. All that separated them was a burly businessman in a pale raincoat mottled with drips of water. Erika pulled her collar closer, so that it touched the blonde hair at the nape of her neck.

She's single and alone. Grieving. She could be suicidal. So many people are. I'd love to pay her a call, the scrawny bitch—surprise her in bed. Hold that skinny throat where the tendons bulge out and watch her eyes go dark. But there's someone else who is due a visit…

The crowds reached Bond Street tube station and ground to a halt. Erika inched forward so she could just get under the large awning as she waited for the crowds to move forward. The figure edged closer, among the packed-in crowd, and slipped a neat white envelope into the pocket of Erika's leather jacket. Seconds later, the blockage at the station entrance cleared. The figure left Erika and moved on through the crowd, blending in: just another person eager to get somewhere fast.

CHAPTER 28

When Erika emerged from the concourse at Brockley Station, she was confused to see her new home in daylight. The street was busy; a Royal Mail van moved past and parked at a post box. A fresh-faced young postman got out and opened the box, pulling out a full sack of letters. There was a café opposite the station where two women sat at a table outside, huddled in jackets against the cold and smoking cigarettes, thick red lipstick smeared on the edge of their white china cups. A handsome waiter with a pierced lip came to their table. He said something as he took their empties, and the women shrieked with laughter.

Erika fumbled in her bag and pulled out her cigarettes. Her hands shook as she lit up. Her feeling of anxiety had increased during the train journey back. Her heart was pounding in her chest and it was like she was seeing the world through slightly blurred glass. The handsome waiter was still chatting to the woman, and they were flirting back with ease.

"Ooh—no, no, no, no, no," said a voice.

Erika looked round. A paunchy man in a South West Trains uniform stood beside her. He had gray hair and a graying mustache.

"Excuse me?" asked Erika.

"You just quite fancy a one thousand pound fine, do you love?"

"What?" she said, feeling dizzy.

"It's illegal to smoke at train stations. But I know how we can resolve this. All you need to do is take one step forward, go on."

Erika, confused, stepped forward.

"There love, all solved, you're no longer on station property!" He pointed to her feet, where she now stood on the smooth tarmac running past the station concourse.

"Okay," she said uneasily.

The man regarded her warily. It was only then that she realized he was being kind, but it was too late and he went off, muttering. Erika stumbled away, heart racing faster, drawing on her cigarette. The women at the café were now browsing the wine list, laughing and chatting with the handsome waiter. An old man twirled a metal stand of greeting cards around outside a newsagent's on the corner. Two old ladies walked slowly, weighed down by shopping bags and deep in conversation.

Erika grabbed the low wall outside a house and steadied herself. It occurred to her that she had no clue how to be a "normal" person. She could look at dead bodies and deal with interviewing violent sex offenders, she'd been spat at and threatened with a knife, but living in the real world as a member of society, it frightened her. She had no clue how to be single, alone, with no friends.

The enormity of what she had just done came back to her. She'd hijacked the press conference of a major murder inquiry. What if she was wrong? She hurried back to the flat, the dizziness intensifying, a cold sweat prickling under her collar.

When she was indoors, she slumped into the sofa. The room was spinning and a fuzzy blur was creeping into the side of her vision. She blinked, looking around the small living room. The blur moved with her vision. She felt her stomach contract and she ran to the bathroom, only just making it as she threw up in the toilet. She kneeled and retched, and threw up again. She flushed and washed her mouth out in the sink, having to hold on to its sides as the floor seemed to lurch and sway underneath. The reflection staring back at her was gruesome: sunken eyes, her skin tinged white-green. The blurry patches were growing, spreading in the center of her vision. Her face was now a blur in the mirror. What was happening to her? She staggered back through to the living room, holding on to the wall, the door-frame, then making a dash for the edge of the sofa. The center of her vision was now flooded with a blur. She tilted her head, having to use her peripheral vision to locate her leather jacket, half-hanging over the armrest. She found her phone in one of the pockets, and tilting her head, she saw it was still switched off from the press conference.

Blood roared in her head and nausea and panic rose in her. She was dying. She was going to die alone. She found the button on the top of her phone and switched it on, but a spinning disc on the screen told her it was booting up. She slumped forward, face on the sofa. She was terrified; a powerful headache was forming at the back of her skull. She realized that this could be the start of a migraine, just as the room seemed to give an almighty spin and then everything went black.

CHAPTER 29

Erika felt she was moving through darkness, fumbling toward a far-off ringing. It seemed to move closer, and then her ears popped and it was close to her head. The side of her face was pressed against something soft with a faint smell of fried food and cigarettes. Her knees were against a hard wooden floor. She sat back on her heels, and lifted her head, realizing she was in her new flat. Her phone was ringing. It dark outside and the street light was shining through the bare window.

The phone glowed and vibrated on the coffee table and fell silent. Her mouth was dry, and she had a terrible headache. She pulled herself up unsteadily and went to the sink and drank a large glass of water. She put the glass down and it all came flooding back. One glimmer of hope was that her vision had returned to normal. Her phone rang again, and, thinking it was Marsh, she answered, wanting to get it over and done with.

A familiar voice said, "Erika? Is that you?"

She bit back tears. It was Mark's father, Edward. She'd forgotten how much he sounded like Mark, with his warm Yorkshire accent.

"Yes, it's me," she said, finally.

"I know it's been a long time—well, I've phoned to say I'm sorry," he said.

"Why are you sorry?"

"I said things. Things I regret."

"You had every right, Edward. I can't bear to look at myself half the time..." Her diaphragm lurched and she was sobbing, hiccupping, the words coming out in a jumble as she tried to tell the man who she'd loved like another father how sorry she was, that she had failed to protect his son.

"Erika, love, it wasn't your fault...I read a copy of the transcript from the hearing," he said.

"How?"

"I requested it. Freedom of Information Act...They hauled you across the coals."

"I deserved it. I should have dug deeper, could have triple-checked things..." she started.

"You can't live your life by should and could, Erika."

"I will never forgive myself. If only I could go back again, if only. I would never..." she said, wiping hot tears away with the heel of her hand.

"Now, that's enough of that, I don't want to hear another word, or there'll be hell to pay!" he joked.

The joke felt forced. There was a silence.

"How are you?" Erika asked. *Stupid question*, she thought.

"Oh. I'm keeping busy...I'm playing bowls now. Never thought I would but, well, you have to keep busy. I'm a mean bowler for an old duffer..." He trailed off again. "Erika love. There's now a gravestone. I've had the stone put in for Mark. It looks grand."

"It does?" said Erika. She closed her eyes. She thought of Mark underground, and morbidly wanted to know what he looked like. Just bones, bones, in a nice suit.

"And you are welcome to come and see it. You're welcome anytime, love. When do you think you'll be coming home?"

Home. He called it home. Erika had no clue where home was anymore.

"I'm back at work; I'm in London," said Erika.

"Oh. Right."

"I will come. But right now I have to work."

"That's good, love. What work are you doing?" he asked. Erika felt she couldn't tell him she was hunting a brutal killer. She wondered if he had seen the press conference on the news.

"I'm with the Met Police, a new team."

"That's good, lass. Keep yourself busy... When you get some holiday, I'd love to see you."

"I'd like that."

"I go past your house a lot. There's a young couple renting it. They seem nice, although I haven't been and knocked on the door or nothing. Not sure how I'd explain who I was."

"Edward, everything is in storage. I didn't throw anything away. We should go through the boxes. I'm sure there are things..."

"Let's take it one step at a time," said Edward.

"How did you get my new number?" asked Erika, realizing she was on her new phone.

"I phoned your sister. She said you'd been kipping on her sofa; she gave me your number. I hope that's okay?"

"Of course it is. Sorry. It's just the copper in me, always wanting to work things out..."

"I just want you to know, Erika, that you're not alone. I know people weren't kind up here, and you can't blame most of them, but you lost him too..." Edward's voice cracked. He went on, "I just hate to think of you being alone. You've got me, love, for what it's worth."

"Thank you," said Erika softly.

"Well, this will be costing me a fortune, ringing up London, so I'll be off... It's good to hear your voice, Erika. Don't be a stranger."

"You too—I mean, no, I won't."

There was a click and a beep, and he was gone. Erika put her hand on her chest and took a deep breath. A rush of warmth flooded through her and she had to blink back the tears.

Her phone rang again in her hand. She saw it was Moss.

"Boss. Where are you?" she said.

"Home."

"You're not gonna believe this. Another body has been discovered. This time in the water at Brockwell Park."

"Is there an ID on the victim?" asked Erika.

"Yes. It's Ivy Norris."

CHAPTER 30

The Brockwell Park and Lido in Dulwich was less than three miles from the Horniman Museum, where they'd discovered Andrea's body. Erika hurtled past the clock tower, which was lit up and showing it was ten-fifteen. Large drops of rain burst on the windscreen and rapidly became a downpour. Erika flicked on the wipers and leaned forward to see through the whirling water. Two uniformed officers swam into view, standing beside a cordon at the lido entrance. Erika came to a lurching stop, and emerged into the rain, which was roaring as it hit the surrounding parked cars.

"DCI Foster," shouted Erika above the noise and holding up her ID. The officers lifted the tape and she passed through.

The park and lido were popular in the summer for swimming and picnics, but in the darkness of a rain-lashed January night they were bleak and depressing. Moss and Peterson were waved through the police tape just behind Erika, bringing a powerful torch, its beam illuminating their way along a series of concrete paths, past a boarded-up ice-cream hut and a pavilion with its paint peeling away. They emerged into a clearing, unable to make out anything. Thunder rumbled in the distance and lightning lit up the vast open-air swimming pond. Up ahead was the glowing outline of a large white forensics tent. A path of polythene had been marked out along the muddy water's edge. Three crime scene assistants in white overalls were kneeling in the mud, working fast to take an impression of a set of footprints. A crime scene officer met them at the tent, and they quickly suited up as the rain continued to roar on the canvas.

A bright halogen light shone down on the still form of Ivy Norris. She lay on her back in the mud, among a churned up mess of brown, smearing her clothes and body.

"Please stand on the boxes," said a CSI, indicating where a series of platforms had been placed around the body to preserve evidence in the mud underneath.

They approached Ivy's body, moving from platform to platform until they were at her side. Her greasy hair was pulled back from her yellowing face and her face was frozen in the same wide-eyed fear as Andrea. Her nose had been flattened among a mess of clotted blood. She wore the coat and jumper Erika had seen her in a few days previously, but she was naked from the waist down. Her legs were painful to look at: emaciated, with clusters of scars, bruises and needle marks. Her pubic hair was gray and matted.

A crime scene photographer took a picture and the tent was filled with a flash and a high-pitched squeal. Isaac Strong stood silently on one of the boxes. He nodded at them all.

"Who found her?" asked Erika.

"A group of kids who'd climbed the fence for a dare."

"Where are they now?"

"Your officers are with them at the community center over the road. We've already taken DNA."

"Did they see anything?" asked Erika.

"No. It was dark. One of the boys tripped over her body and fell."

"He must have been terrified," said Moss, looking down at Ivy.

"Her nose is broken. I think her cheekbone also. There are extensive ligature marks on her neck," said Isaac, crouching down and gently pulling down the folds of Ivy's sweater. "I also think four ribs are broken; I'll have more idea about internal damage when I conduct my autopsy. She was carrying a hundred pounds in cash. The notes were folded inside her bra."

"So we could rule this out as a random assault or robbery?" asked Moss.

"I don't want to be drawn on that until I've done my autopsy. But obviously when a body is left with money, it indicates that robbery wasn't on the assailant's mind. Sex was, though. On a first examination, there is semen present in her vagina."

"Ivy was a well-known prostitute," explained Moss.

"Perhaps whoever did this had lured her with the cash?" added Peterson.

"We can't assume because of that, that the sex was consensual," said Isaac sternly. "There is extensive bruising around the pelvic area."

"Where are her arms?" Erika asked, dreading for a moment that they'd been hacked off.

"Her arms are bound behind her back," said Isaac. One of his assistants approached and carefully lifted Ivy from the mud; both arms had been pulled tight under her body. They were slick with mud and stones. Isaac wiped at her wrists with a gloved finger.

"See? They've been bound using a plastic tie, often used in industry or product packaging."

"What about her shoes?" asked Erika, seeing Ivy's feet, which were mud-splattered and swollen with a map of broken veins and long dirty toenails.

"We found them in the mud," said Isaac. "There are also patches of hair missing from each temple. They look to have been pulled out at the root."

He tilted Ivy's head and indicated large angry pink patches dotted with dried blood. The photographer crouched in and took a photo. As the flash illuminated her skin, it appeared almost translucent, with threads of blue veins on her forehead.

"Andrea's hair was pulled out," said Erika, softly.

"Time of death?" asked Peterson.

"Internal body temperature leads me to say she hasn't been dead for very long, but the body has been exposed to the freezing temperatures and rain, so I'll need to clarify this."

"We've got officers doing a door-to-door and searching the area," said Peterson.

They watched as the photographer worked, taking pictures of Ivy from every angle. A young woman assisting Isaac gently placed plastic bags over Ivy's hands to preserve any DNA evidence. Isaac moved to a hastily set-up bench in the corner of the tent, returning to them with a clear evidence bag.

"This is what we found on her: a bunch of keys, six condoms, one hundred pounds in cash, a credit card in the name of Matthew Stephens, and a phone number on a scrap of paper."

"That's your number," said Moss, shooting Erika a look.

"I was talking to Ivy the other night in connection to Andrea's murder; she had given me some information but I think she was scared. I said she could call me..." Erika's voice tailed off with the realization that the information had died with Ivy.

"Did she try to call you?" asked Peterson.

"I don't know. I'll need to check my phone."

She hadn't checked her messages since before the press conference. She excused herself and went back through the partition and to the doorway of the tent. A figure was working its way along the bank. When it came closer, Erika saw it was DCI Sparks.

"What are you doing here?" asked Erika. "You're not in the first response unit."

"I've been asked by Chief Superintendent Marsh to take over as Senior Investigating Officer," said Sparks. Despite the gravity of the situation, his glee was bubbling under the surface.

"What? At eleven p.m. at the scene of a murder?" asked Erika.

"You should answer your phone. The Super has been trying to call you," said Sparks.

"I haven't finished here. I can discuss this with Marsh tomorrow," said Erika.

"I have clear instructions. I've been made SIO and I would like you to leave the scene."

"You'd like me to leave?"

"No. I'm ordering you to leave."

"DCI Sparks. I have just been to the crime scene and there are things..." started Erika.

"I said, I'm now in control of this crime scene and I'm ordering you to step aside!" shouted Sparks, losing it.

"I think you'll find, if you have any knowledge of crime scene procedure, that the Forensic Pathologist has ultimate control over the crime scene, and therefore gives the orders," said Isaac, appearing behind Erika with Moss and Peterson. "DCI Foster entered the crime scene as SIO and I will finish my briefing and examination of the crime scene with her present as SIO. Now, DCI Sparks, you are in danger of contaminating the crime scene. If you wish to continue to observe, I'll ask that you follow proper procedure, suit up and shut up."

DCI Sparks opened his mouth to say something, but Isaac looked down at him and raised an impeccably shaped eyebrow, daring him to contradict.

"Eight a.m. tomorrow, there will be a briefing at Lewisham Row where we'll be re-focusing this investigation. Be sure you attend promptly," said Sparks to Moss and Peterson. They nodded. Sparks gave Erika a long, hard look and then stomped away, accompanied by one of the uniformed officers.

"Thank you," said Erika to Isaac.

"I didn't do it to be thanked. I'm not interested in police politics. All I'm interested in is preserving a scene so you can do your job and find who did this," said Isaac.

Erika removed her crime scene overalls, which were bagged up to go to the lab. She found shelter from the pouring rain under the peeling facade of the pavilion, lit a cigarette, and listened to her voice-mails. There were four from Marsh, all growing increasingly angry. Simon and Diana Douglas-Brown had apparently been "horrified" when Erika had "hijacked the press appeal for her own agenda," and Marsh was in agreement. He was ordering her to report to him immediately in the morning. The message finished with him saying, "Ignoring my calls will be seen as a further act of insubordination and a direct challenge to my authority."

When she reached the final message in her mailbox, it began with lots of distortion; she heard a voice swearing and then the sound of coins dropping into a pay phone.

"Yeah, it's Ivy…Ivy Norris. If you can give me some money, I'll tell you what you need to know. I need a hundred quid…" There were three fast pips, more swearing and then the line went dead. Erika listened to the message again. It was timed seven hours ago. Erika put in a call to Sergeant Crane, who answered wearily.

"Hi Crane, it's DCI Foster, are you still at the nick?"

"Yes, boss," he said wearily.

"What was the response like to the appeal?"

"We've had twenty-five calls, boss. They've died off over the last few hours. We're just waiting to see if they run the number again on the evening news."

"Tell me we've got something useful?" asked Erika hopefully.

"Fourteen of them are known nutters and time-wasters; they tend to admit to every television crime appeal. One of these guys still maintains that he killed Princess Diana. We still have to go through and eliminate them all, which is taking time. Another ten calls have been from journalists, fishing, basically."

"I make that twenty-four."

"The last one was from Ivy Norris. She called a couple of hours after the appeal went out. We've traced the call to a pay phone at The Crown public house. She was fairly incoherent, but left her name, and said she wanted to talk to you personally. Did you check your messages? I tried to call you, but there was no answer?"

"Yes, and she tried to call me too. We've just discovered her body."

"Shit," said Crane.

"Yes. Shit indeed. Look, I'll be in first thing tomorrow, let me know if you get anything more."

"Um, boss..."

"What?"

"I've been told to give all new info to DCI Sparks."

"Okay, but the Ivy thing, it's kind of personal too."

"Course, boss."

Erika came off the phone as Moss and Peterson approached. She told them about the message from Ivy.

"She's cried wolf so many times before," said Moss. "And it was only a matter of time before she turned up dead."

"They're about to move the body. The team needs to close down the site for forensics as fast as they can; they're going to have to work fast in this rain," said Peterson. "I take it we report to DCI Sparks?"

"Yes, it seems so," said Erika. There was a moment of silence; Peterson and Moss seemed disappointed.

"Well, I'll see you both soon, then," said Erika.

When she got back to her car she sat inside in the darkness, the rain pummeled on the roof. Moss and Peterson drove past, illuminating the inside of her car before plunging her back into darkness. The death of Ivy felt nasty. She pulled her hand out of her coat and flicked on the light above the mirror. The teeth marks were now fading, the scabs healing fast. What had Ivy been doing? Was she lured out to the Brockwell Lido? Did she go willingly? And what would happen to her grandchildren now she was gone?

Erika started her car and pulled out into the rain.

CHAPTER 31

The figure leaned forward, yanking off the thick balaclava, and threw up violently. The vomit hit the inky water with a nasty, high-pitched splatter, even louder than the rain, which was falling onto the surface of the pond in torrents. It was normal to purge after a kill. The figure then collapsed onto the wet earth, enjoying the sensation of the rain.

It had been easy, tracking down Ivy Norris. At her age she was a creature of habit, and had been lurking under a street light at the bottom of Catford High Street. She'd looked more disgusting than usual, with what smelled like dried vomit on the furry hood of her coat, and blood crusting around her nostrils.

"My name's Paulette, you want oral or full sex?" Ivy had said, her eyes lighting up when the expensive car had pulled up beside her. She only saw the figure properly when she climbed into the passenger side, and the central locking was activated.

"Hello, Ivy…I'm looking for something from you," the figure had said in a smooth voice.

Ivy had started to plead and panic, apologizing, saying it wouldn't happen again, the words tumbling out, spittle flying onto the dashboard of the expensive car. "I'm tellin' you, I had to speak to that copper. She threatened me. She threatened to take me kids away…All she knows is that Andrea girl was with a bloke with dark hair and a girl with blonde hair…And I ain't gonna say no more!"

The figure had then held out a gloved hand, offering Ivy two fifty-pound notes.

"What do you want me to do?" Ivy had asked, uncertainly.

I don't know if she was just so beaten down by life, or if she thought there was a chance I would let her go afterward, but she took the money.

Ivy hadn't questioned the remoteness of the location, and when they had got there, she had allowed her hands to be tied behind her back. She hadn't even suggested a safe word.

"Just not me face," she'd said. "I know I'm not much to look at, but it makes life easier if it's not me face..."

It was then that I snapped, and punched her in the face. She didn't look surprised, just disappointed. When I did it again, harder, she looked consigned to her fate. Another disappointment to add to her collection. I ripped handfuls of her hair out...Broke her nose...She only looked surprised when my hands had been on her throat for longer than a minute. It was then that she realized she was going to die.

Far away, across the grass of Peckham Rye Common, a police car streaked past, sirens blazing out. The figure lay deep in the undergrowth next to a pond, enjoying the sensation of being cleansed by the rain.

My car is a few blocks away, but I can't go back for it yet.

Not yet.

When it gets light.

When I'm clean.

CHAPTER 32

Erika didn't sleep for a long time. She lay awake, listening to the rain pounding relentlessly against the window. She couldn't get the image of Ivy out of her mind. Of her blank eyes wide with horror, as if still seeing her killer's face. Erika wondered what that face looked like. Was it old or young? Dark or fair? Was the killer physically threatening, or an everyman who just blended in?

She didn't remember drifting off to sleep. She opened her eyes and the light was filtering softly through the curtains in her bedroom. The day had dawned and for the first time since she could remember, it had been a dreamless sleep. She pulled the curtain to one side and saw it had stopped raining but the sky was a pale gray. It was light. She leaned over to the bedside table and picked up her phone to see the time. It was on its charger, but dead.

She cursed, moving through to the living room where she saw the digital clock on the oven was dark. She opened the tiny cupboard housing the electricity box, yanked out Marcie's blotchy painting and flicked the mains switch on and off, but nothing. Peering out of the front bay window at the empty street below, she had no clue what the time was. She opened her front door, crossed the landing to the door opposite and knocked. A few seconds later she heard a key turning, bolts shooting back and the rattle of a chain. The door opened a few inches and a small elderly lady with a meringue of white hair peered through the gap.

"Sorry to bother you," said Erika. "Could you tell me what the time is?"

"Who are you? Why do you want to know the time?" the lady asked suspiciously.

"I'm your new neighbor. I think we've had a power cut, and my only clock is on my phone, which is also dead."

The old lady pulled back the thin sleeve of her cardigan and peered at a tiny gold watch biting into the flesh of her wrist. "It's ten and twenty past," she said.

"Ten-twenty in the morning?"

"Yes."

"You're sure?" said Erika in horror.

"Yes dear, I'm the one with the watch. My electricity seems to be working," she said, flicking her hall light on and off. "I think you need to feed your meter, dear. The tenants before you got very behind on their bills. The police even came in at one point—I don't know why the police were wasting their time chasing up unpaid bills. Although your landlord is apparently quite a high-up policeman, so I'd be careful…"

Erika arrived breathlessly at Lewisham Row Station at quarter to eleven. Woolf was on the front desk. He crossed round to her side.

"DCI Foster, I've been asked to take you in to see Chief Superintendent Marsh; it's urgent."

"I know where it is," snapped Erika. She went through to Marsh's office and knocked. Marsh opened the door.

"Come in and sit down," he said coldly. Assistant Commissioner Oakley sat in Marsh's chair. Marsh had been relegated to a chair beside his own desk. His office had been hastily tidied.

The corner of a Christmas card poked out from one of the cupboard doors.

"Good morning, DCI Foster. Please have a seat," said Oakley, in calm, clipped tones. He was immaculately dressed: his uniform crisp, his gray hair neatly parted, not a hair out of place. His skin was tanned and shiny. He was like a sleek fox. Not in any way sexual, but cunning and immaculately groomed. Erika remembered she'd read that if foxes are fed on the finest food they have the glossiest coats. Erika sat and noticed that Marsh was pulling on a pair of latex gloves.

"Please can we see your mobile telephone?" said Oakley.

"Why?"

"You are the last person to have received a phone call from the murder victim Ivy Norris. The voice-mail and your phone is now evidence in the investigation." His tone was final; no questions were to be asked. Erika took out the phone and handed it to Marsh.

"It's not switching on," said Marsh, turning the phone over and pressing the power button.

"The battery's dead," said Erika.

"This is your designated phone, for work purposes, and it's dead?" asked Oakley.

"I can explain..."

"Please read out the serial number," said Oakley, ignoring Erika. Marsh worked quickly, pulling the back off the phone and reading the number out as Oakley wrote it down.

"It's possible to access my voice-mail independently, without needing the handset," said Erika, as Marsh placed her phone into a fresh plastic evidence bag, and sealed it up.

Oakley ignored her and opened a file. "DCI Foster, do you know why you are here?"

"I think so, sir. I'm not sure why you are though?"

"Three days ago, an official report was filed by Desk Sergeant Woolf. It details an incident between yourself and Ivy Norris's seven-year-old grandson, Matthew Paulson. Ivy Norris, whose body was discovered last night."

"I'm aware of that, sir. I was one of the first responders at the scene," said Erika.

"It says in Woolf's report that during the incident in the reception area of this station you physically struck the boy on the back of his head. What do you have to say about that?" The Assistant Commissioner looked up at her from the file.

"Is it also mentioned in the report that at the time, the boy had latched onto my hand with his teeth?" said Erika.

"What were you doing in such close proximity to the child?"

"He was sitting on my suitcase, sir. He wouldn't get off."

"*He was sitting on your suitcase*," repeated Oakley, leaning back. He tapped his pen against his teeth. "Were you injured during this attack by a small seven-year-old boy?"

"Yes, my hand was cut," said Erika.

"Yet there is no further entry to this incident in the report. Procedure would dictate that you are examined by a doctor, who can verify this. Were you examined by a doctor?"

"No."

"And why not?"

"It wasn't life-threatening. Unlike some people, I like to engage more in police work than pushing paper around."

"Not life-threatening. Yet these things can fast become *career-threatening*," said Oakley. Erika looked to Marsh but he said nothing.

Oakley flicked through the file. "I had CCTV images pulled from the reception area, which does indeed show the full altercation. Ivy Norris threatened you with a knife, and the situation was diffused by the desk sergeant. However, six minutes later you are seen in the car park where Ivy Norris and her three grandchildren get into your car."

He passed a large photo across the desk that showed a remarkably sharp image of Ivy and the children outside Erika's car. The next image showed Erika holding something out through the open window, and the next was of Ivy and the children climbing into Erika's car.

"It was freezing cold. I felt sorry for them, I gave them a lift."

"And what were are you holding out to Ivy in the photo?"

"Cash."

"You gave them a lift? Where?"

"To Catford High Street."

"And then what happened?"

"I dropped them where they wanted to go."

"Which was?"

"By a Ladbrokes betting shop; Ivy didn't want me to see where she lived. They left the car and vanished in between the shops."

"Left the car, or fled the car? What happened when they were in your car? Was there any further physical violence, from either party?"

"No."

"You were then seen again twenty-four hours later with Ivy Norris, this time harassing her at a private wake."

"It was a glorified lock-in, sir, and Ivy was in a public place. I wasn't harassing her."

"Did you know the landlord of The Crown filed an official complaint about police harassment?"

"Did he? Was that in-between working as a police informant? Or was that part of his work as a police informant?"

"I would tread very lightly here, DCI Foster," said Oakley, icily. "These allegations are stacking up in quite an alarming fashion. Your phone number was found at the crime scene on

Ivy Norris's body, plus she was found with a hundred pounds in cash. You are in this photo giving her cash…"

"I gave her my number, and asked if she could call me with any information."

"We have a transcript of the voice-mail she left on your phone, where she states, I quote, 'If you can give me money I'll tell you what you need to know. A hundred minimum should do.'"

"Hang on, you've already pulled my private mobile phone messages? Are you suggesting I murdered Ivy Norris?"

Erika looked at Marsh, who had the decency to look away.

"No, we are not suggesting you murdered Ivy Norris, DCI Foster. Looking at this evidence though, it's building a picture of an officer who is frankly a concern, perhaps a little out-of-control," said Oakley.

"Sir, you know we all have our narks. Our informants who we take for a drink and a chat—a little money and a little information changes hands, but I did not give Ivy Norris one hundred pounds."

"DCI Foster, can I remind you that it's not official police policy to pay for information," said Marsh, finally speaking up. Erika laughed at this ludicrous statement.

Marsh's voice went up an octave. "You also directly defied my order with regards to the official statement we made at the press appeal. You jumped in, unapproved, unscripted. Used it as a mouthpiece for a wild hunch. Who knows what damage you have done…"

"Hunch? Sir, I have a strong lead on a man who was seen with Andrea Douglas-Brown just hours before she was killed, and this was witnessed by a barmaid and Ivy Norris."

"Yes, the barmaid who doesn't seem to exist, and an unreliable witness, who is now dead," said Assistant Commissioner Oakley, remaining irritatingly calm. He went on, "Do you have an agenda against Lord Douglas-Brown?"

"No!"

"His role supplying defense contracts has been controversial, and has impacted policy in all departments of the police and armed forces."

"Sir, my only agenda is to catch the killer of Andrea Douglas-Brown, and Ivy Norris. Am I going to be the first who says that the circumstances are remarkably similar?"

"So you now believe that the murders are linked?" said Assistant Commissioner.

"Can I just add, sir, that this is not the line of inquiry we are pursuing," said Marsh, spinelessly.

Erika paused. "Yes, I believe these murders are linked. I believe to pursue my line of investigation would be in the best interests of catching this killer."

"I repeat that this is not the line of inquiry we are pursuing," said Marsh.

"Then what line of inquiry are we pursuing?" asked Erika, fixing Marsh with a stare. "DCI Sparks had a prime suspect for all of three hours, before he came back with an alibi!"

"You would know, DCI Foster, if you had bothered to attend the briefing this morning at eight," Marsh said.

"I had a power cut, at home, and my phone wasn't charged. So I didn't have access to any messages or alerts. You will know from my records that this has never happened before."

There was a silence.

"How are you? In yourself, DCI Foster?" asked Assistant Commissioner Oakley.

"I'm fine. How is that relevant?" asked Erika.

"The past few months you experienced would have been stressful for anyone. You lead a team of twelve officers on a drug raid in Rochdale; only seven of you came back…"

"I don't need you to read my own file back to me," said Erika.

Oakley went on, "You went in with insufficient intelligence... It seemed you were *keen to get on with it*, like you are now. Can you see how this might be construed as impulsive behavior on your part?"

Erika gripped the arms of her chair; she was trying to remain calm.

The Assistant Commissioner continued, "Five officers died that day, including, tragically, your husband, DI Mark Foster. You were subsequently suspended. It seems you had the chance to learn a valuable lesson, but you didn't, and—"

Erika found herself out of her chair, leaning over the desk and grabbing the file. She tore it in two and threw it back on the desk. "This is bullshit. I took the lead yesterday because I believe Andrea was seen with two people who could provide information about her killer. Simon Douglas-Brown didn't like it, and he's now dictating how this investigation should be run!"

She remained standing, in shock.

Assistant Commissioner Oakley sat forward in his chair and said, in a practiced tone, "DCI Foster, I am formally relieving you of duty, pending an investigation into your conduct and a fresh psychiatric evaluation of your ability to serve in the police force of England and Wales. You will surrender any weapons, formal identification and official vehicles and await further correspondence. You will continue to receive full pay pending results of our investigation and you will present yourself, when requested, to be examined by an official police psychiatrist."

Erika bit down hard on the inside of her cheek, willing herself not to say any more. She handed over her ID badge. "All I want to do is catch that killer. It seems you both have another agenda." She turned and left the room.

Woolf was waiting outside with two uniformed officers. "I'm sorry. We have to see you out," he said, his jowly face hanging guiltily.

Erika walked with him to the front entrance, passing the incident room. DCI Sparks was by the whiteboards, briefing the team. Moss and Peterson looked up and saw Erika being escorted out. They looked away.

"Airbrushed out," said Erika, under her breath. They reached the front desk, where Woolf asked her to hand over her car keys.

"Now?"

"Sorry, yes."

"Come on, Woolf! How do I get home?"

"I can arrange for one of the uniformed officers to run you home."

"Run me home? Fuck that," said Erika. She put her car keys on the counter, and walked out of Lewisham Row Station.

Outside on the street, Erika searched for a bus stop or taxi, but there was nothing in sight on the busy ring road. She set off for Lewisham station, checking in her bag for loose change, but all she had was her credit cards. She was searching through the old tissues and rubbish in the deep pockets of her leather jacket, when her hand felt something small square and rigid. She pulled out a little white envelope. It was thick and looked expensive. There was nothing written on the front. She turned it over and pushed her finger under the flap, opening it. Nestling inside was one sheet of folded paper.

She stopped dead in the street, the cars rushing by. It was a printout of a newspaper article about the raid where Mark and four of her colleagues had lost their lives. There was a photo of the path leading up to the house in Rochdale where dead bodies lay covered, surrounded by pools of blood and broken glass; another of police helicopters hovering above the house, airlifting two of her colleagues who would later die in hospital; and there was a grainy black-and-white picture of a barely recognizable officer lying on a stretcher and soaked in blood, his hand raised with limp fingers. It was the last photo taken of Mark alive. Above it was written in red marker pen:

YOU'RE JUST LIKE ME, DCI FOSTER. WE'VE BOTH KILLED FIVE.

CHAPTER 33

Over the next few days, there was a shift in the media coverage of Andrea's murder, and Erika's statement at the press appeal kindled a more negative press reaction. It smoked, at first, with hints of Andrea's past relationships, then slowly sputtered to life with fiery revelations of Andrea's many lovers, and the suggestion that she'd enjoyed both male and female partners. By the end of the week, the tabloids ignited in a fireball of disclosures. One of Andrea's ex-boyfriends, who described himself as performance artist, came forward and sold his story to one of the tabloids. Stills from a video emerged of them engaging in oral and anal sex, and of Andrea being tied up and flogged in a sex dungeon while wearing a see-through plastic dress and a gag ball. The tabloids had prudishly pixellated the images, but readers could be in no doubt as to what she was doing. The broadsheets condemned the tabloids while simultaneously offering their own thoughts and opinions, stoking the fire. The right-leaning newspapers had found a new way to attack Simon Douglas-Brown, and in their eyes Andrea might, *just might*, have asked for it.

Erika passed four long and lonely few days in her new flat, attempting to settle in. She got her electricity sorted out and watched the media coverage unfold. She went for a medical check-up, taking the bus to Lewisham Hospital where she explained she was a police officer and she had been exposed to blood and bodily fluids. Samples of her blood and urine were taken, and she was told she would have to return for a further blood test in three months' time. The whole encounter was cold and clinical, and made her feel very small and insignificant in the world. Alone in her flat, she kept staring at the note, trying to work out how it had been placed in her pocket. Was she losing it? How could she have not noticed something? Her mind went back over the days leading up to finding it, over all the places she had been—but it could have been anyone anywhere. For now, she kept it in a clear plastic evidence bag. She knew she should hand it in, but something in the back of her mind told her to keep hold of it.

On the fifth morning, Erika arrived at the newsagent opposite Brockley station to buy the day's papers, when she saw the front page headline of the *Daily Mail*: **TOP COP SUSPENDED FROM ANDREA CASE.**

It detailed how, after a series of high-profile mistakes and blunders running the Andrea Douglas-Brown murder inquiry, DCI Erika Foster had been suspended from duty pending a full inquiry. It stated that Foster had been accused of erratic behavior, of leaking information to the press relating to the case, and of misplacing confidential information regarding police informants, which "most probably" resulted in the death of Ivy Norris.

There was a photo taken of Erika through the passenger window of a car. Her eyes were wide and mouth gurning as she reached out for the dashboard. Under the photo the caption read: **BLUNDERING COP ERIKA FOSTER.** The photo had been taken by the press outside the Horniman Museum crime scene, when Moss's car had slipped on the ice.

Erika threw the newspaper down and left without buying anything.

When she got back home, she made a strong coffee and switched on the television. The BBC News channel counted down to the hourly headlines, and then Andrea Douglas-Brown's face appeared on the screen with the announcement that the police had arrested a man called Marco Frost in connection with her murder.

The report flicked back to the newsreader. "Twenty-eight-year-old Marco Frost was originally eliminated from police inquiries, but was subsequently found to have lied about being abroad when Andrea Douglas-Brown was murdered."

The footage then showed Marco, a handsome, dark-haired young man, emerging handcuffed from the entrance to a block of flats. He had his head down and was led away by two uniformed officers to a police car. They held the back of his head as he was loaded in, and then the car sped away.

The camera cut to Simon Douglas-Brown and Giles Osborne, standing with Marsh outside the revolving Scotland Yard sign.

"This morning, police raided the home of Marco Frost and discovered material of a disturbing nature related to the victim. It is believed the suspect had developed an unhealthy obsession with Andrea Douglas-Brown in the months leading up to her abduction and murder," said Marsh.

Simon then stood forward, his face pained, his hands twitching at his suit jacket pockets. "I would like to thank the Metropolitan Police for their diligence and continued efforts in what has been a problematic investigation. I would like to say that I have full confidence in the new investigative team and I thank them for their continued efforts in tracking down Andrea's killer. We will, of course, continue to work closely with the police. Thank you."

The report flicked back to the newsreader and moved on to another story. Erika grabbed the new prepaid phone she'd bought the previous day and called Lewisham Row. Woolf answered.

"It's Foster, can you put me through to Sergeant Crane?"

"Boss, I'm not supposed to..."

"Please. It's important."

There was a beep and then Crane answered.

"Surely there isn't enough on this Marco Frost to make an arrest?" said Erika, getting straight to the point.

"Give me your number and I'll call you back," said Crane. He hung up and ten minutes went by. Erika was just thinking he had given her the brush-off when her phone rang.

"Sorry, boss, I need to be quick cos I'm on my mobile freezing my tits off in the car park. Marco Frost lied about being in Italy. We only found out after trawling through hours of CCTV from London Bridge station on the night Andrea vanished. He boarded a train on the Forest Hill line twenty minutes after Andrea. Course, there's no CCTV evidence to put him at the scene, but he's damned himself by lying about his whereabouts and getting his aunt and uncle to give him a false alibi."

"It could have been an unlucky coincidence," said Erika.

"His girlfriend, who lives out in Kent, has given him another alibi, but now he's lied we have a motive. We're holding him for the next three days."

"What about the murder of Ivy Norris?"

"It's been taken over by Vice," said Crane. "Look, boss. It's not looking good for your theory."

"Oh, theory now, is it?" said Erika. Crane did not respond. Erika could hear the cars whooshing past the station car park.

"Are you okay, boss?"

"I'm fine. And please spread the word on that. I'm sure everyone has seen the papers."

"I didn't know about your other half. Sorry."

"Thanks."

"Anything I can do?"

"You can keep me in the loop. Even if it does mean freezing your tits off in the car park."

Crane laughed. "I'll keep you in the loop as much as I can, boss, okay?"

"Thanks, Crane," said Erika. As she hung up, she reached for her coat. It was time to pay Isaac Strong a visit.

CHAPTER 34

It was early evening, and Isaac Strong was in his office adjacent to the morgue. Shirley Bassey's *Performance* album was playing, and he was preparing to write his report on the Ivy Norris autopsy. He relished this calm time. His favorite music, the lights low in his office. It was in stark contrast to the violence of slicing open a body, weighing its organs, analyzing the contents of bowel and stomach, swabbing and scraping for DNA evidence, and piecing together the acts of violence inflicted on the corpse to form a narrative—the story of its demise.

A cup of peppermint tea steamed lightly by his computer monitor, the delicate mint leaves still twirling in the freshly poured cup. There was a faint beeping sound, and a window popped up on his computer screen. It was a blue-gray CCTV image of DCI Erika Foster standing in the hallway outside the lab. She looked up at the camera. His hand hesitated, and then he buzzed her in.

"Is this an official visit?" asked Isaac when he met her at the door of the lab.

"No," she said, hitching her bag up her shoulder. She wore jeans and a jumper. Her tired face was free of makeup. She looked around at all the freshly scrubbed steel.

"Officially, you have no authority to be here. You've been removed from the case."

"Yep. No ID, no car. I'm just Jo Public."

Isaac paused, regarding her for a moment. "How about a cup of tea then?" he said.

He took her through to his office. *The Girl From Tiger Bay* was playing softly, and Erika chose a comfy armchair next to his desk. Isaac went to a kettle on a table in one corner. His neat office was crammed with bookshelves. An iPod glowed in a Bose sound system. The shelf next to the sound system differed from the others, which were filled with medical reference books. This shelf contained fiction—mainly crime thrillers.

"Surely you don't read police procedurals in your spare time?" asked Erika.

Isaac turned from switching on the kettle and laughed wryly. "No. They're complimentary copies, sent from the publisher. I was an adviser on a couple of the DCI Bartholomew books…How does peppermint tea grab you? I'm afraid I try to avoid caffeine."

"Sounds good. I should have avoided caffeine today—she says, four coffees later."

There was a small mint plant by a tiny high window. Isaac twisted the pot round and selected a couple of leaves.

"My ex-partner is Stephen Linley, author of the DCI Bartholomew books," he said.

"Oh."

"Oh, I'm gay, or oh, how odd to be with someone who writes crime thrillers?"

"Oh, to neither."

Isaac dropped the leaf into the cup and waited for the kettle to boil.

"Actually, that is a bit odd, that you dated someone who writes crime thrillers," said Erika.

The kettle came to the boil and Isaac poured in water. "He based one of his forensic psychologists on me. Then killed the character off when our relationship ended."

"How?"

"Gay bashed and dumped in the Thames."

"Sadly the pen is mightier than the sword," said Erika, taking the steaming cup.

Isaac took a seat at his desk and twirled the chair round to face her. "Ivy Norris had two types of semen inside her vagina. Her arms were bound, and she was strangled. Our attacker had not long departed. She'd been dead less than an hour."

"Anything from the DNA database?"

"We've run both samples of semen, but nothing has come up."

Erika nodded, and almost subconsciously looked at the back of her hand.

"Is that a bite mark?" asked Isaac.

"Yes. It was Ivy's grandson."

"Ivy's blood work came back. She was a heroin addict and HIV positive. It's feasible she passed it on to her grandson."

"When he bit me, he broke the skin," said Erika, sipping her tea.

"Then I'd advise an HIV test." Isaac wrote a number on a piece of paper and handed it to her. "Here, it's the drop-in clinic I use when I get tested. It's fast, clean and anonymous. It can take up to six or nine months for the virus to show itself, so to speak. You'll have to get tested again."

"Thank you."

"What are you going to do?"

"I have to attend a formal hearing. Psychiatric evaluation. A medical, no doubt."

"If you are diagnosed with HIV…"

"I'll deal with that if it happens. Right now a fear of dying is well down my list."

The album had finished and there was a comfortable silence in the room. Isaac looked at her, debating whether or not to say anything.

"Don't give up on this case," said Isaac.

"I think the case has given up on me," said Erika.

"I've been back through my records. There were three cases, autopsies I conducted, where the victims were Eastern European girls, all suspected of having been trafficked to the UK. All three were found raped and strangled, hands bound, dumped in water around London, hair pulled out, no clothes below the waist."

"What? When?" asked Erika.

"The first was March 2013, the second was November of that year and the third was February 2014. Just under a year ago."

"What? Why was this never flagged?" asked Erika, sitting forward.

"Circumstance often overrides putting the evidence together. Sadly the three girls were all prostitutes, whether they'd had a choice in the matter or not. They got lost among all the other killings; a prostitute is almost expected to lose her life. They were never linked, and the cases remain open."

"Dirt-poor Eastern European prostitute found strangled—oh well, shit happens. Young daughter of titled millionaire found strangled…"

"Yes, it reads rather differently, doesn't it?" agreed Isaac.

"Why didn't you mention it before?" asked Erika.

"Something about Ivy's death flagged it in my mind. Of course, Andrea differs from these because she hadn't been raped. However. The other three girls were found in a state of decay, and they were sex workers. It's possible they had been raped, but not at the same time as being killed. Ivy Norris was also a prostitute and was found with two types of semen. It's possible that her killer didn't rape her, either."

"Jesus!" said Erika, standing up. "This is a major breakthrough. We now have four deaths linked with Andrea."

"And I did, of course, pass this information across to DCI Sparks as soon as I made the discovery."

"When?"

"Yesterday morning."

"And what did he say?"

"I haven't heard anything. I think he's concentrating on his prime suspect, the Italian lad."

"He should at least be running these dates, checking where Marco Frost was when these murders happened. Jesus! Can I see the file?"

"No."

"No?"

"I thought about telling you. And I wasn't going to. And then you show up, and, well I have a good instinct for people..." His eyes traveled up to the shelf of crime thrillers. "Well, a good instinct for everyone except lovers."

"Please can I see the files?"

"No. I'm sorry. I think it's grossly unfair, what's happened to you in the press, but you do need to cool down. You need to think tactically. Can't one of your colleagues furnish you with the information?"

"Possibly. And you're really not going to tell me any more?"

He reached for a pad of paper. "I'll give you their names and dates of birth. But this will not come back to me. Do you hear?"

"I promise," said Erika.

Isaac watched Erika through the CCTV monitor as she hurried off down the corridor, clutching the list of names, and hoped that she would remain true to her promise.

CHAPTER 35

Erika went straight to the coffee shop when she got back to Brockley Station. She ordered a coffee, booted up her laptop and started to search the Internet. Armed with names and dates, it didn't take her long to find details of the girls. The first victim was nineteen-year-old Tatiana Ivanova from Slovakia. A lone swimmer at Hampstead Heath ponds found her body in March 2013. It had been a warm start to spring, and her body was badly decayed. The press used a photo of Tatiana at a dance competition. She was dressed in a black leotard with sparkly silver fringing, striking a pose, hand on hip. She must have been part of a dance troupe, but the other girls had been cropped out. She was dark-haired, very beautiful, and looked younger than her years.

The second victim was Mirka Bratova, aged eighteen. She was originally from the Czech Republic, and was found eight months after her disappearance, in November 2013. One of the park wardens in the Serpentine Lido discovered her body floating in the water among leaves and rubbish by the sluice gate. In the press photo, she was also dark-haired and very beautiful, and pictured holding a black kitten on a sunny balcony. Behind her, blocks of flats stretched away in the distance.

The third victim was Karolina Todorova, again aged just eighteen. Her body was discovered in February 2014. A man was out walking early in the morning and his dog found her body by the edge of one of the lakes in Regent's Park. Karolina was originally from Bulgaria. The press had used a photo taken in an automatic photo booth. She was dressed up for a night out, in a white low-cut top, and she had a streak of pink in her dark hair. Another girl was hugging her in the picture, presumably a friend, but her face had been blurred out.

It frustrated Erika that she couldn't see more; details were sketchy and almost dismissive in the press reports of the deaths.

One other thing mentioned about all the girls was that they had come to England to work as au pairs, and that they had then "fallen into" prostitution. Erika wondered if it had been that gradual. Had the girls been lured to the UK on the pretense of a better life, of a good job? The chance to learn English?

Erika looked up from where she sat in the window of the café. Outside, it was raining hard. It hammered on the awning out front, where several people had gathered to shelter. She took a sip of her coffee, but it was cold.

Erika had left Slovakia when she was just eighteen, for the same reason, to be an au pair. She'd left the bus station in Bratislava on a bleak November morning, traveling to Manchester in England with little knowledge of English.

The family she'd worked for had been okay. The kids had been sweet, but the mother had had a cold attitude toward Erika, as if somehow Eastern Europeans were worth a bit less as human beings. Erika had found the suburban street where they lived to be sinister, and the atmosphere in the house was always tense between husband and wife. They'd refused to let her return home early that first Christmas, when Erika's mother had fallen ill with cirrhosis of the liver, and eighteen months later, when they had decided they no longer needed an au pair, they had given Erika three days' notice to leave. They hadn't asked if she had anywhere to go.

Erika realized she was lucky, though, and blessed in comparison. Had Tatiana, Mirka, and Karolina said good-bye to family just like she had? Erika remembered the crumbling bus terminal in Bratislava: rows and rows of bus platforms. Each platform had rusting metal poles holding up an enormous long shelter, and it had been so damp. She had wondered if it was damp from the tears of all those teenagers who had to say good-bye, to leave a beautiful country where the only way to succeed was to get out.

Had the parents of the three dead girls cried? They had not known that their girls would never return. And what had happened when the girls arrived in London? How had they ended up working as prostitutes?

Tears rolled down Erika's face, and when the waiter came to take her coffee cup, she turned her head away and angrily dried her eyes.

She had cried enough tears to last a lifetime. Now it was time for action.

CHAPTER 36

The next afternoon, Erika felt like she had exhausted all the options she could take as a civilian. She was making another cup of coffee and weighing up her options, when she heard a bell ringing. It took her a few moments to realize it was the front door. She left her flat and went down to the communal front entrance. When she opened the door, Moss was waiting on the front step, her face giving nothing away.

"Are you making home visits?" asked Erika.

"You make me sound like a bloody Avon lady," said Moss with a wry grin.

Erika stood aside to let her in. She hadn't expected to ever receive visitors in the flat, and had to clear off the sofa for Moss. She grabbed several days' dirty plates off the coffee table, and the teacup overflowing with cigarette butts. Moss didn't comment and sat down, shrugging off a backpack she was carrying.

"Do you want some tea?" asked Erika.

"Yes please, boss."

"I'm not your boss anymore. Call me Erika," she said, tipping the dirty plates into the sink.

"Let's stick with boss. First names would be weird. I wouldn't want you to call me Kate."

Erika stopped, her hand hovering over a box of teabags, "Your name is *Kate Moss*?" She turned to see if she was joking, but Moss nodded ruefully. "Your mother called you Kate Moss?"

"When I was given the name Kate, the other, slightly thinner..."

"Slightly!" laughed Erika, despite herself.

"Yes, the *slightly* thinner Kate Moss wasn't a famous supermodel."

"Milk?" said Erika, grinning.

"Yes, and two sugars."

She finished making the tea while Moss busied herself pulling paperwork from her backpack. Erika came over with mugs and biscuits.

"That's a good cup," said Moss, taking a sip. "How did you learn to make such a good tea? Not in Slovakia?"

"No, Mark, my husband. He ingrained in me the tea ritual, and so did my father-in-law..."

Moss looked uncomfortable that she'd led the conversation down this path. "Shit, sorry, boss. Look, none of the team at the station enjoyed reading about... about, well, you know. And we didn't know about..."

"Mark. I've got to start talking about him sometime. When you lose someone, not only are they gone, but everyone around you doesn't want to talk about them. It drives me slightly crazy. It's like he's been deleted... Anyway, why are you here, Moss?"

"I think you're on to something, boss. Isaac Strong sent some case files over. DCI Sparks is refusing to see the link, but there were three young girls killed in similar circumstances to Andrea and Ivy. All three found in water with their hands bound, hair missing from their scalp. They'd been strangled. There was evidence of rape, but they were sex workers."

"Yeah, I know about those," said Erika.

"Okay, well, there's more. The phone box we found under Andrea's bed. Crane requested a trace on the IMEI number written on the box. It matches the IMEI number of Andrea's old iPhone, the one she reported missing. Crane then got in contact with network providers and gave them the IMEI number. They've confirmed that the handset is still active."

"I knew it! So Andrea reported the phone missing, but kept it and bought a new SIM card," said Erika, triumphantly.

"Yes. A signal was last traced for that handset near to London Road on the 12th of January," said Moss.

"Someone's nicked it and they're using it?"

"No," said Moss, pulling out a large ordinance survey map and starting to unfold it. "The signal came from a storm drain running twenty feet below ground. It runs off London Road, beside the train track to Forest Hill Station, and then on toward the next station on the line, Honor Oak Park."

Erika peered at the map.

"The storm drain is a major tributary," Moss went on, "and over the past few days an enormous amount of meltwater from the snow and rain has seeped into the ground and will have rushed through the storm drain."

"Pushing anything with it, including a phone," finished Erika.

"Yeah."

"So the phone battery is now dead, obviously?"

"Nothing has been detected. It's an iPhone 5S, and the network tells us that it will still broadcast its location to phone masts for five days after the battery has discharged—of course, that's now passed."

Erika looked at the map; she saw Moss had drawn a red line from London Road along to Honor Oak Park. It covered just over a mile and a half.

"So, what? The theory is that the phone was chucked or dropped into a drain when Andrea was taken?"

"Yeah. But it's not a theory that DCI Sparks or Superintendent Marsh want to hear. They're convinced they have their man in Marco Frost, and they're under pressure from Oakley *et al* to make a conviction. They've been through his laptop and there's a lot of Andrea on there. Photos, letters he'd written to her, Google search history about places she'd been, and was going to..."

"This is a major breakthrough, but why are you here, Moss?" asked Erika, getting up to make more tea.

"I've been there when we questioned Marco, and he is—was—obsessed by Andrea. But, he just doesn't seem like he's got it in him. He also has very large hands. Isaac showed us the handprints on Andrea. And I don't know, it's not much more than a hunch."

"You don't think he did it."

"I have doubts, but they are a hunch. I think that this phone could open up the investigation," said Moss.

"Well, you've got to get a team down in that drain, to at least have a look," said Erika.

"Yeah, but under whose authority, boss? I haven't got any. Your hands are tied. It would cost a huge amount, plus the manpower involved, who would sign off on either of those right now? The team is now focusing resources toward the prosecution of Marco Frost."

Erika thought. "Does anyone else share your doubts about Marco Frost?"

Moss nodded.

"Peterson? Crane?"

"And others. We've made copies of the files on Tatiana Ivanova, Mirka Bratova and Karolina Todorova."

She handed them to Erika, who flicked through, looking at the photos of the girls—all lying on their backs, naked from the waist down, their wet hair plastered to their pale faces. Fear in their eyes.

"Do you think he deliberately leaves their eyes open?" asked Erika.

"Possibly."

"If it *is* the same killer, how the hell does Andrea fit in with this?"

"Whoever it was ventured out of their comfort zone? She's a different kind of girl," said Moss.

"Only because she was rich. The girls are all similar. Dark, beautiful, good figures."

"Do you think Andrea was working as a prostitute? Did you see the stuff in the papers?"

"She didn't need the money. I think first and foremost she saw sex as a thrill," said Erika.

"The thrill of the chase," finished Moss.

"What if Andrea had fallen for the man who is doing this? She's attracted to dark, handsome men."

"But what about Ivy Norris? Her death bore hallmarks of the previous killings, but she doesn't fit the pattern. She wasn't young. Or attractive like the rest of these girls."

"Maybe it wasn't about that? She shares the common thread that she was a prostitute. What if she saw Andrea with the killer, in the pub? And she was killed to shut her up."

Moss had no reply to this.

Erika became aware that they were sitting in the dark. The sun had set. Erika went to the kitchen drawer and took out the note she'd received. She came back and placed it in front of Moss on the coffee table.

"Shit. Where did you get this?" Moss asked.

"I found it in my pocket."

"When?"

"Just after I was suspended."

"Why didn't you hand it in?"

"That's what I'm doing now."

Moss looked up at Erika.

"I know. Jeez, this means we've got a serial killer out there," said Erika.

"A serial killer who got close enough to put this in your pocket. Do you want me to arrange for a car outside?"

"No. They think I'm crazy enough. I've been asked to attend a psych evaluation. The last thing I need is to stoke things up. Saying I've got a stalker..." Erika saw Moss's face. "Over the years, I've had plenty of disgusting hate mail."

"But was it all hand delivered?"

"I'm fine, Moss. Let's focus on what we can do next."

"Well, okay... I've got Crane cross-checking the dates against Marco Frost's movements, but we don't know the exact time of death for these girls."

"We need to get that phone. Andrea could have been communicating with this guy. There could be his number, voicemails, and his e-mail. Even pictures on the phone itself. That phone is the key," said Erika.

"We need the resources to retrieve it," said Moss.

"I'll have a crack at Marsh," said Erika.

"You sure? Isn't that a bit risky?" asked Moss.

"I've known him a long time."

"He was an ex?"

"God, no. I trained with him, and I introduced him to his wife. That's got to count for something," said Erika. "And if it doesn't, well, what have I got to lose?"

CHAPTER 37

Chief Superintendent Marsh was forcing himself to eat his second crème brûlée. He was already full, but they were just so good. He gripped the ramekin and plunged his spoon through the crisp caramel with a satisfying crunch. Marcie had bugged him for one of those cook's blowtorches for Christmas, promising she'd make him crème brûlée every week. She'd almost kept her promise.

He looked at her, bathed in the candlelight of their dining room. She sat next to him at the long dining table, and was deep in conversation with a round-faced man with dark hair whose name escaped Marsh. He'd been listening out all evening to see if Marcie mentioned this man by name, but so far she hadn't. Forgetting the name of the head of her art class would guarantee nothing would happen in the bedroom later—and Marsh wanted her badly. Her long dark hair hung loose over her shoulders, and she wore a long floaty white dress which clung to the curve of her breasts. He looked around the table at their other three guests, thinking how unattractive they were in comparison: a middle-aged woman with scarlet lipstick, who was managing to look both grubby and elegant, an old man with a straggly beard and long fingernails, who Marsh was convinced had only come along for the free food, and a thin camp guy with mousy hair tied back in a ponytail. They were deep in conversation about Salvador Dali.

Marsh was wondering if it would be rude to offer them coffee while dessert was still being eaten, when the front door knocker clattered. Marcie tilted her head to Marsh and frowned.

"Don't let me disturb you, I'll go," he said.

Erika reached up impatiently and knocked again. She could see people were home; the curtains were drawn at the large bay window, and laugher seeped out with the soft glow of light. Moments later, the hall light came on and Marsh opened the door.

"DCI Foster. What can I do for you?"

She noted he looked quite handsome in crisp beige chinos and a blue shirt rolled up at the sleeves.

"Sir, you're not picking up my calls and I need to talk to you," she said.

"Can it wait? We've got company," said Marsh. He noticed Erika was clutching a pile of what looked like case files.

"Sir, I believe the murders of Andrea Douglas-Brown and Ivy Norris are linked to three other murders. Young girls found in the same circumstances as Andrea. The murders have happened periodically since 2013. All found dumped in water in the Greater London area…"

Marsh shook his head, exasperated. "I don't believe this, DCI Foster…"

"Sir. They were all young Eastern European girls," said Erika. She flicked open a file and held up the crime scene photo of Karolina Todorova. "Look. This girl was just eighteen; strangled, her hands were bound behind her back with a strip of plastic and her hair was pulled out at the temples. She was dumped in the water like rubbish."

"I want you to leave," said Marsh.

She ignored him and pulled out two more photos, "Tatiana Ivanova, nineteen and Mirka Bratova, eighteen. Again, strangled, hands bound in exactly the same way, hair pulled out and dumped in water. All in a ten mile radius around central London. Even the type of girl is the same. Dark, long hair, hourglass figure... Sir, DCI Sparks has had this file for two days. The similarities are so obvious, even to a copper straight out of—"

A door down the corridor opened, releasing a burst of laughter. Marcie approached the front door. "Tom, who is it?" she said. Then she saw the picture Erika held up, of Karolina half-naked and rotting in the water.

"What's going on?" she said, looking between Erika and Marsh.

"Marcie. Please go back inside, I'm dealing with this..."

"Let's see what Marcie thinks," said Erika, opening another folder and holding up a large photo of Mirka Bratova's body photographed lengthways, her face staring in terror. Leaves and vegetation clung to her pale flesh; her pubic hair was matted with blood.

"How dare you! This is my home!" cried Marcie, putting her hand over her mouth. Erika refused to close the file.

"This girl was just eighteen, Marcie. Eighteen. She came to England thinking she had work as an au pair, but she was forced into prostitution, no doubt raped regularly, and picked up and brutally strangled. Time goes so fast, doesn't it? How old are your two little girls now? They'll be eighteen before you know it..."

"Why is she here? Why aren't you dealing with this at work?" cried Marcie.

"That's enough, Erika!" shouted Marsh.

"He's not dealing with it at work!" said Erika. "Please, sir. I know that there has been a trace on a phone belonging to Andrea Douglas-Brown. Give me the resources to find that phone. There's stuff on that phone about Andrea's life. Stuff she kept secret. I believe that information could lead us to catch who killed her and these girls. Look at their photos again. Look at them!"

"What is this? Tom?" asked Marcie.

"Marcie, go back inside. NOW."

Marcie took one more look at the pictures and went back into the front room. There was a moment of loud laugher and then it was snuffed out as she shut the door again.

"How dare you, Erika!"

"No, sir, how dare *we*. This isn't about me. Yes, I'm out of order to show up on your doorstep; it's bang out of line. But I can live with being a cunt. What I can't live with is what happened to these girls. Can you really sleep tonight not knowing we tried? Think back to when we first joined the force. We had no power. You can make this decision now, sir. *You*. Fuck it, you can bill me for the search team, fire me at the tribunal, I honestly don't care right now—but look at these, take a look!" Erika held up the photos again.

"That's *enough*!" shouted Marsh. He slammed the front door and Erika heard the locks shoot home.

"Well, at least I tried," she said to the photos. She closed the file, placed it gently back in her bag and walked back onto the street.

CHAPTER 38

The figure had materialized in the alleyway opposite Erika's flat when darkness fell, just before DI Moss had come out of the front door and driven away in her car.

What was the fat little lezzer doing there? This is a new development.

Watching DCI Foster's movements had become almost addictive. Coupled with the torrential rain, it had been easy to follow her with a hood up, head down and three different waterproof jackets in a backpack.

The secret of blending in, is don't try to. Everyone is so fucking self-obsessed.

The figure's eyes were drawn upward to Erika, who was staring out of the window, smoking.

What is she thinking? What was that other cop, Moss, doing there? DCI Foster is supposed to be off the case…

Abruptly, Erika got up and closed the blinds. Moments later, she came out of her front door. She was carrying her bag and headed toward the station. The figure retreated and sprinted back down the alleyway to a car, and then drove out onto the main road, trying to keep slow, be normal, blend in.

Erika was just turning into Brockley Station when the figure turned the car in to the station approach. Another car started to pull out of a space in front, and the figure used the opportunity to stop, watching Erika as she passed over the footbridge to the opposite platform. The driver in front finished pulling away from the space, and waved a hand in thanks. The figure grinned and waved in return, then sped back down Erika's road, past her dark flat, and parked a few streets away.

When the car engine fell silent, the figure took a moment to visualize the back of DCI Foster's building. A high wall curled round the back of the property with an alleyway running along one side. When it had been converted from a big house into flats, the back had been left a mess of old and new windows, downpipes, and guttering.

The figure climbed out of the car and took a backpack from the boot.

I wasn't going to do this now, but it seems things have accelerated. Watching from outside is no longer giving me enough…

On the way back to DCI Foster's flat, a couple of commuters walked past, deep in conversation, oblivious. Once outside Erika's flat, the figure climbed up onto the surrounding wall, having thought carefully about how to get up to the top floor.

Inch along the wall to the back of the building, step onto the windowsill, grab the downpipe, hook one leg up to a higher windowsill and climb up, using the pipe.

The windowsills were smooth stone and the figure, breathless from the exertion, stopped for a moment. It had worked so far…

Use the lighting rod, a thick gutter pipe for leverage and then there are three more windows, staggered in a line. Tic, tac, toe…

The figure reached Erika's bathroom windowsill, drenched in sweat from the exertion. The window was closed, and this was expected. However, there was a small extractor fan beside the window. It was conveniently cheap and had been poorly fitted. Covering the square plastic grille vent with a gloved palm, the figure gripped the edges and pulled. There was a crack and it came away, exposing a silver-lined ventilation pipe. The figure pushed an arm inside, feeling leather-clad knuckles come into contact with the back of the ventilator's plastic housing on the inside wall. A swift punch and it was knocked out. It rattled and scraped against the bathroom wall as it swung loose from its wire.

The figure pulled a length of coat hanger wire from a side pocket of the backpack and inserted it through ventilation pipe. It took a few fumbling attempts, but the wire finally hooked over the handle of the window inside and it popped open with a click. The figure moved quickly, crawling through headfirst, hands out, and connecting with the toilet seat.

I'm in.

It was exhilarating after so long watching DCI Foster from afar. The bathroom was small and functional. Opening the bathroom cabinet, the figure saw it was filled with a box of tampons, thrush cream, and a dusty packet of waxing strips. The expiry date had passed.

How heartbreaking. She carries a packet of old waxing strips with her.

The figure gathered up the contents of the bathroom cabinet and moved through to the sparse bedroom. It smelled neutral. The smell of women could sometimes be interesting and exotic. The smell of others could repel…

All I get is stale cigarettes…fried food. A hint of cheap perfume.

The figure pulled back the bedcovers, neatly laid out the contents of the bathroom cabinet on the mattress, and replaced the covers, before moving through to the living room. It was dark, save for the orange glow of a street light. Strewn on the coffee table, among dirty cups and an ashtray were copies of police files.

The figure lifted one with a gloved hand, rage surging. There were pictures of Mirka Bratova. Mirka Bratova alive, and then dead and decayed in the water.

DCI Foster knew. She'd connected the dots, and the fat little lezzer bitch was helping her!

There was a noise on the landing, a creaking of stairs, and the figure crept to the front door and peered through the spy hole.

An old woman with white hair reached the landing. She came close to the front door, her face bulging obscenely in the peep hole. She listened for a moment, then turned and went to her front door.

The figure felt a sudden need to get out of there, to go away, to plan.

DCI Foster has forced my hand.

I'm going to have to kill her.

CHAPTER 39

When Erika returned home to the flat, she took a long, hot shower and wrapped herself in a towel. She came through to the bedroom and sat on the bed, running through the evening's events in her head. They didn't play back much better than when they had happened the first time round.

She went to plug in her phone, and then stopped. She pulled back the duvet cover. Underneath, the contents of her bathroom cabinet had been laid out on the mattress.

She stood quickly and went to the bedroom window. It was closed, and there was a sheer drop down to the alley below. She moved to the front room and flicked on the light. The room was as she'd left it. Blinds closed. Files and coffee cups littering the table. She passed the front door. There was no letterbox. Had she locked the door? Of course she had, she thought. She went back into the bathroom and opened the cabinet above the sink. It was empty.

The window had been closed when she'd taken her shower, and she hadn't opened it. No, she thought; she was just tired and forgetful. She must have taken the things out of the cabinet herself. She noticed how steamed up the bathroom was and pulled the cord on the tiny extractor fan. She pulled it again. Nothing happened.

"Shit," she said, wiping the condensation off the mirror with the back of her hand. Why did Marsh have to be her landlord too? The last thing she wanted to do was contact him. She flicked off the light, went back to the bedroom and took the things out of her bed, feeling uneasy. Had she taken them from the bathroom cabinet? And then there was the note she'd received.

But how had someone got in? They would have needed a key.

The next morning, Erika tidied the flat and was contemplating calling in to the station that she may have had a possible intruder—possible being a very accurate word—when she heard the post land on the mat downstairs. After sorting through the bills for her neighbors and leaving them on the table by the door, she found a letter addressed to her. Her first piece of mail in her new flat. It was a request from the Met Police that she attend a psychiatric evaluation in seven days' time.

"I'm not crazy, am I?" said Erika to herself, only half joking. When she came back up to the flat, her phone rang.

"Erika, it's Marsh. You've got six hours with a team from Thames Water. If you don't find the phone, then that's it. You understand?"

Hope rose in Erika chest. "Yes. Thank you, sir."

"There's virtually no chance it's down there. Have you seen the rain we've been having?"

Erika looked out as the rain hammered against the window.

"I know sir, but I'll take those odds; I've solved cases on less."

"But you won't be solving this. You're suspended. Remember? And you'll pass any evidence over to DCI Sparks. Immediately."

"Yes, sir," said Erika.

"Moss will be in touch with the rest of the details."

"Very good, sir."

"And if you ever pull a stunt like that again, showing up on my doorstep and waving sick crime scene photos in my wife's face…You won't just be suspended. Your career will be over."

"It won't happen again, sir," said Erika. There was a click and Marsh hung up. Erika smiled. "Behind every powerful man is a woman who knows how to push his buttons. Good on you, Marcie."

Erika walked over to meet Moss and Peterson. The manhole accessing the storm drain was beside the graveyard at Honor Oak Park Church, only a couple of miles from Erika's flat. The church was a few hundred yards past the train station, perched on a hill. The rain had stopped, and there was a slight break in the clouds when Erika met Moss by a large van bearing the Thames Water logo. Peterson had a tray of takeaway coffees and was handing them out to a group of guys wearing overalls.

"This is Mike. His team will be coordinating the search," said Moss, introducing them.

"I'm Erika Foster," she said, leaning over to shake hands. The guys didn't mess about. They gulped down their coffee and within minutes they were levering up the giant manhole cover and rolling it to one side with a clink.

"Good to see you, boss," said Peterson, handing her a coffee with a grin.

Mike took them into the tiny van. It was equipped with a bank of monitors, a small shower, and radio comms for all the men going down into the drain. On one of the monitors, a satellite weather map continually refreshed, showing streaks and bulges of charcoal gray across a map of Greater London.

"That's the difference between life and death," said Mike, tapping a biro against the screen. "The sewers below combine storm water and waste water. A sudden downpour of rain can flood the sewers, and very quickly you have a tidal wave of water making its way toward the Thames."

"What did you do before all this technology?" asked Peterson, pointing at the television screens and satellite weather maps.

"Good old fashioned noise," said Mike. "If a storm came, we'd lift one of the nearest manhole covers six inches and let it crash back down. The clanking sound would echo down the tunnels and hopefully give the blokes down there enough of a warning to get the fuck out."

"Is it just blokes who work down there?" asked Moss.

"Why? You want to apply for a job?" quipped Mike.

"Very funny," said Moss.

They came back out of the van and looked at the sky. The cloud above seemed to be clearing, but was growing darker on the horizon.

"We'd best get on with it," said Mike, moving over to where the four men had set up a winch above the manhole, and were attaching themselves to safety harnesses. Erika went and peered down the shaft where iron rungs stretched away into blackness.

"So what are we looking for, a phone?" asked Mike.

"It's an iPhone 5S, we believe it's white, but it could be black," said Moss. She handed them each a laminated photo.

"We realize it's been down there for almost two weeks, but if you find it, please can you avoid touching. We need to preserve any remaining forensic evidence. I'll give you these evidence bags, which it will have to be placed into immediately," said Erika.

They each took a clear evidence bag. They looked skeptical.

"So, what? We're meant to levitate this phone out of the shit?" said one of the lads.

"We really appreciate your helping out here, lads," said Peterson. "You've joined us at a crucial stage in a very harrowing case involving young girls who have been murdered. Finding this phone is a large piece of our puzzle. Just try not to touch it with bare hands."

The men's attitude changed completely. They rapidly put on their helmets, and started checking their lights and radios. When they were ready, they all stood around the manhole as Mike lowered in a probe.

"We're checking for poisonous gases," he said. "It's not just shit and piss we have to worry about down there. There's carbonic acid, which miners used to call *chokedamp*; carburetted hydrogen, which explodes; and sulfurated hydrogen, the product of putrid decomposition... You've all got your chemical detectors in your suits, lads?"

They all nodded.

"Jeez, wouldn't you all rather work in a supermarket?" asked Moss.

"This pays much better," said the youngest of the lads as he went first and was slowly winched down into the manhole.

They watched as the remaining men were lowered down into the darkness, their lights illuminating the brown grimy interior of the storm drain. Erika looked across at Moss and Peterson as they leaned over. They exchanged tense glances.

"Like looking for a needle in a haystack," said Peterson. Slowly, the torchlight below began to fade and they were left in silence. Mike went into the van to watch their progress.

An hour later there was nothing to report, and they were stamping their feet in the cold. Then a call came through on the police radio. There was an incident at a supermarket in Sydenham. A man had pulled a gun, and shots had been fired.

"We're on call today," said Moss, looking up at Peterson. "We'd better scoot. Marsh said this wasn't high priority."

"You guys go; I can stay here and wait," said Erika. Moss and Peterson hurried off and she was left alone, realizing again that she had no badge, no authority. She was just a woman hanging around an open sewer. She stepped into the van and asked Mike how they were getting on.

"Nothing. We're almost at the point where I don't want them to go any further. The network branches off in several directions toward central London."

"Okay, where does it all end up?" asked Erika.

"Sewage treatments plants around London."

"So..."

"So the chances of a tiny little phone showing up are slim," he said. "It's not like a dog who's swallowed a diamond ring and you..."

"Yes, I get the message," said Erika. She came back out of the van, perched on a tree stump and smoked a cigarette. The church loomed above her in the cold, and a train clattered past in the distance. The men emerged an hour and a half later, caked in mud, exhausted and soaked in sweat. They shook their heads.

"As I thought, it could be anywhere right now. Out to sea even. The storm drains have been opened twice since the 12th of January, and so much would have flowed through, nothing would stay down there under that amount of water pressure," said Mike.

"Thank you," said Erika. "We tried."

"No. They tried," said Mike, pointing at the men. "I said to your boss, it was bloody hopeless, a wild goose chase."

Erika wondered if that was the reason why Marsh had arranged it. As she walked home in the rain, she remained convinced that Andrea's phone had to be found. She thought of the letter she'd received and the things left in her bed.

She felt like the only person who knew that the police had arrested the wrong man.

CHAPTER 40

Three days passed with no word from Moss or Peterson. All Erika's enthusiasm and positivity drained away, made worse by having nothing to do. On the third day, she was poised to call Edward and face up to visiting Mark's headstone, when her phone rang in her hand.

"Boss, you're not going to believe this," said Moss. "Andrea's phone has just shown up."

"What? In the sewer?" asked Erika, gripping the pen.

"No. A second-hand mobile phone shop in Anerley."

"That's only a few miles away," said Erika.

"Yeah. Crane circulated the IMEI number around local second-hand phone dealers, saying that if a handset with this number came into their shop they were to contact the incident room urgently."

"And they did?"

"He also said they'd be paid the value of a new unlocked iPhone 5S, which must have sweetened the deal."

"How did it show up in Anerley?" asked Erika.

"A woman found it. The huge amount of rain and melt water last week caused the drains to overflow on the lower end of Forest Hill Road. The drains were so overloaded that high-pressure water was forced up through the sewage system, tearing through the tarmac. We've figured the phone came with it. She saw it, and even in the state it was in thought she could get a few bob for it."

"And it's okay? It works?"

"No, and the screen is badly cracked, but we've whisked it over to the cyber team who've put it at the top of their work queue. They're trying to get everything they can off the internal memory."

"Moss, I'll come in."

"No, boss, stay put. If you're going to come down here, wait until you have a reason to storm in and read them the riot act."

Erika started to protest.

"Seriously, boss. I promise I'll phone you the second I know anything." Moss hung up.

Six long, tense hours later, Moss called to say that the Cyber Crime Unit had pulled a substantial amount of data from Andrea's phone.

Erika took a cab to the address Moss had given her, and met her outside the central London Cyber Crime Unit, which was based in a nondescript block of offices near Tower Bridge. They took the lift up to the top floor and emerged into a huge open-plan office. Every desk was busy; sitting at each was a weary officer poring over computer screens, beside them a phone or laptop in pieces, or a mess of wires and circuit boards.

On the far back wall was a row of what looked like viewing suites with tinted windows. Erika shuddered to think of the things these officers had to watch behind those screens.

A short, handsome man wearing a threadbare wooly jumper met them at the water cooler. He introduced himself as Lee Graham. They followed him through the office to a large storage room with racks and racks of computers, phones, and tablet computers, all bagged up and sealed. They passed one low shelf where a laptop was wrapped in plastic and encrusted with dried blood.

He took them over to a messy desk in the far corner where Andrea's phone lay, battered and cracked. The back was off and it was hooked up to a large PC with twin screens.

"We got a lot off this phone," said Lee, sitting and adjusting one of the screens. "The hard drive was in good condition."

Moss pulled over a couple of chairs and they sat beside Lee.

"There are three hundred and twelve photos," Lee continued, "sixteen videos, and hundreds of text messages going back from May 2012 to June 2014. I've run all the photos through our facial recognition software; this crunches through the National Criminal Database and uses facial recognition to look for any matches. It flagged up one name."

Erika and Moss looked at each other, excited.

"What was his name?" asked Erika, keenly.

Lee tapped away at his keyboard. "It wasn't a he, it was a she," he said.

"What?" said Erika and Moss in unison. Lee swiped his way through a series of thumbnail images, then clicked on one: a familiar face.

"Linda Douglas-Brown is in the police database?" asked Moss, in surprise. In the picture, Linda and Andrea sat at a table in a bar; Andrea stared confidently down the lens and looked immaculate in a cream blouse. The buttons were open, displaying a dark, full cleavage with a silver necklace nestling between her breasts. Linda, in comparison, was ruddy-faced with unkempt hair. She was wearing a roll-neck black jumper, which rode high enough to nestle just under her double chin. The jumper was embroidered with images of small poodles cavorting across the fabric. A large gold crucifix hung around her neck. Her hand was slung around Andrea's and her face wore a drunken grin.

"Is this is the victim's mother?" asked Lee.

"No, the victim's sister; there's four years between them," said Erika. They let that hang for a moment.

"Okay. Well, I've pulled her criminal record; it's just printing off for you now," said Lee.

CHAPTER 41

Lee found them a spare workstation in the office, where they first read through Linda's file.

"Jeez, Linda has a considerable record going back several years. Arson, theft, shoplifting…" said Erika. "Between July and November last year, Andrea's fiancé Giles Osborne made three complaints to the police, saying Linda was harassing him and sending him threatening mail."

"Officers spoke to her on all three occasions," said Moss, reading.

"Yes, so no arrest. Giles Osborne's first complaint was in July 2014, concerning abusive e-mails he received from Linda; in one she threatened to kill his cat first, and then him. The second complaint was a month later. His flat was broken into and his cat was *poisoned*. Linda's fingerprints were found in the property, but her lawyer successfully claimed that her fingerprints *would* be in there because she had recently been a guest at the dinner party he threw to celebrate his engagement to Andrea.

"Linda was also caught on CCTV in the next street to Giles Osborne's flat within minutes of the break-in. She then capitulated and stated that she went into the house *after* the break-in to try and save the cat, who seemed in distress when she looked through the window."

"Sounds like she's got a damn good lawyer," said Moss.

"Perhaps, but there wasn't enough proof to substantiate this either way. The third complaint was October last year when

Linda caused eight thousand pounds' worth of damage to Giles's office. She threw a brick through one of the large glass window panels. Here, they even caught her on CCTV."

The picture was over-exposed and black and white, but a bulky figure could be seen in a long overcoat, a baseball cap pulled down over her face. The coat had opened when the figure pulled back to throw the brick, and a jumper could be seen underneath, bearing an illustration of dancing poodles.

Moss was carrying her laptop in a bag. She pulled it out and switched it on. "Let's work through the photos from Andrea's phone," she said, fitting a USB key into the drive, which contained the contents of Andrea's phone. They waited while the laptop whirred and hummed and booted up. The tiny little light on the USB key began to flicker, and then a scattergun of photos began to skim by on the screen.

Andrea was pictured at several parties: there were many selfies, pictures of Andrea topless in her bathroom mirror, cupping a breast seductively, tilting her head back. Then a series of photos that had been taken on a night out at a bar. It looked to be at the same bar as in the picture with Linda.

"Stop, go back!" said Erika.

"I can't stop, we have to let them load," said Moss.

"Come on," said Erika, impatiently, as the laptop paused on a blurred photo of blackness, obviously taken in error—then the photos began to load again and finished. Erika began to flick through.

"Yes. Here we go, these are the most recent ones, from the bar," said Erika.

"Who's that, do you think?" asked Moss as they peered at the screen. A tall and broad man in his early thirties was pictured with Andrea. He was very dark with large brown eyes, and he had close-cropped stubble on his handsome, chiseled face.

The first few photos were taken by Andrea holding out the camera. In all of them, she was leaning into the man's chest. He was incredibly handsome.

"Dark-haired man," said Erika, in a soft, excited voice.

"Let's just steady on," said Moss, who also sounded excited. Erika clicked forward through the photos. They were all taken at what looked like the same party: people filled the background, sitting at tables or dancing. Andrea had gone mad taking pictures of herself with the man, and he'd happily let her. The poses began with them side-by-side, Andrea staring up at him with the love-light in her eyes. The pictures progressed to him kissing Andrea, their mouths locked with a glimpse of tongue, her red fingernails grazing his chiseled stubbly jaw.

"These were all taken on the 23rd of December last year," said Moss, noting the date stamp of the pictures.

"That picture of Linda with Andrea. It was taken the same night. That's the same party…"

The picture from which the National Criminal Database had recognized Linda's face popped up again.

"It's toward the end of the evening by the look of it; they look a bit worse for wear," said Erika.

"So Linda was there at the same time as that guy. He could have taken this photo," said Moss.

They pressed on through the photos. The date stamp showed a gap of a few days, and then they came across photos taken on a bed with pale sheets. Andrea lay with the dark-haired man, again holding out the camera to take the shots. His chest was powerful and covered in a smattering of dark hair. Andrea had her arm hooked under her naked breasts. The photos progressed to become more explicit: a close-up of the man with Andrea's nipple drawn up between his white teeth, a full frontal picture of Andrea laying back on the bed, smiling. And then Andrea's face filled the screen. Her lips were locked around the base of the man's penis. He looked to be cupping her chin. One of his large thumbs rested on her cheekbone.

The next photo was abruptly less X-rated. Andrea and the man were pictured on December 30th, hand-in-hand on the street. They were both dressed for winter. A familiar clock tower was in the background.

"Shit. That's the Horniman Museum," said Moss.

"And that's four days before she went missing," said Erika.

"Do you think this is the guy she was seen talking to in the pub?" asked Moss.

"This could be the guy who killed her," said Erika.

"But he's got no record that we know of; the National Criminal Database software didn't flag him..."

"He looks Russian, or—I don't know—Romanian? Serbian? He could have a record overseas."

"But we don't have a name, and that could take time," said Moss.

"But we do know someone who could have his name. Linda Douglas-Brown," said Erika. "She's pictured the same night. In the same bar as him."

"Should we bring her in?" asked Moss.

"Now, hang on," said Erika.

"What do you mean, hang on? She's obviously withholding information, boss."

"But we need to be very careful before we bring her in. The Douglas-Browns will lawyer up the second we do anything. It seems they have spent a fair bit of cash keeping Linda on the straight and narrow."

Moss paused. "You know what your flat could do with, boss?"

"What?"

"Some nice fresh flowers."

"Yes. We should pay a visit to a florist," said Erika.

CHAPTER 42

Jocasta Floristry was tucked between an elegant jeweler's and a polished granite office block on Kensington High Street. The window was optimistically decorated for early spring. There was a carpet of real grass, and daffodils, tulips and crocuses pushed up in reds, pinks, blues and yellows. Several china Easter bunnies sat on the grass, or peered out from behind toadstools and giant speckled eggs. At the front, up close to the glass, a small picture of Andrea, smiling into the camera, sat on a red velvet cushion.

Moss went to open the glass entrance, but saw next to it a small white bell and a neatly printed sign with the words: RING FOR SERVICE.

Erika pressed the button. Moments later, a small elderly woman with severely scraped-back hair peered up at them from under hooded eyelids. It was the same lady who had answered the door at the Douglas-Browns' house. She waved them away dismissively. Erika held down the bell again. They realized how thick the glass was when she pulled open the door and the sound of the bell amplified.

"What's this about?" she snapped. "We've spoken to the police, you have a man in custody. We're preparing for a funeral!" She went to slam the door, but Moss grabbed it.

"We'd like to speak to Linda, please, if she's here?"

"You've got someone in custody, haven't you? What more do you need from the family?" the woman repeated.

"We're still building our case, Madam. We believe Linda will be able to help us to confirm a few details which could lead to a swift conviction," said Moss.

The old woman regarded them, eyes darting from side to side under the hooded lids, the skin crinkling and twitching, reminding Erika of a chameleon. She opened the door, and stood to one side to let them in.

"And wipe your feet," she said, eyeing the wet pavement outside.

They followed her through to an open-plan seating area decorated in white. Along the back wall, an enormous clear-glass conference table glowed and changed color. Adorning the walls were photos of the previous work Jocasta Floristry had undertaken: society weddings, product launches. The old lady vanished through a door at the back, and a moment later Linda emerged, carrying armfuls of yellow daffodils. She wore a long black A-line skirt, and another cat jumper poked out from behind a white apron. This time it was a giant tabby cat with languid eyes.

"My mother isn't here. She's taken to her bed," she said. Her tone of voice seemed to suggest that her mother was slacking off. She crossed to the large table, laid the daffodils on the glass and began to sort them into bunches. Erika and Moss joined her at the table. "What are you doing here, DCI Foster? I thought you'd been taken off the case…"

"Surely you of all people should know not to believe everything you read in the press," said Erika.

"Yes. Journalists. They're all beasts. One of the tabloids described me as a 'moon-faced spinster.'"

"I'm sorry to hear that, Linda."

"Are you?" snapped Linda fixing them with a stare. Erika took a deep breath.

"When we spoke to you before, we asked if you had any information that could help us with our inquiries. You failed to mention to us that Andrea had a second phone," said Erika.

Linda went back to bunching daffodils.

"Well?" said Moss.

"You didn't ask me a question. You made a statement," said Linda.

"Okay. Did Andrea have a second phone?" asked Erika.

"No. I wasn't aware she did," said Linda.

"She reported it stolen in June 2014, but kept the handset and bought a pay-as-you go SIM card," said Moss.

"So, what? You're here on behalf of the insurance company to investigate insurance fraud?"

"We found your criminal record, Linda. You have quite the rap sheet: assault, shoplifting, credit card fraud, vandalism," said Erika.

Linda stopped bunching the daffodils and looked up at them. "That was the old me. I've found God now," she said. "I'm a different person. If you look close enough, we all have a past we regret."

"So when did you find God?" asked Moss.

"I beg your pardon?" asked Linda.

"Well, you're still on probation, and you caused eight thousand pounds' worth of damage to Giles Osborne's offices four months ago. Why did you do it?"

"I was jealous," said Linda. "Jealous of Andrea, of Giles. She found someone, and as I'm sure you can imagine, I'm still looking."

"And what did Andrea and Giles have to say about your harassment?"

"I apologized, I said it would never happen again and we all made up."

"He forgave you for killing his cat too?" said Moss.

"I DID NOT KILL HIS CAT!" cried Linda. "I would never do something like that. Cats are the most beautiful, intelligent creatures... You can stare into their eyes, and I think they know all the answers... If only they could talk."

Erika shot Moss a look, not to go too far.

Linda's puddingy face clouded over and she slammed her hand down on the glass table. "I didn't do it. I am not a liar!"

"Okay, okay," said Moss. "Can you tell us who this man is in the picture with Andrea?" She placed the photo of Andrea at the party with the dark-haired man next to the pile of daffodils.

"I don't know," said Linda, glancing at it.

"Look at it properly, please, Linda," said Moss, holding up the photo in front of her face.

Linda looked at the photo and back at Moss. "I told you, I don't know."

"How about this one?" said Moss, pulling out the picture of Linda with Andrea. "This photo was taken of you and Andrea on the same night, at the same bar. He probably took this photo."

Linda looked at the photo again and seemed to compose herself. "You see, officer, your use of the word *probably* is quite telling. I came to that bar a few minutes before closing for a drink. I'd been working here all evening. When I arrived, Andrea was alone; whoever she'd been there with had gone. She'd waited for me so we could have a drink and a catch-up before the family Christmas events took over. This man may well have been there, but not at the same time as me."

"Did Andrea mention him?"

"Andrea always had a lot of male attention when she went out. I only agreed to meet her if she promised not to go on about boys all evening."

"Don't you like boys?"

"*Boys*," Linda snorted. "You know, two intelligent women can pass an evening without having to talk about men, surely?"

"What was the name of the bar?" asked Erika.

"Um, I think it's called Contagion."

"Who was Andrea there with?"

"I told you, I don't know. Andrea had a revolving door of party mates."

"Where was Giles?"

"I would have thought that he'd left by then so he could avoid having to see me."

"Because you harassed him, vandalized his offices, and killed his..." finished Moss.

"How many more times, I did not kill Clara!" cried Linda. Tears welled up in her eyes. She pulled down a sleeve of the tabby jumper and wiped her eyes. "Clara was... she was a lovely animal. She would let me hold her. She wouldn't let many other people, not even Giles."

"Then who poisoned her?"

"I don't know," said Linda, softly. She pulled out a lump of balled tissue paper from the pocket of her jumper and scrubbed at her eyes until they started to look red.

"What can you tell us about this?" asked Moss, placing down the clear evidence bag which contained the letter that Erika had received.

"What's this? No, no, no. I don't know anything!" Linda said, fresh tears appearing on her red face.

"I think Linda has been accommodating enough," said a voice from the back of the room. The Douglas-Browns' house-keeper with the hooded eyes, had materialized and was coming toward them. "If you want to talk to her further, perhaps we can arrange something more formal, with the family solicitor in attendance?"

"Linda. This man," said Moss, tapping the photo of the handsome man with Andrea, "is also a suspect in the rape and murder of three young Eastern European women over the past two years, and the recent murder of an elderly lady."

Linda's eyes widened. The housekeeper was now holding out her arm for them to leave.

"Linda. Please contact us if you think of anything, however small," said Erika.

"She either doesn't know who that guy is, or she's a very good liar," said Moss, when they were back out on the street.

"The only thing I believed her about was the cat. She didn't kill that cat," said Erika.

"But we're not investigating cat murders."

"I think we should go and pay Giles Osborne a visit," said Erika. "See what he has to say about Linda, and these photos."

CHAPTER 43

"She's totally crazy," said Giles Osborne. "To the point where she frightens me and many of my staff."

Moss and Erika sat in Giles's glass office, overlooking the back gardens of a row of terraced houses. A train clacked past behind the houses, and on an industrial estate to one side, four giant gas sumps rose up, slick with rain. It seemed absurd to build such an elegant state-of-the-art building with such a dismal view.

Giles looked as if he hadn't slept, and the skin on his face was loose and haggard. Erika also noted that he'd lost weight in the two weeks since Andrea's body was found.

"The family is all aware of Linda," Giles went on. "Seems she's been the black sheep for many years. She was thrown out of every school they put her in. When she was nine, she stabbed her teacher with a compass. The poor woman lost an eye."

"So you think Linda has psychological problems?" asked Erika.

"You make it sound far more mysterious and exotic than it is. She's just mad. It's a sort of tedious madness. But throw cash and an influential family into the mix and it's all heightened. The problem is that Linda knows there's no real consequences for her actions."

"Yet," said Moss.

Giles shrugged. "Sir Simon is always there to throw money at problems, or have a word in an influential ear… In the end, he bought the teacher a house, and she lives in the top half and rents out the bottom. Almost worth losing an eye, don't you think?"

There was silence. Another train clacked past on the track and blared its siren.

"Sorry. I don't mean to be cruel. I'm arranging Andrea's funeral. I thought I'd be arranging our wedding, I never dreamed…Linda is doing the flowers; she's insisted on the church she attends in Chiswick. I'm sitting here staring at a blank screen, trying to write her eulogy."

"You have to know someone well to write their eulogy," said Moss.

"Yes, you do," said Giles.

"Was Andrea religious?" asked Erika, steering the conversation away from choppy waters.

"No."

"Is David?"

"If all nuns had big tits and low-cut tops, I'm sure he'd be a Catholic," laughed Giles dryly.

"What do mean by that?"

"Oh Lord, do you have to take everything literally? It was a joke. David likes girls. He's young. He's remarkably normal. Takes after his mother more than…"

"Linda," said Moss.

"Yes, it's just him and Linda," said Giles. He wiped a tear away.

"And Linda attends church regularly?"

"Yes. I'm sure God isn't too overjoyed at having to listen to her warped little prayers each night," said Giles.

"Has Linda been to your office on many occasions?" asked Erika.

"She came once with Andrea, to see the place. Then she showed up a couple of times alone."

"When was this?" asked Moss.

"July, August, last year."

"And why did she show up alone?"

"She came to see me, and it very quickly became apparent that she wanted, wanted to… Well, she wanted to have sex."

"And how did she indicate this?" asked Moss.

"How do you bloody think!" said Giles, growing red. He looked around, desperate to be somewhere else. "She lifted her sweater and exposed herself. Told me that no one would know."

"And what did you do?"

"I told her where to go. Even if she wasn't Andrea's sister, she's not exactly…"

"Not exactly?"

"Well she's not exactly a looker, is she?"

Moss and Erika remained silent.

Giles went on, "As far as I'm aware it's not a crime to find someone…"

"Repulsive?" finished Erika.

"I wouldn't go quite that far," said Giles.

"And then things turned nasty. Linda vandalized your office and, according to the records, broke in and poisoned your cat."

"Yes, and I don't know. You've read the case files, then?"

Erika and Moss nodded.

"I found myself with an unfortunate dilemma with Linda. Sir Simon asked me to drop the charges. What could I do?"

"I'm sorry to have to bring this up, Giles, but were you aware that Andrea was seeing other men when you were together?" asked Erika.

Giles paused. "I am now."

"And how does that make you feel?"

"How do you bloody think that makes me feel?! We were engaged. I thought she was the one. Sure, she liked to flirt and play, and I should have seen it, but I thought she might calm down once we were married, and then we'd get sprogged up."

"Sprogged up?" asked Erika. "You mean, have children?"

"Yes. I had no idea she had several men on the go. She was so stupid to get involved with that hateful creature Marco Frost. He scared Andrea with his *obsession.* Do you think you have enough evidence to secure a prison sentence?"

Erika looked at Moss. "Mr. Osborne, can I please ask you to take a look at this photo?" She placed the picture of Andrea with the dark-haired man on the table. He glanced at it.

"No. I don't know him."

"I didn't ask if you knew him. Please take a good look; this was taken just four days before Andrea disappeared."

Giles looked at the photo again. "Well, what am I looking at? He was probably one of the many men who make eyes at her."

"What about this? Or this…or this?" asked Erika. She placed the series of photos in front of Giles: Andrea lying in bed with the dark-haired man, naked, her nipple drawn between his teeth, then Andrea with her lips spread wide and his penis in her mouth.

"What are you people doing?" cried Giles, pushing his chair back and getting up. There were tears in his eyes. "How dare you come in here and take advantage of my good will!"

"Sir, these are from Andrea's second mobile phone which we recently recovered. We showed these photos to you for a reason. They were taken just a few days before she vanished."

Giles stood and went to the glass door. "Thank you, officers, but I came into my office today to remember Andrea, and write about her life. I have been asked to speak at her funeral, and you come here and sully my memories of her with hardcore pornographic photos!" He opened the door and indicated that they leave.

"Sir, we believe that the man pictured with Andrea is also involved in the killing of three Eastern European girls who worked as prostitutes, and the murder of an elderly lady. We also believe that Andrea was with this man on the night she died," explained Erika. She looked at Moss. Giles saw their exchange.

"Hang on. What about Marco Frost? I thought he was your man? Chief Superintendent Marsh assured me, and Assistant Commissioner Oakley..." said Giles.

"This is another line of inquiry we are pursuing," said Erika.

"So you really have no idea who killed Andrea? Yet you come over here hassling me, on a hunch? Andrea was a flawed human being, and she had secrets. But all she did was love, all she wanted was to love..." Giles broke down, heaving and sobbing. He put his hand to his mouth. "I just can't take this much longer. Please! Leave!"

Erika and Moss went back to the table, gathered up the photos and left, leaving Giles to sob.

"Oh fuck," said Moss, when they came back to the car parked a few roads away.

"I said it, not you," said Erika.

"Boss, I have to go and report this all to DCI Sparks, and Marsh."

"I know. And that's fine."

Moss dropped Erika home and despite all that had happened, all the revelations, Erika felt no closer to the truth, and very far away from being reinstated and getting her badge back. When she came into her living room she switched on the light, seeing herself and the image of the room reflected back in the window. She went to the light and turned it off. She peered out of the window and down into the deserted street, but everything was still. Quiet.

CHAPTER 44

Over the next two days, Moss and Peterson had to appear in court and give evidence in the case involving an armed gunman at the supermarket in Sydenham. Much of the original team investigating Andrea's death had been reassigned, now that Marco Frost had been charged with her murder. Erika was stuck in limbo, awaiting her misconduct hearing. She'd had a call from Marsh that morning.

"Did you and Moss visit Linda Douglas-Brown and Giles Osborne?" he demanded.

"Yes, sir."

"I've had complaints from them both, and Sir Simon is threatening to make a formal complaint."

So you answer their calls, but not mine? Erika wanted to say. She bit her lip. "Sir. I was there as an adviser to Moss; in both instances I wasn't asked to produce identification."

"Leave it out, Erika."

"Sir, you are aware we recovered Andrea's second mobile phone?"

"Yes, I'm aware. Moss filed her report."

"And?"

"*And*, you withheld evidence. The note you received."

"But the note, sir..."

"The note could have come from several places. Think back to your colleagues in Manchester. There's still a great deal of anger toward you..." Marsh tailed off. "I'm sorry. That was unfair...I think, Erika, that you need to let this go."

"What? Sir, have you seen the pictures?"

"Yes, I've seen the pictures, and I've read Moss's report very carefully. Although I can hear your voice when I read it. It still proves nothing, you have no grounds whatsoever to prove that this...person, whoever he is, was involved in the deaths of Andrea or Ivy."

"Or Tatiana, or Karolina, or Mirka?"

"What you have succeeded in doing is pissing off a lot of people and metaphorically pissing on the memory of Andrea Douglas-Brown."

"But sir, I didn't take those pictures she..."

"She had a secret phone for God's sake! Everyone has secrets."

"I take it this conversation is off the record?"

"Yes, it is, Erika. And I must remind you that *you* are off the record. You are suspended. Now, be sensible. Enjoy the full pay. I have it on good authority that if you lay low and keep your mouth shut, you'll be reinstated next month."

"Lay low, until what? Marco Frost goes down for something he didn't do?"

"Your orders—"

"Come from who?" she said, cutting him off. "Do they come from you, or Assistant Commissioner Oakley, or Sir Simon Douglas-Brown?"

Marsh was silent for a moment.

"It's Andrea Douglas-Brown's funeral tomorrow. I don't want to see you there. And I don't want to hear you've been poking your nose in anywhere else. And when this is over, and *if* you are reinstated, I'm going to make sure you're transferred to a nick a long, long way away. Have I made myself clear?"

"Yes, sir."

Marsh hung up. Erika sat back on the sofa. Fuming. She cursed Marsh, and then herself. Had she lost the plot? Were her instincts off on this one?

No. They weren't.

She had a cigarette and then went to pick out something suitable for a funeral.

CHAPTER 45

Erika woke before it was light, and sat smoking and drinking coffee by the front window. The day stretched ahead in front of her, full of obstacles, and she had to navigate it as smoothly as possible. She took a shower, and when she emerged just after nine, the sky still had a gray-blue tinge. Erika felt it wasn't right to be going to the funeral of someone so young. Perhaps the day was protesting, refusing to begin.

She'd searched through her suitcase for something suitable to wear to Andrea's funeral, only to realize that most of her wardrobe was suitable for a funeral. At the bottom, she found the elegant black dress she'd worn over a year ago to a Christmas party organized by the Manchester Met Police. She remembered that night so clearly; the lazy afternoon beforehand when she and Mark had made love, and then he'd run her a bath, pouring her favorite sandalwood oil into the steaming water. He'd sat on the side of the bath and they'd chatted and drunk wine as she'd wallowed in the water. When it came time to put on the dress, it had felt snug, and she'd protested she was fat. Mark had slipped his arm around her waist and pulled her into him, telling her she was perfect. She'd gone to the party, proud to be on his arm, the warm feeling of being loved, of having someone special.

Now, as she pulled the dress on in front of the tiny mirror in the bare damp bedroom, it hung loose on her slender frame. She closed her eyes and tried to imagine that feeling of Mark beside her, pulling her into him for a hug. She couldn't conjure it up. She was alone. She opened her eyes and stared at her reflection.

"I can't do this without you. Life... Everything..." she said. Then, in her head, she heard what Mark used to say when he thought she was being over-dramatic: *Get off the cross, someone needs the wood!*

She laughed, despite her tears, saying, "I need to get a grip, don't I?"

She wiped her eyes and reached for her makeup bag, untouched for months. She wasn't a massive fan of makeup, but she applied a little foundation and lipstick and stared at her reflection. She'd been wondering why she was going today, defying her bosses again. She was doing it for Andrea, for Karolina, Mirka... Tatiana.

And for Mark. As with the girls, the person who'd killed him had never been caught.

The church of Our Lady of Grace and St. Edward on Chiswick High Road was a dreary, industrial-looking building. Its square red brick structure was more suited to being a Victorian water pumping station than a church. In its tall plain tower, a bell tolled, but the traffic moved past unceasingly. A hearse gleamed in the gray morning light, the back windows packed with a rainbow of flowers. Erika waited on the opposite side of Chiswick High Road, watching between the traffic as the mourners filed in.

She could just make out, among the gloom of the front doors, Simon, Giles, and David. They were dressed in black suits and giving out the order of service. The mourners were well dressed, and much older than Andrea. As Erika watched, three former members of Tony Blair's cabinet climbed out of a sleek Mercedes and were greeted warmly by Simon when they entered the church. A small group of photographers had been permitted to attend the funeral, and they were stationed on the pavement at a distance, their shutters clicking almost respectfully.

It was a story that needed no prompting or staging. A girl had died, far too young, and people were here to grieve. Of course, this wasn't the final chapter. Marco Frost was due to stand trial in the coming months, and no doubt the complex and sordid details of Andrea's life and death would be replayed, rehashed, and debated anew. However, for now, this was a full stop, the closing of one part.

A smart BMW pulled up at the curb. Marsh and Assistant Commander Oakley emerged in black suits. Marcie and the Assistant Commander's smart middle-aged wife followed behind, also in black. They moved quickly to the church entrance, pausing to talk to Simon and Giles, and to hug David, who seemed vulnerable, despite being taller than both Giles and his father.

The last mourners to arrive were Andrea's mother, Linda, and the elderly lady with the hooded eyes. A limousine pulled up at the pavement and Linda bustled out and round to the opposite door, where she helped Diana from the car. Both she and the old woman, whose name Erika still didn't know, were painfully thin, chic and elegant in black. Linda was swathed in a shapeless black tent, a dark woolen jacket, and she had a large wooden crucifix hung around her neck. Her mousy hair was neat, but looked as if someone had placed a bowl on her head and cut round it. Her face was devoid of makeup and she looked, even in the chill, to be sweating. The photographers took a keen interest and clicked away. Diana and the old woman bowed their heads, but Linda stared up at the cameras defiantly. Erika waited a few more minutes until it looked like the last mourners were inside, crossed the road and slipped into the church.

She took a seat at the end of a pew at the back of the packed church. A beautiful ornate wooden coffin rested on a plinth in front of the altar, decked in a spray of white flowers. The Douglas-Brown family sat on the front pew, and as the church organ petered out, Erika noticed Diana looking frantically around as the church hushed. The vicar, dressed in crisp white robes, moved to the front and seemed to look for a signal that it was appropriate to begin. However, Simon shook his head. He then leaned in under the brim of Diana's huge hat, where they seemed to confer. Linda leaned in on the other side and joined the discussion. Erika realized what they were talking about: David was missing from the pew. Linda then got up, and standing at the front in full view of the congregation, just a few feet from Andrea's coffin, placed a call on her phone. The vicar was now waiting awkwardly by the altar. Linda said a few words before being cut off. She tried the number again, and held the phone out to her father.

"Linda... *Linda*," said Simon, beckoning her over. Linda huffed and stood her ground, before relenting and walking over. Her father took the phone and the conversation became quite heated. Erika couldn't make out what was being said, but his angry tone reverberated around the church. The congregation was now shifting uneasily. The scene juxtaposed uncomfortably with the polished, flower-topped coffin. The murmur of Simon's voice stopped abruptly, and Erika shifted in her pew to see what was happening.

It was then that she heard, from her seat by the door, the faint sound of a mobile phone ringtone. Simon stood and moved off to the side of the church, a phone to his ear. Erika rose from her seat and slipped out of the church.

Houses and shops were heavily built up nearby, leaving the courtyard out front and a thin strip of flagstones along one side of the church, which backed onto a high wall. David stood by the high wall with an unlit cigarette between his teeth. He tucked his phone inside his suit jacket.

Erika moved over to him. “Need a light?” she asked, pulling out her cigarettes and lighter.

He peered at her for a second and then leaned in to her lighter, cupping his hands around the flame, and puffing furiously as the end of the cigarette glowed red. Erika lit one herself and took a drag.

“You okay?” she asked, tucking her cigarettes back in her coat pocket. David was painfully thin, with sunken cheeks. His skin was honey-colored, and there was a smattering of acne under his cheekbones. Despite this, his face was still handsome. He had the same brown eyes and full lips as Andrea. He squinted at Erika and shrugged.

“Why aren’t you in there for the service?” asked Erika.

“It’s all bullshit... My parents have planned this pretentious tribute, which is *nothing* to do with who Andrea was. She was a slut, she was loud and crass, and she had the attention span of an insect. But she was so good, so much fun to have around. I hate that phrase, ‘she lit up a room.’ It’s trotted out all the time, but it was true of her. God, why did it have to be Andrea and not Lin...” His voice tailed off and he looked ashamed.

“Linda?”

“No. I didn’t mean that. Although I think Linda is so desperate for attention she’d quite like to be brutally murdered. It would be more interesting to write on her Facebook profile than, ‘I work as a florist and I like cats...’” David began to cry.

"Shit, shit, shit; I vowed I wouldn't use these," he said, pulling a little pack of tissues from his pocket.

"Look. David. You'll regret it if you don't go in there. Trust me, you need closure. Another overused phrase, I know."

David blew his nose and pulled another tissue from the pack. "Why are you here?" he asked.

"I've come to pay my respects."

"You know, my parents blame you for the media coverage."

"And what do you think?"

"I think Andrea was always honest about dating men, about loving sex."

"What about Giles?"

"He wanted a trophy wife. A nice thoroughbred to mix up the gene pool. Too many cousins have married in his family. You must have noticed he's a little carny."

"Carny?"

"Little carnival circus folk…"

"Right."

"Sorry, I'm being an arse."

"You've got the right to be one, today of all days," said Erika.

"Yes, and you've caught the killer. Marco Frost."

Erika took a drag of her cigarette.

"You don't think he is the killer, do you?"

"How's your mum coping?" asked Erika.

"If you want to change the subject, choose a less stupid question. You look far from stupid, though," said David, taking a deep drag on his cigarette.

"Okay," said Erika, pulling out a copy of the photo of Andrea in the bar with the dark-haired man. "Have you ever seen this man?"

"Smooth segue," said David.

"David. Please. It's important," said Erika. She watched his face. He took the photo and chewed his lip.

"No."

"You're sure?"

"Yes."

"Because Linda was there that night as well."

"Well, I wasn't," said David.

"I don't believe this," said a voice. Erika turned and saw Simon was approaching across the courtyard. His head was tilted to one side and his brown eyes flashed with anger. Diana teetered behind on high heels, her hat and shades giving little away.

"Do you have no respect?" he said, squaring up to Erika, his face close to hers. She refused to be intimidated and stared back at him.

"David, why are you out here?" said Diana when she reached them, her voice breaking.

"I'm asking David if he's seen this man; a man I believe…" started Erika. Simon snatched the photo, crushing it into a ball and throwing it down. He grabbed Erika's arm and started to drag her across the courtyard.

"I'm sick of you fucking around in my business," he shouted. Erika tried to pull away from his grip, but he held on fast and kept dragging her toward the road.

"I'm doing this for you, for Andrea…" said Erika.

"No. You're doing this to advance your grubby little career. If I catch you near my family again, there'll be a restraining order. My lawyer says I have grounds!"

They reached the curb just as a taxi was pulling past. Simon put up his arm and it dived into the space in front of them. He wrenched open the door and shoved Erika inside, cracking her head on the door as he did.

"Take this cunt far away," he spat through the driver's window, throwing down a fifty-pound note.

Erika stared at him through the door. His brown eyes were raging.

"You all right, love?" said the taxi driver, looking at her through the rearview mirror.

"Yes, just go," she said.

The taxi pulled out into the traffic and Erika watched Simon Douglas-Brown glaring after her from the curb. David was slowly walking back to the church entrance, his mother's arm hooked through his.

Erika rubbed her arm through her leather jacket, throbbing from Simon's powerful grip.

CHAPTER 46

Erika arrived at Brockley Crematorium a few hours later. It was on a small residential street, set back from the main road and within walking distance of her flat. She walked along the winding driveway, past tall evergreen trees, and saw Sergeant Woolf outside the glass double doors of the crematorium. He was dressed in an ill-fitting suit, his jowly cheeks red from the cold.

"Thanks for coming, boss," he said.

"It was a good idea," she said. She took his arm as they went inside. The chapel was pleasant, if a little institutional. The soft red curtains and carpet were faded, and the rows of wooden seating were a little chipped.

At the front was a small cardboard coffin placed on a box with wood paneling, which, on closer inspection, was a conveyor belt.

A middle-aged Indian social worker sat in the front row with Ivy's three grandchildren. They had been cleaned up; the two girls were wearing matching blue dresses, and the little boy was wearing a suit a little large for him. They scowled at Erika and Woolf with the same wariness they reserved for the rest of the world. Three more mourners sat near the back: the large woman Erika had seen at the pub with Ivy, and another thin, hard-faced woman who had yellow-blonde hair topped by three inches of black roots. Seated behind them was the landlord of The Crown. His strawberry-blond hair had been combed flat and he was just as big and imposing in a smart suit. He nodded at Erika as they slipped into seats near the door.

A priest rose and rattled through a respectful but impersonal service, calling her Ivy Norton throughout. Everyone was encouraged to say the Lord's Prayer, and then Erika was surprised that Woolf got up and squeezed past her. He went to the lectern and put on a pair of reading glasses. He took a deep breath and started to speak:

"When I am gone, release me, let me go.
I have so many things to see and do,
You mustn't tie yourself to me with too many tears,
But be thankful we had so many good years.

I gave you my love, and you can only guess
How much you've given me in happiness.
I thank you for the love that you have shown,
But now it is time I traveled on alone.

So grieve for me a while, if grieve you must,
Then let your grief be comforted by trust.
It is only for a while that we must part,
So treasure the memories within your heart.

I won't be far away for life goes on.
And if you need me, call and I will come.

Though you can't see or touch me, I will be near.
And if you listen with your heart, you'll hear,
All my love around you soft and clear.

And then, when you come this way alone,
I'll greet you with a smile and a 'Welcome Home.'"

When Woolf finished, Erika was tearful and felt almost angry. The reading had been a touching and beautiful thing to do, but she had expected to sit through a sad but inevitable funeral. Woolf's reading had moved her deeply and transported her to a place she didn't want to go. When Woolf came back to his seat, he saw Erika crying, gave her an awkward nod and made for the door. Music then played, and Ivy's coffin rolled toward the curtain, which opened and closed with a whirr.

Woolf was waiting by a circle of small empty flowerbeds outside the main entrance when Erika emerged.

"All right, boss?"

"Yeah, fine. That poem was beautiful," she said.

"I just found it on the Internet. It's called, *To those whom I love and those who love me* by Anon. I thought Ivy deserved something to see her off," he said, embarrassed.

"You coming to the wake?" said a voice. They turned to see the landlord from The Crown.

"There's a wake?" asked Erika.

"Well, a few drinks. Ivy was a regular."

Erika's eye was caught by the two women, fat and thin; they stood smoking under a tree in the small memorial gardens.

"Hang on, I'll be back in a sec," she said. She hurried over, pulling out a copy of the photo of Andrea and the dark-haired man from her bag.

"You've got a nerve," said the large woman, when Erika reached them.

"I need to ask you," started Erika, but the woman tilted her head back and spat in her face.

"You've got a nerve to sit there sobbing yer crocodile tears when you as good as killed Ivy, you bitch!"

She stalked away, leaving the ratty blonde to stare at Erika's shock.

"Yeah. And we don't know anything," she said, eyeing the photo before moving off after her large companion. Erika fumbled in her bag for a tissue and wiped her face.

When she came back, she saw Woolf had gone, but the landlord was waiting for her.

"Your mate got a call and had to go," he said. "You fancy a drink?"

"You really want me back in your pub after last time?"

"Oh, I dunno. I seem to be drawn to difficult blondes." He grinned and shrugged. "Come on, you owe me. I got you out of a sticky spot."

"As tempting as being picked up at a wake is . . . sorry, I've got to head off."

"Suit yourself," he said. "Is that who you're after? George Mitchell?"

Erika stopped in her tracks. "What?"

"That picture," he said. "What's George been up to now?"

"You know this man?"

He laughed. "I know of him. I wouldn't count him as a friend, though."

Erika held the photo up. "This man is called George Mitchell?"

"Yes. And now you're worrying me. He's not someone you want to fuck around with. This isn't going to come back on me, is it?"

"No. Do you know where he lives?"

"No, and that's all I'm gonna say. I don't know anything else. I never spoke to you, okay? I'm serious, okay?"

“Yes. Okay,” said Erika. All talk of a drink had vanished and she watched him walk out of the crematorium, get in his car and drive away. Erika turned to look back at the low building with its immaculately manicured grounds. A stream of black smoke trailed from a long tall chimney.

“Go on, Ivy. Now you are free to fly,” said Erika, excitedly. “I think I’ve just found the bastard who did this to you.”

CHAPTER 47

It was shortly after ten p.m., and Erika had left several messages for Moss, Peterson, Crane and even Woolf. No one had been available when she'd called Lewisham Row, and she'd left messages on their mobile phones.

She had no clue if they were working still, but guessed that unlike her, they all had social lives outside work. When she'd come back from the funeral, she'd headed for the coffee shop and searched for George Mitchell online. Nothing had come back on the George Mitchell she was interested in finding.

She went to the fridge to pour herself another glass of wine, but saw the bottle was empty. She suddenly felt tired; she needed sleep.

Erika switched off the light, went to the bathroom and took a long, hot shower. When she climbed out of the shower the combination of the cold air and whirling steam irritated her. She missed the luxurious bathroom of her house, which was now rented out, and she also missed the house in general. Her furniture, her old bed, the garden. She tried the extractor fan once more, and then rubbed at the mirror, wiping away the condensation. She decided if she didn't hear from someone by morning, she would pay a visit to Lewisham Row Station.

As she climbed into bed, she tried Peterson again and then Moss. She left messages for both of them, repeating that she knew the name of the man in the photo. Then, feeling frustrated and pissed off, Erika switched off the light.

Shortly before midnight, Erika was sleeping softly. Commuters from the last train had walked past the flat, and the road outside settled into silence. A soft glow from the street lights bled through the living room, falling on the back wall of the bathroom. Erika rolled over in her sleep, shifting her head on the pillow. She didn't hear the sound of the ventilator fan in the bathroom as it popped out of the wall and swung from side to side with a scrape.

Erika woke suddenly from a dreamless sleep. It was dark and her bedside clock glowed red, showing 00:13. She shifted her pillow and had turned over to go back to sleep, when she heard a very faint creak. She held her breath. The creak came again. A few seconds passed and then she heard a rustling of paper in the living room. Then she heard a drawer being opened, very quietly. Her eyes darted around the bedroom for a weapon; something to defend herself with.

There was nothing. Then she spied the bedside lamp. It was made of metal, and heavy, like a small candlestick. Very slowly and quietly, without taking her eye off the door, she leaned down beside the bed and eased out the plug. Holding her breath, she wound the cable round the base of the lamp, and heard a faint creak outside her bedroom door.

Bracing the lamp in her hand, she eased herself off the bed. She heard a creak further down the hall, moving away from the door. She stopped and listened. Silence. Erika moved lightly to where her phone was charging on the floor by the wall, and switched it on, wishing she'd had a landline put in. She heard another creak. This time it was coming from outside the bathroom. Part of her just wanted whoever it was to realize that there was nothing worth taking, and then leave. As Erika crept toward the door, taking care to lay her bare feet down evenly and softy on the wooden floor, her phone blared out its start-up tone. It rang through the silence.

Shit, what a fucking idiot mistake. Her heart started to race. There was silence, and then the sound of footsteps walking toward the bedroom. It was now a heavy footfall, confident, no creeping about and scared to be heard.

It happened suddenly: the door was kicked open, and a figure, head-to-toe in black, rushed at her and gripped her by the throat with a black leather glove. Eyes glittered through a balaclava. Erika was shocked at the power in the hand and she felt her throat and windpipe crushed. She grappled for the lamp, but it slipped from her grasp onto the bed. The figure pushed her back onto the bed, all the time gripping her throat.

Erika kicked, swinging her leg, but the figure twisted deftly to one side, pinning both of her legs down with a hip. She reached up with her hands, trying to grab at the balaclava, but the figure pinned her upper arms down painfully with sharp elbows.

The hands tightened around her neck. She couldn't breathe, couldn't do anything. She felt drool from her open mouth, running down her chin. Blood seemed trapped in her face and head, and the hands kept squeezing, squeezing so hard that she felt her head might explode before she suffocated. The figure was so quiet. So calm. Breathing rhythmically, arms trembling from the effort of maintaining the grip on her.

The pain was now unbearable; thumbs on her trachea pushing, crushing. She was starting to see black spots in her vision. They spread and grew.

And then Erika's doorbell rang. The grip on her throat tightened and the last of her vision began to fail. The bell rang again, longer. There was a bang on the door, and she heard Moss's voice.

"Are you there, boss? Sorry to call so late but I need to talk…"

She was going to die, she knew it. She was overpowered. She flexed her fingers and felt the lamp on the bed beside her. Her vision was flooding with blackness. She summoned up all the energy she could and pushed her fingers against the lamp. It budged a little. Moss knocked once more. Erika used last of her energy and shoved at the lamp. It slid off the bed and hit the floor with a crash, the bulb shattering.

"Boss?" said Moss, hammering on the door again. "Boss? What's happening? I'm going to break down the door!"

Suddenly the grip loosened on Erika's neck, and the figure fled from her bedroom.

Erika lay there, gagging, attempting to draw air into her ravaged throat, down to her lungs. There was a thud as Moss attempted to break down the door. Erika gasped once, twice, heaved, and as a little oxygen reached the rest of her body, her vision swam back into view. With a superhuman will she crawled to the edge of the bed, tumbling off onto the wooden floor with a crash, feeling shards of the broken bulb pierce her forearm. She scrambled toward the door, not caring if the figure was still there.

There was now a louder thud as Moss shouldered the door. On the third attempt it burst open with a crack and a splinter.

"Jesus, boss!" shouted Moss, hurrying toward where she was lying on the floor. Erika was still gagging and clutching her throat. Blood from the cut poured down her arm, and was smeared over her chin and throat. Her face was gray and she sank back in the doorway.

"Boss, shit, what happened?"

"Blood…just my arm," Erika croaked. "Someone was…here…"

CHAPTER 48

Moss moved fast, calling for backup, and within minutes Erika's flat was teeming with police. Then a team of CSIs arrived and took swabs from her fingernails and neck, and then they said they'd need to take all her clothes.

The elderly lady next door had been reluctant to open her front door to Moss, but when she'd seen the police, ambulance and forensics surging up and down the stairs, her attitude had softened and she'd let them in.

Erika wore a set of white overalls; everything in her flat was now part of a crime scene. Two paramedics came through and bandaged her arm as she sat on the little sofa in the old lady's front room. Two budgies hopped and pecked in a cage high up on the wall.

"Oh dear, would you like a cup of tea?" the woman asked, as a male and female paramedic examined Erika.

"I don't think hot tea is a good idea," said the male paramedic.

Erika caught sight of herself in a gilt mirror above the mantelpiece, which was tilted at an angle to show the whole living room. Her throat and neck were swollen with angry red weals; the whites of her eyes were pink and streaming. In the corner of her left eye, a spot of red bloomed.

"You've burst a small blood vessel in your left eye," confirmed the paramedic, shining a pen torch into her eyes. "Can you open wide for me? It's going to hurt, but wide as you can manage, please."

Erika swallowed painfully and opened her mouth.

The paramedic shone the torch into her throat. "Okay, that's good, now can you keep your mouth open and make a sighing noise…"

Erika tried, but began to gag.

"Okay, easy does it…I don't see any evidence of laryngeal fracture, or upper airway edema."

"That's good, yes?" asked Moss, who had appeared in the doorway. The paramedic nodded.

"How about a nice cold drink? I've got some blackcurrant cordial in the fridge," suggested the old lady, who stood by in a long dressing gown, a neat row of blue curlers under her hairnet.

"Just a little plain water," said the female paramedic. "Do you have any other injuries? Apart from the arm," she added. Erika shook her head, wincing.

"Just stay put for now, boss. I'm going to talk to the team who are inside your flat," said Moss, leaving.

"We'll be downstairs waiting; we'll need to get that arm sewn up," said the female paramedic, who had applied a pressure bandage to the cut. Erika nodded as they clipped up their first aid box and left. The old lady came back in with a small glass of water. Erika took it gratefully, and gingerly sipped. She coughed and choked and the old lady rushed forward with a tissue.

"Try again dear, take very tiny sips," she said, holding the tissue under Erika's chin. Erika managed a tiny sip, but it burned.

The woman went on, "This area. When I first moved here in 1957 we all knew each other. You could leave your door open; we had a real community. But these days…Not a week goes by without you hearing there's been a robbery or a break-in…You'll see I've got bars on all my windows, and I have a personal response alarm."

She tapped a small red button round her neck. There was a knock on the front door. The woman got up, and came back a few moments later.

"There's a tall black feller who says he's a police officer," said the woman, cautiously coming into the room with Peterson.

"Jeez, boss," he said.

Erika smiled weakly.

"You're his boss?" asked the woman. Erika shrugged, and then nodded.

"You're a policewoman?"

"She's a Detective Chief Inspector," said Peterson. "We've got a ton of officers doing a house-to-house but, nothing... Whoever it was, scrammed."

"*My God*. And to think this happened to a Detective Chief Inspector! What about the rest of us? Whoever did it must have no fear. What are you?" asked the old lady, of Peterson.

"I'm a policeman."

"Yes, dear; what rank are you?"

"Detective Inspector," said Peterson.

"You know who you remind me of?" said the woman. "What's that program about the black policeman?"

"*Luther*," said Peterson, trying not to look annoyed.

"Ooh yes, Luther. He's very good. Has anyone ever told you, you look a bit like him?"

Despite everything that had happened, Erika smiled.

"People like you normally do," said Peterson.

"Oh, thank you," said the old lady, not getting what he meant. "I do try to watch quality drama on television; none of those reality shows as they call them. What rank is Luther?"

"A think he's a DCI. Look..."

"Well, if he can do it, so can you," said the old lady, patting him on the arm.

"Would you please excuse us for a minute, madam?" asked Peterson. The woman nodded and left. He rolled his eyes. Erika tried to grin, but it hurt.

"Jeez, boss, I'm so sorry." Peterson pulled out his notebook and thumbed through to a clean page. "Was anything taken?"

Erika shook her head and then shrugged. She could only nod or shake her head and Peterson asked all the standard questions, but beyond the figure being tall and strong, she couldn't give any information.

"It's pathetic," swallowed Erika painfully. "I should have…" She mimed pulling off a balaclava.

"Boss. It's okay. It always seems simple in hindsight," said Peterson. Moss came back in, carrying the housing of the extractor fan.

"He got in using the ventilation pipe," she said.

"It was—I don't know, I think it was a him," croaked Erika.

"Boss, they're going to be working through the night with forensics. Do you have anywhere you can stay?" asked Peterson.

"Hotel," croaked Erika.

"No, boss, you're staying with me," said Moss. "I've got a spare room. I've also got something you can borrow to wear…You look like you're about to go out clubbing in the late 1990s."

Erika tried to laugh again, but it was painful. In a weird, warped way she felt pleased. He'd come for her. She was on to him.

CHAPTER 49

The figure sped down Camberwell High Street, screaming and raging inside the car, not caring about the speed.

I was so fucking close! SO CLOSE!

The figure's nostrils flared, eyes streaming with tears. The tears were of rage and pain. The exit from DCI Foster's flat had been terrifying, slithering down the back wall of the building, barely managing to hold on, and then crashing down onto the brick wall before crumpling onto the pavement. The figure hadn't worried about the pain, but kept running through the darkness, out into the street lights. Not caring who saw, just running, drenched in sweat. The fear and pain joining together for a final burst of mad energy.

DCI Foster had been so close. The light in her eyes had just been starting to dim, and then…

A set of red traffic lights was hurtling toward the windscreen. As the figure slammed on the brakes, the car screamed to a halt, just overshooting a crossroads with a pub on the corner. A group of students stepped off the pavement and surged around the car, laughing and pointing.

Shit, I'm still wearing the balaclava.

Some students hammered on the back of the car as they passed. A group of girls peered through the windscreen as they walked in front of the car.

Calm down, pull it off, act like them—a stupid student.

The figure pulled the balaclava off with a flourish, and made goofy faces at the students through the window. The madness must have shone through, because the group of girls screamed and shied away, as one guy lurched forward and threw up beside the window.

The lights turned green and the figure floored the accelerator, screeching away toward The Oval and Blackfriars Bridge.

She didn't see anything, she couldn't have. I had my face covered. I had my face covered…

The fear was replaced with anger.

She denied me the kill.

CHAPTER 50

Moss took Erika to Lewisham Hospital where her throat was X-rayed, and the cut in her arm was given twelve stitches. She was ordered to rest for a week, and more importantly, not to speak.

It was after four in the morning when Moss drove them back. The adrenaline that had been flooding through Erika's body had ceased, and a crashing tiredness overwhelmed her. She was shaking when she followed Moss through the small front gate of a smart terraced house in Ladywell. A pretty blonde woman opened the front door, cradling a small dark-haired boy wearing blue pajamas.

"He woke up, so I thought you could say a quick hello before I put him back down," she said.

"Sorry I missed bedtime," said Moss, taking the boy in her arms as they stepped indoors. She planted a huge kiss on his cheek. He rubbed his eyes shyly and smiled.

"This is my wife, Celia, and our son, Jacob," said Moss, as they came into the cozy hallway.

"Hi, Erika," said Celia, not quite knowing how to deal with the sight of Erika's battered neck, pink eyes and the fact she was wearing crime scene overalls.

"Are you a space woman?" asked Jacob, a serious look on his little face. Erika's face broke into a weak smile and they all laughed. It broke the ice.

"No..." croaked Erika.

"Yes, no criminals in space. I bet it would be very peaceful," said Celia. "I'm just going to put this little one to bed. Please, make yourself at home, Erika. Do you want to have a shower?"

Erika nodded.

"Kate, get Erika one of the towels from the airing cupboard whilst I put Jacob back down. Say night-night, Jacob."

"Night-night Jacob," he said with a grin.

"The bed in the spare room is made up and I've put the little heater in there," added Celia.

Moss gave Celia and Jacob a kiss and they left the room.

"Nice family," croaked Erika, perching on the edge of the sofa, not quite knowing what to do with herself.

"The doctor said no talking, boss... Thanks. I'm very lucky. Jacob came along a few years ago. Celia gave birth to him. I'd love to have a little girl. We always said that we'd have one each. It's just—work gets in the way."

Erika croaked something.

"What was that?"

Erika shook her head frustrated, and croaked, "Don't leave it too late... kids."

Moss nodded sagely. She went to the kitchen and came back with two glasses of orange juice. Erika's had a straw.

"You look like you could use some sugar."

They sipped for a moment.

"I got one of the night-duty officers to run George Mitchell through the database. Nothing."

Erika swallowed and shook her head.

"Boss, someone just tried to kill you. Do you think it's connected?"

Erika felt like she was done. She didn't know if it was shock or exhaustion, but she didn't care. She wanted sleep. She nodded. "Shower?" she asked, looking down at herself in the overalls.

"Sure thing, yeah, boss," said Moss. She regarded Erika for a moment. Worry, mixed with a little pity.

Erika stood under the shower for a long time, her bandaged arm extended to avoid the water. She inhaled the steam, trying to take away the terrible rawness in her throat. Moss had lent her a pair of pajamas, and Erika pulled them on. She looked at herself in the bathroom mirror. Her eyes bulged out with a pinky tinge, and her throat was now so swollen that it gave her a toadish look. She opened the medicine cabinet but there were only painkillers in there, and Night Nurse. Erika had hoped for some anti-anxiety medication or sleeping pills. She gingerly took some Night Nurse, the pain almost unbearable as she swallowed.

When she emerged from the bathroom, the house was dark and quiet, save for a small night light in the hallway. On her way to the spare room she stopped outside Jacob's bedroom. His door was ajar, and he was sound asleep under a blue blanket. A mobile turned above his bed, soft lights sliding across the walls as a lullaby played.

Moss put her life on the line most days, mingling with the crazies out there with knives and guns, vendettas and grudges. Jacob slept, his chest slowly rising and falling. His world was his two mummies, his toys, the mobile slowly turning above his head, its calming tune winding down. For the first time, Erika questioned if it was all worth it. You arrest one bad guy, and ten more fill the void.

She found the tiny back bedroom at the end of the house, climbed into the single bed, pulled the covers over her head and tried to sleep. Every time she closed her eyes she saw the figure looming over her, squeezing the life from her body. The blank face under the woolen mask, just a pair of eyes glittering in the half-light.

Was it fate that Moss had called at her door at the precise time she had? Why had Erika been spared? Mark was a much better person than she could ever be. He was kind and patient; a brilliant police officer. He'd carved out a place in this world for himself. He'd done much good, and he was capable of so much more.

Why had he been taken, when she was spared?

CHAPTER 51

Erika stayed with Moss and Celia for a few days. At first, she was exhausted and was able to sleep. But soon the pain from her throat and arm, the frustration of being unable to communicate, and the claustrophobia of Moss's tiny back bedroom got to her.

Celia was very kind, bringing up trays of warm soup and magazines, and Jacob came to visit her when he got back from school. A couple of times he brought his little DVD player and they sat in bed and watched *Minions* and *Hotel Transylvania.*

The details of the case went round and round in Erika's mind. She went back to when Andrea's body was found under the ice, then to meeting her family—Simon and Diana, who lived such busy lives that they parented at arm's length. Linda and David were like chalk and cheese, and had had vastly different relationships with Andrea, neither knowing what their sister was doing on the night she vanished. Not knowing why she went to a grotty, dangerous pub in South London to meet George Mitchell and the as yet still unidentified blonde-haired woman. And then there was Ivy Norris, who had seen Andrea and her companions that night, quite by chance. So too had the barmaid, Kristina. Neither of them was around to tell the full story.

And then there were the three dead girls. Out of loyalty and kinship, Erika refused to call them prostitutes. Was there a link with Andrea? With Ivy? Or were they just on the wrong street corner at the wrong time? And then there was Marco Frost, whom DCI Sparks had seized upon as their prime suspect, using tenuous, yet compelling evidence which had linked him to Andrea.

The details of the case spun and tangled in Erika's head, like a giant cat's cradle. Somewhere, there was a missing link. Something that could link the man who'd tried to kill Erika to all of the other deaths.

In her dream, the man visited Erika again, but as he gripped her throat she was able to reach up and pull away the balaclava covering his head.

It was a different face every time: George Mitchell, Simon Douglas-Brown, Mark, David, Giles Osborne—even Linda. In Erika's final dream, when she pulled off the balaclava it was Andrea, just as she had appeared in death, with eyes staring, teeth bared and her long dark hair wet and full of leaves.

As the days passed, Erika heard nothing from Marsh. Moss was busy with court appearances and other cases, and was only able to snatch brief chats in the evenings. The police database had drawn a blank with George Mitchell, and a search of electoral records and financial databases also yielded nothing. There was one development: a tiny hair follicle had been recovered from Erika's nightclothes, which could have come from her attacker—but again, it was run through the DNA database and nothing came back.

On the fourth morning, her throat was starting to heal, and she was able to speak. Erika knew she had to face up to things and go back to the flat. She thanked Celia and hugged little Jacob good-bye. He gave her a picture he'd drawn, of Erika dressed in a white boiler suit getting into a UFO to go up into space with a group of Minions.

It pretty much summed up how she felt.

It was quiet in the car as they drove back, Erika wearing a borrowed set of clothes from Celia. Moss eyed her from the driver's seat.

"Boss, you all right?"

"Yeah."

"What are you going to do?"

"I dunno. Wind up the police tape, and then I'm going to go and see my father-in-law."

"What about the case?"

"Find George Mitchell, Moss. He's the key."

"But what about you?"

"What about me? I'm suspended. The sensible thing to do is to wait it out until the hearing, where hopefully I'll get my badge back without losing my dignity. Well, I don't give a shit about my dignity, but I can't do anything without my badge."

They'd arrived at Erika's flat.

"Thanks. I really appreciate everything," said Erika.

"Want me to come in?"

"No, you get to work."

"I won't give up on the case, boss," promised Moss.

"I know. But you've got a family. Do what you have to do."

When Erika got back to the flat, it was in disarray. The surfaces were covered in the black magnetic powder used to dust for fingerprints, and crime scene tape still adorned her front door. She went to the bedroom and stared at the bed. She could see the outline of her body in the duvet, and the long legs of her assailant, the marks deeper at the knees where he'd lain on top of her. She reached over and pulled the edge of the duvet. The imprint vanished. She worked quickly, packing her suitcase. She went to the bathroom and gathered up her toiletries, noting the fingerprint powder on the mirror, and the taped-over hole where the extractor fan used to be. She left the house and wheeled her suitcase round to the station. It was a cold, bright day and she stopped at the coffee shop opposite the station, thinking she'd attempt a coffee, even if it hurt.

"Sugar, or are you sweet enough?" grinned a handsome waiter with a pierced lip as he took her order.

"I need sweetening up," said Erika.

"That can be arranged," he said. She watched him as he worked and when he handed over her coffee he did so with a wink. Erika grinned back and walked over the road to the station.

"Morning, I hope you're not going to be smoking on my nice concourse," said the ticket officer, opening the ticket machine beside Erika.

"No, I've given up," said Erika. She chose a single ticket to Manchester Piccadilly Station, and fed in her credit card.

"Good for you, love," said the ticket officer, closing the machine. He grinned and walked back off to the station. Erika's ticket shot out into the little steel drawer.

There were a smattering of people on the platform. She pulled out her phone and dialed Edward's number. He answered after a few rings. His voice lit up when he realized who it was. Erika explained that she was coming up to see him, adding, "I hope it's not too short notice?"

"No, not at all, love. I just need to make up the bed in the spare room," he said, sounding happy. "Give us a bell when you're close and I'll pop the kettle on."

"It'll just be a couple of days..."

"You stay as long or a short as you want."

Erika ended the call as the train rounded the track up ahead. She had drained the last of her coffee and was looking for a bin, when her phone rang.

"Boss, it's me," said Moss, breathlessly. "Marco Frost has just been released."

The train passed under the footbridge and carriages blurred past.

"Released? Why?" asked Erika.

"The solicitor has been working on Marco's alibi. He found some CCTV from a newsagent's shop in Micheldever."

The train was now slowing; Erika could now make out commuters inside the carriages.

"Where's Micheldever?" she asked, feeling excitement prickling in her stomach.

"An hour south from London Bridge Station. Marco stated, in his second alibi, that that's where he was going on the night of the eighth of January. As you know, there was insufficient evidence to back that up. Micheldever is a tiny station with no CCTV... That's been the story of this case, no CCTV," said Moss.

The train came to a stop. People on the platform rushed at the train.

"The CCTV from the newsagent shows Marco Frost stopping outside to light a cigarette at 8:50 p.m. The newsagent's is a thirty-five minute walk from the train station, so he did arrive off the 8:10 p.m. train from London Bridge."

The train doors opened with a beep, and passengers surged around Erika.

Moss continued, "So Marco Frost can now be placed an hour and thirty-five minutes from London around the time Andrea vanished. It's highly unlikely he could have made it back to the station for the last train into London that evening. He's in the clear."

The passengers had now boarded the train. The guard stood on the edge of the platform, waiting as the seconds on the electronic clock ticked by to the departure time.

"Of course, now Marsh is shitting a brick. The CPS had been crowing to the press how we've caught Andrea's killer, and now a duty solicitor who phoned up a newsagent and asked for a copy of their CCTV video has blown all the case apart…You still there, boss?"

"Yes, I am," said Erika.

The guard blew his whistle. "Get back if you're not boarding the train!" he shouted, signaling for Erika to get behind the yellow line. She looked at the inside of the carriage. There was a seat just by the door, and warm air flowed out. The doors lit up and gave the warning beep.

"I thought you'd be really pleased, boss?" asked Moss.

"I am, this means…"

"I wanted to give you the heads-up, because I think Marsh is going to call you."

The train doors were about to close, when a man in a leather jacket came thundering down the stairs from the footbridge. He reached the platform and dived onto the train just as the doors closed on him. With a beeping sound, the doors opened again to free him.

There was a ping on Erika's phone. She saw that she had Marsh on her call waiting.

"He's calling me now."

"Okay, I'll get off the line," said Moss. "Let me know what's happening."

The doors were now closing. This was her last chance to get on the train and go up north. The doors closed. Erika answered her phone.

"DCI Foster. How are you?" asked Marsh, sounding insincere and panicky.

"I now know how a chicken feels seconds before death," she quipped.

The train clicked and whirred and pulled away from the platform.

"Sorry I didn't get in contact, it's been—"

"Yes, I've heard you had to release Marco Frost."

"Would you be willing to come into the station? We need to talk," he said.

Erika paused and watched the train move into the distance, vanishing round a bend. "I can be there in fifteen minutes, sir," she said. She picked up her case, looked at the real world, which she had briefly felt she might join, and then hurried toward the station exit.

CHAPTER 52

There was a fight going on in the reception area when Erika entered Lewisham Row Station. Two teenage boys hit the concrete floor with a hollow thud, and began to roll around, goaded on by assorted siblings and their equally young mothers. The larger boy clambered on top of the smaller and started to punch his face, the teeth of the smaller boy blurring pink with blood. Woolf waded into the fray, supported by a couple of uniformed officers. Erika ducked through the fighting and was buzzed in through the inside door by Moss.

"Shit, it's good to see you back here," she said, as they started down the corridor.

"Steady on. I've just been summoned, not invited," said Erika, feeling nervous and excited.

"Well, Marsh is freaking out," Moss explained.

"That's what happens when you let outside parties dictate an investigation," said Erika.

They reached the door to Marsh's office. Moss knocked and they went straight in. Marsh was pale and standing over his computer, watching the breaking news running across the BBC News website announcing that Marco Frost had been released.

"Thank you, Detective Moss. DCI Foster, please sit."

"I'd like Moss to stay, sir. She's been working on this whilst I've been—"

"I'm aware of your, *investigations*."

There was a brisk knock at the door and Marsh's secretary poked her head round. "I've got Sir Simon Douglas-Brown on the line, says it's urgent."

Marsh pushed his hand through his short hair and looked harassed.

"I'm in an important meeting here, please relay that, and I'll call him back asap, thanks."

The secretary nodded and left, closing the door.

"I'm your important meeting?" asked Erika. Marsh came round to his desk and sat. Erika and Moss each pulled up a chair.

Marsh attempted a smile. "Look, DCI Foster—Erika. What has happened is unfortunate. I admit you may have been treated unfairly, and I will address this properly in due course. However, we find ourselves suddenly in the midst of a crisis. We're on the back foot here. I need all the information and insights you have from your alternative investigation."

"Which, I hope, will now become your priority investigation?"

"I will be the judge of that. Just tell me everything you've got," said Marsh.

"No," said Erika.

"No?"

"Boss. I'll tell you everything, and I'll outline my theories, when you've returned my badge and reinstated me as SIO on this investigation." Erika sat back and stared at Marsh.

"Who do you think you are, to come in here—" he started.

"Okay. I'll leave you to your chat with Sir Simon. Say hi from me." Erika got up to leave.

"What you're asking is near impossible. You've got a serious allegation against you, DCI Foster!"

"I call bullshit. Assistant Commissioner Oakley was acting on orders from Simon Douglas-Brown to remove me from this case.

Little Matthew Norris has been in and out of youth detention for years. He's assaulted several social workers and, I'll repeat, at the time I hit him, his teeth were latched into the back of my hand. Now if that's what this whole case swings on, then fine, but you'll be waving good-bye to someone who can catch this guy. And of course, I'll repeat this to the press, because I won't go quietly."

Marsh ran his fingers through his hair.

"Sir, Marco Frost has just pulled together an alibi and made you all look like a bunch of bumbling comedy policemen. Didn't DCI Sparks think to do a few background checks? I mean for God's sake. CCTV from a newsagent! Oh, and I'll also make sure that the press know there's a killer still out there on the loose thanks to you, DCI Sparks, and of course the sleek fox himself, Assistant Commissioner Oakley."

Marsh looked as if he were going to explode. Erika stared at him, not looking away.

"Put me back on the case and I'll catch this bastard," she said.

Marsh got up and went to the window, looking out at the bleak January landscape. He turned. "For fuck's sake. Okay. But you are on a very short leash, do you understand, DCI Foster?"

Moss gave Erika a small, triumphant smile.

"I understand. Thank you, sir."

Marsh came and sat back down. "Well, go on, give me your insights."

"Okay. Let's go public with this. Launch a fresh appeal, and if you can pull some strings, let's get a television reconstruction going. We're going to face flack for Marco Frost, sir, and you need to be ready to bombard the press with all the things we *are* doing, so they concentrate on that, not all the things that we didn't do."

Marsh looked at Erika. She went on, "We've already celebrated once that we caught the killer. We can't do it again unless we really do catch him. So let's get ahead of the news cycle. Make George Mitchell our main focus. Flood the press with the image of him with Andrea...We also need a scapegoat. The press will want to see that someone is paying for this fuck-up. And I know just the person."

CHAPTER 53

Erika took a deep breath and opened the door to the incident room. DCI Sparks stood talking at the front by the whiteboards, which were stripped bare. The rest of the team sat around the room despondently.

Sparks looked angry and haggard, his long dark hair pulled back from his face and spots of grease blooming where his hair touched his collar. "I'll be talking to you one by one, and I'll be asking tough questions. We're going to go back to the beginning and root out exactly who failed to check the basic fucking timeline of Marco Frost's journey from boarding the train at London Bridge to…"

Sparks's voice tailed off as he saw Erika enter with Moss.

"You here to pick up your P45, Foster?" he sneered. The rest of the officers remained stony-faced.

"No, my badge, actually," said Erika, flashing it to Sparks. He looked confused. "Do you take the title SIO seriously, DCI Sparks?"

"Well, seeing as only one of us has it, yes," he said. "Can I help you? I'm in the middle of a briefing here."

"SIO means Senior Investigating Officer. The 'senior' part doesn't mean you're older than everyone and entitled to bully them when the shit hits the fan. It means you take responsibility for your fuck-ups."

"I don't understand," said Sparks, losing a little of his resolve.

"That's been the problem. I've been reinstated as SIO. And my first order is that you need to piss off to Marsh's office."

DCI Sparks froze.

"Now, DCI Sparks."

He stared at Erika, along with the rest of the incident room, and then he went slowly to his desk, picked up his coat and walked out. Before he was out of the door, Crane started to applaud. Other officers joined in, and Peterson put his fingers to his lips and whistled. Erika was touched, and looked down as she blushed.

"All right you lot," she said. "It's much appreciated, but there's still a murderer out there." The applause died down. Erika went to the whiteboard at the front. She pinned up the picture of Andrea and George Mitchell.

"This is our prime suspect, George Mitchell. Andrea Douglas-Brown's lover, and ultimately, her killer. Also suspected in the rape and murder of Tatiana Ivanova, Mirka Bratova, Karolina Todorova and Ivy Norris."

The room was silent.

"Until today, the focus has been on the murder of Andrea Douglas-Brown. Her face has been on the front of every newspaper, Internet browser and television screen, and has worked its way into the national conscience. Yes, she was rich and privileged. But she experienced a terrible death: alone, scared and helpless. Tatiana Ivanova, Mirka Bratova, Karolina Todorova and Ivy Norris may have been prostitutes, but I can guarantee this was not a world they entered into willingly. Given different circumstances, they could have been as lucky as Andrea in life. They, too, had a harrowing demise. I say all this because I want you to forget where these women stood in society. Don't do what we do in this country, day in, day out, and divide them into their social classes. They are all equals, all victims, and they deserve our equal attention."

Erika paused. Crane had started to pin up photos of the victims.

"So, this is our person of extreme interest and our main focus," said Erika, pointing to the photo of George Mitchell. "He was in a sexual relationship with Andrea, and they were photographed together four days before Andrea went missing. I also believe she met him and an unidentified blonde woman on the night she was taken. I want you all to review the full contents of Andrea Douglas-Brown's second phone on the intranet. Please look at them with fresh eyes. There are no stupid questions. We find this man, and I believe we unlock this case."

The officers nodded in unison.

Erika went on, "This afternoon we're going to make a fresh public appeal for information. We're going out with full guns, naming George Mitchell as a suspect. Hopefully it will lead to new information, or flush him out from wherever he is hiding."

Erika paused, checking that she had their full attention. She continued. "Please also focus on our other victims. The murders of Tatiana Ivanova, Mirka Bratova, and Karolina Todorova are unsolved cases which have never been linked before. I want the evidence pulled on all three murders and revisited. Look for links, any similarities; did the victims know each other? If so, how and why?"

There was a knock at the door of the incident room, and Colleen, the police press officer, entered.

"Sorry to interrupt, DCI Foster; I'm expecting a conference call from Reuters at any moment. I thought you'd want to sit in on it," she said.

"Right, thank you everyone. We need to get ahead on this.

Put Marco Frost to the back of your minds. Tune out the press; drop your pre-conceived ideas. Concentrate on what is in front of us here and now. We get ahead of the news cycle and we'll start to win this."

Erika rose and left the incident room as it began to buzz with activity.

CHAPTER 54

The press appeal was in stark contrast to the previous press conference in Marble Arch. Erika had insisted it was held on the steps of Lewisham Row Station, and that it should be more genuine and urgent than the polished nature of the previous press conference, with its video screens and elegant conference room.

In addition, Erika had insisted that Marsh not be present, which hadn't gone down well. The light was fading by the time that Erika, Moss and Peterson gathered on the steps of Lewisham Row in front of the assorted television and print journalists. A harsh light was trained on them, which bounced off the chipped wood of the station's main entrance behind.

"Thank you for attending today," Erika began, raising her voice above the crowd. She was faced with scores of lenses. The televisions cameras trained their lenses on the stairs, and cameras fired off flashes. Moss and Peterson stared straight ahead.

Erika continued, "I guess that many of you here today might already have written this story, and made up your minds about what I'm going to say. But before you drift off and metaphorically file your copy in your head, writing luridly about police incompetence, or before you decide that Andrea's death is more newsworthy than that of someone who wasn't born into a life of privilege, think back to why we are all here today. Our job is to catch the bad guys; your job is to report on that in a fair and just manner. Yes, we do use each other. The police use the press to further our cause, and to spread a message. You sell column inches. So, ladies and gentlemen of the press, I ask that we work together today. Let me give you a new story to run with."

Erika paused. "Marco Frost was today released from custody due to insufficient evidence. He was able to supply us with an alibi and we had no choice but to release him. He's an innocent man. But that is not your story. Your story is that the killer of Andrea is still out there, at large in society. After reviewing the evidence and refocusing the investigation, we have strong reason to believe that the death of Andrea wasn't an isolated crime. The man we are looking for has killed previously. We believe he is responsible for the death of three young Eastern European women: Tatiana Ivanova, Mirka Bratova and Karolina Todorova. They all came to London in the belief that there would be a good job here for them. What happened, however, is that they were trafficked as prostitutes and forced to work to pay off a debt. We also believe that the same individual is responsible for the death of forty-seven-year-old Ivy Norris. Now, please, you will see a photo of our prime suspect in this case. His name is George Mitchell…"

Back in the incident room, Chief Superintendent Marsh was watching the press conference with Colleen as it went out live on the BBC News channel.

"It looks amateurish, and she's coming across a bit schoolmarmish," he said, as the picture cut away from Erika, Moss and Peterson in the glare of the cameras to a photo of George Mitchell.

"Of course, a woman is confident of her opinion and she's *schoolmarmish*," said Colleen.

A number and e-mail address flashed along the bottom of the screen. After a few moments, the screen cut back to Erika.

"Please if you have any information about this man, contact us using the details on your screens. Your call will be dealt with in confidence. We also advise anyone who sees this man not to approach him. I thank the members of the press for your time and for your help with this matter."

There was a pause on screen, and then journalists began to shout out questions.

"Will Marco Frost be entitled to compensation?" shouted one voice.

"Marco Frost's case will be treated in the same way as all others. The Crown Prosecution Service will be looking into it as a matter of urgency," said Erika.

The journalists started to bombard Erika with more questions.

"Are these murders linked to the business activities of Sir Simon Douglas-Brown?"

"I think what we need to remember is that Sir Simon is a father whose daughter died in a horrific manner. Just like the other girls—they also have family who feel their loss every day. This investigation has already been hampered by the perceived manner in which we should do things. What we realize now is that Andrea's secrets are the very thing that will lead us to the killer. Please don't judge her, or her family."

"Christ, I knew this was a bad idea," said Marsh.

"No. This is good. She's really connecting with people. This press conference is much more real and genuine than before," said Colleen. Marsh gave her a sideways glance, but she was glued to the screen.

The press conference then cut away to a wide shot as Erika, Moss, and Peterson made their way up the steps and back into the station. The television cut back to the BBC News studio, where the news anchor asked the reporter at the scene for his comments.

"This is a bold move by the police, who after several weeks still have very little in the way of evidence. With a suspect at large, time is running out."

"What does he mean, running out?" scoffed Marsh.

On the screen, the reporter carried on, "Sir Simon Douglas-Brown has been faced with a fresh round of newspaper revelations over his links to Saudi Arabian arms deals. An extramarital affair has also been hinted at."

The camera then cut back to the news anchor.

"This press conference was a marked departure in the police investigation. Whereas in previous weeks the Met seemed to be dancing to the tune of the Douglas-Brown family, are they now putting forward a credible line of inquiry, based upon evidence which the family would perhaps rather be kept out of the media?"

The camera cut back to the reporter outside Lewisham Row. "I think yes. I believe this press conference may have hurt the relationship between the establishment and the police force, but it may well give the police more credibility and autonomy, which will, I'm sure, help to gain back the support of the public."

"There, you see; that's the angle we're looking for. I'll make some calls and get the tape of these comments circulated," said Colleen.

Marsh felt a prickle of sweat forming on his brow and he felt his phone vibrate in his pocket. Pulling it out, he saw it was Simon Douglas-Brown.

CHAPTER 55

The past few days had passed in a haze of frustration. To have come so close, and then to have to pull back, had left the figure raging inside. Not only had DCI Foster survived, she'd come back from it stronger.

She's been put back on the fucking case!

After witnessing the appeal from Lewisham Row, where DCI Foster had publicly linked the murders, the figure was torn. There was an instinct to flee far away, to start again, but there was also an itch which needed to be scratched. The link had been made, but the police had nothing. The figure was sure of this.

So, at six p.m., the figure drove up to Paddington Train Station, where the cabs dropped off and picked up passengers, and where the girls hung around…

The girl looked confused when the figure pulled up in the car. She was standing a little way down the end of a dirty slip road which was used by cabs to turn around, or by people on the lookout for a good time.

"I can give you a good time," she said, automatically. She was a thin girl with a strong Eastern European accent. She shivered in tight leggings, a spaghetti strap top and a large, ratty, fake fur coat. She had pale pointed features and shoulder length, poker-straight hair. Her eyes were surrounded by glittery eye shadow and she was chewing gum. She leaned back against the skip, waiting for a response.

"I'm looking for a good time...Something a bit different, a bit rarer."

"Oh yeah? Well, you know, when stuff is rare, it costs more."

"I know your boss," said the figure.

She scoffed at him. "Yeah, they all say that...If you're looking for a discount, you can fuck off," she said, going to turn away.

The figure leaned forward and told her a name. She stopped and came back to the window, dropping all pretense of being alluring. Her eyes were frightened. Fear surrounded by glitter.

"Did he send you?" she asked, looking around at the cars roaring past.

"No. But he knows I put a lot of business his way...So he'll expect me to get what I want."

The girl narrowed her eyes. Her instincts were good. This might be harder than expected.

"So, you come here and drop the name of my boss. What do you want me to do?"

"I like outdoor scenes," said the figure.

"Okay."

"And I like it when the girl plays scared..."

"You mean you want a rape fantasy?" said the girl bluntly, rolling her eyes. She looked around and pulled down her top, showing her small pert breasts. "That will cost more."

"I can afford it," said the figure.

She pulled her top up. "Yeah? Show me."

The figure pulled out a wallet and opened it, pushing it under her nose. The money was in a crisp block, glinting under the street lights.

"Fifteen hundred. And we have a safe word," she said, pulling a mobile phone from her leggings. The figure put a hand out and covered the phone.

"No, no, no, no. I want this as real as possible. Within the realms of fantasy. Don't tell anyone where you're going."

"I have to call."

"An extra five hundred. The boss doesn't have to know."

"No way. He finds out, and I don't get to have a safe word."

"Okay. All above board. Two grand. And the safe word is Erika."

"Erika?"

"Yes. Erika."

The girl looked around and chewed on her lip. "Okay," she said. She pulled open the door and got into the car. The figure drove off, activating the central locking, telling her this, too, was part of the game.

CHAPTER 56

The incident room was rather quiet after the press conference. Officers milled around as the occasional phone rang. An air of expectation needed to be quenched. The few calls that did come through were from the usual time-wasters.

"Jesus. You'd think that someone would come forward with information," said Erika, looking at her watch. "I can't bear this; I'm nipping out for a cigarette."

She had just reached the steps of the police station when Detective Crane appeared behind her.

"Boss, you'll want to take this," he said.

"Who is it?" asked Erika.

"We've got a young girl on the line who says she's Barbora Kardosova, Andrea's long lost best friend," said Crane.

Erika hurried back with him to the incident room and took the call.

"Is this the police officer who was on the television this afternoon?" asked a young female voice with an Eastern European accent.

"Yes. This is Detective Chief Inspector Erika Foster. Do you have information about George Mitchell?"

"Yes," she said. There was a pause. "But I can't talk on the phone."

"I can assure you that anything you say here will be treated confidentially," said Erika. She looked down, and saw it was a withheld number. Erika looked over at Crane, who nodded to show he was already working on a trace.

"I'm sorry, I won't talk on the phone," the girl said, her voice shaking.

"Okay, that's okay. Can I meet you?" asked Erika. "It can be anywhere you like."

Peterson was hastily scribbling on his notepad. He held up a sign, which read: GET HER TO COME IN TO STATION?

"Are you in London? Would you like to come to the station here at Lewisham Row?"

"No... No, no..." The girl's voice was now panicky. There was a pause. Erika looked up at Crane, who mouthed that it was a pay-as-you-go phone.

"Hello, Barbora, are you still there?"

"Yes. I'm not saying any more over the phone. I need to talk to tell you things. I can meet you tomorrow at eleven a.m. Here's the address..."

Erika scribbled it down hastily and went to ask more, but the line was dead.

"It was a pay-as-you-go, boss; no joy," said Crane.

"She sounded really rattled," said Erika, replacing the phone.

"Where does she want to meet?" asked Peterson. Erika tapped the address into her computer. A picture on Google Maps popped up on screen. It was a vast expanse of green.

"Norfolk," said Erika.

"Norfolk? What the hell is she doing in Norfolk?" asked Moss.

Erika's mobile phone rang. She saw it was Edward. "Sorry, I just have to take this. Can you work out a route, and we'll decide how to proceed when I come back," she said, and left the incident room.

The corridor outside was quiet and she answered her phone.

"So lass, I take it you're not coming?" said Edward. Erika saw that it was five past five.

"I'm so sorry…You're not still waiting there? On the platform?"

"No, lass. I saw you on the telly this afternoon, and I thought, unless you can fly, you wouldn't be here at five o'clock."

Erika thought back. The morning seemed like a million years ago.

"You did well for that press conference, love," said Edward. "You made me care about that girl, Andrea. She hasn't been getting very nice things said about her in the papers, has she?"

"Thank you. It all happened at once. I was called in this morning, I was about to get on the train to you and…"

"And it all got away from you, eh?"

"Yes," said Erika, softly.

"Listen love. You do what you have to do. I'll be here for you."

Moss appeared at the door, signaling that she wanted to speak.

"Sorry. I have to go. Can I phone you back later?" asked Erika.

"Yes, love. Take care of yourself, won't you? You catch that bloke, lock him up and throw away the key."

"I will," said Erika. There was a click, and Edward hung up. "I will. I promise I will," she repeated.

Taking a deep breath, she went back into the incident room, wondering exactly when she'd be able to honor her promise.

CHAPTER 57

Erika, Moss and Peterson set off early from London the next day to meet Barbora Kardosova. They had tried a search on her several times, but it had brought up a blank. Her National Insurance, passport and bank account numbers had ceased activity more than a year previously. Her mother had died two years previously, and she had no other living relatives.

Just as the sun broke through the clouds, they plunged into the gloom of the Blackwall Tunnel. When they emerged a few moments later, the sun had vanished again behind a bank of steel-colored clouds.

"Now we've crossed the river, we're looking for the A12, boss," said Moss. Peterson sat in the back, engrossed in his phone. They'd stopped for petrol just before Greenwich, and Moss had indulged her sweet tooth with packets of red licorice bootlaces.

The built-up sprawl of London soon gave way to the A12 dual carriageway which was neglected and crumbling in places, and they noticed how flat the landscape was. Brown fields with bare trees whizzed past, and toward Ipswich they turned off the dual carriageway and slowed as they hit a single-lane road.

"It's quite eerie, isn't it? This straight road through nothing," remarked Peterson, speaking for the first time in a hundred miles. The road carved its way through a vast expanse of flat fields, and the wind roared across the bare soil, buffeting the car. The road rose up a little, and they crossed a metal bridge over a canal of choppy water. Dead gray reeds lined the straight waterway all the way to the horizon. Erika wondered if the water reached the edge and poured away into nothingness.

"It's an old Roman road, the A12," said Moss, stuffing another red bootlace into her mouth and chewing.

"They burned hundreds of witches in Suffolk and Norfolk," added Peterson, as they passed a deserted windmill in a field next to the water.

"I'll take high prices, door-to-door traffic, smog, and a crowded Nando's over this any day," said Moss, shivering and turning up the car heater. "How far?"

"There's about six miles to go," said Peterson, consulting his iPhone.

The trees thickened and the landscape changed to woodland. The car sped along under a canopy of bare trees, and Erika slowed as she spied a lay-by with a picnic area, which was no more than a scrub of soil and a picnic bench. A wooden sign had the number 14 painted on it.

"What did she say, picnic area 17?" asked Erika.

"Yes, boss," said Peterson, tapping on his phone. They carried on a little more as the wood seemed to get denser. The road wove to the left and right, past picnic area 15. They took a sharp bend, and a picnic bench with the number 16 slid past. The picnic area was overgrown. The bench was rotten and had collapsed.

"Advise on your status," said Detective Crane's voice, bursting through with static on the police radio mounted on the dashboard.

"We'll be approaching within the next few minutes, skip," said Moss.

"Okay, keep an open line of communication. That's what the Super asked for," said Crane.

Chief Superintendent Marsh had been against sending three of his officers off to Norfolk on what he thought was a wild goose chase.

"Boss, Barbora Kardosova was one of Andrea's closest friends, and she says she knows George Mitchell," Erika had pointed out, when she was sitting in his office.

"Why hasn't she come forward before? Andrea has been in the newspapers for weeks. And why don't we get the local plod to take a statement? You'll be gone for a whole day. You've just launched a major appeal in London," said Marsh.

"Sir, this is our strongest lead. We'll leave early, we'll be in contact the whole time. Again, I'd like you to entertain my hunch on this one."

"Why was she using an unlisted number? We've no idea of her whereabouts," said Marsh, leaning back in his chair and rubbing his eyes.

"Maybe she doesn't want to be found. That's not an offense is it?" asked Erika.

"It would make everything far more bloody easy if everyone was tagged at birth with a GPS tracker. It would save a fortune..."

"I'll be sure to pass that along to the next journalist I meet," said Erika.

"Keep me informed every step of the way," he had said irritably, waving her away with a hand.

The sky had grown heavy, and Moss had to put on the car headlights. The surrounding woodland was now thick, and the bare branches seemed impenetrable. The sign with the number 17 appeared up ahead, and they came to a stop at a patch of bare soil. The bench had been removed, leaving four deep impressions in the soil. Moss killed the engine and the lights, and they were left in silence. When Erika opened the door, a cold breeze floated past, bringing with it the smell of damp and rotting leaves. She buttoned up her coat as Peterson and Moss joined her.

"So now what?" asked Moss.

"She said she'd meet us here; she was very specific," said Erika, pulling out the scrap of paper where she'd written the original directions. They looked at the road beside them. It was empty in both directions.

"There looks like a track up ahead here," said Moss. They made toward a gap in the dead brambles and undergrowth. After squeezing through for several meters, it opened out onto a track for walkers. It was well-kept, under a huge canopy of trees stretching away to a corner, where the track disappeared. Erika imagined that in the summer this bleak and creepy woodland corner felt different.

They waited for almost forty minutes, the radio clicking and beeping as Crane, back in London, checked their status.

"It's a bloody wind-up," said Peterson. "No doubt it was the woman who said..." His voice trailed off as they heard the crack of a stick breaking, and the whoosh of leaves being disturbed. Erika put her finger to her lips. There was a rustling, and through the undergrowth came a woman with short blonde hair. She wore a pink waterproof jacket and black leggings. She held a knife in her hand, and what looked like a canister of mace in the other. She stopped fifty yards from where they stood.

"What the fuck?" said Moss.

Erika shot her a look. "Barbora? Barbora Kardosova? I'm DCI Erika Foster; these are my colleagues, Detective Moss and Detective Peterson."

"Take out your IDs and throw them over here," said Barbora. Her voice shook with fear, and as she came closer they could see her hands did too.

"Hang on," started Moss, but Erika put her hand in her pocket, pulled out her ID and slung it across. It landed a few feet from Barbora. Moss and Peterson reluctantly did the same. She picked them up, and keeping the canister of mace trained in their direction, looked through their IDs.

"Okay, you can see we are who we say we are. Now please put the knife and the mace away," said Erika. Barbora put them down on the ground, and came cautiously toward the three of them. Erika could just make out the face from the picture she'd seen on Facebook. It was still beautiful, but the nose was now smaller and straighter. The face was fuller, and the long dark hair was now short and dyed blonde.

A dark-haired man and a blonde-haired girl... thought Erika.

"Why are we going through all this just to talk to you?" started Moss. "You know we could nick you here and now for having that knife. It's more than seven inches long, and don't get me started on the mace..."

Barbora had tears in her eyes. "I'm so scared, but I have to talk to you. There are things I have to tell you or I'll never forgive myself...I shouldn't have contacted you using my real name," she said. "I'm in the witness protection program."

CHAPTER 58

They froze for a moment, Moss, Peterson and Erika. The wind rushed through the treetops above.

"I'm not going to tell you my new name," said Barbora, shakily.

"No," said Erika, holding up her hand. "Don't say anything more."

"Shit, this should have been bloody obvious," said Moss. There was a faint beep from the open car window, and they heard Crane ask for their status and position.

"We've got to call this in, boss... If someone in witness protection reveals themselves or is revealed, then we have to call it in," said Moss.

"You'll need a new identity," said Peterson, trying to hide his annoyance.

"Wait. Please. There are things I have to say," said Barbora. "I met you because I have to talk to you about George Mitchell..." She swallowed and shook even more. "I should tell you his real name."

"What's his real name?" asked Erika.

Barbora gulped, and it seemed like a physical effort to say it. "Igor Kucerov," she said, finally.

Peterson made for the car where the radio was.

"Please! Let me tell you everything before you... Before you make it official."

There was another pause. Crane's tinny voice floated from far away, asking for their status and position.

"Peterson. Tell him we're still waiting. All is okay...And please, Peterson, nothing about this until we've heard her out," said Erika.

He nodded, and then sprinted off back to the car.

"We don't want to know your new name, or where you're living around here," said Erika.

"I live far away from here. I have more to lose than all of you put together, but I've made up my mind to finally speak," she said. "If we double back a bit, there's a picnic spot up ahead."

They followed, leaving Peterson to man the radio in the car. After a five-minute walk they came into a clearing with a picnic bench. The light had difficulty penetrating a canopy of branches high above. Again, Erika thought it must be beautiful on a summer's day, but in the cold and gloom it was oppressive. She pushed this to the back of her mind and she and Moss sat down opposite Barbora, the table between them.

Erika offered Barbora a cigarette, and she took one gratefully from the pack. Her hands shook as she leaned in, cupping her hand for a light. Erika lit her own and Moss's, and they inhaled in unison.

Barbora looked as if she was going to throw up. She ran her hand through her short blonde hair. It was bleached cheaply, with a yellow, straw-like appearance. She gulped and started to speak, her voice shaky.

"I first met George Mitchell...*Igor Kucerov*...three years ago, when I was twenty. I lived in London, and I was working two jobs. One in a private members' club in central London called Debussy's." She took another drag on her cigarette, and went on, "I worked shifts there, and at the same time I worked in a café in New Cross called The Junction. It was a fun, vibrant place, where local artists, painters and poets met. It was also where I first met Igor. He was a regular customer, and every time he came in, we started to talk. Back then, I thought he was gorgeous and so funny. I was flattered he spent his time talking to me…One day, I was in work and very upset. My little iPod had broken, and it had songs and photos on it that I couldn't replace. He was kind, but I didn't think anything of it. When I came for my next shift a few days later, he was there, waiting with a gift bag, and inside was a new iPod…Not like the tiny little one I had, but the newest and most expensive, worth several hundred pounds."

"And that's when you started a relationship with George / Igor?" asked Moss.

Barbora nodded. It was growing darker, and a cloud was looming above.

"At first, he was so wonderful. I thought I was in love and that I'd found the man I would spend the rest of my life with."

"What did your family think of him?"

"It was just me and my mother. She came to England when she was in her twenties. She wanted to meet a man and live a nice middle-class life, but then she fell pregnant with me. Her boyfriend at the time didn't want to know, so she had me on her own and struggled as a single mother. Then, when I was ten, she was diagnosed with multiple sclerosis. It was slow at first, but when I was sixteen she got really bad. I had to leave school and look after her. I took these jobs in the mornings at the café and nights at the club."

"So how long were you in a relationship with Igor?" asked Moss, gently moving her story forward.

"About a year. He did so much in that time. Helping us out. He paid for a special bathroom to be put in for my mother. He cleared my credit cards…" Barbora smiled off in the distance, the memory still alive in her mind. She took a drag on her cigarette and her face clouded over.

"Then, it was a few months into our relationship. One night we'd been to the cinema in Bromley... These boys had been making comments about me when we bought our tickets, stuff about my body. Igor had got angry, but I told him to leave it. We went inside and watched the film, and I thought he'd forgotten about it. When we came out it was late and there weren't many people around. Igor saw one of the boys leave and he walked in front of us to the car park. When we were near our car, he just went for him, punching and kicking. He was like an animal. This boy went down on the ground and Igor just kept on kicking him, stamping on his head. I'd never seen him like this; it shocked me... I tried to pull him away but he punched me in the face too. Finally, when he had no more energy, he just walked away. He left the boy lying on the ground in the dark..."

Barbora began to cry. Moss pulled out a small packet of tissues. She held them across the table and Barbora took one. She took a deep breath and wiped her face.

"And I followed him," she said. "We just left the boy on the ground between two cars... Igor made me drive, even though I wasn't insured on his car, and I did. He grabbed my handbag and found my makeup remover wipes and cleaned the blood off his knuckles, and some that had sprayed on his face. And then he dropped me home. I didn't see him for a few days, until he showed up with a gift, and my mum was so happy to see him. I just took it and carried on as if nothing had happened."

"What happened to the boy?" asked Erika. Barbora shrugged. There was a far off rumble of thunder and a flicker of lightning.

"So where does Andrea come into all this?" asked Moss.

"A few weeks after I started work in the club Debussy's, behind the bar, Andrea came in for a drink. It was quiet and

I served her a drink and we got chatting. She started coming in more regularly, and I slowly got to know her. She said how much she hated all the snobby trust fund girls she'd been to school with. When she heard I lived south of the river, she said she'd love to come and visit me. She said it like she was going off on a package holiday or something... but New Cross is only ten minutes on the train from Charing Cross." Barbora laughed bitterly.

"So, did Andrea come to your house?"

Barbora shook her head. "No, she used to come to The Junction, the coffee place where I worked. She loved it. It was so bohemian, and there were always interesting people there; people who'd lived life free, not in a cage, that's what she said... I said her cage was gilded, but she didn't get that. I don't think she knew what the word 'gilded' meant."

"When did she tell you who her father was?"

"Not at first, and she made this big thing about keeping it a secret. But then she spent more time at the café, and became quite competitive with some of the girls who'd hang around the artists and painters. She started to let it drop into conversation."

"And what did people say?" asked Erika.

"Most of them were quite blasé... but George—Igor—took interest. When he found out, it was like he suddenly noticed Andrea..."

"Did he have an affair with Andrea?"

Barbora nodded. "It happened so fast, and I was so brainwashed by it all."

"At this stage, was he being violent with you, Barbora?"

"No—well, sometimes. It was more the threat of the violence, the control... When I found out about Andrea, that's when he first properly hit me."

"Where was this?" asked Erika.

"At home. It was a Sunday night and my mother was in the bath. I don't know why it came up at that time, but it did and I confronted him."

"What happened?"

"He punched me in the stomach. It was so hard I threw up, and then he locked me in the cupboard under the stairs."

"How long for?"

"Not long; I was pleading because my mother was in the bath and getting cold. I had to help her out. He said he'd only let me out if I promised not to mention him and Andrea again."

"And did you?"

Barbora shook her head.

"What happened next?" asked Erika.

"Things were normal for a while. It kind of calmed down. Then I was at home one day. Igor arrived at the kitchen door at the back of our house. He had this young girl with him. She could only have been eighteen. She could barely stand, and was dressed in skinny jeans and a tight T-shirt. Her face was a mess of blood; some of it was dry and some of it was new, and it was all down the front of her T-shirt. She was crying and—what was I supposed to do? I let them in, but Igor didn't want to help her. He went to that cupboard under our stairs and he put her in there and he locked it. He was crazy, swearing he just wanted to know where his phone was. He said this girl had taken it..."

The storm was coming close now, and under the tree it was very gloomy.

"What happened to the girl?" asked Erika, softly.

"Igor sent me upstairs. He told me to stay in my room or there would be trouble. I heard the girl screaming and crying. It went on for what seemed like hours...And then it went quiet. Igor opened the door and asked to go to my mother's room. She smiled when she saw him. She'd slept through it all. He asked for my sports bag, the big one I used when I went away. I went to the wardrobe and I pulled it out and he took it... He was so calm. I went downstairs a few minutes later and he was leaving with the bag over his shoulder."

"What was in the bag?" asked Moss, even though they knew the answer.

"The girl," said Barbora. "She was in the bag, and he just left."

"What did you do?" asked Erika.

"I cleaned up the mess in the cupboard. There was blood and other stuff..."

"And then?"

"He came back later, and he told me I'd done a good job. He even gave me some money..." Barbora's voice was full of self-loathing. "And then we carried on again, as if nothing had happened. But he started to tell me about his work. How he'd meet girls from the buses at Victoria Coach Station; how they came to work for him."

"To work as what?" asked Erika.

"Prostitutes. The more I knew, the more Igor kept giving me money. He bought my mother a new electric wheelchair she could use herself. She didn't have to be pushed anymore. It changed her life."

"And how is Andrea part of this?"

"I was so stressed I couldn't eat; my periods stopped. Igor just didn't look at me that way anymore, so Andrea took over. She provided him with that service."

"Was all this going on when you went on the family holidays with Andrea?"

"Yes."

"Did you know that later on, Andrea got engaged?"

Barbora nodded, and accepted another cigarette.

"And did Andrea know about Igor? Did she know what kind of work he did?" asked Erika.

"I don't know. I never discussed it with her. We'd been close at first, and we still were weirdly close on the holidays with her family, but I withdrew into myself. I think Andrea had this romantic notion that Igor was some kind of roguish London gangster, like in those stupid Guy Ritchie films."

"So how did you come to be in the witness protection program?" asked Moss.

"The body of the girl was discovered in my bag a few months later."

"Where?"

"A landfill in East London. The bag had an old store card belonging to me in the inside pocket. It led the police to my door. They said they'd been watching me for a long time, and that I could strike a bargain for giving evidence."

"And you did?"

"Yeah. Igor seemed to trust me by now. He wanted me to start coming to Victoria Coach Station to meet the girls. They thought they were coming to England to work as housekeepers. He figured if I was there they'd trust me, and get in the car..."

"Igor was trafficking women to London, to work as prostitutes?" asked Erika.

"Yes."

"Was he working alone?"

"No. I don't know; it was all so complicated. There were other men involved, and their girlfriends."

"Where were the girls taken? How many girls were there?" asked Moss.

"I don't know," Barbora started. She broke down, heaving and crying.

"It's okay," said Erika, reaching out across the dark table to take Barbora's hand. She flinched and pulled it away.

"So what happened?" Erika continued. "Igor was arrested?"

"Yes. It went to trial," said Barbora. Erika looked across at Moss. Even in the darkness, she could see the shock registered on her face.

"Trial, what trial? We have no record... What happened?"

"The prosecution's case collapsed. There wasn't enough solid evidence. The jury couldn't rule either way... I think Igor got to some of the other witnesses. He... he knows too many people." Barbora now looked blank. "I realize how I must come across; the terrible things I've done. I know what a terrible person I am. All from loving a man," she said. Erika and Moss were silent. "When I saw those girls on the news, when you made your appeal, I remembered one of them—Tatiana. When she arrived in London. She was so excited, and... I had to speak to you. You have to get that bastard."

"Have you seen Andrea since?" asked Moss.

Barbora shifted uncomfortably. "Yes."

"Was it the night of the eighth of January, in a pub called The Glue Pot?" asked Erika.

"Yes."

"Was Igor with her?"

"What? No! I never would have gone near her if... Was he there?"

"No," said Erika. Moss shot her a look. "Why were you there in London? You're in the witness protection program."

"I go to London every month, to visit my mother's grave. I tidy, and I lay fresh flowers. Do you know how hard it is to be a stranger, to have a new identity? I texted Andrea thinking we could meet for coffee. I know it was stupid. But Andrea kept changing where we were going to meet and... I know I shouldn't have gone, but I missed her."

Moss was finding it hard to mask her disbelief.

"We only met for a little bit. She was on her own. She said she was meeting a new boyfriend later on…It was like nothing had ever happened with her. She wasn't surprised that I'd vanished and that now I was back. She didn't care."

"When did you leave The Glue Pot?"

"I don't know. Before eight. I knew there was a train from London Liverpool Street just before nine."

"And you didn't see anyone else?"

"No, Andrea said she was going to have a drink at the bar. There was a girl working…I wanted to say to her, watch out, that was me once, but I didn't."

"But all this, we'll need you to go on record, Barbora."

Barbora was suddenly silent. When she spoke, her voice sounded far away. "I've had my mobile phone on, recording this," she said, handing her phone over. "I have a little more to tell you, but first I really need to use the bathroom."

"Really? It's dark and…"

"Please, I have to," she repeated, urgently.

"Okay. Well, don't stray too far…We'll be here," said Erika.

"Here, use this little torch," said Moss, pulling one out of her coat pocket. Barbora took it, got up and went off into the undergrowth. The thunder was rumbling now with increased frequency. A flash of lightning lit up the inside of the clearing.

"I'm calling Peterson," said Erika. "When she comes back we should make a move. Take her back to London. I mean, she's just revealed herself so the new identity is no use. I don't know the procedure for any of this."

"Jesus, boss, what about that trial? There is no record of George Mitchell or Igor Kucerov. And when they ran the photo of him through the national database, nothing came back…I don't like it; this is getting weird."

Erika nodded and lit a cigarette. "We need to confirm her new identity. Then cross-check all she's told us…"

"Another complex twist in the murder of Andrea Douglas-Brown," said Moss. Erika looked at the phone for the first time and fiddled with the buttons, managing to play back a little of Barbora's voice.

"We've got her on record. It's grounds to bring this George Mitchell, or Igor Kucerov, in. We need an address from her when she gets back," said Erika.

Moss got on her phone and called Peterson, trying to explain where they were, but the signal was bad.

"It's breaking up, boss; I can't get through." Thunder rumbled and a flash of lightning lit up the sky above. "Jesus!" she cried. "I'm not using my bloody mobile when there's lightning above. Peterson can wait."

"Okay, okay, calm down; let me try," snapped Erika. She tried her phone and then Moss's again, but there was no signal; the call wouldn't even go through.

A strange creeping feeling was crawling over her.

"She's been gone a long time for a pee," said Moss. The light from Erika's phone cast a glow across their faces.

They jumped up at the same time, and moved in the direction where Barbora had left the clearing, ducking under a large branch. They pushed through some dead brambles and came back out onto the long track.

Rain began to pelt them as they left the shelter of the trees. Lightning flashed, and then they saw, up ahead, a tall tree with several long branches.

A rope creaked and swung, and on the end of a noose hung Barbora. Her feet were still, and her body swung in the breeze.

CHAPTER 59

The rain had become torrential, roaring on the treetops and turning the muddy track to a blur of white. Thunder rumbled, and flashes of lightning illuminated Barbora where she hung with her eyes open, folds of skin around her neck bunched up by the rope under her chin. Moss attempted to climb the tree, but the rain hampered her efforts.

"Stop, come down!" shouted Erika above the noise. "It's too late... She's dead. Go back to Peterson and call for backup. I'll stay here."

"You sure, boss?" shouted Moss, above the roar of the rain.

"Yes, go!" shouted Erika.

Moss ran off into the trees, and Erika waited. She paced up and down in the mud, not caring that she was getting wet. Her mind was whirring. The further they dug into this case, the more complex it became.

The storm seemed to be right above; the rain roared and the air fizzed with electricity. Erika was forced to stand under the tree, putting the thick trunk between her and the body.

Eventually the rain slowed, and storm began to move on. She was trying to find a signal on her phone when she heard the sound of a police siren. A squad car appeared far up the track and slowly made its way toward her, its wheels churning up the waterlogged mud. Two young male officers got out, and Erika walked to meet them, holding up her ID. They looked up at Barbora's body.

"You haven't touched anything? We need to secure the area," one of them said.

"It was suicide," said Erika. "She was with us before she did it."

It was several hours before Erika, Moss, and Peterson were cleared to leave the scene. The fact that Barbora had been in witness protection had hampered efforts to discover who she was. It was getting dark as they drove back toward London. Erika and Moss filled Peterson in on the details.

"So, this Igor Kucerov is responsible for the deaths of Andrea, the three Eastern European girls, and Ivy?" asked Peterson.

"And the girl he killed at Barbora's house. The one he stashed in the sports bag."

"He was arrested for this and went to trial, and he's not in any system or database?"

"He's not in any system as George Mitchell," said Erika. On cue, there was a hiss and a beep as Crane came over the radio.

"Boss, we found an address for Igor Kucerov from the council tax records. He lives in Kilburn; he's thirty-seven, of Romanian-Russian descent. He's married, too. House is in the wife's name, a Rebecca Kucerov. They've got a five-year-old son."

"Jesus," said Moss.

"How long has he been married?" asked Erika.

"Ten years," said Crane.

"Any employment history?"

"He runs a landscape garden maintenance business. He's down as director, but the company is in his wife's name. We're just running our computers to find out if he had any contracts in the locations where the dead girls were found."

There was a pause.

"Do you want us to bring him in?" asked Crane. Erika looked at the clock glowing on the dashboard. It was past five p.m.

"We should be back in London in about two hours," said Peterson, reading her mind.

"No. Hold off bringing him in. I want to be ready for him. Put a surveillance team outside his house. Don't let him know you're there. And keep him in sight."

"Yes, boss."

"We'll be back at Lewisham Row in a couple of hours. In the meantime I want everything you can find on him: bank statements, e-mails, companies he owns, any bankruptcy. Also, check out the wife—full profile. I bet anything else he's hiding stuff in her name too. And try to unlock the new identity they gave Barbora Kardosova. Now she's dead it should be easier."

"We're already working on it," said Crane. He added, "Are you all okay? We heard she topped herself right in front of you."

"We're fine," said Erika. "Now get off this radio and concentrate on Igor Kucerov."

Outside the car it was pitch black. The fields and fens around them were invisible. There were no moon or stars, and barely any light pollution; just the road in front, illuminated by the arc of the headlights. Erika longed to get far away from the bleakness of the fens, from where Barbora's body had swung creaking from the tree. She needed to be back in the city, where buildings crowded around her; where there was noise, and time didn't stand still.

She pulled down the mirror above the passenger seat and its light flicked on. She saw she had mud on her face. Peterson's reflection stared back from behind, bathed in the light.

"It doesn't get any easier, does it, boss? Seeing a dead body," he said.

"No, it doesn't," said Erika. She wiped at the mud with a tissue, and then snapped the mirror shut, plunging the interior of the car back into darkness.

They rode the rest of the way back in silence, conserving their energy for the night ahead.

CHAPTER 60

Erika, Moss, and Peterson arrived back at Lewisham Row Station just after seven p.m. The torrential rain had moved with them during the journey back from Norfolk, and was pelting the car park as they dashed into the reception area. They were met by Crane, who buzzed them through from reception. Erika was impressed to see that the full team had stayed, and the incident room buzzed with activity.

"Good evening, everyone. I take it that Crane has briefed you on what happened?" said Erika. There was a murmured nodding. "Good. Now, what can you give me?"

One of the officers had brought up some towels from the police gym in the basement and threw one each to Moss, Peterson and Erika. They took them gratefully.

"We've gone back through records and found that the girl who was found dumped in the sports bag was seventeen-year-old Nadia Greco. A trial was held in Southwark Crown Court," explained Crane.

"And?" asked Erika, rubbing at her hair with the towel.

"And this is where it gets weird, boss. The trial records have been marked as CMP—closed material procedures."

"What?" asked Erika. "Why would Igor Kucerov's trial be put on the same legal footing as a classified secret intelligence trial?"

"I don't know; as I said, very little is available. The transcripts have been redacted, names blanked out," said Crane.

"How do we know it's his case then?"

"It matches the keyword search I did for the murder—the location where the body was found and the details of the victim weren't classified."

"Are there any details of the trial verdict?" asked Erika.

"It says that the trial collapsed due to insufficient evidence."

"And there's no record of an arrest for an Igor Kucerov or a George Mitchell?"

"No. We've done a Google search on Igor Kucerov, and several of the search results have been removed under the European data protection law. And if Igor Kucerov had a record, it's been wiped. There's nothing for him, or for a George Mitchell, in the database."

"I don't like the sound of this."

"We're gonna keep working, boss."

"What about unlocking Barbora Kardosova's real identity?"

"We're working on it now, but the courts won't open until nine a.m. tomorrow. Witness protection is a highly secretive department; they work on a different computer network."

There was a silence. Erika stood and went over to the whiteboards, where photos of all the victims were pinned up. There were also CCTV stills of Andrea's last sighting, when she had boarded the train, and next to these was the photo taken of her with George Mitchell, now known as Igor Kucerov. There was also a new photo of Igor Kucerov taken from his driving license, and at the end were family photos of the Douglas-Browns on holiday with Barbora Kardosova, before she'd cut her hair short and dyed it blonde, and vanished in the witness protection scheme.

"Okay. I know it's been a long day," said Erika, turning back to face the room. "But we need to get out our spades and start digging. I'm asking a big favor of you all, and I'd like to work on for a few more hours. I want to go back to basics and go over everything to do with this case with a fine-tooth comb. Everything. I'll order in food, coffee; I'm buying. We just have to find *something*. There's a link between Andrea Douglas-Brown, Igor Kucerov and the rest of the murders. We need to find it, and it could be the tiniest thing we've missed. As I always say, there are no stupid questions.

"Now, with this trial being classified, we're dipping our toes into dangerous waters here, but don't be afraid to dig deep, in particular with Sir Simon. He was off-limits before, but he isn't now. We have Barbora Kardosova's recorded statement; I'll get it uploaded to the intranet. Now, who's willing to stay?"

Erika looked expectantly at the full incident room. Slowly, people put their hands in the air. She looked at Moss, who grinned and raised her hand, as did Peterson.

"If I wasn't such a bitter old cow I'd kiss you all. Thank you. Right. Let's make the next few hours count and get to it."

The officers in the incident room sprang into action.

"Where did you get those doughnuts from last time?" asked Crane, coming over with a pile of files.

"Krispy Kreme. You have free rein to order," said Erika. "Where's Marsh?"

"He left early. He's got the weekend off; taking his missus to some kind of art retreat," said Crane.

"I didn't know he was into painting, too," said Erika.

"No, he's dropping her off; it's in Cornwall. I think he's getting some tonight though; he's told us he's not on call...under any circumstances."

"Typical; we're at a crucial point in our investigation and he decides to bugger off on a mini-break."

"You want me to get him on the phone?" asked Crane.

"No, hold off on contacting Chief Superintendent Marsh," said Erika, realizing that this could work to her advantage.

CHAPTER 61

The next morning, Chief Superintendent Marsh lay with Marcie in a beautiful hotel room—the name of the hotel escaped him, but he knew it was far from London with a sweeping view of Dartmoor. Her head lay on his bare chest, and he had that warm post-coital rush. The feel and smell of his wife's skin was intoxicating. It was now light, and they'd woken from a night of repeated love-making, something unheard of since the twins had come along.

The phone beside the bed screamed out, breaking the silence. Marsh rolled over and saw it was nine-thirty in the morning. He reached over, lifted the receiver, and dropped it down into the cradle again.

"Did you order a wake-up call?" murmured Marcie.

"Course not," he said.

"Ooh. That turns me on the most, you not answering the phone," purred Marcie. She kissed him, sliding her hand down over his stomach…

The phone rang again. Marsh cursed, rolled over and yanked the cord from its plug on the wall. He rolled back to her and grinned. "I believe you were about here," he said, placing her hand on his growing erection.

"*Again*? Chief Superintendent." She grinned.

Suddenly, there was a hammering on their door. "Sorry, hello… it's the front desk," came a voice.

"What the hell!" exclaimed Marsh, as Marcie was poised to unroll a condom over the head of his stiff cock.

"Tell him to piss off; this is the last one in the pack," said Marcie.

The hammering came again. "Sir, sir?" quavered the voice of the young boy from the front desk. "I know you said not to bother you under any circumstances, but there's an Assistant Commissioner Oakley waiting on the line. On your phone... Sir? He says if you don't pick up there will be consequences... That's me quoting him... that's what he said."

Marsh leaped up out of bed and scrabbled to reconnect the phone into the wall socket.

"Where the hell have you been, Marsh? We have a situation!" snapped Oakley when Marsh picked up the phone.

"I'm sorry, sir, I didn't know it was you..."

"One of your officers, that bloody Foster woman, showed up on Sir Simon Douglas-Brown's doorstep at five this morning with an armed response unit. She's taken him and his daughter Linda into custody. She's taken Giles Osborne into custody too."

"What the hell?"

"Now I'm up in Scotland, Marsh, on a much needed bloody holiday and I do not want to have to return to London. I trust you will rectify this."

"I will, sir."

"You'd better. I don't often get woken up before nine by someone from the bloody cabinet office. Heads will roll on this one if we're not careful, Marsh."

The call was abruptly disconnected. Marsh stood there, naked, his penis now shriveled to nothing. He picked up the phone again and dialed, shouting that he wanted to speak to DCI Foster. Immediately. Marcie pulled the bedclothes up around her, and bit back her tears. This would be yet another holiday ruined by her husband's work.

CHAPTER 62

Erika and the rest of the team were struggling after little sleep. They had worked into the early hours, piecing the evidence together with the new information, and at one o'clock in the morning they'd experienced a breakthrough. A frenzy of planning had ensued, and at three a.m. Erika had sent everyone home to grab a few hours' sleep, before they came back at first light to begin the first phase of Erika's plan.

It was now eleven a.m. and Erika sat with Moss, Peterson and Crane in the observation suite at Lewisham Row. In front of them were four screens. Each screen showed a police interview room.

In interview room one, Linda Douglas-Brown was agitated and paced up and down, wearing a long dark skirt and a vast tea-stained white jumper covered in black kittens. On the next screen, in interview room two, her father, Simon Douglas-Brown, sat impassively with his hands on the table, staring ahead. Despite being pulled out of bed by a group of officers in armed response gear, he had dressed smartly in dark slacks, a freshly ironed blue shirt, and a V-necked jumper.

On the next screen was interview room three, where Giles Osborne cut a curious figure. He was dressed in skintight bottle-green jeans, his belly barely constrained by a tight T-shirt with a tropical print of palm trees. His greasy hair was parted to one side and he stared up at the camera.

"He hasn't looked away from the camera for twenty minutes," said Crane, tapping his biro against the screen.

"The only one who looks like he hasn't got a care in the world is Igor Kucerov," said Erika, watching the screen of interview room four.

Igor sat behind the table, slouched back in his chair with his legs spread wide. He'd been working out when the police arrived to arrest him at his house on a pleasant middle-class street in Kilburn. He wore a tight white T-shirt with a Nike tick emblazoned across the front, shiny black Nike running shorts and trainers. His body was lean and muscly, and his skin a baked olive color. The stubble he had in the pictures with Andrea was gone. His black eyes flicked up and regarded the camera.

"Let's have a crack at him first," said Erika. Moss and Crane remained in the observation suite, as Erika left with Peterson. They met Igor's solicitor in the corridor, who was a thin, graying man with a neat little mustache. He started to protest as to why his client was being held.

"I will be recommending that my client answers none of your questions until you have credible..."

They moved past the solicitor and entered interview room four. Igor stayed slouched back in his chair. His black eyes looked Erika up and down as she filed in with Peterson. There was a long tone as the recording equipment kicked in.

"It's five minutes past eleven on the morning of January the 24th. I'm Detective Chief Inspector Foster, and with me is Detective Inspector Peterson. Also present is solicitor John Stephens."

Erika and Peterson took a seat opposite Igor and his solicitor. She spent a few moments checking over her paperwork, and then looked up at Igor.

"Okay, Mr. Kucerov. Or should I call you George Mitchell?"

"Call me what you want, darling." He grinned. His voice was deep, with a trace of a Russian accent.

"Could you explain why you use two names?"

He shrugged.

"Do you work for MI5 or MI6? Or are you a secret agent involved in espionage? Perhaps you've signed the Official Secrets Act?"

Igor gave her a lopsided grin, and rubbed at his chin. "No," he said, finally.

"I'm sorry, but these are absurd questions," said the solicitor.

"No, these are valid questions. Were you aware, Mr. Stephens, that your client was tried for the murder of a young woman called Nadia Greco? Her decomposing body was found dumped in a quarry, zipped up in a hold-all."

Erika pushed a photo of Nadia across the table. Her bloated, blackened body could be seen through the open folds of the hold-all.

"The hold-all was traced back to Mr. Kucerov's then-girlfriend, Barbora Kardosova. Nadia Greco had been beaten to death at Barbora's house. Igor's DNA was found at the scene, and Barbora testified against him at his subsequent trial. However, the jury failed to reach a verdict, and the trial collapsed."

The solicitor glanced to one side at Igor.

"Prove it," said Igor, shrugging.

"That's the problem, Igor. The records and transcripts from your trial are now marked as CMP: closed material procedures. This classification is only reserved for criminal trials involving matters that could damage national security. Are you aware of this, Mr. Stephens?"

"I'm aware of what closed material procedures are, yes," said the solicitor, flustered.

"So you'll understand how unusual this is, that this restriction was imposed on your client's murder trial, when he has nothing to do with the secret service," finished Erika. Igor stretched his arms above his head, then moved his neck from side to side with a crack of his joints.

"Maybe I look a bit like James Bond," said Igor.

"No, we don't see that when we look at you," said Peterson, coldly.

"Don't look so sour, mate. Aren't they always talking about having a black James Bond? You could still be in with a chance," replied Igor.

Peterson paused, and slid the photo of Nadia Greco's body closer.

"Please look at the photo, do you recognize this girl?" he asked.

"I'm advising my client not to answer that," said Stephens.

"Okay. How about this photo? This is you and Andrea Douglas-Brown. Are you aware of the Douglas-Brown murder? This photo was taken four days before she died, and this and this..."

Peterson pushed the series of photos across the table, starting with Igor and Andrea standing together outside the Horniman Museum grounds, and moving to the sexually explicit pictures. Igor pursed his lips and sat back.

"This is the same Andrea Douglas-Brown who was found murdered."

"Yes, we're all aware of who she is," snapped the solicitor. "Are you charging my client with her murder?"

Erika ignored him. "You were seen with Andrea just hours before she died, at The Glue Pot pub in Forest Hill..."

"I don't have to answer your questions. I want to leave," said Igor, getting up from his chair.

"Sit down," said Erika. He pursed his lips and folded his arms, still standing. "And you do have to answer my questions. As I said, you were seen with Andrea."

"No. I wasn't seen anywhere, because I wasn't in the UK the night Andrea went missing. I was in Romania from the 31st of December to the 15th of January. I have tickets, and you can check my passport records."

"Is that the records of you, or George Mitchell?"

"You know, it's not against the law to change your name," said Igor. "You're Slovak, yes? And you have a name like Foster?"

"It's my married name," said Erika.

"Married?" asked Igor, raising an eyebrow. "How did that work out?"

"I'll ask that you sit down," shouted Erika, slamming her fist down on the table.

"If you are going to charge my client..." started Mr. Stephens.

Erika stood and left the room.

"DCI Foster has just left the interview room. I'm stopping this interview at eleven-twelve a.m.," said Peterson, rising, then following her out.

"He's a bastard, isn't he?" said Erika when she was outside with Peterson. She was shaking with anger. "I shouldn't have lost it so early with him. He's just so smug... Can you get Crane to check out his alibi, that he was out of the country?"

"Yes, boss. Just don't let him get under your skin. We've only just started. You want to go back in?"

Erika took a deep breath and shook her head. "No. I want to have a crack at Simon Douglas-Brown."

CHAPTER 63

Simon Douglas-Brown's solicitor was equally as gray as Mr. Stephens, but he wore a much better suit. He was waiting outside the interview room, straightening his tie.

"We're in here," said Erika, pointing to the door of interview room one.

"I'll be advising my client not to answer any of your questions until..." he started, but Erika and Peterson moved past him.

Simon glowered at them as they filed in to the interview room. "Just be aware that when I've finished with you, you'll be directing bloody traffic on the Old Kent Road. For the rest of your years on the force!"

Erika and Peterson ignored him, and they all sat. She went through the formalities for the tape and then opened a folder in front of her on the table.

"Where is Linda?" he said. Erika ignored him. "I have a right to know where my daughter is!"

"Linda has been arrested, and is here in detention," said Peterson.

"You leave Linda out of this, you hear me? She's not well!" shouted Simon.

"Not well?"

"She's under a lot of stress; she's not fit to be interrogated."

"Who informed you that we're going to interrogate her?" asked Erika.

"When police officers rock up at my door at the crack of dawn in riot gear with guns, they don't want a chat. I presume of course... I'm warning you..."

"Your wife is in reception. Where is your son, David?" asked Erika.

"He's on a stag weekend, with friends, in Prague."

"Where is he staying?"

"I don't know, a pub or hotel; could be a youth hostel for all I know. It's a stag party."

"A stag party for who?" asked Peterson.

"One of his friends from university is getting married. I can get the information from my secretary; she booked it all."

"We'll do that," said Peterson. There was a pause as Erika flicked through her file.

"You run several companies in connection with your business and personal affairs, is that correct?" she asked.

"What a stupid question. Of course that's correct."

"One is called Millgate Ltd, yes?"

"Yes."

"And you have another one called... Peckinpath."

"Yes."

"Quantum, Burbridge, Newton Quarry..."

The solicitor leaned across the table toward Erika.

"I don't see why you feel the need to read this out to my client, DCI Foster. He's well aware of his business interests; these are all public limited companies and this information is in the public domain."

Simon sat back, alert but furious.

"Yes, that's correct," said Erika. "I just needed confirmation for the tape, before I proceed. Sorry to waste your client's *valuable time*... So, I'll ask again."

"Yes, yes, yes. Is that loud enough for your bloody tape?"

"I would like to draw your attention to one of your bank statements from the month of September last year." Erika took a sheet of paper from her folder and laid it on the desk. Simon leaned forward.

"Hang on, why do you have this? On whose authority?"

"On *my* authority," said Erika. "A payment was made by you to Cosgrove Holdings Ltd, which is the registered company behind Yakka Events—Giles Osborne's Yakka Events. The sum was for forty-six thousand pounds." Erika tapped the figure on the statement with her finger.

"Yes, I've invested in the company," said Simon, sitting back and eyeballing Erika.

She took out another bank statement. "I also have one of Giles Osborne's bank statements. For Cosgrove Holdings Ltd, for the same date, which shows the forty-six thousand pounds goes in to the account..."

"Where is this going?" asked the solicitor. Erika held up her hand and carried on.

"But on the same day, your forty-six thousand pounds goes back out again."

Simon started to laugh, and looked around the room to see if anyone would laugh with him. Peterson remained stony-faced. "Why don't you ask Giles? I'm not involved in the day-to-day running of his company. I'm a sleeping partner."

"But you invested forty-six thousand pounds. That's a lot to be just a sleeping partner?"

"Define a lot? To me, forty-six thousand pounds is not a vast sum of money...I'm sure for you, with a police salary, it's a lot more."

"With that taken into account, surely you and Giles would have at least agreed what your investment would have entailed?" said Erika.

"I trust Giles and, if you remember, before the brutal murder of my daughter, I was welcoming Giles into my family as my son-in-law."

Simon's angry mask cracked, and they saw the raw pain from the loss of Andrea.

"Okay, so as your son-in-law, did Giles share with you why the forty-six thousand pounds was paid straight out to a company called Mercury Investments Ltd?"

Simon looked across at his solicitor.

"Yes or no? It's a simple question," said Erika. "Yes or no, did Giles share why the forty-six thousand pounds was paid back out to a company called Mercury Investments Ltd?"

"No."

"Do you know of a company called Mercury Investments?"

"No."

"It's registered to a Rebecca Kucerov, wife of this man—Igor Kucerov. Just in case you need reminding, we recovered Andrea's second mobile phone with these pictures."

Erika took the explicit photos from the folder and laid them out in front of Simon. He glanced down at them. He closed his eyes and began to shake.

The solicitor leaned in and started to gather them up. "I object to my client being shown these distressing photos of his daughter, who has only just been buried..."

"But what does your client have to say about this forty-six thousand pounds? We believe this man, Igor Kucerov, is linked to the illegal trafficking of young Eastern European woman to the United Kingdom. He was also tried for the murder of a young girl called Nadia Greco."

"Was he convicted?" asked Simon, sharply.

"No, but even without a conviction it adds up to a damming link. So I'll ask you again. Do you know why Giles

Osborne transferred the forty-six thousand pounds to Igor Kucerov?"

Simon sat back, looking rattled.

"My client has no comment."

"Right," said Erika. She gave Peterson a look and they both stood.

"And?" asked the solicitor.

"We're suspending this interview for the time being," said Erika.

"What time did you say it was?" asked Simon.

"It's twelve-fifteen p.m.," said Erika.

"I'd like to talk to Linda, NOW," he said.

Erika ignored him as she and Peterson left the interview room.

CHAPTER 64

"He looks like he's going a bit nuts in there," said Moss when they were back in the observation suite. They looked at the four screens. Simon was in the middle of a rant about "that bitch policewoman" having no right to deny him access to his daughter.

"Perhaps they all need to sweat it out for a bit," said Peterson.

"Yes, but remember we've only got them for twenty-four hours. If we can't charge them, then we have to let them go."

"If only we could re-arrest Kucerov for the murder of Nadia Greco," said Moss.

"We don't have any new evidence. And our time wouldn't be used effectively trying. We need to get him on this link with the money from Simon and Giles," said Erika. "And Linda is the link to Andrea and Igor."

On the next screen, Linda was now sitting with her head on the table of the interview room, absentmindedly tracing circles on the scratched tabletop.

On the screen below, Igor sat back, legs splayed, resting his head against the wall. Giles remained impassive too, sitting in his chair and looking around, almost as if a waiter had forgotten his order.

"Let's take a few minutes," said Erika. She grabbed her cigarettes and made her way outside.

When she came out onto the steps of the front entrance, Diana Douglas-Brown was just lighting up a cigarette. She stood at the bottom of the steps, and wore a long, black fur coat. Her hair was immaculately blow-dried and feathered around her exhausted face.

Erika was about to turn and go back inside when Diana noticed her.

"DCI Foster, what's happening?"

"We're conducting our interviews," said Erika, with an air of finality.

She went to go back indoors but Diana said, "Please, would you give this to Linda?" She reached into the folds of her coat and held out a tiny stuffed cat on a key ring. It was black with soft brown eyes and a tiny piece of faded pink material for a tongue.

"I'm afraid I can't, I'm sorry," said Erika.

"Please…you don't understand, Linda needs familiarity." Diana took a drag on her cigarette. "When I gave birth to her, she was starved of oxygen. She has emotional problems. She can't cope with the world!" The last part was almost shouted.

"Our Duty Sergeant can have a doctor here within minutes, but Linda is fine, I promise you. We just want to ask her some questions."

Diana burst into tears. She bowed her head and her hair fell forward, covering her face. She brought the tiny stuffed cat to her face and sobbed. Erika turned and went back into the reception area.

"It checks out," said Crane, meeting her when she arrived back in the incident room. "I have a passenger manifest saying Igor Kucerov left the country on December 31st from London Luton Airport on a flight to Romania. He flew back on January 15th."

"Shit!" said Erika. All eyes turned to her. "What if he did something in-between? Have you got CCTV evidence of him walking through that departure gate?" she added.

"Boss, this is information from Passport and Immigration."

"I know, but we've got stuff here from the CPS and court records which have been altered. It shows Igor Kucerov was given some special treatment during a trial! Someone has been in and altered official records...Could he have come back on a bus, a car or a coach, and then gone back and..."

Crane scratched his head. "It's feasible, boss, I suppose."

"Let's stop supposing and find out. I want pictures from passport control, CCTV when he arrived in Romania; a digital footprint confirming that Igor Kucerov left the country on December 31st and came back on January the 15th."

"Yes, boss."

"And remember, the clock is ticking," said Erika, looking at her watch. "We've got nineteen hours."

Erika came back outside and met Peterson and Moss in the corridor. She told them that Igor Kucerov could have been out of the country when Andrea vanished.

"So this means that he didn't kill Andrea, or Ivy. We can't pin him directly to their murders," said Moss.

Erika shook her head.

"What about the other girls? Tatiana Ivanova, Mirka Bratova and Karolina Todorova? We have the dates when they were discovered. Can we find out where he was?" asked Peterson.

"There are only loose forensics for the first three girls, and for the times when they vanished. Besides, I came out publicly and linked those three murders with Andrea and Ivy. And I believe they are linked. Unless it's a copycat? Jesus, this is just so complicated," said Erika, rubbing her face. She saw a look pass between Moss and Peterson. "What is it? Spit it out."

"Simon Douglas-Brown's solicitor is really kicking off. He's been trying to phone the Assistant Commissioner," explained Moss.

"He's trying to phone Oakley?"

"Yes. And it wasn't through the switchboard; he has Oakley's direct line."

"Did he get through?"

"No, not yet. Oakley is away on a mini-break."

"He's on a mini-break. Marsh is wining and dining his wife on a painting holiday... Who the hell is in charge around here?"

"Well, boss. Technically, you are," explained Peterson.

"Good point. Okay, well, let's have a crack at Giles Osborne," said Erika, determinedly.

CHAPTER 65

Giles Osborne sat in the interview room with an embittered face, as Erika and Peterson filed in with Giles Osborne's solicitor, another gray man in a good suit, called Phillip Saunders.

After Erika had read out the formalities for the tape, she put the same questions to Giles, asking about the forty-six thousand pounds he had received from Simon Douglas-Brown and why he had then transferred it to Mercury Investments, owned by Igor Kucerov.

Giles leaned toward his solicitor, his mouth close to the man's ear, murmuring.

"My client would need to appraise his accounts fully, to answer on this matter," said the solicitor.

"Here's the bank statements," said Erika, pushing them across the table. "You can clearly see the money coming into one account, and going out to the other. How much more do you need to appraise? Mercury Investments is a landscape gardening company. Yakka Events have very little in the way of gardens."

Giles tapped his finger to his lips, pausing. Finally, he said, "I believe that the money was used to source a rare tree from New Zealand."

"What?" said Peterson.

"I wanted it to be the centerpiece of my courtyard, the tree. I forget its name," said Giles, smoothly. "I can, in due course, produce an invoice with proof of this. You are aware that Mr. Kucerov owns a landscape gardening business?"

"Yes," said Erika.

"Then, mystery solved. That is why I transferred forty-six thousand pounds to his account."

"He trims hedges and mows lawns, albeit on a large scale," said Erika.

"And Simon Douglas-Brown has no knowledge of this deal?" added Peterson.

"And why would he? He was a sleeping partner. We agreed he would buy a certain amount of shares, making him a part owner in Yakka Events. I believe he now owns 13.8%, to be precise. But, as you can see, I can't access that information because you dragged me out of bed first thing in the morning and confiscated my devices." Giles smiled at Erika sarcastically.

"How were you introduced to Igor Kucerov?" asked Erika.

"Through Andrea," he said.

"And you are aware that Andrea was involved in a sexual relationship with Kucerov?"

"At the time, no. You've since shown me photographs, of course."

"Do you know how Andrea met Igor Kucerov?"

"I think she said something about, um, a friend—Barbora something..."

"Kardosova, Barbora Kardosova?"

"I think so, yes."

"And did you know that Barbora Kardosova was involved in a relationship with Igor Kucerov?"

Giles looked baffled and shook his head.

"My client has answered your questions in relation to the forty-six thousand pound investment; I don't see why he has to answer questions about the friend of his fiancée's private relationships," said the solicitor.

Erika and Peterson stared at Giles across the table.

"That's all for now," said Erika.

"And my client can leave?" asked the solicitor.

"I didn't say that." Erika and Peterson stood up.

"And what now?" asked the solicitor.

"We'll be back," said Erika.

They filed out into the corridor and back to the observation suite.

"Bloody hell," said Erika, eyeing Moss and Peterson.

"Do you think the rare tree bullshit will fly in court, if we got there?" asked Moss, who had been watching everything on the screens.

"We've seen his office, full of pretentious touches. It fits with what he's saying," sighed Peterson.

"Yes, but where is the tree?" asked Erika. "The money was paid over a year ago."

"Maybe they're waiting for it to grow," remarked Moss, darkly.

There was a knock on the door of the observation suite. It was Woolf.

"Boss, I've got Marsh on the phone. He's demanding to talk to you. He's in his car on his way back to London."

"Does he say where he is?"

"Still in Devon," said Woolf.

"Tell him you can't find me."

"Boss, he knows you're interviewing them all."

"Use your brain, Woolf. Make something up. I'll face the consequences; just get us more time."

"Yes, boss," said Woolf. When he'd gone, they looked back at the screens.

"Let's see what Igor has to say about this," said Erika. "And then let's bring Linda into the mix."

CHAPTER 66

"He wanted me to find a tree for his office," said Igor, sitting back in his chair and stretching his arms above his head. Erika noticed he had yellow patches under his arms, and that the interview room was now starting to smell of stale sweat.

"And you can do that, in your capacity as a landscape gardener?" asked Erika.

"This is London; most people want crazy stuff in their gardens, and with the Internet it's easy."

"Why is the company in your wife's name?"

"It just is."

"And who introduced you to Giles?" asked Peterson, even though they knew the answer.

"Andrea, of course." Igor grinned.

"And does your wife know about Andrea?"

"What do you think?"

"Did she know about your relationship with Barbora Kardosova?"

"My wife is a good woman!"

"What does that mean? She knows when to keep her mouth shut? Looks the other way? Does she know you are involved in the trafficking of young Eastern European girls to London? That you pick them up at Victoria Coach Station?" asked Erika.

"My client doesn't have to answer these questions. This is mere speculation. You have no evidence," interrupted the solicitor.

"We have a recorded interview with Barbora Kardosova where she states all of this, and that you murdered Nadia Greco."

"And where is this witness?" asked the solicitor.

"She committed suicide shortly after the interview," said Erika, watching Igor. "She was so scared of speaking the truth about you, that she killed herself."

"I hardly call that a credible witness, a suicidal woman. And this wasn't a sworn deposition," said the solicitor.

Igor sat back in his chair, smug and confident.

Igor's solicitor continued. "Whilst you have been flitting between interview rooms, I took the opportunity to review the trial documents in question. What you claim is nothing more than that: a claim. Great swathes of the trial records have been redacted. From a legal standpoint, they don't exist. You realize that very soon you are going to have to charge my client? Time is ticking, Miss Foster."

"It's DCI Foster," said Erika, trying to hide her frustration. She added that she was suspending the interview, and after reading out the time stamp for the tape, she and Peterson left.

CHAPTER 67

Erika, Moss, and Peterson were about to file into interview room three to speak to Linda, when the solicitor reminded them that legally their suspects were due a meal break. An hour later, and it was late afternoon. The day seemed to be vanishing.

"Linda, do you know why we've arrested you?" asked Erika.

Linda sat back in her chair, cool and collected. "You think I have information. You think that I knew someone who killed Andrea? You think I killed Andrea, or perhaps you think I shot JR? Or President Kennedy."

"This isn't funny, Linda. This is Igor Kucerov; he's also been using the name George Mitchell. Andrea was involved in a sexual relationship with him before and while she was with Giles," said Erika, pushing his photo across the table.

Linda stared at the photos laid out in front of her, regarding the explicit ones impassively.

"We know he took this photo of you and Andrea," Erika added.

"You don't know that," Linda sniffed, her eyes darting between the officers. "How can you know that?"

"Because we've arrested Igor Kucerov on suspicion of Andrea's murder, and the murders of Tatiana Ivanova, Mirka Bratova, Karolina Todorova and Ivy Norris. Right now he's being interviewed in the next room," said Erika.

"You're lying, and I don't talk to liars. Do I have to talk to these liars?" asked Linda, looking to her solicitor.

"Do you have evidence that this photo of my client was taken by the man you state?" asked the solicitor.

Erika ignored him. "Do you remember a girl called Barbora; she was friend of Andrea's?"

"Yes."

"She accompanied your family on a couple of summer holidays?"

"She was sweet; perhaps a little too sweet—and eager. Even so, too good for Andrea, and surprise, surprise, Andrea chased her away."

"How did she chase her away?"

"Oh, the usual. At first she thought Barbora was the bee's knees, then her excitement cooled and she made the girl feel like the poor relative. When she joined us on our last holiday, Barbora had lost a lot of weight; she was emaciated. Andrea thought it was the height of fashion. That was probably enough to excommunicate the poor girl."

"Did Andrea say where Barbora went?"

"She just said she moved away. Why?" asked Linda, narrowing her eyes.

Erika explained Barbora's connection to Igor, and that she had been sexually involved with Igor at the same time as Andrea.

"May I remind you that this information has been redacted," said the solicitor.

"The fact that Barbora was in a sexual relationship with Igor Kucerov and that she went into the witness protection scheme and committed suicide is not redacted," said Erika. She noticed that Linda was shaking, her eyes filling with tears which spilled down her cheeks.

"How did she do it?" asked Linda.

"She hung herself. She was terrified. So now do you see how important it is that we find out the truth about Igor Kucerov? He is linked directly to Andrea."

Linda wiped away her tears. "I met him a couple of times, at a club in Kensington and a pub in Chiswick. As I've said before, Andrea got loads of male attention; she was always stringing them along. Andrea used men like tampons: she was happy to have them up her for a short time, but then she flushed them away."

There was a silence. The solicitor couldn't hide his distaste. Erika opened a folder, took the note she'd received, and placed it in front of Linda.

"What can you tell me about this?" asked Erika, watching Linda's face.

"It's the same note you showed me before. When you came by the florist." She looked up at Erika. "It was sent to you?"

"Yes. You can see that as well as being personal to me, it taunts the police about the death of Andrea, and the other murder victims."

"And why are you showing me?" asked Linda, icily.

"Linda, we've seen your record. You've made it quite a habit, sending threatening mail. You've previously sent letters to Giles Osborne, and others. Teachers, a doctor, Andrea's friends. You even sent letters to Barbora. She spoke of it in her interview, which we have on record."

"Again, DCI Foster, this is all circumstantial," said the solicitor. "You are crudely attempting to connect the dots, and trying to trick my client into talking. She won't."

"Well, she can talk, or her silence can be just as damning. Linda, it's you, your father, Giles, Barbora, Igor. You are all connected. We have your laptop and the hard drive is being searched. We've seized computers from your father and Giles. It's only a matter of time before we link it all together. Talk to me, Linda; I can help you."

"No. I won't," said Linda, sitting back in her chair. She picked some fluff from her jumper, and then regarded the officers. She now seemed in full control of her emotions. Erika could barely hide her frustration.

"You like cats?" asked Peterson.

"Oh dear, we are desperate, aren't we?" Linda smiled, flirtatiously. "Mr. Lloyd should I go ahead and answer that? I wouldn't want to implicate myself in a cat scandal too."

The solicitor rolled his eyes and nodded.

"Yes, DI Peterson, I like cats."

"Do you have a cat?"

"Not right now," she said, stiffly.

"Do you have any other *relevant* questions?" asked Mr. Lloyd.

"No. That's all for now," said Erika, trying to save face. When they came back outside into the corridor, Woolf was waiting.

"What?" she snapped.

"It's Marsh."

"Not now. I'll call him back."

"He's here, in his office, and he wants to speak to you."

CHAPTER 68

Marsh was pacing up and down in front of the window when Erika knocked on the door of his office. When she entered, he stopped and stared at her. He wore crisp white chinos, an open-necked shirt, and had an arty flat cap on his head. Despite everything, Erika had to suppress a smile.

"Are you going for the David Beckham look, sir? Or is that your painting outfit?"

"Sit down," he said, pulling off the hat and chucking it on the papers piled high on his desk. "Are you out of your mind, DCI Foster? Do you know the shit storm you've stirred up, arresting the Douglas-Browns? I've had calls coming in from the cabinet office."

He seemed weary, fed up of the whole situation.

"Sir, if you'll listen..."

"No. I'm ordering you to release Sir Simon, Linda, Giles Osborne *and* Igor Kucerov from custody, do you understand? You've exposed someone in the witness protection scheme, you've been openly discussing the details of a criminal trial marked CMP..."

"Sir, Barbora Kardosova killed herself, which means she is no longer in witness protection." Erika went on to explain the money transfer between Simon, Giles and Igor, and the statement from Barbora, linking Igor to the trafficking of Eastern European women. She left out the doubt about him being in the UK at the time of Andrea's murder. "You've got to admit, sir, even as a coincidence all this stinks."

Marsh had listened intently. He was now breathing heavily, and continued to pace up and down. She could almost see the cogs turning.

"What time is it?" he asked.

"It's coming up to five," said Erika.

"And when is their twenty-four hours in custody up?"

"Nine a.m. tomorrow."

"Have they had an evening meal break?"

"Not yet."

"Okay, and they are entitled to an uninterrupted eight hours' rest."

"I know, sir. I need more time. Will you consider extending, giving me another twelve hours? I can't authorize it and you can. I'm waiting on forensics. They took Simon's laptop, and Linda's too. There are also bank statements we're going through."

"No. I can't extend." Marsh came and sat down. "Look, Erika. You are a brilliant officer…"

"Sir, you always say that, right before you tell me not to do something."

Marsh paused. "I say it because it's true. Also, because I can see how this is going to end. You're going up against powerful people here, and the odds are not in your favor."

"Sounds very *Hunger Games*…"

"I'm serious, Erika. Release your suspects and I will do the best I can to protect you."

"Protect me?" asked Erika, incredulously.

"Erika, are you blind to how things work? The establishment always wins. We've both seen it. You lack credible evidence. Please. Walk away. Save your career. Sometimes you have to let things go."

"No. I'm sorry, sir. That's not good enough. Five women have died. *Five*. What right do people in the so-called establishment have to get away with covering it all up? So they can make more money? Keep hold of their cozy lives?"

"You know what will happen, don't you? You could lose your badge, your reputation."

"Sir, I've had almost everything taken from me. Mark, a life I loved up north surrounded by friends, a place I can call home. The only thing I have to hold on to is a sense of morality, and that until nine a.m. tomorrow I might still get justice for these women."

Marsh stared at her. The anger between them had gone. All that was between them was a messy desk, but it was as if they sat on either side of a vast canyon. And Erika was on the side that had the least stability.

"Okay. You've got until nine a.m. tomorrow to make a case. And you'll take the consequences," said Marsh.

"Thank you, sir."

Erika got up and left his office, noting the sadness in his eyes.

CHAPTER 69

Erika and her team continued to question the suspects, but as early evening slipped away, the case seemed to go with it. Igor, Simon, Giles and Linda sensed their lack of evidence and grew confident, clamming up and running circles around their questioning. Their solicitors were incredulous when Erika announced that they would be kept overnight and questioned again in the morning.

It was close to midnight, and Crane and Erika were the last two left in the incident room.

"Is there anything else I can do, boss?" said Crane, appearing at her shoulder. "We're still waiting on the airport CCTV on Igor Kucerov. I don't think anything will come through for the next few hours."

Erika was reviewing the details of the case going back to Andrea's abduction. Her computer screen blurred in front of her. "No. Go home and get some rest," she said.

"You too. Are you back at your flat?"

"No. The Met has sprung for a hotel room. Until I get sorted."

"Where are you?"

"Park Hill Hotel."

Crane whistled. "It's nice. Had my nan's ninetieth there. Nice golf course, too. Night."

"See you tomorrow, bright and early," said Erika as he left.

It was after midnight when she arrived at the hotel. When she came into her smart, elegant room, she felt a million miles away from the case. The distance didn't help.

She woke at four-thirty, drenched in sweat, from the now familiar dream. Gunshots ringing around her, and Mark collapsing to the ground. She closed her eyes, the last image burned into her brain: the back of his head blown away by a shotgun.

It was sweltering. She got out of bed and went to the window, feeling the radiator underneath pumping out heat. Her room was on the sixth floor, and beyond the inky blackness of the golf course she could see houses, rows of houses packed together toward Lewisham. A few had lights on, but most were in darkness. The window only opened two inches. An anti-suicide lock stopped it.

"I just want cold air," she said. "I'm not going kill myself."

Erika dressed and went downstairs to the large plush lobby, which was empty save for a bleary-eyed receptionist. He looked up from playing solitaire and gave her a nod.

She relished the sensation as she hit the freezing air outside. There was a row of benches along the front of the building. She chose the first, and pulled a cigarette from the packet, lighting up and exhaling a stream of smoke into the night sky. She shivered, shaking the dream off her, and forced her thoughts back to the investigation.

Maybe this would be that case. The one that got away. Every police officer was haunted by an unsolved case. She flicked her ash on the gravel and there was a meow as a large black cat appeared from under the bench and rubbed itself against her legs.

"Hello," she said, leaning down to stroke it. The cat purred and strutted off to a couple of little dishes under one of the bay windows. It lapped at some water and then sniffed the bowl next to it, which was empty.

Linda Douglas-Brown came to the front of Erika's mind. *Linda the cat lady.* So much evidence linked back to her. Linda was supposed to meet Andrea that night at the cinema, but didn't. She'd watched the film with David. They knew that much, but what had happened afterward? Linda, and her obsession with cats. What did she know about Linda? Was she a victim in life? She was obviously not a favorite with her family. She was bitter and envious. She *could* have killed Andrea, but what about the other women? The prostitutes who had been involved with Igor? Linda knew of Igor, she'd met him. What if she also knew that Igor had killed the three prostitutes? She could have seized the opportunity to make Andrea's murder look like a copycat killing? Copycat. Linda the cat lady.

It went round in Erika's mind. Yet Linda didn't have a cat. Peterson had asked her in the interview if she had a cat. She had answered him weirdly—*not right now*—and a look had passed across her face, a strange look. Erika hadn't picked up on it at the time, but now it blared out at her.

Erika went back up to her room, where she dressed quickly, and, after passing the disinterested lad on reception for the second time, she drove over to Lewisham Row Station. It was now just after five in the morning. She wasn't familiar with the night desk sergeant, but he signed out the keys to her for the Douglas-Brown house.

The roads were quiet as she drove over to Chiswick. The office buildings loomed tall and empty as she navigated her way through Elephant and Castle, crossing the Thames at Blackfriars Bridge and then following the river along the Embankment. The view of the water was dimmed by a low fog, which turned blue as the dawn broke.

Erika placed a call to Moss, but she got her answering machine.

"Hi, it's Erika. It's coming up to five-thirty. I'm just on my way over to the Douglas-Brown house. Something is bugging me about Linda. I want to take a look at her bedroom. If I'm not back by seven, interview her again—and get Peterson to lead; she seems to have taken a shine to him. Get her talking about cats; I know it sounds mad but I think there's something there, I can't put my finger on it... She's cat crazy, but she doesn't have a cat..."

Her phone gave three bleeps and then cut off.

"Shit!" Erika cried, looking down at her dead phone. She'd barely been back at the hotel long enough to charge it.

She arrived on Chiswick High Road. She tucked her phone in her pocket and parked on one of the back streets, realizing she would have to be quick, and would need to travel back on the underground to have any hope of making it to the station before the twenty-four hours expired.

CHAPTER 70

The Douglas-Brown house sat resplendent at the end of the cul-de-sac, dominating the street like a polished, buttery block. Mist hung in the air, and the street lights blinked off as she reached the house. The front gate was well-oiled and opened soundlessly. The bay windows stared back at her blankly. She went to the front door and pressed the bell, hearing it ring deep from within the house. A moment passed, then she started to try the bunch of keys in the front lock. The third key she tried opened the door. She listened for a moment and then came inside, closing the door behind her.

She made for the hallway, past the grandfather clock with its swinging pendulum, and into the vast steel and granite kitchen. It was still and immaculate. Copper pots hung from a frame above a large black granite island, and the back wall was floor-to-ceiling glass. Beyond, she could see the landscaped garden. A blackbird landed on the smooth grass, but seeing Erika move inside, it took flight.

Erika came back out and climbed the sweeping staircase up to the second floor, moving past smart, neutral guest rooms, a marble bathroom, until at the end of the corridor, at the back of the house, Erika found Linda's room. The door was closed with a small sign saying: *WELCOME TO LINDA'S BEDROOM, PLEASE KNOCK BEFORE ENTERING.* Under it, and almost obliterated with crossings-out, was written: cos i might not be wearing any knickers! Erika couldn't help but smile, and thought it must have been David. Little brothers liked to tease. She opened the door and went inside.

CHAPTER 71

"I've had a message from the boss," said Moss, when she came into the incident room. Peterson had arrived at the same time, bringing in a tray of coffee. He was handing them out to the officers who were arriving bleary-eyed and taking off their coats.

"She wants us to go ahead and bring Linda back first for questioning."

"Has her solicitor showed up yet?" asked Peterson.

"Yeah, I just saw him in reception. He doesn't look happy, being pulled in at this ungodly hour."

"Oh well, it will all be over by nine," said PC Singh, coming up and going to grab the last coffee.

"Sorry. I need that one," snapped Moss. "Go and get one from the machine."

"That was a bit harsh," said Peterson, when Singh had walked off.

"She made it sound like we're just clock-watching until nine a.m.... Like it's a formality."

"Isn't it?" asked Peterson, awkwardly.

"No," said Moss, pointedly. "Now listen, the boss has had an idea..."

CHAPTER 72

Linda's bedroom was small and gloomy. A sash window with a deep cushioned window seat overlooked the garden, and from above Erika could see that the lawn was still dotted with a few patches of dirty snow. A heavy dark wardrobe stood beside the window. The door creaked as Erika opened it. On one side hung a selection of dark voluminous skirts; next to these was a block of crisply ironed white blouses, some with lacework on the collar; and the rest of the wardrobe was taken up by a huge selection of cat jumpers, all thick and heavy. At the bottom of the wardrobe was a jumble of court shoes, some sensible sandals, a pair of powder-blue running shoes, a dusty pair of ice skates, and a pink Thighmaster.

A single bed with a dark wood frame was tucked in the corner against the back wall, and above its curved wooden headboard was a thick metal crucifix. A line of toy cats sat guard on the neatly made patchwork bedspread. They were arranged in descending height order. Their Disney-esque eyes looked heartbreakingly optimistic among the sad gloom. Erika paused for a moment to consider that Linda had made her bed and arranged the cats before she was hauled into a police car.

On the bedside table was a small, Tiffany-style lamp, and a little curved plastic box containing a clear plastic bite guard. There was also a small picture in a frame taken a few years back, of Linda sitting on a swing chair in the garden with a beautiful black cat on her lap. It had white fur on its paws. Erika picked up the frame and turned it over, unhooking the metal clasps and pulling off the cardboard backing. On the back of the photo, in a neat hand was written:

My darling boy, Boots, and me.

Erika held on to the photo as she carried on looking around. An old-fashioned secretary desk in matching dark wood was against the wall at the end of the bed. It was filled with pens and a girly stationery set. A large square in the dust showed where the police had removed Linda's laptop. A dressing table between the window and the secretary desk held the bare minimum of makeup, a large pot of E45 cream and a bag of cotton wool balls. A brush lay on its side, and strands of Linda's mousy hair caught the light from the window. Beside the door was a large bookcase crammed with novels by Jackie Collins and Judith Krantz, and scores of historical romance novels. There were a couple of photos from the family holidays in Croatia, Portugal, and Slovakia—mainly of Linda and Andrea with various stray cats—and there was a photo of Linda standing at the base of a cliff with a large tanned guy with dirty blond hair. Linda wore climbing gear and a red plastic hard hat. She was grinning so hard that the chinstrap cut into her shiny tanned face. There was nothing written on the back of the photo.

On the wall beside the door was a large pinboard with a photo collage. The photos were pinned overlapping and were all of Boots, the beautiful black cat with the white paws: Linda sat astride a bike with a wicker basket where Boots perched on a blanket; Linda on a swing in the garden with Boots on her lap; Andrea and Linda eating breakfast in the kitchen, Boots sprawled on his back across the middle of the breakfast bar holding a piece of toast in his white paws. Linda and Andrea's heads were thrown back laughing. There was a picture of Boots on Simon's desk, lounging on a pile of paperwork. Despite him being in the middle of something, he had allowed Linda to take a photo of his work being disrupted. Erika began to remove the pins and take away the photos. In several of the photos, where they overlapped, a figure had either been cut out, or the end of the photo had been snipped off unevenly. Scanning the photos of family gatherings, Erika realized who the missing person was.

CHAPTER 73

Linda looked drained when Peterson entered the interview room. Her hair was tousled, and she didn't look like she'd got much sleep in her cell. The solicitor finished polishing his glasses and put them back on.

"Here, I got you a coffee, Linda," said Peterson, sitting opposite and pushing the takeaway cup toward her. The solicitor saw Peterson had a coffee of his own, and looked annoyed that he hadn't been included.

Peterson tilted up his cup to the light. "Look, they never get it right; I said my name was Peterson. They've written 'Peter Son.'"

Linda stared at him for a moment, and then reached out for her cup and checked the side.

"They got my name right," she said. She turned the cup and her face broke into a smile. "Oh, and they drew a little cat! Look!" She twisted the cup round so Peterson could see.

"I thought you'd like that." Peterson grinned.

Linda's eyes narrowed. "I see what you're doing," she said. She sat back and pushed the cup away. "I'm not that easy."

"I never thought you were," said Peterson. He read out his name and the time and the interview tape started recording.

"Linda, you said yesterday you didn't have a cat."

"No. I don't," she said, cautiously sipping at her coffee.

"Did you?"

"Yes, I did," she said softly. "His name was Boots."

"Boots?"

"Yes, he was black, but he had four white paws, like he was wearing boots..."

The minutes ticked by, and Linda became quite animated, talking about Boots. She was just telling Peterson about how Boots used to sleep under the covers with her, with his head on her pillow, when the solicitor interrupted.

"Look, DI Peterson, what has this got to do with your investigation?"

"I'm talking about my cat, thank you very much," Linda snapped back.

"I'm working for you here, Miss Douglas-Brown..."

"Yes, you are, and I'm talking about my fucking cat, okay?"

"Yes, very well," said the solicitor.

Linda turned back from the solicitor to Peterson. "I'm sick of people who think cats are just pets. They're not. They're such intelligent, beautiful creatures..."

Back in the observation room, Moss and Crane were watching. "Keep her talking about Boots," said Moss into a microphone. Inside the interview room her voice came quietly through the earpiece Peterson wore.

"Did Boots have a middle name? I had a dog called Barnaby Clive," said Peterson.

"No. He was Boots Douglas-Brown; that was quite enough. I wish I had a middle name, or even a nicer name than just boring old Linda."

"I dunno; I like the name Linda," said Peterson.

"But Boots is so much more exotic..."

"And, what happened to Boots? I take it she's not still with us?" asked Peterson.

"He, Boots was a HE...And no. He's not with us," said Linda. She gripped the edge of the desk.

"Are you okay? Is this upsetting to talk about how Boots died?" pressed Peterson.

"Of course it was upsetting. He DIED!" shouted Linda.

There was a silence.

"Okay, this is good, Peterson, keep on at her. We're breaking her down," said Moss, in his ear.

CHAPTER 74

The Douglas-Brown house was silent, and felt heavy and oppressive with secrets and unanswered questions. Erika hadn't noticed how long she'd spent in Linda's bedroom, staring at the family photos and absorbing the sadness emanating from Linda's possessions. She was now moving down the corridor, still clutching the photos of Boots the cat, and checking to see what was behind the doors. She passed empty guest bedrooms, a large bathroom, a huge linen closet, and two picture windows in the corridor which looked onto the bare back wall of the house next door.

At the other end of the floor, at the furthest point from Linda's room, Erika found David's bedroom. The door was open.

In comparison to Linda's, it was stylish and bright with a large metal-framed double bed, and a long mirrored wardrobe. A poster of Che Guevara was framed on one wall, next to a Pirelli calendar showcasing a beautiful blonde for January, her arms crossed over her bare chest. There was a faint smell of expensive aftershave, and on a large desk was a silver MacBook laptop, which was open, and beside it an iPod, docked into a large speaker set. On the wall above was a rack with six pairs of Skullcandy headphones in assorted bright colors. Erika spied a phone charger snaking out from behind the desk, and she pulled out her iPhone and hooked it up. A few moments passed and, when she saw it starting to charge, she switched it on. She went to the open MacBook, and brushed her fingers over the trackpad. The screen lit up, showing that a password had to be entered. Large black-and-white prints of Battersea Power Station, The National Theatre, and Billingsgate Fish Market adorned the remaining wall space. A large set of shelves was stuffed with books on architecture, ranging from paperback guides to enormous coffee table photo books.

As Erika glanced along the bookshelves, a bright blue cover caught her eye: *Swimming London: London's 50 Greatest Swimming Spots.* Erika pulled the book out and began to leaf through photos of swimming pools and lidos in London. A creeping feeling began to emerge from the pit of her stomach.

CHAPTER 75

Back at Lewisham Row, Moss and Crane were watching the interview unfold on the video screens. Peterson was listening as Linda talked about Boots, her beloved cat. There was a knock, and Woolf put his head round the door.

"This just came through for DCI Foster," said Woolf. He handed Moss a piece of paper. She scanned it quickly.

"This is from Linda Douglas-Brown's private Harley Street physician. He states she is mentally unfit to be questioned by the police."

"Jeez, what are we dealing with here?" said Crane.

"Who brought this in?" asked Moss.

"Diana Douglas-Brown; she's shown up with another lawyer," said Woolf. "You need to stop this interview."

"We've been told she knows nothing, and yet this document is hand-delivered just before seven in the morning?" said Moss.

"You know I have your back, but this goes high up. Establishment stuff. I can see the edge of the cliff approaching," said Crane.

"Just a few minutes more, Woolf. Go back out, come back in ten."

Woolf reluctantly nodded and left.

"Okay, Peterson, push her harder," said Moss, into the microphone.

* * *

"How did he die, Linda?" asked Peterson, back in the interview room. "How did Boots die?"

Linda's bottom lip was now trembling and she gripped the coffee cup, running her finger over the tiny cartoon cat. "None of your business."

"Were your family upset when Boots passed?"

"Yes."

"Andrea and David, they must have been younger, too?"

"Of course they were younger! Andrea was upset, But David..." Linda's face clouded over; she bit down hard on her lip.

"What about David?" asked Peterson.

"Nothing. He was upset too," said Linda, flatly.

"You don't look too convinced. Was David upset, or wasn't he, Linda?"

She started to breathe fast, sucking in air and blowing it out, almost hyperventilating. "He...was...up...set...too," said Linda, her eyes wide, looking at the floor.

"David was upset?" pushed Peterson.

"I JUST SAID HE WAS! HE WAS FUCKING UPSET!" shouted Linda.

"I think this is getting—" started the solicitor, but Peterson went on.

"David's away at a stag party, isn't he, Linda?"

"Yes. I was surprised at how hard it was to let him go," she said. She froze, and frowned.

"He's only gone for a few days, hasn't he?" asked Peterson.

Linda was now crying, tears pouring down her cheeks.

"It's okay...He's coming back, Linda...David is coming back," said Peterson. Linda was now gripping the desk and her face was red, her mouth curled up.

"My client is..." started the solicitor.

"I don't want him back," Linda hissed.

"Linda, why don't you want David back? It's okay, it's me; you can tell me," said Peterson. He could feel the air almost prickling with intensity in the interview room.

"Far away," said Linda darkly. "I want him gone far away... Gone... GONE!"

"Why, Linda? Tell me why; why do you want David gone far away?"

"BECAUSE HE KILLED MY CAT!" she suddenly cried. "HE KILLED BOOTS! Killed Boots! No one believed me! They all thought I was making it up, but he killed my baby cat. He killed Giles's cat too, and made it look like it was me! That fucking bastard..."

"David? David killed your cat?" said Peterson.

"Yes!"

"How did he kill him?" asked Peterson.

Linda was now turning purple, gripping the desk, trying to rock it, but it was bolted to the floor. The words were pouring out of her now. "He strangled him... He strangled him... Like, like..." Linda bit down on her lip so hard that a spot of blood oozed out.

"Like who, Linda?"

"Like those girls," she finished, in a tortured whisper.

CHAPTER 76

Erika's hands were shaking as she began to leaf through the book in David's bedroom. As she flicked through the pages, her heart pounded faster. She saw a section for the Serpentine Lido, another for Brockwell Lido, Hampstead Heath Ponds, The Serpentine Lido—all of the murder scenes, apart from the Horniman Museum. In each section, notes had been written around the photos and text in a manic hand. On some pages, the notes filled all of the blank space around the photos, noting where the entrances and exits were, whether there were CCTV cameras, what the opening times were of each location, where the best place was to take a car and conceal it nearby.

Then Erika reached a double-page map in the back, where all the locations had been marked out and circled. It was identical to the map in the incident room. Erika dropped the book with a thud, and went to the desk, where her phone was now switched on and charging. She picked up the phone and started to scroll through, searching for Moss or Crane's extension number back at Lewisham Row.

Then she sensed movement and a shadow behind her. A hand closed over hers, ripping the phone from her grasp.

CHAPTER 77

Chief Superintendent Marsh had entered the observation suite just as Linda had broken down, revealing David as the killer. He watched with Moss and Crane in horrified silence as Linda lost control. She was raging, pulling at her hair, her face red, spittle flying from her mouth,

"David killed Boots in front of me; he strangled her! No one believed me when I said he did it! No one! They all thought I was lying! That I did it!"

"You said David killed girls? Which girls?" asked Peterson.

"Girls... The type you pay for. He spent so much on those girls..."

"What do you mean, spent so much?"

"Money, you fucking idiot!" roared Linda. "And not his own money. Oh no! Daddy paid it off. Daddy paid it off, but wouldn't buy me a new cat... Because they said I'd lied about David killing her; they believe HIM over ME. A fucking murderer. Am I worth less than a murderer? AM I? Dad was happy to spend thousands. THOUSANDS!"

"Why did he have to spend thousands, Linda? Who did he give the thousands to?" asked Peterson.

"To Igor, Andrea's fucking fuck buddy! For the girls."

"And your father paid him off?" asked Peterson.

"He gave Giles the money to pay him off! And he's given David money to leave the country. ALL THAT MONEY AND HE WOULDN'T BUY ME A LITTLE KITTEN!"

Linda tilted her head back and brought it crashing down on the tabletop. She lifted it and brought it crashing down again.

"Stop! Stop!" cried Peterson. The solicitor had now retreated to the corner of the room. Peterson went to the wall and triggered the panic alarm. It blared out around the station. He turned and looked up at the camera. "I need help in here, NOW!"

"Where's DCI Foster?" asked Marsh, back in the observation suite.

Moss paused, the color draining from her face. "Jesus. She's gone to the Douglas-Brown house."

CHAPTER 78

Erika spun round and found herself face-to-face with David, who was standing across from her in his bedroom. He was dressed in a green sweater, a dark body warmer, and jeans. He pulled the SIM card from her phone and broke it in two with a small snap. He dropped the handset, and there was a cracking, splintering sound as he ground it into the carpet with the heel of his boot.

Erika regarded David's face. It was as if his mask of youth and attractive confidence had fallen away. His nostrils flared; his eyes blazed. He looked evil. She could see it all so clearly now. She had been so stupid.

"I thought you were away, David?" said Erika.

"I will be away. On a *stag weekend*..."

Erika looked down at the book. It lay on the carpet, its pages open to the map of London.

"It's not marked in the book, but you killed Andrea, too, didn't you?" said Erika, evenly.

"Yes. I did. Pity really; she was much more fun than Linda," said David. "I can see what you're thinking. Why Andrea and not Linda?"

"Is that what you're thinking, David?"

"No. Linda has proved to be an asset. She'll take the rap for Andrea's murder. Igor Kucerov will go down for the whores—they were *his* whores after all. And Ivy Norris—well, that piece of trash belonged in the ground."

"Can you hear yourself?"

"Yes, I can," sneered David.

"Why did you do it?"

David shrugged.

"You can just shrug it off? That I don't believe," said Erika.

"Believe it," he hissed. "You think you can analyze me. Rationalize what I did, why I killed? I did it because I CAN."

"But you can't, David. You won't get away with it. There will be consequences."

"You wouldn't know what it's like to grow up privileged and powerful. It's intoxicating. Watching how people defer to you, and to your parents. Power reeks from your pores, and it infects people around you. Power corrupts, envelops, entices... The more powerful my father becomes, the more he fears losing it."

"So he knew you killed Mirka, Tatiana, Karolina?"

"Of course... Not that he was thrilled, but they were Eastern European girls; they all think they can suck and fuck their way to greatness."

"What about Andrea? She was your sister! Your father's favorite!"

"She was threatening to tell Mother; she said she was going to go to the fucking press! Stupid girl. First lesson of life in the establishment: keep your mouth shut. Or someone will shut it for you, permanently."

"I can't believe your father was willing to cover even that up; to let it go that you killed his beloved daughter."

"Shut up. You don't know what you're talking about. He fears a fall from grace more than anything else. He fears that the other wolves will descend and tear him apart... Fear is more powerful than love. He found himself with the choice to save Linda or me. Linda's halfway to being off her fucking rocker anyway, and she hated Andrea so much, she probably would have done it herself."

"Linda wouldn't have killed Andrea," said Erika.

"You're sticking up for her now? Jesus. Well, I suppose most people feel pity for her when they've paid a visit to her bedroom... You know, when my friends used to come for sleepovers we'd find her little cat and lock it in one of the huge petty cash tins from my fathers' office... We'd make her do all sorts to get the key back."

Erika forced herself to keep eye contact with David. "Boots. That was her cat."

"Yes, dear old Boots... Linda used to go into terrible rages when she didn't get her way. I used one of these to dispose of Boots... Strangulation, in case you were curious. Have you ever tried to strangle a cat?"

"No."

"Kill a rabbit? You Slovaks like a bit of bunny, don't you?"

"No."

"It's the *claws* with cats. They go ballistic. They put up an admirable fight for survival."

"Your parents are intelligent people. They must have known it was you who killed the cat?" said Erika.

"That's the problem when you delegate your child's upbringing. Hiring nannies, you just play a walk-on role. You see the children before bath time, an hour here and there. *Don't come too close, darling; I'm dressed up for the evening out*... Your child becomes a bunch of statistics: he got an A in Maths, he can play *Für Elise* on the piano... Let's get him a polo pony so we can mix with the polo set..."

David seemed to drift off for a moment, and then came back to the room. "Anyway. I take it your questioning of all concerned has been fruitless? My father has made their silence very lucrative. And Linda will take the rap for killing Andrea; I made her promise."

"Why would she promise?"

"I said that if she did, she could have another cat and not have to live in fear of me disposing of it."

"You can't be serious," said Erika.

"I am. She'll plead insanity; end up in some expensive clinical facility for a few years. My father will probably bung some orderly a few quid to poke her in that aching place between her thighs... They might even let her have a cat. She'll give a little pussy to get a little pussy..." David started to laugh. It was high-pitched, unhinged.

Erika took the opportunity and made a dash for the bedroom door, but David was quicker. He grabbed her, his hands encircled her neck and he slammed her into the bookcase, knocking the air from her lungs. But this time she was ready for him; she brought her arm up and punched him in the nose with the heel of her hand. There was a satisfying crack as the cartilage snapped, and his grip loosened. Erika managed to push him away and made for the door, but he caught her arm just before she was through, and wheeled her back round. She slammed into the desk, and he was on her again. Blood was now gushing down his chin, and a look of pure rage contorted his face. Erika kicked and flailed, all the while gasping and trying to force air back into her winded lungs. She thrashed under his grip but he held on, trying to control her arms, climbing on top of her. He successfully pinned one of her arms down using his knee.

With her free hand, she scrabbled around on the desk and grabbed a smooth paperweight, and smashed it against his ear. He lost grip on her and she managed to scramble from under him, again making for the door, but he recovered quickly, throwing out one of his long legs and tripping her up. She fell, and he loomed over her, his face now a mess of blood, coating his teeth as he gave a manic grin. She fought, scratching and kicking, fighting like an animal to get out from under him, but he pinned her down. Lifting his arm, he punched her in the face: once, twice. When he struck her the third time, Erika felt one of her teeth hit the back of her throat, and then everything went black.

CHAPTER 79

"Sir, DCI Foster switched on her phone half an hour ago. The signal came from the Douglas-Brown house," said Peterson. The incident room was now up and running with a full-scale man hunt for David Douglas-Brown.

"I want a team of officers sent over to the house now. I want a full armed search conducted. Close off a five-mile radius around the house. Put out an arrest warrant on David Douglas-Brown. Circulate his photo."

"Sir, we were told by Simon and Diana Douglas-Brown that David had left the country and was attending a stag party in Prague. Passport and Immigration show he's still here. He never left the country," said Crane.

"I want him found, now. And fast. DCI Foster could be in danger," said Marsh. "And get Simon Douglas-Brown out of his bloody cell and stick him in an interview room..."

"Of course, you realize all this is inadmissible," said Simon, twenty minutes later, when Marsh had outlined Linda's confession. "My solicitor has informed me that you were faxed a statement from Linda's physician to show that, basically, anything that comes out of her mouth is inadmissible. She's gaga; always has been. As for David, he changed his plans without telling me; no crime in that. They must have moved the stag party."

Simon rose from his seat in the interview room. "Now, I will be calling Assistant Commissioner Oakley later, where I'll be recommending that..."

"Shut your mouth, Simon," said Marsh.

"I beg your pardon?" said Simon.

"Shut your mouth and sit down. You are still detained under caution and I'm not finished with you. Sit. Down."

Simon looked shocked, and slowly sank back into his chair.

"Now. An arrest warrant is out for your son, who we believe is responsible for the deaths of five women, including your own daughter."

Simon was silent.

"We've also discovered that the phone Andrea lost and claimed on insurance was in your name. Andrea lied that it had been stolen and we have the handset as evidence." Marsh opened an envelope and dropped the plastic-wrapped cracked handset on the table. "So, I see it like this. At best, you'll be done for insurance fraud. And you know how hard the government has lobbied for this. It could mean prison time, and as well as you being a very unpopular boy in prison, it will no doubt open the floodgates to all kinds of people with grievances toward you. Journalists, politicians. Add into the mix that your own son killed your daughter, and you knowingly told him to skip the country whilst stitching up your other daughter..."

"All right! ALL RIGHT!" shouted Simon. "All right. I'll tell you..."

"Simon Douglas-Brown, Baron of Hunstanton, I'm arresting you on charges of perverting the course of justice and concealing criminal activity. We also suspect that you used your position of power to influence the outcome of one or more Crown Prosecution trials. Okay. Start talking, and fast," said Marsh.

CHAPTER 80

David had quickly cleaned himself up in the bathroom, packing his nose with tissue to stop the bleeding. He then grabbed his bag, passport and money, and carried Erika downstairs over his shoulder. He was surprised how heavy she was for someone so scrawny. They emerged into the underground garage, and the lights blinked on. He approached the boot of the car. Inside was the prostitute with the long dark hair he had picked up at Paddington Station.

They'd driven round for a while, he and the prostitute; the girl attempting to make him hard, her hand inside his trousers, but that hadn't interested him. It had been a busy night, and all his usual places, the parks and lidos, had too much action going on. People walking about; police cars moving slowly past.

He had been forced to bring her home. She had been so excited when he'd driven up to his parents' house. Checking her face in the small mirror above the passenger seat. As if she hadn't been hired to fuck; she seemed to think she might be introduced to his parents. He wondered if she'd watched *Pretty Woman* too many times. He'd laughed when he thought this, and she'd joined in.

Stupid bitch.

Once they were in the underground garage, and they were out of the car, he'd slammed her face into the concrete wall. She never regained consciousness. This had made the moment when she died disappointing.

Still, he now had the ultimate prize. *DCI Foster.*

When he opened the boot of his car, the dead girl lay on her back. He had checked on her three times since he had strangled her to death, and each time it fascinated him to see how she'd changed: through the rigid wide-eyed stare of rigor mortis, to the tinge of purple on her skin where she looked as if she were sleeping, and now, her sharp cheekbones buried beneath swollen, bloated flesh, making her bruises bloom dark like ink stains. He laughed at her swollen face; she would hate to see how fat she was getting. He heaved Erika's limp body in beside her, closed the boot, and locked it.

It was still early in the morning when he pulled out of the underground garage and into the cul-de-sac, but he drove carefully for the couple of miles to the M4 junction. Once on the motorway, he was able to join the rush-hour traffic, whipping round the M25 motorway, orbiting the outskirts of London.

Erika felt herself regain consciousness, but the darkness was absolute. Her face was pressed against something rough. One arm was pinned under her at an angle. She brought the other arm up to touch her face, but her hand hit a solid mass a few inches above her head. She shifted, feeling the pain shoot through her face. She tasted blood and swallowed painfully. There was a rumbling, swaying motion underneath her. She felt around her the curved sides of the confined space, the metal above her, the inside mechanism of the lock, and realized she was in the boot of a car. Then a foul, pungent smell hit her. It had a tang of rot, and she heaved, barely able to catch her breath when she was forced to suck the rancid smell back into her lungs in the confined space. The car sped up and took a turn, the road bumping unevenly underneath. The gravitational force pushed Erika across to the edge of the boot, and something heavy rolled against her.

It was then that she knew she was in the back of the car with a body.

CHAPTER 81

Information was coming through to the incident room fast, and Moss and Peterson were realizing with horror that DCI Foster could be the next victim. The Douglas-Brown house had been searched, and was empty. Erika's car had been found parked two streets away and the number plate for David's car had been photographed leaving the west section of London's congestion charge zone.

"Simon Douglas-Brown's secretary bought David a one-way ticket on the Eurostar to Paris," said Crane, coming off the phone.

"So, not Prague," said Moss.

"Shit. What about DCI Foster?" asked Peterson.

"She's not in the house. She's not in her car. She must be in his," said Moss. "Crane, how fast can we scramble a helicopter?"

"When Chief Superintendent Marsh gives the order, four minutes," said Crane.

"Okay, I'm calling Marsh," said Moss.

CHAPTER 82

The junction sign for Ebbsfleet International Train Station loomed above, and David indicated and took the exit off the M25, slowing as he hit the ramp, which curved round and changed to a single lane carriageway. The A2 was busy with cars, but they peeled off at the turning for the Bluewater Shopping Center, its futuristic glass spires emerging from where it sat deep in an old chalk quarry. David drove on, speeding past empty industrial wasteland, grass, and the occasional tree dotting the scrubland. He slowed when he saw the lay-by up ahead, and then turned off. He came to a halt, and had to get out of the car to unhook a chain which hung across a small dirt track.

Erika had struggled to control the fear climbing her throat—the fear of being boxed in with a dead girl, and of what would happen when they reached their destination. She had forced herself to check for signs of life, and during this had discovered the body was that of a girl with long hair, whose life had long since left her. Her eyes had adjusted to the dark, and she could make out two tiny pinpricks of light next to the inside of the locking mechanism. She had run her hands over it, slowly at first, feeling its sharp greasy contours for a weakness, a way to prize it open. The car had lurched and the body had rolled against her again, and for a brief moment she'd panicked, clawing at the lock and breaking two of her fingernails below the quick. The pain had pulled her away from the brink of losing it, and she'd forced herself to think. To remain calm.

To survive.

She'd found a small hole in the carpeting underneath her, used to pull out the layer of carpet where underneath were kept the tools and spare wheel. She'd had to lie to one side, on top of the dead girl, to get the carpet up far enough to reach under, where she'd found a wrench. She had it now, in her grip. It was cold, but her hands were sweating. She felt the car come to a stop and braced herself. A door opened, and weight shifted. Moments later, the car lurched as David got back in. She heard a door close again, and then the car set off slowly, lurching from side to side, its suspension creaking. She felt the body beside her move, and the weight shifted so that it rolled onto her, the hair on its scalp pressing against the back of her head. She closed her eyes and tried to think; to focus on what she would do.

David drove slowly along the bumpy track, which opened out to a vast, disused chalk quarry. In the center was a deep pit filled with water. He came to a stop twenty yards from the edge, and killed the engine. He got out of the car and walked to the edge. The quarry walls were smooth. Tufts of grass grew in patches, and a small tree emerged from a break in the rock. Fifty feet below, the water was still and the weak morning sunlight bounced off dim blurry patches where the water was still frozen. To the left, the Bluewater Shopping Center sat low on the horizon, and a couple of miles in the opposite direction, a high-speed train left Ebbsfleet International, streaking past silently on its way to the Eurotunnel crossing to Paris.

David checked his watch; there was just enough time. He removed his rucksack and placed it on the ground a few feet from the car. He opened the back passenger door and made sure the child lock was activated. He then grabbed the heavy steering wheel lock from the passenger footwell and moved round to the boot of the car. He listened for a moment, braced himself with the steering wheel lock, and then opened the boot.

The stench was worse in the clean air of the quarry, and the putrid smell rose up, hitting him in the face. Both bodies were still. He leaned in to pull Erika out, but her arm shot out and she caught him on the side of his head with a wrench.

He staggered back for a moment, seeing stars, but as she started to climb from the boot, he swung the steering lock round and hit her in the side of her left knee. She collapsed onto the ground, groaning. He did the same to her right knee. She cried out again. David grabbed her and dragged her round to the rear passenger seat.

"Don't fight me," he said.

"David. It doesn't have to end like this," gasped Erika through the pain, seeing the vast expanse of water stretching out below them. She couldn't move her legs, and one of her arms was dead from being pinned under her in the car. Her head was still woozy where she had been hit, and she was fighting to think. Her head struck the doorframe as David hauled her body into the car. The door slammed and she looked around, seeing she was in the back, sitting behind the driver's seat. She caught sight of her face in the mirror. Her blonde hair was slick with blood on one side, and plastered against her scalp. One eye was so blackened and swollen that it was closed. She tried the door beside her, but it wouldn't open. She leaned across, groaning in agony, and tried the other passenger door. It, too, wouldn't open.

The front passenger door opened, sucking out the air, which was replaced by the stench of death. David was carrying the body of the dead girl, looking more horrific than Erika had imagined. The girl had long dark hair, but her face was swollen with two black eyes and multiple cuts. Strands of hair had been pulled out from the side of her head. Erika looked down and saw strands of the girl's hair stuck to her own jacket.

David shoved the girl into the front passenger seat, and her head flopped to one side. Erika could see that her eyes were a pearly blur, and her tongue had swollen, oozing from her mouth like a huge, purple-black slug.

"David, listen. I don't know what you're planning, but you won't get away with it... If you surrender now, I can..."

"You really are an arrogant bitch, aren't you?" he said, peering through the seats. "Here you are with the shit beaten out of you, stuck inside a car in the middle of nowhere, and you think I'm going to surrender to you."

"David!"

He leaned over and punched her hard in the face. Her head jerked back and bounced off the window. Blackness flooded her vision for a moment. When she came to, she felt a seat belt being pulled around her and fastened with a click. The door beside her slammed shut. David peered through the seats, taking off the handbrake. She felt the wheels jerk free.

"It looks like it's going to freeze again tonight," he said. The driver's door slammed, and seconds later the car began to roll forward, toward the edge of the quarry.

The car quickly picked up speed. David broke into a run, still pushing. He pulled back a few meters from the edge, and the car surged forward and vanished over the edge.

Erika felt the wheels leave the edge of the quarry. The horizon seemed to fly upward, and was replaced by bright blue, hurtling toward the windscreen. David had strapped both her and the dead girl in, but the whiplash from the impact was excruciating nevertheless. The car was submerged in bright blue for a moment, and then righted itself and broke the surface, the interior blazing with natural light. Erika searched frantically for the seat belt clasp, but it wouldn't open. The windows had been left open a few inches, and ice-cold water was surging inside, rapidly filling the car. Erika had expected to have time to react; she tried to open the door but the child lock was still activated. Water flooded in the windows, and within seconds the freezing water rose to her chest. Panicking, Erika grabbed as deep a breath as she could, and the roaring sound from above ceased as she was submerged. The car began to sink at a terrifying rate, down, deeper and darker. The weight of the engine sent them into a head-on collision with the bottom of the quarry.

The police helicopter reached the edge of the quarry as, far below, they saw David's car roll over the edge and hit the water. Moss and Peterson were in the helicopter with a police pilot. They had an open radio link to the incident room in Lewisham Row, and backup vehicles and an ambulance were on their way.

"Suspect is running," said Moss, training the gyroscopic camera fixed to the bottom of the helicopter, beaming the images back to the incident room. "Put police on alert. Suspect is running from the scene, north, toward Ebbsfleet Station."

"Shit, what if she's in that car? How far are the backup vehicles?" asked Peterson.

"Backup vehicles are four or five minutes away," said Marsh, over the radio.

"DCI Foster must be in that car. Land, land, land!" yelled Moss into the radio. The helicopter descended fast. The white chalk of the quarry came rushing up toward them, and the helicopter had barely set down before Moss and Peterson jumped out, ducking under the spinning blades, holding their hands up against the flying dust. The seconds were racing past, and below, bubbles were flooding up to the surface and rippling out into a large circle in the water.

"You are authorized to shoot, but we want him brought in alive," they heard Marsh say on the radio.

Peterson made for an access slope at the side of quarry, running flat out to reach it. Moss followed, shouting into her radio.

"We believe there is an officer in the car which went over the side and into the water. I repeat, an officer is trapped in the car underwater."

"Three minutes away," came a voice.

"Shit, we haven't got three minutes!" cried Moss.

The helicopter hovered above, flew over the lip of the quarry and sank down until it was just above the spreading bubbles on the surface. Peterson was now at the water's edge, and without hesitation, ripped off his jacket and gun and waded into the water, swimming out, arms arcing from side to side. He reached the spot where the car had submerged, and dived under.

"Can you report? Suspect is on the run, do we have backup at Ebbsfleet Station? I repeat, do we have backup? If he gets on the fucking train..." came Marsh's voice, over the radio.

"Backup on its way, and the station is being shut down," answered a voice.

"Moss, report. Our visual shows Peterson is in the water."

"Yes, sir, DI Peterson is under the water. I repeat, DI Peterson is under the water," said Moss, into her radio. She was now standing at the water's edge.

"Jesus!" said Marsh.

There was radio silence as the helicopter roared and hovered, pressing an oval shape into the water. Seconds ticked by.

"Come on, please, come on!" said Moss. She was about to wade in after Peterson, when he broke the surface, holding Erika's limp body.

The quarry above was suddenly filled with the screaming sirens of an ambulance, fire engine, and police support cars. Above the water, a safety line came down from the helicopter, and Peterson managed to hook it over both himself and Erika. He gave the thumbs up and they were lifted out of the water, their feet skimming above as they were half-carried, half-dragged over toward Moss at the edge.

"DCI looks badly injured, and she appears unconscious," said Moss into her radio. "There's an access road to the left side where you've come in, we're down by the water. I repeat, DCI Foster looks unresponsive!" cried Moss.

Peterson and Erika reached the edge of the water, and the helicopter set them down. Four paramedics raced down the slope to the water's edge. They unhooked Erika from the safety line and gently laid her on the ground.

Peterson was drenched and shivering, and a foil blanket was quickly put over him. The paramedics started to work on Erika. There were a tense few moments, and then Erika gasped, coughing up water.

"It's okay, on your side," said the paramedic, tipping her into the recovery position. She coughed, and more water shot out of her mouth. She gasped, pulling clean, cold air into her lungs.

"DCI Foster is out of the water and she's alive," said Moss. "Thank fuck, she's alive."

CHAPTER 83

There was a soft hissing sound and a rhythmic beep as Erika's vision slowly swam into focus. She was in a hospital room, beside a window. The blinds were closed and a soft night light filled the room. In the corner of her vision was another bed. The bedcovers moved up, and then down, matching the hissing sound that she had heard. She rolled her tongue around her dry mouth, and realized that the patient in the bed next to her was on a ventilator.

Blue blankets were pulled up around her, and great swathes of her body felt completely numb: her legs, one arm, the left side of her face. She felt no pain, just an uneasy feeling that pain was close by. Right now, she was floating above the pain, but it would come soon and then she would have to deal with it. For now she could float above it, observing; numb body, numb emotions.

She closed her eyes and drifted off.

When she woke again it was dark, and Marsh was sitting beside her bed. He wore a smart shirt and his leather jacket. The pain was starting to encroach: her face, her legs, her arm. She also felt closer to her emotions, to the fear. The memories. That she thought she was going to die. The burning in her lungs when she hadn't been able to hold her breath any more, and she'd pulled in water... The dead girl in the back of the car with her, and then the girl's blurred face when the car had submerged, her dark hair spreading out in a halo around her head.

"You're going to be okay," said Marsh, reaching over and gently taking Erika's right hand. She noticed her left was bandaged, and that she could only hear on one side—the opposite side to where Marsh was sitting.

"You've had an operation. You've got a pin in one of your legs, and a fractured cheek..." Marsh tailed off. He was clutching a bunch of grapes on his lap. It was almost comical. "You'll make a full recovery... I've put a card on your bedside table. Everyone at the station has signed it... You did well, Erika. I'm proud of you."

Erika tried to say something. On her third attempt, she managed it: "David?"

"They arrested him at Ebbsfleet. He's in custody, along with his father, Giles Osborne and Igor Kucerov. Isaac went back through the forensic evidence and has found a match to some small hair fibers found on Mirka Bratova, the second victim. They match David's DNA. And we have Linda's testimony, and forensics are all over the car. They pulled it out of the quarry with—with the girl inside..."

Marsh smiled awkwardly. He reached out and took Erika's hand. "Anyway, there's plenty of time to tell you everything. What I really wanted to say is that I'm here if you need anything. And I'm here as a friend... Marcie sends her love, and she went out and got you some toiletries. I've put them in your locker."

Erika tried to smile, but the pain was becoming sharp and angry. A nurse came in and checked Erika's chart. She went to the drip and pressed a button.

"Peterson... I want to thank Peterson," said Erika.

There was a beep, and Erika felt a coldness trickle through her hand. Marsh and the hospital room blurred to a pain-free whiteness.

EPILOGUE

Erika breathed deeply, feeling the clean air fill her lungs. Next to her, on the wooden bench, Edward did the same. It was a comfortable silence, as they stared out at the moors, which spread away in greens and browns. Clouds hung heavy in the distance, twirling into a knot of blue-black, which was heading their way.

"There's a storm brewing," said Edward.

"Just a minute longer... I love it here. Even the grass is greener up north," said Erika.

Edward laughed beside her. "Is that a metaphor, lass?"

"No. It really is greener." She grinned. She pulled her eyes away from the beautiful view to Edward, who sat next to her, swaddled in his thick winter coat. A thin gravel path separated Mark's headstone from the bench where they sat.

"I'm finding it easier to come here now," said Edward. "Once you get over being confronted with those letters in gold, his date of birth and the date when he, you know... I come here a lot and I talk to him."

Erika started to cry again. "I don't know where to begin; what to say to him," she sobbed, searching her coat for a tissue.

"Just begin," said Edward, handing her a little pack of tissues. He tilted her face up to his. Her hair was starting to grow back at the patch on the side where she'd had a long row of stitches.

"Okay," she said, pulling out a tissue and wiping her face.

"Tell you what, I'll nip back, put the kettle on. You just talk. Course, you'll feel like a lunatic at first, but there's no one about..."

He patted Erika on the shoulder and started off down the path. She watched as he walked away. He turned and smiled, before picking his way cautiously through the graves and down to the village. She noticed how similar his gait and his movements were to Mark's. She turned back to the grave.

"So, I solved five murders...And I narrowly escaped the murderer, twice," she said. "But, that's not what I came up here to tell you..."

Her phone rang in her pocket. She pulled it out. It was Moss.

"Hello, boss. I thought, it's been a couple of months, and I'd give you a call..."

"Hello," said Erika.

"Is it a bad time?"

"No, well, I'm...I'm just at Mark's grave."

"Oh, bugger, I'll call back."

"No. I've been trying to talk to him. My father-in-law says I should talk to him. He says it helps. I just don't know what to say..."

"You could tell him that your murderer is going to trial in May. Did you see today's news? David Douglas-Brown was declared fit to stand trial. They've also expelled Sir Simon from the Lords...And it looks like Igor Kucerov will be retried for the murder of Nadia Greco. We're just waiting on the CPS about Giles Osborne. I'm confident he'll be done for perverting the course of justice...You there, boss?"

"Yes. And I did see. And Mark doesn't want to hear all that."

"If I were stuck laying six feet under, I'd want my loved ones to keep me up-to-date on current events..."

There was a silence. The wind rippled across the grass. The knot of black cloud was almost above her now.

"Sorry, I'm being crass," said Moss.

"No, you're being honest, which is far better. Did Peterson get my card?"

"Yes. But you know him. The strong, silent type. He came to see you after, in the hospital, but you were out of it."

"I know he did."

There was another silence.

"So. When you back, boss?"

"I don't know. Soon. Marsh has told me to take as long as I need. I'm going to stay up here with Edward for a bit."

"Well, we're looking forward to you coming back, boss. You are coming back, aren't you?"

"Yeah, I'm coming back," said Erika. "I'll call you."

"Good. Well enjoy yourself up there, and when you…you know…talk, to Mark, say hi from me."

"That's the weirdest request for passing on a hello," said Erika, wryly.

"I just wish I could have met him," said Moss.

Erika came off the phone as thunder began to rumble overhead. She turned back to the grave and stared at the gold letters on the black granite.

IN MEMORY OF
MARK FOSTER
1ST AUGUST 1970–8TH JULY 2014
LOVED AND REMEMBERED ALWAYS

"That's the toughest word, Mark," said Erika. "Always. I'll always be without you. I don't know how I can live without you, but I have to. To move on, I have to let you go at some point. I have to keep going, Mark. Keep working. Keep living my life. Most days I don't think I can go on without you, but I have to.

There's so much bad stuff out there that the only way I think I can cope with it all is to keep working. To try and make some kind of difference to the world."

Water splashed on to Erika's cheek, and for once, it wasn't a tear. The rain began to fall, spattering on the gravel and Mark's gravestone.

"Your Dad's making me a cuppa… So I'll be off. But I'll be back, I promise," said Erika. She got up, put her fingers to her lips and pressed them against the cold stone, just under Mark's name.

Erika hitched her bag over her shoulder and set off across the graveyard, back toward tea and cake, and the warmth of Edward's kitchen.

A NOTE FROM ROBERT

Hello, and a huge thank-you to you for choosing to read *The Girl in the Ice*. If you did enjoy it, I would be very grateful if you could tell your friends and family. Word of mouth is one of the most powerful tools, and it helps me reach out to new readers. Your endorsement makes a big difference! You could also write a product review. It needn't be long, just a few words, but this also helps new readers find one of my books for the first time.

If you'd like to get in contact with me, and tell me what you thought about the book, or just to say hi, you can find me through my social media links below.

I'm excited to say that Erika will be returning shortly in *The Night Stalker*.

Until then...

Robert Bryndza

girlintheicebook.com

twitter.com/robertbryndza
facebook.com/bryndzarobert
Instagram @robertbryndza

robertbryndza.com

ACKNOWLEDGMENTS

Thank you to Oliver Rhodes, Claire Bord, Keshini Naidoo, Kim Nash and the wonderful team at Bookouture. Special thanks to my editor Claire Bord, for your encouragement and pushing me to make this book better than I ever dreamed it could be.

Thank you to Henry Steadman for the stunning cover, which has now gone around the world and graces so many of the international editions, and thank you to my agent Amy Tannenbaum and Danielle Sickles and all at the Jane Rotrosen Agency. Thank you to Beth de-Guzman, Lindsey Rose, Nidhi Pugalia and all the fabulous team at Grand Central, for bringing Erika Foster to a whole new audience!

Thank you to Stephanie Dagg, and to my mother-in-law, Vierka, who seems to have a psychic ability, when the going gets tough and the writing goes late, to turn up at the front door with delicious hot food, and love and kindness, which always cheers me up. And thank you to my husband, Ján, who manages to heap praise and encouragement when needed, but is not averse to shouting to make me stick to deadlines. Keep the praise and encouragement coming, and the shouting is essential too. Without this tough love and unwavering support, I would still be toiling away in a job I didn't enjoy, just dreaming of being a writer.

And lastly, thank you to all the wonderful readers, and book bloggers, all over the world, both the new ones who have discovered my work and those who have followed my work from my Coco Pinchard romantic comedy novels to crime. Word of mouth really works, and without you all blogging about my books, and telling your friends and family, I would have far less readers. Thank you.

Please turn the page for a preview of

The Night Stalker

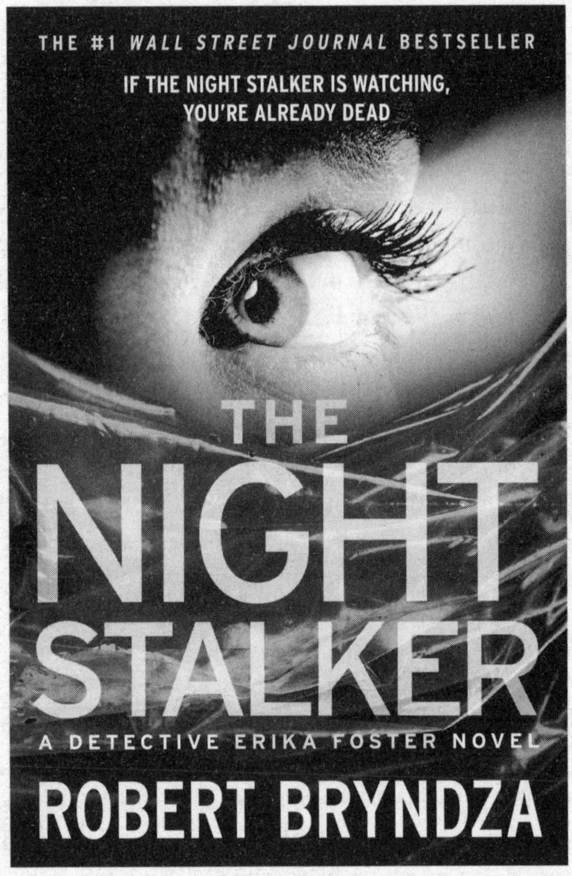

Robert Bryndza's next exciting detective Erika Foster thriller, available soon from Grand Central Publishing.

CHAPTER 1

It was a sweltering summer night in late June. The black-clad figure ran lightly, streaking through the darkness, feet barely making a sound on the narrow dirt path, ducking and twisting gracefully to avoid contact with the dense surrounding trees and bushes. It was as if a shadow were sweeping silently over the leaves.

The night sky was just a thin strip between the trees high above; the light pollution from the city cast the undergrowth in dusky shades. The small, shadow-like figure reached a gap in the undergrowth on the right, and stopped abruptly: poised, breathless, heart racing.

A strobe of blue light lit up the surroundings as the 9:39 p.m. train to London Bridge switched from diesel, extending its metal arms to the electrified lines above. The shadow ducked down as empty glowing carriages rumbled past. There were two more flashes and the train was gone, plunging the narrow strip of undergrowth back into darkness.

The shadow moved off again at speed, gliding soundlessly as the path curved slightly away from the tracks. The trees began to thin out to the left, exposing a row of terraced houses. Snapshots of back gardens slid past: neat dark strips with patio furniture, tool sheds, a swing set—all still in the thick night air.

And then the house came into view. It was a Victorian terrace, like the others in the long row—three stories of pale brick—but its owner had added a large glass extension at the back, which jutted out from the ground floor. The small shadow knew everything about the owner. Knew the layout of the house. Knew the owner's schedule. And most importantly, knew that tonight he would be alone.

The shadow came to a stop at the end of the garden. A large tree grew against the wire fence that backed on to the dirt track. In one place the trunk had grown around the metal, the folds of wood biting down on the rusting post like a large lipless mouth. A heavy halo of leaves burst upward in all directions, obscuring the view of the train tracks from the house. A few nights previously, the shadow had taken this same route and had neatly clipped the edges of the wire fence, loosely tacking it back in place. The fence now pulled away easily and the shadow crouched down and crawled through the gap. The grass felt dry and the soil below was cracked from weeks of no rain. The shadow came up to its feet under the tree and in a fast, fluid motion crossed the lawn in a swoop of black.

An air-conditioning unit was attached to the rear wall of the house. It whirred loudly, masking the faint crunch of feet on the gravel that lined the narrow path between the glass extension and the house next door. The shadow reached a low sash window and ducked down underneath the wide sill. Light shone out, casting a square of yellow on the brickwork of the neighboring house. Pulling up the hood of the running suit, the shadow slowly inched upward and looked over the wide windowsill.

The man inside was in his mid-forties, tall and well-built, dressed in tan trousers and a white shirt rolled up at the sleeves. He moved around the large open-plan kitchen, took a wineglass from one of the cupboards, and poured himself a glass of red. He took a long gulp and topped up his glass. A ready meal lay on the counter, and he picked it up, slipped off its cardboard sleeve and pricked at the plastic lid with the corkscrew.

Hatred rose in the shadow. It was intoxicating to see the man inside, knowing what was about to unfold.

The man in the kitchen programed the microwave and placed the meal inside. There was a beep and the digital countdown began.

Six minutes.

The man took another gulp of his wine and then left the kitchen. Moments later, a light came on in the bathroom window directly above where the shadow crouched. The window swung open a few inches, and there was a squeak as the shower was turned on.

Heart hammering, the shadow outside the window worked fast: unzipping a money belt, pulling out a small flat screwdriver and easing it into the crack where the window met the sill. With a small amount of pressure, it popped open. The sash window moved up smoothly and the shadow slid in through the gap. This was it. All the planning, the years of angst and pain...

Four minutes.

The figure stepped down into the kitchen and moved swiftly, pulling out a small plastic syringe and squirting its clear liquid into the glass of red wine, swirling the wine around before gently placing the glass back on the black granite counter.

The shadow stood for a moment, listening, enjoying the cool waves from the air-conditioning. The black granite countertop sparkled under the lights.

Three minutes.

The shadow moved quickly through the kitchen, passing the wooden banister at the base of the stairs, and slipped into a pool of darkness behind the living room door. A moment later, the man came down the stairs, wearing just a towel. The microwave gave three loud beeps to say it was finished. As the man padded past barefoot, the smell of clean skin wafted through the air. The shadow heard a clink as the man pulled cutlery from the drawer, and a scrape of a stool on the wooden floor as he sat down to eat.

The shadow exhaled deeply, emerged from the shadows and quietly climbed the stairs.

To watch.

To wait.

To exact long-awaited retribution.

CHAPTER 2

FOUR DAYS LATER

The night air was close and humid on the quiet South London street. Moths fizzed and bumped in the orange arc of light cast by a streetlamp illuminating a row of terraced houses. Estelle Munro shuffled along the pavement, arthritis slowing her progress. When she drew close to the light, she stepped down from the pavement and onto the road. The effort to step down off the curb made her groan, but her fear of moths outweighed the pain in her arthritic knees.

Estelle eased her way through a gap between two parked cars and gave the streetlight a wide berth, feeling the heat from the day's sun radiating off the tarmac. The heatwave was in its second week, pressing down on the residents of London and the southeast of England, and along with thousands of other old people Estelle's heart was protesting. The siren of a far-off ambulance blared, seeming to echo her thoughts. She was relieved to see that the next two streetlights were broken, and slowly, painfully, she edged between two parked cars and rejoined the pavement.

She had offered to feed her son Gregory's cat while he was away. She didn't like cats. She'd only offered so she could have a good nose around the house, and see how her son was coping since his wife, Penny, had left him, taking Estelle's five-year-old grandson, Peter, with her.

Estelle was out of breath and pouring with sweat when she reached the gate of Gregory's smart terraced house. In her opinion, it was the smartest house in the whole street. She pulled a large hanky out from under her bra strap and wiped the sweat off her face.

Light from the orange streetlight rippled across the glass front door as Estelle fished out her key. When she opened the door, she was hit by a wall of stifling heat and she stepped reluctantly inside, onto letters strewn over the mat. She flicked the light switch by the door, but the hallway remained in darkness.

"Bloody hell, not again," she muttered, pulling the door closed behind her. As she felt around to pick up the post, she realized this was the third time the power had tripped while Gregory had been away. The lights in the fish tank had done it once before, and another time Penny had left the bathroom light on and the bulb had blown.

Estelle fished her mobile phone from her handbag and, with an awkward fumble of gnarled fingers, unlocked the screen. It cast a dim halo of light a few feet in front, illuminating the pale carpet and narrow walls, and she jumped as she saw her ghostly reflection in the large mirror on the left-hand side. The half-light gave the lilies on her sleeveless blouse an inky, poisonous quality. She focused the light of her phone down onto the carpet and shuffled toward the living room door, feeling around on the inside wall for the switch, to check it wasn't just the hall bulb that had gone. She flicked the switch on and off, but nothing happened.

Then the screen of her phone timed out and she was plunged into total darkness. Just the sound of her labored breathing filled the silence. She panicked, fumbling to unlock the phone. At first her arthritic fingers wouldn't move fast enough, but finally she managed it and the light came back on, casting the front room in a circle of dim blue.

It was stifling inside: the heat pressed down on her, closing off her ears. It was as if she were underwater. Dust particles twirled in the air; a cloud of tiny flies floated silently above a large arty china plate filled with brown wooden balls on the coffee table.

"It's just a power cut!" she snapped, her voice resonating sharply off the iron fireplace. She was annoyed that she'd panicked. It was just the circuit breaker, nothing more. To prove there was nothing to be scared of, she would first have a drink of cold water, and then she would get the electricity back on. She turned, shuffling purposefully off toward the kitchen, her arm outstretched with the phone.

The glass kitchen seemed cavernous in the phone's half-light, extending out into the garden. Estelle felt vulnerable and exposed. There was a distant whoosh and a click-clack as a train passed on the track beyond the bottom of the garden. Estelle went to a cupboard and pulled down a glass tumbler. Sweat stung, as it dripped into her eyes; she wiped her face with her bare arm. She moved to the sink and filled her glass, wincing as she drank the lukewarm water.

The light went out on the phone again, and a crash from upstairs broke the silence. Estelle dropped the tumbler. It shattered, glass spraying out on the wood floor. Her heart pulsed and pounded, and as she listened in the darkness there was another scuffling sound from above. She grabbed a rolling pin from a pot of utensils on the counter and went to the bottom of the stairs.

"Who's there? I've got pepper spray and I'm dialing 999!" she shouted up into the darkness.

There was silence. The heat was oppressive. Thoughts of snooping around her son's house were gone. All Estelle wanted to do was to go home and watch the Wimbledon highlights in her cozy, brightly lit house.

Something darted out of the shadows and came straight at her from the stairs above. Estelle stepped back in shock, almost dropping the phone. Then she saw it was the cat. It stopped and began to rub at her legs.

"Bloody hell, you gave me a fright!" she said, relieved, her pounding heart slowing. A foul smell floated down from the landing above. "Just what I need. Have you done something nasty up there? You've got a litter tray, and a cat flap."

The cat looked up at Estelle nonchalantly. For once, she was glad of its presence. "Come on, I'll feed you."

She was comforted as the cat followed her to the cupboard under the stairs; she let it rub against her legs as she found the electricity box. When she opened the little plastic flap she saw that the power had been turned off at the mains. *Strange.* She flicked it on and the hall filled with light. There was a distant beep as the air-conditioning whirred to life.

She came back into the kitchen and turned on the lights. The room and her reflection bounced back at her from the huge windows. The cat jumped onto the counter and watched her quizzically as she swept up the broken tumbler. Once she had dealt with the glass, Estelle opened a sachet of cat food, squeezed it into a saucer and placed it on the stone kitchen floor. The air-conditioning was working fast. She stood for a moment and let the cool air wash over her, watching as the cat daintily licked and nibbled at the square of jellied food with its small pink tongue.

The bad smell was intensifying, rushing into the kitchen as the air-conditioning sucked air through the house. There was a clinking as the cat licked the last of the empty saucer, then darted to the glass wall and vanished through a cat flap.

"Eat and run. Leave me to clear it up," said Estelle. She grabbed a cloth and an old newspaper and moved to the stairs, climbing slowly, her knees complaining. The heat and the smell got worse the higher she climbed. She reached the top and moved along the brightly lit landing. Methodically, she checked the empty bathroom, the spare room, under the desk in the small office. There was no sign of a present from the cat.

The smell was overpowering when she reached the door to the master bedroom. It caught in her throat and she gagged. *Of all vile smells, cat mess is the worst,* she thought.

When she entered the bedroom, she flicked on the light. Flies buzzed and whined in the air. The dark blue duvet was thrown back on the double bed, and a naked man lay flat on his back with a plastic bag tied tight over his head, his arms tied to the headboard. His eyes were open, bulging out grotesquely against the plastic. It took her a moment to realize who it was.

It was Gregory.

Her son.

Then Estelle did something she hadn't done in years.

She screamed.

CHAPTER 3

It was the least enjoyable dinner party DCI Erika Foster had attended in a long while. There was an awkward silence as her host, Isaac Strong, opened the dishwasher and began to load plates and cutlery, interrupted only by the low whirr of a plug-in electric fan in the corner. It barely made a dent in the heat, instead just pushing waves of warm air across the kitchen.

"Thank you, the lasagna was delicious," she said, as Isaac reached over to take her plate.

"I used half-fat cream for the Béchamel sauce," he replied. "Could you tell?"

"No."

Isaac went back to the dishwasher and Erika cast her eye around the kitchen. It was elegant, with a French-rustic theme: hand-painted white cabinets, work surfaces of pale wood, and a heavy Butler sink in white ceramic. Erika wondered if, as a forensic pathologist, Isaac had deliberately steered clear of stainless steel. Her eyes came to rest on Isaac's ex-boyfriend, Stephen Linley, who sat across from her at the large kitchen table, watching her suspiciously with pursed lips. He was younger than Erika and Isaac: she guessed thirty-five. He was a strapping Adonis of a man with a beautiful face, but its expression had sly flashes that she didn't like. She forced herself to defuse his attitude with a smile, then took a sip of wine and willed herself to say something. The silence was beginning to stretch uncomfortably.

This didn't usually happen when she had dinner with Isaac. Over the past year they'd shared several meals in his cozy French kitchen. They'd laughed, divulged a few secrets, and Erika had felt a strong friendship blossom. She'd been able to open up to Isaac, more than she had to anyone else, about the death of her husband, Mark, less than two years previously. And, in turn, Isaac had talked of losing the love of his life, Stephen.

Although, whereas Mark had died tragically in the line of duty during a police raid, Stephen had broken Isaac's heart, leaving him for another man.

This was why it had been such a surprise to Erika to see Stephen when she'd arrived earlier that evening. In fact, not so much a surprise—it had felt more like an ambush.

Even though she had lived in the UK for more than twenty-five years, Erika had found herself wishing this dinner were happening back in her native Slovakia. In Slovakia, people were direct.

What's going on? You could have warned me! Why didn't you tell me your idiot ex-boyfriend would be here? Are you insane to let him back into your life after what he did to you?

She'd wanted to shout when she'd come through to the kitchen, and had seen Stephen sitting languidly in shorts and a T-shirt. But she'd felt awkward, and polite British convention dictated that they all gloss over it, and pretend things were normal.

"Would anyone like coffee?" asked Isaac, closing the dishwasher and turning to face them. He was a tall, handsome man, with a head of thick dark hair swept back from a high forehead. His large brown eyes were framed by thinly shaped eyebrows, which could be arched or drawn together to communicate all manner of wry emotions. Tonight, however, he just looked embarrassed.

Stephen swirled the white wine in his glass and looked between Erika and Isaac. "Coffee *already*? It's barely eight o'clock, Isaac, and it's bloody hot. Open more wine."

"No, coffee would be great, thank you," said Erika.

"If you must have coffee, at least use the machine," said Stephen. He added, territorially, "Did he tell you? I bought him the Nespresso. Cost a fortune. From my last book advance."

Erika smiled blandly and took a roasted almond from a dish in the center of the table. As she chewed, it seemed to crackle through the silence. During the awkward meal, Stephen had done most of the talking, telling them in great detail about the new crime novel he was writing. He'd also taken it upon himself to tell them all about forensic profiling, which Erika had thought was a bit rich, considering that Isaac was one of the leading forensic pathologists in the country, and that Erika herself, as a detective chief inspector with the London Metropolitan Police, had successfully solved a string of murder cases in the real world.

Isaac started to make coffee and switched on the radio. "Like a Prayer" by Madonna cut through the silence.

"Turn it up! I love a bit of Madge," said Stephen.

"Let's have something a bit more mellow," said Isaac, scrolling through the radio stations until the sweet mournful strings of a violin replaced Madonna's squeaky voice.

"*Allegedly,* he's a gay man," said Stephen, rolling his eyes.

"I just think something more mellow would suit right now, Stevie," said Isaac.

"Christ. We're not eighty! Let's have some fun. What do you want to do, Erika? What do you do for fun?"

Stephen, to Erika's eyes, was a host of contradictions. He dressed very straight, like an American Ivy League athlete, but his movements had a camp lightness to them. He crossed his legs now and pursed his lips, waiting for her answer.

"I think…I'm going to go and have a cigarette," she said, reaching for her bag.

"The door's unlocked upstairs," said Isaac, looking at her with apologetic eyes. She pulled her face into a smile and left the kitchen.

Isaac lived in a townhouse in Blackheath, near Greenwich. The spare bedroom upstairs had a small balcony. Erika opened the glass door, went outside and lit up a cigarette. She exhaled smoke into the dark sky, feeling the intensity of the evening heat. The summer night was clear, but the stars were faint against the haze of light pollution floating up from the city stretching out in front of her. She followed the path of the laser from the Greenwich Observatory, craning her head to where it vanished among the stars high above. She took another deep drag on her cigarette and heard the crickets singing in the dark back garden below, mixed in with the hum of traffic from the busy road behind.

Was she being too harsh in her assessment of Isaac allowing Stephen back into his life? Was it just that she was jealous that her single friend was no longer single? No—she wanted the best for Isaac, and Stephen Linley was a toxic individual. She reflected, sadly, that there might not be room in Isaac's life for both herself and Stephen.

She thought of the small, sparsely furnished flat she struggled to call home, and of the lonely nights she spent in bed staring into the darkness. Erika and Mark had shared their lives in more ways than just as man and wife. They had been colleagues, joining the Greater Manchester Police in their early twenties. Erika had been a rising star in the force and was rapidly promoted to detective chief inspector, senior in rank to Mark. Mark had loved her all the more for it.

Then, almost two years previously, Erika had led the disastrous drug raid that had resulted in the death of Mark and four of their colleagues. Afterward, the grief and burden of guilt had at times seemed too great to bear, and she had struggled to find her place in the world without her husband. A fresh start in London had been tough, but her work in the Homicide and Serious Crime Command within the Metropolitan Police was the one thing she had been able to pour her energy into. But where she had once been a rising star in the force, now she was tainted, and her career progression had ground to a halt. She was direct, driven and a brilliant officer who didn't suffer fools—but she had no time for the politics of the force, and she had clashed repeatedly with her superiors, making some powerful enemies.

Erika lit another cigarette, and she was just deciding she would make an excuse to leave quickly when the glass door opened behind her. Isaac poked his head round and came onto the balcony.

"I could use one of those," he said, closing the door and moving over to where she stood by the iron railing. She smiled and offered him the packet. He teased one out with a large, elegant hand and leaned over as she lit it for him.

"Sorry, I really screwed up tonight," he said, straightening up and exhaling smoke.

"It's your life," said Erika. "But you could have given me a heads-up."

"It all happened so quickly. He showed up this morning on the doorstep and all day we've been talking and... I won't spell it out. It was too late to cancel, not that I wanted to cancel."

Erika could see the angst playing over his face. "Isaac, you don't need to explain yourself to me. Although, if I were you, I'd pick lust as your explanation. You were overcome by lust. It's much more forgivable."

"I know he's a complicated individual, but he's different when we're alone together. He's vulnerable. Do you think if I approached it in the right way, if I set proper boundaries, it could work this time?"

"Possibly...And at least he can't kill you off again," said Erika wryly.

Stephen had based a forensic pathologist in one of his novels on Isaac, only to kill the character off in a rather graphic gay bashing.

"I'm serious. What do you think I should do?" asked Isaac, his eyes filled with angst.

Erika sighed and took his hand in hers. "You don't want to hear what I think. I like being friends with you."

"I value your opinion, Erika. Please, tell me what I should do..."

There was a creak as the glass door opened. Stephen emerged barefoot, carrying a full tumbler of whisky and ice. "Tell him what he should do? About what?" he asked tartly.

The awkward silence was broken by a message alert tone chiming from the depths of Erika's bag. She pulled out her phone and read the message, frowning.

"Everything okay?" asked Isaac.

"The body of a white male has been discovered in a house in Laurel Road, Honor Oak Park. Looks suspicious," said Erika, adding, "Shit, I haven't got my car. I took a cab here."

"You'll need to assign a forensic pathologist. I could take you in my car?" said Isaac.

"I thought you had the night off?" Stephen demanded, indignantly.

"I'm always on duty, Stevie," replied Isaac, looking eager to leave.

"Okay, then, let's go," said Erika, and couldn't resist adding to Stephen, "looks like coffee from your machine will have to wait."

CHAPTER 4

Erika and Isaac arrived at Laurel Road half an hour later, their awkward dinner party rapidly forgotten. Police tape closed off the road in both directions and support vehicles added to the cordon: a police van, four squad cars and an ambulance. The vehicles' blue lights pulsed across the long row of terraced houses. In several of the front windows and doorways, neighbors stood gawking at the scene.

Detective Inspector Moss, one of Erika's most trusted colleagues, walked over to meet their car as it pulled into a space a hundred yards down from the police cordon. She was a short, solid woman and was sweating profusely in the heat, despite her knee-length skirt and thin blouse. Her red hair was pulled back from her face, which was awash with freckles—a small group of them clustered under her eye, forming what looked like a tear. However, in contrast to this, she was upbeat, and gave Erika and Isaac a wry grin as they got out of the car.

"Evening, boss, Dr. Strong."

"Evening, Moss," said Isaac.

"Evening. Who are all these people?" Erika asked, as they approached the police tape, where a group of tired-looking men and women stood staring at the scene.

"Commuters from Central London, arriving home to find their street is a crime scene," said Moss.

"But I live just there," one man was saying, pointing with his briefcase to a house two doors down. His face was flushed and weary, his thinning hair plastered to his head. When Moss,

Erika and Isaac drew level with him at the police tape, he looked to them, hoping they had come to give different news.

"I'm DCI Foster, the senior investigating officer, and this is Dr. Strong, our forensic pathologist," said Erika flashing her ID at the uniformed officer. "Get in contact with the council, organize these people beds for the night."

"Very good, ma'am," said the uniformed officer, signing them all in. They ducked under the police tape before they could get involved with the commuters protesting at the thought of a night on camp beds.

The front door of 14 Laurel Road was wide open, and lights blazed from the hallway, which was busy with CSIs wearing dark blue overalls and face masks. Erika, Isaac and Moss were handed overalls, and they suited up on a patch of shingle in the tiny front garden.

"The body's upstairs, front bedroom," said Moss. "Victim's mother came over to feed the cat. Thought he was away on holiday in the south of France but, as you'll see, he never made it to the airport."

"Where is the mother now?" asked Erika, stepping into the thin overalls.

"She was overcome by the shock and heat. Uniform just went with her to University Hospital, Lewisham. We'll need to get a statement when she's recovered," said Moss, zipping up her own suit.

"Just give me a few minutes to examine the scene," said Isaac, as he pulled up the hood of his own suit. Erika nodded, and he went off into the house.

The heat, volume of people and bright lights all helped to tip the temperature in the upstairs bedroom to over forty degrees centigrade. Isaac, with his team of three assistants and the crime scene photographer, worked in an efficient, respectful silence.

The victim lay naked on his back in the double bed. He had a tall, athletic frame. His arms were pulled up and outward and tied to the headboard with thin twine, which was biting into the flesh of his wrists. His legs were splayed, feet apart. A clear plastic bag was molded to his head, the features distorted underneath.

Erika always found naked corpses much more difficult to deal with. Death was undignified enough, without being exposed in this way. She resisted the urge to place the sheet over his lower body.

"The victim is Dr. Gregory Munro, forty-six years old," said Moss, as they stood around the bed. His brown eyes were wide open and surprisingly clear beneath the plastic, but his tongue was beginning to swell and poke through his teeth.

"Doctor of what?" asked Erika.

"He's the local GP. Owns and manages the Hilltop Medical Practice on Crofton Park Road," replied Moss. Erika looked over at Isaac, who was standing on the opposite side of the bed, examining the body.

"Can you give me a cause of death?" asked Erika. "I'm assuming asphyxiation, but..."

Isaac released the victim's head, the chin coming to rest on the bare chest. "The evidence points to asphyxiation, but I'll need to determine that the bag wasn't placed over his head post-mortem."

"A sex game gone wrong? Autoasphyxiation?" asked Moss.

"Hypothetically, yes. But we can't rule out foul play."

"Time of death?" asked Erika, hopefully. She was now sweating profusely under her crime scene overalls.

"Don't push it," said Isaac. "I won't be able to give you a time of death until I've had a closer look and opened him up.

Extreme heat or cold slows putrefaction: in the case of the heat in this room, it's drying out the body. You can see the flesh has started to discolor." He pointed to where the skin was blooming in shades of green around the abdomen. "This could indicate he has been here for a few days, but, as I say, I'll need to perform the post-mortem."

Erika cast her eye around the room. A long wardrobe of heavy wood lined the wall next to the door, and in the nook of the bay window there was a matching dresser with a mirror. To the left of the window was a tall set of drawers. Every surface was clear: there were no books or ornaments, or any of the general detritus that accumulates in a bedroom. It was very neat. Almost *too* neat.

"Was he married?" asked Erika.

"Yes. The wife is no longer on the scene. They've been separated for a few months," said Moss.

"It's very tidy, for a newly single man," said Erika. "Unless the attacker cleaned up," she added.

"What? Had a vacuum round before he scarpered?" asked Moss. "I wish he'd pay me a visit. You should see my place."

Despite the heat, Erika saw a couple of the crime scene officers working around the body hide their smiles.

"Moss, not the right time."

"Sorry, boss."

"I think the arms were tied post-mortem," said Isaac, gently indicating the wrist area with his latex-gloved finger. The skin around the armpits was stretched in white lines against the shades of waxy skin underneath. "There's very little abrasion on the wrists."

"So he was already in bed when the attack happened?" asked Erika.

"Possibly," replied Isaac.

"There's no discarded clothes. He could have undressed normally for bed and tidied them away," said Moss.

"So someone could have been hiding under the bed or in the wardrobe, or could have come through the window?" asked Erika, blinking as sweat ran down her forehead into her eyes.

"That's for you to find out," said Isaac.

"Yes, it is. Lucky me," replied Erika.